BROTHER OF A FIRE WITCH

A romantic fantasy

By

John Boyle

Book 3 of

Beneath the Jeweled Moon

This book is dedicated in memory of my wife,

Deborah Katherine Woolley

Copyright © 2016 John Boyle

Cover copyright © 2016

Cover art created by Benjamin P. Roque

All Rights are reserved. This is a copyrighted work. It's offered only for private reading. Except for brief quotations in a review, no part of this text can be reproduced without permission, in writing, from the author.

This is a made up story. None of the characters are intended to represent anyone living or dead.

The Jeweled Moon Series:

Book 1 – Daughter of a Fallen Angel

Book 2 – Outcast City

Book 3 – Brother of a Fire Witch

Acknowledgements:

I would like to express thanks to the many people who helped me turn this book into a readable manuscript.

A special thanks to Benjamin P. Roque for creating the cover.

As this is the third book in the series, it helps to know that Haruko is the son of Matthew Sharpe, a displaced high school science teacher who ended up in the magical world and married to Kimiko, the queen of all the people.

Most of my writing is futuristic science fiction. I'm starting to publish my trilogy: **The Rise and Fall of Synfood**. The first installment, *Clericals, Courtesans and Superconductors* is now available. Note that all my books are complete stores, and it's only mildly useful to read them in order.

Besides writing novels, I'm working to develop a new kind of thermionic electric generator which has the ability to make direct solar energy cheap enough to compete with oil and coal generators.

Real science takes longer (and alas, more money) to accomplish than wishful thinking, but this new principle can create thousands of jobs while ending the global warming danger. All the generator's principles are explained on my website, where I also include pictures of the various prototypes along with information about my upcoming books. I'd appreciate it if you would visit my website and see the reasoning behind the ferromagnetic generator and why it could be important in securing our future.

www.ferrogenerator.com   Thanks, John.

CHAPTER 1

My sister, Tanoshi, bent over to inspect the steam engine's condenser and made sure to press her body against Yushin. The engineer drew back to put some space between them.

"It sucks the used steam from the cylinder, which makes the piston move faster." Yushin explained.

I groaned. Airi, sitting next to me on the coal tender, muttered a ripe Earth-oath and shook her head. Tanoshi looked at Yushin and muttered, "Oh, I see."

"After all the time your Dad spent teaching him thermodynamics," Airi whispered, "he still doesn't know shit." My sister's best friend, and my unofficial protector, Airi, didn't suffer fools easily.

"Yeah, what a dickhead," I agreed, also speaking in English; the secret language we three shared with my Earth-born father. "Tanoshi is pretending to be impressed, even though she knows better. She really wants Yushin to like her."

"He's a pretty face, but she can do better," Airi said. "Besides, it's obvious he doesn't want anything to do with her."

"But it stinks," I replied. "The only reason Dad brought Yushin into our house and taught him to become an engine driver was so he could spend enough time around Tanoshi to learn she's not a monster."

Airi put her hand on my shoulder. "We'll find her someone better. There's got to be a guy with an open mind somewhere."

I agreed, but thought, not in this world. It wasn't as if we hadn't been looking. But how do you find a guy willing to marry a witch? And not just any witch. Tanoshi wasn't one of those spell chanting, crystal hugging witches. She was the other kind. The really scary kind.

When she was five, she'd stopped a two-thousand man army dead in its tracks just by picking up a knife. In the intervening years, the stories of her abilities had only escalated. Mothers still used the frog incident to threaten misbehaving children, and few remembered Tanoshi had turned those bullies back to normal after a few days. A dumb move, but at the time it'd stopped those kids from taunting her for being an evil witch. However, the echoes of her childish temper tantrum still made everyone look away when she approached.

Of course, the whole town knew Tanoshi loved fire. When she wasn't making fireworks for our annual Freedom Day celebration, she would sit and play with flames as if they were loving pets. This meant people blamed her for every house fire, even though she always used her magic to suck away the flames. But the whispers continued, and if it wasn't for myself and Airi, my big sister would have no friends.

Yushin announced the steam was up to operating pressure. Just to make Airi bite back another curse, he began cranking the backup water pump. Even Tanoshi broke her 'act nice' resolve and told him they'd just equipped this engine with Airi's new steam injector. He didn't need to pump water into the boiler by hand.

"I can't risk an untested device with our future king on board." Yushin said. "The boiler will explode if the water gets too low."

"Damn," I said to Airi. "He knows I hate it when people dump that monarch crap on me. He really is a dickhead."

"Haruko," Airi began massaging my shoulder. "You're destined to become king. You've got to accept it. They won't let you spend your whole life building steam engines."

"Mom's pregnant," I said quietly. "Maybe she'll have a girl and well…you know. I'm sure everyone will jump at the chance for a queen."

Airi shook her head. "My mother tested Kimiko's urine. The herbs say you're going to have a little brother. Our colony needs you to accept the throne. By taking a wife from one of Takamatsu's leading families, you can reduce the animosity between our cities."

Relations between little Kyoto and big Takamatsu remained uneasy. The important families hated Queen Kimiko for forcing them to honor their promise to free their slaves. They also resented the queen of all the people spending most of her time in the ramshackle colony we optimistically named Kyoto, instead of staying in her vast royal estates overlooking the great city on the lake. For those proud citizens, losing a war because a five-year old girl had put their entire army on its knees and begging for mercy must still rankle. It'd take a few more generations before they could see the humor in it.

I needed to accept my fate. Airi's mother, Shizuku, was the best doctor in either city. If she said my mother was going to have a boy, then a boy it would be. I knew this little adventure was just a farewell gift before they shipped me up the lake to a life of pomp and boredom. I hated politics.

Remembering Tanoshi's checkered past made me look at her. No one could say she wasn't beautiful. Her body, while taller than most, had the proportions women lusted after. But, other than my father, she was the only person in the land under the jeweled moon with brown skin. And, unlike the rest of us, her long, luxurious hair was not green, but the deepest shade of radiant black imaginable. Plus, mimicking her father, her ears were rounded. Something which seemed to disturb people far more than it should.

I'd been lucky. While Tanoshi and I had the same Earth-born father, my mother, the queen, possessed a magic tuned to the kingdom's needs. So, while I was larger than most people, my hair was the acceptable green and my ears came to a very impressive point.

Tanoshi stood next to the firebox and continued smiling at Yushin, but behind her back, one hand pointed toward the engine's boiler. No doubt she was pumping magical heat directly into it. Patience wasn't Tanoshi's strong suite. Nor did she ever back down. Her fur-trimmed outfit came from a sixteen foot tall bear who'd thought a small, unarmed girl would make a nice snack.

Actually, myself and Airi also wore some of that bear's fur on our outfits. Because we were transporting workers from Takamatsu, we wore our better clothes in the hopes of impressing them enough to move to our colony. Everyone in Kyoto wore thigh-high boots made from red and yellow snakeskin. Tanoshi and Airi's leg-hugging boots were each decorated with a long row of gold buttons. For reasons I didn't understand, girl's seemed to like gold, even if it was common and not especially useful. Once, I'd made a bear claw necklace for Airi, but she'd insisted I put a gold bead between each claw, 'to make it pretty.'

Otherwise, we dressed almost alike with seal-leather jackets, although the girl's were cut differently. I preferred a looser fit, while they'd tailored theirs to tightly follow those wonderful curves that made female chests so nice to look at. Plus, as they were both unmarried, as was traditional, their skirts were much shorter than my kilt, short enough to show quite a bit of thigh.

Yushin turned to me. "Everything's ready, permission to get the train underway?"

We called this a train, but it didn't run on tracks. It was a mobile single-cylinder steam engine with wide, cast-iron wheels and made to pull three wagons. It didn't look like the pictures my Dad had drawn of steam locomotives on Earth. Instead of a horizontal boiler, ours used a vertical boiler. Necessary, as the hastily-made dirt road had steep grades which would put a horizontal boiler in danger of allowing water to slosh to one end and leave the other end dry. Dad had warned us about exploding boilers, which was why the people carriage brought up the rear. Besides the rope and other goods we were bringing to the harbor, the last carriage held workers going to improve the road to the salt mine.

Yushin vented live steam into the single cylinder with the water cocks on both the head and crank ends full open. The resulting roar and accompanying white cloud made us jump.

Once the cylinder quit spitting condensed water, he closed the cocks part-way and the main crank began moving. Roaring steam billowed around us as the cylinder took up the load. The flywheel spun and the train began inching forward. The roaring quieted as Yushin closed the drain cocks to the running setting while diverting the exhaust steam to the smoke stack. The noise changed to the thump-thump of a loaded steam engine, while the stack shot giant puffs of smoke, steam and hot cinders.

"He does it well," Airi conceded. "He wasted very little pressure getting us moving."

"Exactly as we taught him," I admitted. "In truth he's a great train engineer. There are many little details necessary to keep this baby running, and I doubt he'll ever forget one. But he'll never go beyond following the instructions." I picked up the coal shovel and shoved my goggles down to protect my eyes. With the engine's steam increasing the draft, the firebox would need more fuel. Airi, anxious to cut in her condenser and see if it increased the engine's power, went to stand next to Yushin.

I could see Yushin didn't like his future king doing the stoker's job, but, for someone who'd grown up working heavy iron, shoveling coal didn't even make me break a sweat. Plus, it let me ride in the cab and keep an eye on Tanoshi. I knew Yushin's attitude hurt her and we didn't need to spend another three months training a replacement driver. Tanoshi's magic was so strong it could be triggered just from her emotions. While she'd never gotten pissed-off enough to kill anyone, a couple of times it'd been a close-run thing.

Twelve hours later, after several water stops and breaks for our passengers to get out and move around, we pulled into the harbor station. The noise and smoke had alerted everyone to our approach, so all rushed to greet us. Aunt Maki the Pirate jumped into the cab, the heavy cutlass on her belt slamming into Yushin as she spun to give me a hug. Speaking in a heavy accent, which revealed her off-world origins, my Aunt grilled me on my current heath and whether I had a girlfriend.

"Haruko's doing that test," cut in Airi rather loudly. "We

explained it to you."

Maki looked at her and smiled. "Why of course, Airi. How could I forget?"

It wasn't really a test. Just something Airi had suggested when we both realized Tanoshi was going to have trouble finding a man. If it wasn't for her magical powers, my big sister would be dead by now, as everyone in this world lived under the curse laid on us by the Moon Goddess. Namely, once we reached maturity, sex became a daily necessity. All adults needed the affections of a mate lest they sicken and die.

I'd just reached the age where the yokubo, as we called the condition, should start affecting me. But Airi's mother, Shizuku, had suggested we males weren't born with the affliction, but caught it after becoming intimate with a female who desperately needed attention lest she die. Since my status as a prince, and the brother of scary Tanoshi, gave me some isolation from the general populace, I'd agreed not to seek out female companionship for a few years and see if the yokubo left me alone. As Tanoshi used her magic to keep the condition at bay, Airi prevailed on her to see if she could do the same for her and perhaps find a clue to lifting the curse. That made the three of us the oldest virgins in the land under the jeweled moon.

Airi inspected the train's condenser. She'd been disappointed in its performance. The condensers we'd installed on the stationary engines back at our foundry had produced a significant power boost, but on this locomotive it was hard to notice any improvement.

Airi looked up while holding her slide rule and scribbled notes. "It's because of the delayed valve cutoff. The engine is working so hard it has little adiabatic steam expansion. Until we can build larger two-cylinder engines, installing condensers isn't going to be worthwhile."

I nodded. "That's too bad. Still, it'll make Yushin happy. Tell him we'll yank it off as soon as we get a chance. One less thing to break and one less thing for him to maintain."

Yushin wasted no time in getting away from Tanoshi and now basked in fawning attention from the girls in the

Takamatsu road crew. No doubt any of them would be glad to land him as a husband. Being a locomotive engineer was one of this world's glamour jobs. He'd have all the company he wanted tonight. Tanoshi stood next to me pretending to be interested in Airi's calculations, but her tight lips betrayed her disappointment.

I spoke a little too loudly. "Let's go down to the beach and inspect Maki's new boat. The last time we were here, it was only ribs and cross members. The tide's out, so it's high and dry and we can inspect the twin hulls."

Maki had designed the catamaran for fishing and had already taken it on two shakedown cruises. Because this world was mostly ocean, the bay teamed with fish of all descriptions, each species desperate to use the limited spawning grounds. Those two short excursions had brought back so many fish half had rotted before they could be gutted. Now that more salt had been brought up from the salt caves near the ocean, a third fishing trip was ready to go, and we'd been invited to tag along. Just a little pre-marriage treat before my life as a free man ended.

The catamaran was all Maki and didn't look anything like an Earth boat. She'd designed it for our world and our needs. In this mostly water world, mammoth tides rose and fell up to fifty meters twice a day. Such energetic tidal surges meant the land adjacent the water ended in steep, unclimbable cliffs. In the entire bay, only this one small beach, a slope created by a landslide from an abutting mountain, gave access to the water.

With the low tide leaving it high and dry, the three of us spent an hour looking over Maki's boat. Someone had done a nice job of carving the boat's name, *Asahi'Kaze*, into the stern using the old formal script. Airi translated it for me and explained it meant wind from the morning sun. One of the sailors told me they just called it the *Kaze*. I saw our captain picking her way across the exposed seaweed coated rocks and coming toward us. "Four masts," I shouted down to her, "isn't that a bit much?"

"Really, it's three power masts so we can fight the current," Maki called back. "The little one at the back is only to aid in steering. We need the ability to make sharp turns when we're close to this harbor. The death nozzle is just over there, and if it catches us, it'll rip the boat apart."

Standing on the boat's main deck I could see the narrow gap between the mountains we called the death nozzle. Water from a rising tide speeded up as it squeezed through the constriction, creating a current so strong that when it exited on the other side it became a twenty meter high wave, which surged up the Kohaku River all the way to our lumber outpost. On this bay side of the nozzle, the inrushing current could be swift and unpredictable. I would not venture out with any other captain than Maki the Pirate.

"I came to tell you to go clean up for dinner," Maki said. "It'll be an early morning for us. The outgoing tide occurs before sunup. At least, with the sun and moon in alignment, the receding tide's current should be strong and it'll get us out of the danger zone quickly."

CHAPTER 2

In the dim light of early dawn, I listened to the rigging protesting as we fought our way out of the makeshift harbor. Maki had waited until the receding tide's current reached its maximum, as she needed its power to push us away from the death nozzle. Unfortunately, those two side-by-side mountains also channeled the wind coming off the ocean creating an almost gale-force blast, which tried to push us toward the nozzle. Maki had told me she'd experienced trouble getting out of the harbor and we needed to put as much distance as possible between us and the death nozzle before the tide turned.

We three landlubbers hung onto the aft rail of the pitching catamaran trying not to show our terror while watching our captain shout commands to her crew. This was Maki the Pirate in her element. I suspected she was having fun. My Dad and Sachi had brought Maki here from the dead world. She knew boats and rigging, and had been the driving force behind creating the raft and boat squadron that brought timber, and most everything else our little colony needed, up the Kohaku River.

My Dad called her Maki the Pirate because she looked the part. She'd lost one eye while trying to survive the chaos of her doomed home world and now wore a black patch over the empty socket. But it was the way she dressed that made the pirate name appropriate. Besides the heavy cutlass on the left side of her belt, the right held a half-length katana that Airi's father, Taro, had made for her using the many-folding technique. The same way he'd made his own and my two blades. My dad once told me Maki always carried at least one dagger in her boots. She wore a tight bodice made from bear leather and trimmed with its fur. All topped by a gold-braided three-corned hat made from one of the bears I'd killed.

Maki slammed a hammer on the large gong besides her, the noise was audible over the crashing waves and howling wind. Her crew, moving as one, sprang into action. The two men handing the tiller wheel spun it to full over, while others ran to various rigging lines. The boat lurched over, making Airi and I hang onto the rail in fear of going overboard. I'm sure I saw a red flash of magic surround Tanoshi's body as she steadied herself on the tilted deck. In the dim light I saw, impossibly close, a towering rock wall. We'd crossed the bay and were about to slam into the cliff on the other side.

Except Maki wasn't reacting to the danger. She stood, hands on her hips, watching the rigging, then raised her right hand. The ship spun, one side of the catamaran's twin hulls almost swamped as the other rose out of the water. I could hear the timbers groaning, and I swore the mainmast bent downwards. We slid down the backside of a wave, spray splattered across the deck, and then the cliff was to our aft and we were sailing away from it.

"That was close," I gasped, "We almost slammed into the cliff."

"There's not much maneuvering room," Maki agreed. "I have to watch closely. If I make the turn too soon, the seas are too steep to complete the turn without capsizing. I needed to reach the shelter of those cliffs. Anyway, we survived the hard bit. We'll tack upwind until we're out of the danger zone. The wind will ease as we move away from the mountains, so we won't need to get so close to the cliffs for the other turns."

"You do this every time to put out to sea?" I asked. "If a line breaks or a sail rips, you'll die."

"Today's wind is much stronger than I thought. I guess I should have waited. But, yeah, getting out of our pitiful little harbor is tricky. Honestly, I don't think we're going to be able to operate a fleet of fishing boats from that spot." She jumped down to the main deck and shouted to her crew.

We didn't have much canvas hoisted. Just a storm jib on the forward mast and the aft ketch sail to help in turning. In the strong headwind near the nozzle using anything more would have risked capsizing. On this reach we had more sea room and Maki had her crew unfurl more canvas. The boat heeled over, but Maki needed to hold her heading as the tidal current carried us away from the danger zone.

"It's just a matter of time before a disaster," Tanoshi said.

"Launching boats this close to the death nozzle is too dangerous. I doubt anyone except Aunt Maki could even manage it. We can't use the inlet for a fishing fleet."

Airi nodded. "I didn't realize the harbor and the nozzle were so close together. When this little rockslide was discovered, we thought we'd be able to use it exploit the fish in the bay. If we renege on the deal to provide Takamatsu ten cart loads of salted fish each year, it's going to increase the friction between our cities."

I put my hand on Airi's shoulder. This had been mostly her plan, and it was falling apart. We still needed to improve the trail from the harbor to the salt cave, and if we couldn't supply Takamatsu with the promised fish, they weren't going to give us any more help. They might even get nasty about the outstanding debt.

We were supposed to be one people, with my mother the queen of all, but it wasn't working out that way. The city's powerful families resented our colony and didn't hide that they wanted it shut down. There'd been only one city in this world since the Moon Goddess brought our ancestors here thousands of generations ago. The idea of two cities seemed sacrilegious.

And, of course, the leading families wanted their slaves back.

Much of the problem came from Takamatsu having little need to trade with us. Other than our fish, they didn't want anything we had to offer. Ironically, it was my father's fault. Before my father came, bread and beer, helped by a smattering of cheese and pigeon meat formed the main food staples. But when my father arrived from Earth, his boat held many different fruits and vegetables, adding a great variety to the once-bland diet. And on his trek to the bay, he'd discovered fat birds, which he called chickens, living in the cold forest. Their meat was especially tasty, and some clever breeding created a strain which laid an amazing amount of eggs.

Even his old nemesis, the Clothmakers, now profited from his arrival. The giant cottonwood grove, where thousands of slaves had once toiled to secure the wispy threads to make clothing, now occupied but a quarter of the area. The rest of the fertile land grew many different kinds of Earth vegetables. Plus, they'd copied our discovery. After buying sharp iron beating combs from our foundry, they used them to turn hemp fibers into linen.

But other than a few items, Takamatsu rarely trades with us for anything made from iron. The city's upper class considered it a cursed metal, and as they'd been forced to remove all the bronze neck-rings from their slaves, that recycled metal was now plentiful enough to meet their immediate needs.

Essentially, they didn't need us. Unfortunately, we desperately needed them. Unlike warm weather Takamatsu, we endured several months of cold and snow each year. Our colony was situated on the edge of a great grassland. The nearby swamp provided eels and crawfish in the cold months, but in the heat of summer, no one wanted to battle the snakes and insects that lived there. There'd been a small strand of short, soft pine trees growing on the edge of the western mountains, but we'd cut them down in the desperate early years and now only young trees grew there, none yet big enough to be used for lumber.

All our lumber came from the hardwood forest far down the Kohaku River, and towed to the city by Maki's fleet of rafts. In our colony, wood was precious and no one wasted it.

Other than the coal and ore from our mines, and the vegetables in our fields, most everything our colony needed came upriver, either from the wood outpost or from further down the bay where we could catch fish. The ocean at the far end of the bay provided us with seals, whose leather and fur kept us warm over the winter, and the amazing salt cave which allowed us to preserve meat and fish for the long winter months.

And coal. Coal was the choke point that held us back. Every male in our colony, who was old enough, spent several weeks each year in either of our three coal, two limestone, and one iron ore mine. But it wasn't enough.

Coal was everything when you lived without enough wood

to keep your houses warm and cook your meals. Each house required a large coal stockpile to survive the long winter.

Then there were the needs of our foundry. A blast furnace used prodigious amounts of coal to turn iron ore into cast iron. For the last few years we'd piled up the excess next to the foundry and only run the blast furnace in winter when its heat was more appreciated. Still, we never produced as much as we needed and most of our iron was worked on the hearth using the more plentiful iron meteorites—another item that Maki's crew brought upriver. However, many parts of a steam engine could only be fashioned from cast iron, which was why we'd built so few.

CHAPTER 3

The catamaran zigzagged down the bay toward the ocean. The headwind's intensity dropped as we moved away from the constricting mountains, which allowed the seas to settle. One at a time, Maki ordered her crew to hoist more sails, until we were under full canvas and able to tack close to the wind. We had to be making a good ten knots when Maki turned to a young man standing alongside her.

"All right, Sato. Take command. Hold this heading for another five mirau then come about onto the port tack."

Sato looked nervous but shouted, "Aye aye captain!" as he saluted her.

Maki turned to me. "You look a little green, has Tanoshi been practicing her magic on you again?" She grinned at our running joke. "Let's go into the cabin and talk. Besides, I need to see if Sato can make the turn without me at his side. He's the best I've got, and I want someone who can bring the ship home if I'm hurt. Getting into our shitty harbor is almost as hard as getting out."

"I'm sorry," Maki said as we squeezed onto the small wooden chairs placed around the ship's dining table. "I never should have set sail with the wind so strong. I hope I didn't scare you too much?"

"We needed to see the problem for ourselves," Airi said. "No one back at the colony understood how dangerous launching a boat so close to death nozzle would be. Obviously, we need to abandon the idea of using the collapsed cliff as a base for a fishing fleet. One mistake, one rope or sail failure, and the ship with all its crew, would be lost. It's only a matter of time before it happens."

Maki nodded. "Launching boats off that rockslide looked a lot easier in the planning stages. We wasted a summer building this boat. But I didn't understand how strong the wind becomes when it's channeled between the mountains and how close it'd blow us toward the nozzle. As a place to establish a fishing fleet, it'll not work. At least we can still catch fish from the cliff-side stations."

The windowless cabin remained dark as little early-dawn light came down from the open hatch. Tanoshi touched her index fingers together. As she drew them apart, a pea sized ball of flame, like a miniature sun, appeared between them. Slowly, as if she caressed a pet, the little fireball grew, its glow brightening the cabin. When it reached the size of an apple she released it so it floated to the ceiling, where it continued burning without scorching the wood.

In the reddish light Maki stared at Tanoshi. "You know it spooks the shit out of me when you do things like that," she said. "And how do you keep it burning without fuel?"

"Something from another place flows through me," said Tanoshi, "giving it the food it needs. A little baby like this doesn't want anything from this world, but if I made it larger, it would get hungry and burn the wood. I've been practicing; there are a lot of subtleties to manipulating the physical world, which I didn't understand when I was younger."

Airi interrupted. "All our plans hinged on large catches of fish. If we can't use the harbor, we have a problem."

"We can still fish from the side of the cliff like we've been doing," said Maki. "We've eaten well for years now. We just won't catch many of those big sushi-tuna, which everyone likes so much. It's rare for one of those big-boys to swim close to the cliff edge."

"It's more complicated," I said. "We promised to send ten carts of salted fish to Takamatsu every year. It'll cause problems if we renege."

"Why did you make such a promise?" asked Maki. "Why didn't you wait to see how well this fishing boat idea worked out?" she looked at Airi.

"Don't blame Airi, it was my fault," I said. "After we learned about your two successful voyages and how you'd caught full loads in just a few hours, we thought it was doable. The messenger didn't say anything about the dangers of getting out into the bay."

Maki nodded. "We made those first trips during spring tides with its powerful outgoing current. Plus, we lucked out as the wind coming off the ocean wasn't so strong. Today, we encountered a weaker tidal current and a major headwind. But, such might be more common than not. So tell me, why did you promise to send so much fish to Takamatsu?"

I explained. "We need the trade. Our minimal labor supply can't produce everything we need. The only thing we have, which they need in any significant amount, is fish. Relations between Kyoto and Takamatsu are not good. Actually, they're crap and getting worse. The noble families have never accepted that their queen refuses to live in the royal palace. And they are still seething because Kimiko decreed all the inhabitants of Kyoto are part of her family—the royal family. If the Takamatsu nobles weren't terrified of Tanoshi, they would have taken Kimiko back to their city by force."

"I see," Maki looked at me before turning to Airi. She put her hand on Airi's shoulder. "That explains a lot. You believe things will improve if the Takamatsu nobles have our future king in their city."

Airi looked at the table. "And he's married to the daughter of the powerful Clothmakers."

"I...I can't fight them," Tanoshi whispered. "I might kill someone."

I put my arm around my sister. "Marriage to a noble's daughter is not such a bad fate. I'll be back here often enough."

"You mustn't think of fighting over this," Airi said to Tanoshi. "I could never forgive myself."

I thought I'd best explain to Maki. "Tanoshi's power comes from two sources," I began. "She inherited the magic of her mother Yuki, the most powerful witch this world has ever seen. When the evil one tried to corrupt Yuki, he gave her some of his strength. When Tanoshi's mother died, both powers flowed into her daughter. If Tanoshi uses magic to hurt others, the evil part of her power tries to corrupt her."

One of the sailors rushed into the cabin ending our discussion. He shouted Sato needed Maki's help. Considering the boat was heeled over and the sailor looked ready to piss himself, we decided we'd best stay below and let Maki handle the screw-up.

CHAPTER 4

After the crisis on deck ended, we three remained below, not wanting to interfere with the ship's operation. I'd started dozing when Maki opened the cabin door. "Guys," she shouted. "Come on deck, there's something you should see."

Like the obedient landlubbers we were, we filed out of the cabin, Tanoshi leading the way. I only stumbled once, a sign I was getting my sea legs. Neither Airi nor I wanted to admit we'd be spewing our breakfast on the deck if my sister hadn't used her magic to settle our stomachs.

"Look on top of the cliff," Maki grabbed my arm and pointed. "See those rocks? It's the monument you and your dad erected over Rick's grave. I'm glad it's visible from the water. Once we've come this far, we're free of the death nozzle's current. Now, if the wind dies, we won't get sucked back toward it. From this point onward we can turn our attention to fishing."

We leaned against the rail and stared at the monument. Rick had died before I was born. Tanoshi had been an infant carried on the back of Sachi, the Moon Goddess. But we'd heard the stories of Rick and how he'd died saving Sachi's life. I don't think Aunt Chie had ever gotten over the loss of her first love. Today, she was part of our immediate family, and spent much of her time in Takamatsu, trying to defend our colony against those who'd see us fail. Fortunately, as the daughter of a politician on her home world, she was usually one step ahead of their plots.

"That's a long drop from the cliff top to the water," Airi said. "The story is Aunt Chie grabbed Sachi and jumped from there to escape the bear that killed Rick."

"The tide was at its highest point when she jumped," I explained, while remembering Airi had never traveled this far toward the ocean. "See the line on the cliff about eight meters down from the land. That's the high water mark. Of course, it only gets that high for a few days every month, so they were lucky."

Tanoshi looked at the cliff. "The tide rises up the cliff side every day, doesn't it?" she said. "And this area is beyond the influence of the death nozzle." She turned to Maki. "Could you get closer to the cliff and slow down?"

Maki studied the wind. "I can get in close, but not for long."

"All right," Tanoshi said. "I'm going to trust your crew to keep my secret. I need to find a crack in the rock, so I'm going to fly over to the land. When I find the right spot, I'll come back and direct you toward it."

"You...you can fly?" gasped Maki.

"Tell your crew it's a secret," Tanoshi leaned toward Maki. "People fear me quite enough as it is. Besides, flying takes so much concentration I can't do much else."

Maki nodded, and assured Tanoshi her crew was trustworthy. As Tanoshi rose from the deck and moved toward the cliff, Maki started giving orders, dropping the mainsails and using the aft ketch sail and the small triangular foresail to keep the boat facing the wind. The boat slowed as we followed Tanoshi as she hovered in the air while inspecting the rock face.

"I understand what she's planning," Airi said. "If the top of this cliff was lower, we could launch boats at high tide. They could go out in the bay, fish for half a day and then return at the next high tide. It'd provide the fish we need to meet our obligations."

"I don't like it," I said. "A cliff is a lot bigger than a boulder. It might be too much for her."

Eventually, Tanoshi returned and said she'd found a crack she could exploit. I tried to convince her this was a bad idea and reminded her of how exhausted she'd felt after blasting those rocks away while we were building the road. Tanoshi insisted it wouldn't be difficult. She'd found a deep crack, which she could use to undermine the cliff face.

After Maki got the boat into the right position, Tanoshi extended both arms and, palm toward the cliff, sent a bolt of red fire at the rock. Now the boat was near the cliff, I realized the rock was granite, not limestone like she'd faced when building the road. I shouted at Tanoshi. "Don't do it! That stone is really strong." But she was lost inside her magic and I doubted she heard me. I could only hope she knew metamorphic rock wouldn't yield like limestone. Could she really blast away enough material to collapse part of the cliff? Did my sister really control that much power?

For a long minute nothing happened. Then, small rock flakes began popping free and shooting across the water. Next came larger pieces, which noisily shot from the wall like they'd been blasted by gunpowder. The sailors shouted when an especially large boulder arched through the air and splattered into the water with a splash high enough to send spray across the deck.

I knew these flying rocks were just a side effect, as I could see cracks forming on the lower part of the cliff face. Tanoshi was using heat to expand the rocks and causing the matrix to shatter. Eventually, the weight of all the material above would create a landslide. But to send that much heat into the heart of hard rock? I had no idea she could draw on such power. I saw beads of sweat running down her face, and her arms, formerly held straight out, began sagging. When her knees began shaking, I feared she might collapse.

"We have to help her," I shouted to Airi. "She's never channeled this much magic before." The two of us rushed to Tanoshi's side. I grabbed her around the waist and took her weight. Airi held her arms and helped keep them pointed at the cliff. "Don't overdo it," I shouted in Tanoshi's ear. "We can finish the job with gunpowder." But with so much power flowing through her, she couldn't respond.

The red stream impacting the cliff increased. Tanoshi no longer tried to support herself. If I let go, she'd collapse to the deck and blast the boat apart. I had a horrible feeling she'd lost control and could no longer stop even if she tried. All Airi and I could do was support her and keep her deadly blast pointed at the cliff.

Time seemed to stand still. Tanoshi felt hot in my arms, not feverish hot, but painful to hold hot. Still the stream continued. Finally, a layer of half-melted rock yielded. In slow motion, a great portion of the cliff slid into the water, creating a wave high enough to wash onto the deck and set our boat to rocking. Tanoshi's deadly beam shot into the air when the deck tilted back, then it plunged into the water as the ship rolled forward. Steam rose from the overheated water, making it difficult to see anything.

"She can't stop," I shouted to Maki. "She's killing herself." My arms burned where Tanoshi's skin touched mine. What could I do? There were only seconds before my sister would die, and I had no ideas.

Maki ripped off her leather jacket. She draped it over Tanoshi's head so she could no longer see anything. The narrow red beam widened, became more diffuse. Then cold water splattered against us. I looked over to see Maki had her crew running toward us with buckets of seawater. The icy water felt great against my burning arms. After three dousings, the red magic faded and I held my unconscious sister.

"Is she alive?" whispered Maki.

I removed the jacket covering Tanoshi's face. Her eyes remained closed and her brown face appeared disturbingly white. Airi pressed her fingers against Tanoshi's neck.

"I can feel a pulse," she said. "But it's weak, we should get her back into the cabin. She's going to need a lot of care."

Maki's crew stood silently as I carried my sister to the cabin. Just as I opened the door, Maki began shouting orders. I didn't have to look to know that with everyone focused on Tanoshi, the boat had drifted dangerously close to the cliff.

Airi and I did what we could to make Tanoshi comfortable while on deck the crew went about the task of saving the boat. Some hours later, after everything settled down topside, Maki entered the cabin.

"She opened her eyes," Airi said. "We've been lying against her to try and get her warmed up. She'll recover, but it will take several days."

Maki nodded. "I'm holding position here as we can't risk approaching the harbor until the next outgoing tide. In a few hours we can head back. We'll do our fishing on another voyage. Tanoshi comes first."

Airi patted the edge of the bed. "Come sit. I don't believe

Tanoshi is in any danger. She's completely exhausted, but she'll regain her strength. It's her magical power I'm worried about. I'm sure she used every last drop. It might not return for a long time—if it does at all."

"Tanoshi without power," I gasped, thinking of all the people who wanted her dead. The noble houses of Takamatsu left us alone because they remembered Tanoshi terrorizing their army. "Tanoshi told me, when we were building the road, how it drained her to use a lot of power. She always needed to recover after blasting away heavy rocks. I'm sure her power will return but it could take a week or more."

Airi nodded. "It would be best if we didn't return to the harbor while Tanoshi remains weak. People will talk, word of Tanoshi's limits will spread. The noble houses in Takamatsu will learn she's not as powerful as they fear. Who knows what they might scheme after that. Our plan to have Haruko marry into a noble family and ease the tensions between our cities might fall through. Why, they might even decide Kimiko isn't the true queen."

Maki shook her head and muttered an oath from her own world. "I understand. I'll talk to my crew. Don't worry, none of my river rats will say anything more than how they watched Tanoshi blast a cliff away to create a new harbor. About going back, rather than hang around here, which will look suspicious as there are people on the trail coming up from the salt cave, how about we sail down the bay and into the ocean? It's time someone did a little exploring. We might find all sorts of new resources."

"To boldly go where no one has gone before," I said and got a funny look from Maki. "It's one of my dad's sayings. Something from an Earth story, I think."

* * * *

That evening, Tanoshi revived enough to take a little soup. She didn't feel as cold, and, in a whisper, thanked us for saving her. I explained our plan to delay returning and we now headed toward the great ocean, but it was slow going as we needed to tack against a headwind.

Tanoshi nodded and assured us she'd be walking soon.

She didn't say anything about her magic powers returning, but insisted we place her half-katana on the bed alongside her. She lay down and, clutching her weapon, went back to sleep. Airi said she'd keep watch, so I headed up to the deck.

The moon reflected off the gentle swells coming from the ocean. The wind wasn't as strong as earlier, but the boat had only the small fore and aft sails up so we weren't making much headway.

"I don't want to reach the ocean at night." Maki came over and stood at my side. "The little bit I know about the area where the bay meets the ocean is that the mountains on our starboard side hook around and protrude into the bay. I don't want to tangle with any underwater ridges. In the daytime, we can see obstacles in the water. Plus, the tide will be going out, which should help."

I agreed and we both stood staring at the water and the line on the horizon where the stars began.

"This Clothmaker girl you're going to marry," Maki said quietly. "What's she like?"

"Female," I said. In the following silence I realized I was being petty. "Well, I guess she's pretty enough. Nothing like Tanoshi or Airi, but she dresses real nice, always fancied up, you know. It's just that…ah, we don't have much in common. With her, it's all about the gossip and the intrigues of her friends; whose dress is out of style, what jewelry goes with what outfit. I've spent my life pounding iron and building machines. The metal lathe Airi designed and I built can hold to five thousandth of a centimeter, even my dad can't believe I accomplished it. I tried explaining to Toma what that meant, but she looked at me like I was daft. Iron and steam are considered dirty words in Takamatsu."

"There were rich girls like that on my planet also," Maki said. "I can understand why you're not enthused with the idea of marrying one."

"Maybe I'm being too critical. Actually, we've only met a couple of times, once two years ago, and then last month when Aunt Chie and I went to the city to finalize the fish deal. Who knows, maybe we'll get along."

Maki stared at the water. "Are you sure there's no way you can get out of it?"

"Not if we want Kyoto to survive. Our relationship with Takamatsu is on the edge of collapse. The nobles are furious because Kimiko lives with my dad and refuses to return to the palace. With the Clothmakers powerful again, the lesser families follow their lead."

"You told me the Clothmakers now grow Earth vegetables on their cotton-tree farm. With control of the city's food supply, it's no wonder they've regained power."

I sighed. "It's more about our weakness than their power. We live in a harsh climate. Wood is scarce and needed for many things besides burning, so our main fuel is coal, which we have to mine and transport and store to keep everyone warm through the winter. On top of that, we still have to sow our fields and gather the harvest and do all the other things a town needs."

Maki nodded. "I've always thought it something of a miracle your dad is able to keep his furnaces going. I know a blast furnace uses a lot of coal. Have you considered letting them remain idle until the colony is more established?"

"We decided not to run the big furnace this winter and just forge those meteorites you bring in. Still, it's a shame because steam engines need cast iron parts, but it'll have to wait until this crisis eases."

"It's disappointing its come to this," she whispered. "I really thought this world would be better than my own. But it seems there are always a few assholes willing to make everyone's life miserable."

"My dad still thinks this world is great. He's told me about life on his world, and for all our troubles, I believe we're far better off. I know I wouldn't ever want to live on Earth."

Sato came on deck and said he was ready to relive Maki. After she gave him some directions, the two of us went below.

CHAPTER 5

The clatter of sailors hoisting sails woke me. Light, entering from a porthole, assured me the sun was more than a little above the horizon. I moved, trying not to disturb either Tanoshi or Airi. Airi and I had started the night pressed against Tanoshi, who needed our warmth, but somehow Airi was now snuggled tight against me, her soft breasts pressing against my side and one of her legs wedged between mine. I found the arrangement disturbingly erotic. True, we weren't related by blood, but we'd been raised in the same house and for all of my life I'd considered her my sister.

Big dark pupils outlined with sparkling green and gold irises stared into mine. Airi moved and kissed me on the cheek. "Morning, Haruko," she muttered. "Thanks for keeping me warm." She didn't release me, but for a few seconds hugged my chest as tightly as she could. I gasped when the leg that was between mine moved upwards enough to send what might be politely described as a tingle up my spine.

"I have to use the commode," I blurted, desperate to put a little space between us. I was engaged, and it didn't help to have the most desirable girl in Kyoto pressing her naked body against mine. She sighed and moved enough to let me out of bed.

Later, as I took care of my morning needs, it occurred to me Airi might be suffering. Tanoshi had promised Airi she'd keep her yorubo under control, but my sister had depleted her magic yesterday. Could Tanoshi's lack of magic let the curse affect Airi that quickly? I realized she might be in desperate need of a male, and I found the thought of her grabbing a young sailor and dragging him to her bed utterly devastating. I ran back to the cabin.

Tanoshi and Airi sat on the bed, Airi was combing out Tanoshi's hair. "Oh," I said, "is everything all right?"

"Tanoshi says she feels stronger, but her magic hasn't returned." Airi said. "I explained how we're going to spend a few days at sea, to give her time to recover."

"So you're both feeling. . .normal?"

"I'm a bit cold," Airi replied. "We should put some clothes on. You can't go on deck without your kilt Haruko." She pointed at the problem. "You'll get Aunt Maki all excited. You know she considers any man on her ship fair game."

"My head aches," Tanoshi whispered. "And I'm hungry. Haruko, dear, go see if you can scrounge up some breakfast."

The ship's galley was large for a fishing vessel, as it served as a sleeping area for the crew. Cleverly designed collapsible bunks lined the walls, and the center table was constructed to lower to the floor when not needed. The crew stowed pillows and blankets in every available space. Obviously, Maki had designed The *Kaze* for longer voyages than just day fishing, and she'd made sure her crew, both the males and their communal wives, would have a comfortable space to take care of their daily needs.

With everyone on deck, we had the table to ourselves and found breakfast waiting. After eating, Tanoshi said she was going back to bed, so Airi and I headed up the gangway to the main deck.

The boat was close to the starboard cliffs, the ones marking the land of the giants. It was time for a strong outgoing tide to occur, and Maki explained it would make getting out to sea easy as long as we avoided any underwater ridges. Two sailor wives, whose name I didn't yet know, were stationed on the bow checking the depth with a large gold sounding weight.

"The depth is well over a hundred meters," Maki said. "I'm thinking strong tidal currents scour the bottom, so we shouldn't hit any shallows. I'm going to turn and head out to sea."

Airi and I went to stand next to our captain. With the wind coming off the ocean, we couldn't point our bow directly out of the bay, so Maki put us on a board reach toward the nearby cliff. She explained how when we got close to the rocks, she'd go about on the opposite tack which would be enough to get us to open water.

The *Kaze* lurched across the five-foot swells. I became used to the rhythm, so when it stopped, I looked over the side.

The evenly spaced rollers coming off the ocean had disappeared. Now the water looked flat and streaked, more like a fast-flowing river than a bay open to the ocean. Maki looked at the sea, muttered something in her own language, and shouted orders to her crew. The boat started coming about, it seemed Maki intended abandoning her plan and wanted to head back up the bay, away from this strange current. But the boat didn't respond. It turned sideways before the sails lost their wind and began flapping.

Airi stood at my side. "We're caught in some sort of current. We've lost steerage."

I looked toward the cliff making the edge of the bay. This current now pushed us toward it. Maki took control of the ship's wheel. "We're caught in what's called a maull-hole on my planet. It's where the ocean swirls around and around like water draining out of a tub. They're really big and the hole in the center can go all the way down to the seafloor. They're created when a bay's outgoing tide collides with the next tide coming in. They've been known to swallow small boats."

I spotted a dark hole in the water a few hundred meters away. It grew larger as I watched. We were on the outer edge of the hole's current, but the boat, lacking any control, was in danger of spiraling into its maw.

"Damn," Maki swore. "Maull-holes were never this large on my planet, but we never had tides that changed over fifty meters. This one is huge; it'll draw us into it. Maybe, if I set the sails to catch the aft wind, we can claw our way out of danger?"

I looked at the sea. Even with the wind behind us, I doubted we could escape the hole's grip before we were battered against the fast-approaching cliff.

"No!" shouted Airi. "We must lower all the sails and ride the current. While it'll suck us closer to the hole, it'll get us moving faster and faster. Without the wind pushing us outward, the current will sweep us past the cliff. Once we're on the ocean side of the maull-hole, we'll have the speed we need to break free." She patted my shoulder. "Haruko's dad explained how on his planet they use the gravity wells of planets to speed up their spacecraft so they can escape into deep space. This is the same thing only on water. It's our only chance."

Maki looked at Airi. After a short pause she said; "What do you want me to do?"

Airi started giving directions which Maki shouted to her crew. Soon the sails were down and we bobbed like a cork in the current swirling around the ever-expanding hole. Everyone looked terrified, all except Airi who stood on the deck studying the water as we drew closer and closer to the cliff. As Airi predicted, without our sails catching the wind and pushing us toward the rocks, the hole sucked us toward itself, and we were swept past the towering cliff with less than ten meters to spare. Some sailor-wives screamed.

After several long, breath-holding minutes, the current spiraled us around to the ocean side of the maull-hole. Airi did some calculations on her slide rule. "Now," she shouted. "Hoist all the sails and put the helm over. We have enough speed to break free."

Maki shouted to her crew. Fortunately, their trust in their captain was strong, and all began hoisting the sails. Maki tried to turn the ship's wheel and shouted for me to help. With so much hull-speed and pressure from the current, the wheel didn't move easily. As I strained against it, I feared the jute ropes connecting it to the rudder post might snap. The two of us fought the torque with all of our strength as I watched the connecting rope thinning under the strain.

Maki smiled at me, "Haruko, it's a good thing you're strong. No one else could have turned this wheel."

With the wind in our sails and the rudder hard over, the ship changed course and we began beating our way out of the Maull-hole's grip. Once pointed toward the open ocean, we stared at the water as our speed decreased. For two long minutes the current fought to reclaim us as our inertia and the favorable wind sought to save us.

Airi was leaning far over the side. Eventually she stood. "We're out of the fastest part of the current. The wind will do the rest," she announced. "The *Kaze* is safe."

Maki used her captain-voice and shouted to her crew Airi had saved them. All began cheering, shouting Airi's name over and over. Airi's face went deep red. Maki laughed. "If Airi wants a husband, there are many guys on this boat who'd be happy to oblige her," she elbowed me in the ribs. "Your not-really-your-sister has stolen their hearts. Smart, attractive and cute, all in the same loveable package, what more could any man ask for?"

Confused thoughts raced through my mind. Airi married. We wouldn't be together. She'd be with some other man, someone who might not realize how totally wonderful she was. But I was engaged—

"Haruko," Airi stood at my side, interrupting my thoughts. "Most men don't have your strength. We need to design a ship's wheel and rigging with a greater mechanical advantage. Also, rig up some ropes so Maki can station a lookout on top of the center mast to watch for dangers in the water. Ropes will have to do for this voyage, but when we get back, let's install a proper platform up there so it can be manned comfortably."

She tapped her slide rule against my arm. "I'm going down to the cabin to check on Tanoshi and explain the steering problem to her, come and join us after you get the ropes rigged and someone up on top of the mast."

Maki and I watched her walk away. That was my Airi; she wouldn't let a little praise distract her when problems needed solving.

* * * *

There is something special about being the first people to venture onto the open ocean. The sailors crowded the rails, laughing and speaking loudly, pointing out every detail of the new environment. Out here, the water appeared a lot more blue than the bay, and once away from the land, the sea settled into long-spaced rollers, which the *Kaze* bounded across, propelled by a steady wind. Unfortunately, the wind wanted to push us back toward the shore, so Maki needed to take us quite a way out before turning to follow the coastline.

Late afternoon, Tanoshi, aided by Airi, came on deck. My

sister walked slowly, unsteadily, and I could see she needed Airi's help to avoid falling. After Tanoshi grabbed the rail and looked toward the land, I went to stand at her side and asked how she felt. Sato, Maki's trusted first mate, also came over to see if she needed help.

"I'm a little stronger, but I'm still tired." She turned to look me in the eyes. "There's no sign of my magic returning."

I put my arm around her waist. "Before, after you used too much, it always came back. Give it time. I'm sure you'll be your normal self soon."

"Haruko, what if my power doesn't return? What if I'm not a witch anymore? The Takamatsu nobles might reject you as their ruler. Why, they might decide to disband Kyoto. The city's army is large and strong. They could force your mother to return to her palace, and we have no way of resisting if the nobles, speaking in her name, decree everyone should return to Takamatsu."

Typically, Tanoshi was only thinking of our colony. She hadn't stated the obvious. The first thing the nobles would do would be to arrange for her assassination in case her powers returned. "It's early days yet," I assured her. "Let's give it more time. I know you'll recover. Maki will keep us out here for as long as it takes."

"Staying out here is not a problem," interrupted Sato, who I realized, had listened to our conversation. Well, everyone on board knew Tanoshi had exhausted her magic and Maki trusted them not to tell anyone. I felt sure Sato would not reveal to our enemies overuse could exhaust Tanoshi's power.

I decided to change the subject. "A few hours ago, Maki took us inshore toward those tall cliffs and the beach at the base of them. She came in as close as she dared. We have two telescopes and everyone took turns studying the land of the giants. The mountains have eroded and created an extensive beach, which stretches for miles." I handed her a telescope and pointed to the beach in the distance. "Those big black circles are groups of something like a large seal, but these beasts are massive and have two teeth longer than a man's arm protruding from their mouths."

Tanoshi nodded. "Dad once said that if there were seals, we might find a larger version in colder areas. What name did he call them?...ah, I remember. Wall-rus, I think. They are a bit seal-like but much bigger and fatter. They are very strong and their huge teeth are formidable weapons."

"While on the beach," I explained, "they circle into colonies with the biggest on the outside and the babies in the center. It looks as if bears patrol around the colonies looking for an opening. I suppose they're after the babies. I think the bears are often successful as I spotted red streaks on the beach and in the water. However, when we were closer, I saw dead bears too."

"We almost hit an underwater rock when we were close to the beach," said Sato. "Now our captain insists we say out here. If the *Kaze* was to flounder, a human wouldn't stand a chance on a beach like that. Maki said we'll head north. These mountains and this beach can't go on forever, and this is our chance to see what else might be outside the bay. But those tall rocks poking out of the sea appear more frequent the further north we go. We might have to turn back without ever finding a place to land."

"The land of the giants really is just as dad predicted," Tanoshi said. "This water-world teams with fish and marine life. The wall-rus are plentiful because they feast on abundant sea life, but they come ashore to have babies, which gives the bears a great source of food so they too become large. But those tall cliffs and rugged mountains don't provide enough hibernation caves for the bears when the winter snows arrive. Even with their plentiful food supply, the bear's population is held down by the difficulties they face in surviving the long freezing months. That explains why some females and their cubs risk the dangerous swim across the bay to find winter dens."

"Used to swim across the bay," Airi said as she fingered the gold bead and bear-claw necklace I'd made for her. "We didn't encounter any last year. Our heavy caliber rifles kill them too easily. I think we've eliminated those who knew of the wintering grounds on our side of the bay. It must have been a trick some discovered and taught their offspring, but those with the knowledge are gone now."

"Good for us, bad for them," Tanoshi focused the telescope on the land in the distance. "This beach appears to stretch for miles and I can see dozens of black circles on the sand. There must be millions of wall-rus and thousands of bears living off them. I suppose we didn't substantially change things."

We remained on deck through the rest of the afternoon, alternately staring at the endless ocean or the chain of mountains and the long beach. Airi sat with her back to the mainmast and began calculating and drawing diagrams in her notebook. I asked her what project she was working on.

"Hope for the future," she replied. "Now Tanoshi has created a place where boats can be launched into the bay, it makes more of my ideas possible. Very soon, Takamatsu will have to take us seriously."

"Tell me about it." I said.

"Takamatsu and Kyoto as equals, I never thought I'd live to see it come about." Sato, who'd been standing on the other side of the mast, came around and sat next to Airi.

I felt irritated at Sato's interest in Airi. I remembered Maki telling me he was both smart and ambitious and would soon captain his own boat. Of course he'd be attracted to beautiful and intelligent Airi. The guy was obviously thinking of Airi as a potential mate. I bit back my frustration and tuned in to what Airi was saying.

"We won't need to build large and complex fishing boats like the *Kaze* anymore. We'll create a fleet of smaller vessels, about the size of the lifeboat we're carrying. Two or four person crews will go out and fish during the daytime. Considering how bountiful the bay is, we'll easily meet our quota for Takamatsu and have more besides."

"The harbor Tanoshi created, while big," Sato said, "didn't reach down to low tide level. Boats can only use it when the tide is high."

"That won't be a problem," Airi explained. "Half a day at sea will be about the right for a small fishing boat. Plus, now the initial harbor has been carved out, we can deepen and widen its slope with gunpowder. In time, Tanoshi's harbor will become a major fishing center during the summer months. It'll even have a floating dock to move up and down with the tide." She showed Sato a picture she'd drawn in her notebook. "Fishermen will bring in their catch; others will process the fish and move them to drying and salting buildings. In the future, I hope to have a rail line going from this new harbor to Kyoto. Once there, we'll load the preserved fish onto schooners for transport to Takamatsu. In a few years, hunger will be a thing of the past in the city."

Sato and I stood staring at the diagrams in Airi's notebook. A new harbor; essentially she wanted to create a town to exploit the riches of the bay. We both remained a bit stunned as we realized how much life would change.

"It'll take a lot of manpower to accomplish it," I finally said. "You know our population is hard pressed to meet our current needs. We can barely mine enough coal to keep ourselves warm through the winter, and our iron works use all the excess. I fear we just don't have the people needed to build such a long rail line."

"That's what I was working on when you came over," Airi said. "I haven't calculated the details yet, but I have a plan."

"Can you explain it?" asked Sato. He stepped close to Airi, pressing against her side as he peered at her notebook.

"Aunt Chie sent me a letter saying Takamatsu has many ex-slaves who're not happy. Most continue working for their former masters for what is called pay, but is really just room and board. Many are worse off now than they were as slaves. Although the noble families would fight it, they are technically allowed to leave the city."

She turned and looked at me. "When you go to Takamatsu, I think Tanoshi and your mother should accompany you. With Aunt Chie's political savvy, you and the queen, backed by Tanoshi's unspoken threat, could arrange for a second wave of ex-slaves to come here. After all, you're promising the city all the fish they want. The one thing they don't have. I'm sure many will volunteer. That will give us the people we need to expand our coal mining operations."

"Even with the queen's command and the enticement of fish, the city nobles might not agree," I said. "Takamatsu intends keeping Kyoto as small as possible."

"Haruko has a point," said Sato. "And, Kyoto isn't in a position to absorb great numbers of people. Think about the winter housing they will need. Kyoto doesn't have a surplus of buildings."

Airi opened her satchel and withdrew a second notebook. This one looked old and well-used. "I'm calling it a five year plan," she said while flipping through the pages. "Our first request will be for three hundred ex-slaves. Not enough to get anyone overly upset and we can squeeze them into our current houses until we can erect more buildings."

"You plan to use them in the coal mines?" asked Sato.

"Not really, although, each male will take his turn underground as that's what it means to be a man in Kyoto. But their main job will be expanding our rice field."

"Rice?" I said.

"It's taken us a long time to learn the tricks of growing rice, but we've figured it out now. Rice won't grow in dry Takamatsu, but here we have a freshwater river we can divert to flood a large meadow every spring. Rice grows fast, gives a fantastic yield and is highly nutritious. It'll more than double our available food supply and provide the basis of many new dishes with the fish we catch. With a large rice field supplementing our other crops and abundant fish, we could start absorbing thousands of immigrants. That'll give us the manpower we need to expand our city and divert more coal to our ironworks."

"Yes," I grasped her idea. "Rice is delicious and added to the fish and our many vegetables, it will give us a great variety of food and more than we need to accept all the people who come here."

"I'm not sure why you think growing rice would make a difference," Sato said. "For the number of people we have, our current vegetable fields could keep more people alive. In fact, we should admit one reason the nobles of Takamatsu resent

Kyoto is our great abundance of food. We grow a surplus of all the vegetables Haruko's dad brought to this world. The people eat a great variety with their fish, chicken or Ryu meat. In addition they enjoy first run beer with every evening meal. I believe, with those new iron cooking stoves and pots you designed, everyone here eats better than the richest noble in Takamatsu. And the noble's anger is fueled by the numerous festivals we celebrate, and how everyone stops working when the sun touches the horizon for an evening of relaxation, games and song."

"That is the charge Sachi, the Moon Goddess, laid upon us," Airi said. "She sees all of us as equal and will not tolerate greater or lesser people. That is why Haruko builds steam engines. We cannot permit a class of people needed only for their muscles. His engines will someday take over the difficult back-breaking work. But meanwhile, we go out of our way to make every person's life as comfortable as we can. Kyoto is the seed destined to transform all the Moon Goddess' world."

"Your plan means in five years, Kyoto won't need Takamatsu at all," Sato said quietly. "In fact, with your steam machines, the nobles of Takamatsu must adopt your ways or the city will wither and decline."

"Oh," I said. "Don't forget, my mother is the queen of all the people. She worries about Takamatsu and won't let harm come to it. But our promise to the Moon Goddess is that we'll work to prevent slavery either directly, like we had before, or this new kind the nobles are using—being technically free but forced to work for next to nothing to stay alive. That's the reason the queen has decreed we in Kyoto celebrate many festival days every year. Even while we build our new city, we must not let work dominate anyone's life. For true happiness, humans need a balance."

"Yes," Sato said. "And the stories of how we live reach Takamatsu causing their workers to grumble and demand more food and better treatment. Surely you can see why there is so much hostility directed toward our colony." He looked at Airi. "Oh, I'm not justifying the actions of the nobles, but we must keep in mind why they feel the way they do."

Maki, who'd been in my rig on top of the mast, shouted for her crew to lower her down to the deck. She came over to us. "Those big cone-shaped rocks, which stick up from the sea, appear more numerous ahead," she explained. "And it looks like a storm is heading our way. I'm putting us farther out to sea. We'll come back when it's safe. I'm thinking we're coming to the end of this mountain chain, so the land and beaches might be different. From what I can see through the telescope, there are fewer animals this far from the bay. It'd be good to find out if any places are free of them."

Tanoshi, who'd been sitting on the deck listening to us, stood. "I've been thinking. My father was almost sent back to his world after he entered the ocean and Sachi's magic couldn't hold him to this land. There is something about the open ocean that is magically different, as it's the same on every planet. My heritage is half-Earth. I'm thinking, while I'm out here, my magic can't return. I believe my witch power flows into me from the land." She turned to Maki. "Captain, in the morning, if we see a suitable spot, is there any way you could get me ashore?"

"Just by going onto the land you could get your power back?" gasped Sato. He saw us all turn to look at him and added. "I mean, that would be a great thing. We could head home."

"We've got to survive the coming storm first," Maki said. "But just as soon as we're able, we'll get your feet back on land. But this boat and my crew have never been through a storm. I need everyone to eat and take turns resting. We have a long, hard night ahead of us."

CHAPTER 6

The wind increased after dark. With no stars or moon providing light, the sea couldn't be seen from the wheel deck. Maki sent we three landlubbers below along with those members of the crew who were not needed. As the night wore on, what started as a gently rocking increased to the point where we needed to hang onto something to prevent being tossed around the galley. I heard the timbers creaking under the strain and wondered if the boat could hold up. Then the boat heeled over, far over, and everyone in the cabin tumbled, in a screaming mass, against the port galley wall. We hung there for what felt like an eternity. I felt sure the boat was about to flip upside down, but a sudden lurch sent everyone careening to the other side.

"We must tie ourselves down," Airi shouted, "or suffer broken bones."

As I worked on getting Airi and Tanoshi secured to the trunk of the mast that went through the center of the galley, Maki opened the hatch and shouted. "Haruko! I need you up on deck. Now!"

Sato said he'd finish securing the other sailors and pointed to Maki waiting at the hatch. I nodded and scurried up to the deck. Damn, the wind was loud, Maki needed to shout even with her mouth touching my ear.

"A catamaran this small can't handle such rough seas. Deep ocean sailing vessels use a rounded bottom so they can recover after being heeled over. We can't drop the sails and heave-too like they would, so our only chance is to use the ketch and storm jib to keep the prow facing the waves, but none of my sailors are strong enough to turn the wheel in seas like this. You'll have to do it, I'll guide you, just follow my directions."

In the dark and rain I couldn't see the water, and I knew one-eyed Maki couldn't either. But she seemed to be able to detect the direction of the approaching waves by the wind and feel of the boat. In the weak, flickering light of two wildly swinging lanterns, I watched her arms and turned the wheel in the direction she indicated. First one way, then the other, sometimes franticly, other times only a small trim.

The boat pitched forward and backward. I knew each time the bow pierced an oncoming wave by the spray of icy saltwater flying into my face. With only darkness beyond the wheel deck, sometimes I was sure the boat pointed at the sky or was about to plunge to the bottom of the sea. The wheel fought my grip like an angry giant. After only a few minutes my arms started to ache, my legs screamed for a break. But Maki stood confidently gripping the mainmast with one hand and gave me directions with the other. I could never betray her trust. The two of us battled on through the storm, and in those few pauses when the boat was lined up correctly, I wondered if we were the only two topside. Had everyone else taken shelter from the cold wind and stinging spray below decks?

The storm and darkness dragged on through what felt like an eternity. Just as I thought I had no more energy left, the pitching eased. My face hadn't been splattered by salt-foam in several minutes and the rain was no longer being driven sideways by the wind. Maki turned and gave me a thumbs-up, one of those secret off-world gestures my father had taught us. Five minutes later, when it was obvious the water had settled, Sato emerged and offered to take the wheel. Maki looked around and nodded. I relinquished the wheel and staggered over to her.

I looked at her ashen face. "You're more exhausted than me. We need more of your crew up here. You've got to start trusting them." I reached out and she slumped, unconscious, into my arms. "Sato!" I shouted. "Keep the *Kaze* steady, I'll get Maki below and send up some crew to help you with the wheel. I'll be back soon. I think I understand the trick to keeping us from going sideways to the waves."

I felt exhausted, I struggled to carry Maki below. I shouted to the first two sailors I saw to go topside and help Sato with the wheel. The catamaran began rolling heavily again. Sato was doing a bad job of keeping us facing the oncoming seas. I freed Airi and Tanoshi, telling them to take care of Maki before I headed topside and tried to duplicate Maki's trick of keeping the boat facing the oncoming waves. It was still dark, but these waves weren't as high of those before, so even if I was a bit sloppy, we weren't in great danger. Maki had built a strong ship.

By the time dawn's pale light glowed on the horizon, the swells had decreased. Other sailors had come up on deck and took turns with the wheel. These more normal ocean waves didn't endanger us, so I said I'd go below and rest. Just as I reached the hatchway, I turned and looked over the *Kaze* in the dim light. Broken railings, disheveled rigging, the short foremast was gone, along with the storm-sail it'd held. Two spars on the other masts lay at ridiculous angles. The aft ketch sail still stood, but held only loose ribbons of cloth flapping in the wind. Tiredness pressed against me and I staggered down to the galley and saw a glimpse of Airi running toward me as I passed out.

* * * *

"How do you feel?" Tanoshi sat at the bedside, obviously waiting for me to stir. We were in the little cabin Maki has assigned to the three of us.

I tried to move. Every muscle hurt, my arms felt as heavy as gold. After a few pants, I muttered, "OK" and saw Tanoshi shake her head. "You've slept almost an entire day. Airi bandaged your hands. If they hadn't been callused from working the forge, you wouldn't have any skin left on them. Everyone's in awe of what you endured."

"Maki knew how to save us. I couldn't have done it. Anyway, how is the *Kaze*?"

"Repairs are being made. It seems Maki was clever enough to stow many spare parts and extra rigging. The ship remains seaworthy, but there are other problems."

"The storm swept us out of sight of the land, didn't it?" I voiced my worst fear.

Tanoshi nodded. "Airi's on deck, trying to get a fix on the sun. It's hidden by a thick cloud cover. We knew which way east was when it brightened the horizon this morning, but the boat has turned around several times since then and there's nothing but ocean in every direction."

"But the compass—?"

"Gone," Tanoshi said. "Something must have shattered the glass cover and the needle is missing. Maki had everyone scouring the decks in the hopes it hadn't gone overboard, but no one found it."

We were adrift with no compass in a world that was all ocean except for one lonely island. How could we find our way back? Even if our home was just over the horizon, we could sail right past it.

"Why, why did we set sail with just one compass?" I asked. "I can't believe I didn't make a spare."

"This fishing boat was never intended to go beyond the bay," Tanoshi said. "Maki didn't want to ask for another, as she knew it took you two days to make the one you gave her."

"I could have made another. Our first compass took so long because Dad and I needed to work out how to make it without electricity. We had to try a dozen different iron alloys to find one that didn't lose its magnetism quickly. Each sample needed to be repeatedly heated and cooled while being stroked by the little magnet from his old electric drill. Making a second compass would have taken a couple of hours, tops. I let Maki down."

"No one can think of every possibility," Tanoshi said. "And it might not matter because there's another problem."

"It gets worse?"

"Much worse, during the storm both of the freshwater barrels down in the hold leaked. It looks like the bungs on the bottom popped out. They are both empty."

"Oh, shit, we have no drinking water?"

"Dregs in the bottom and there was a full amphora in the galley. There are fresh fruits and vegetables on board, but in a day or two we're going to be desperate."

"We must rig sails to catch any rain that comes our way," I started to get out of bed. "Let's…"

"Airi's taken care of it." Tanoshi pushed me back. "I can't. . .well, I don't want to go up on deck right now," she said. I could see the tears in her eyes. Tanoshi crying! In all my years I'd never seen my strong, self-assured sister cry. "It's my fault," she sobbed. "I've put everyone in danger. We're in this mess because of me, and I can't do anything to help. I'm useless!"

I realized why Tanoshi had been subdued. It wasn't all due to exhaustion. I reached out and put my arm around her. "I can't imagine how it feels to be the one everyone depended on, and then have your power ripped away." I wanted to say something trite, like, 'I know your power will return.' But my sister knew better, out here on the vast ocean and separated from the land, she was just another human. As one who'd been imbued with unparalleled magical power all her life, she must feel as if her soul had been stripped away. I held her tight, desperate to find words that might give her comfort.

"No matter what comes," I began, "Airi and I will always be at your side. You've protected us, protected everyone in Kyoto for all these years. People have been reluctant to show it, but they know they live free because of you. Don't think you're going to be abandoned. We'll find a way to get off this endless ocean and get you back where you belong. Have faith in us, we'll find land."

Tanoshi shook her head. "There are three hundred and sixty degrees in a circle. How do you decide which one of those headings will take us to our land? Without a compass, we won't even know if we're going in circles. In two or three days we will be suffering from dehydration."

"There are some mighty tall mountains in the land of the giants. If we get anywhere close, we'll see them poking above the horizon. That means there isn't three hundred and sixty different directions we can sail. It's more like four or five. And. . ." I stopped as an idea shot into my head. "Tanoshi! The land is the source of your magic. You might be able to feel where it's located. You can guide us in the right direction."

She looked at me. "But I don't feel anything, I just feel empty."

"Yeah, down here in the cabin with the ocean just beyond the wooden hull, it would be hard to feel anything. But up on deck—no, you need to go up on top of the mast above the water where there's nothing else around you. I know you can do it. The land will call out to you."

She looked at me and began shaking her head. "I doubt it'll work. I can feel the emptiness inside me. Because I was always powerful, I never developed any skills like you and Airi. You have your steam engines and Airi has her math and engineering. You know who you are. I'm a witch with no magic. How useless is that? Why, just standing on the boat's rocking deck, knowing I don't have my power to keep myself steady, scares me."

"No," I said. "You're wrong. You have tremendous strength. For all these years you've kept your power under control. I know it's always calling out to you to abuse it, trying to make you selfish and lazy. Yet you walk when you could fly, sweep the floor and wash the dishes when you could just magic everything clean. And, remember Yushin, the engineer who turned out to be an asshole after all we did for him. He's not hopping around like a frog now, is he? When he pushed you away to go flirt with those other girls, I know I might have changed him if I had your power."

Tanoshi smiled. "It was a close thing, but we did spend all that time teaching him how to operate your locomotive. Wouldn't be cost effective." She sighed, "all right, brother dear, you can hoist me up on top of the mast and I'll make a fool of myself. Who knows, maybe your idea will work."

* * * *

We found Airi, Maki and Sato pouring over a hand-drawn map they had on top of an upturned barrel. The heavy clouds were thinning, and Airi had determined the approximate direction of the sun. That helped, as we knew our island was in this planet's southern hemisphere, since the sun wasn't directly overhead, Airi was explaining how that let her eliminate half the possible directions we should sail.

"I'm looking at the way the wind and waves move," Airi said. "Now the storm is over, the normal weather patterns should reestablish themselves. The wind almost always blows straight into the bay. If we keep the wind to our aft, there's a good chance we'll find home."

Maki agreed, pointing out the boat only needed to get close enough to spot the tops of those tall mountains.

"Tanoshi might be able to help." I explained my idea of hoisting her to the top of the mast, and letting her try to feel the source of her magic. Airi and Maki looked doubtful and Sato shook his head.

"It's worth a try," I insisted. "If Tanoshi can't feel the land calling to her, we have Airi's plan to fall back on."

At Maki's command, two sailors lowered the lookout sitting on the rig I'd made. It wasn't much, just a short plank attached to two ropes which spread from the hoisting rope like a triangle. Sato directed Tanoshi to sit on the plank and to keep her hands on the side ropes even after they attached a safety harness around her waist. Tanoshi had been carrying her half-katana around, but saying she didn't want to drop it overboard, handed it to me for safekeeping.

The rig was makeshift, but I'd only expected experienced sailors to be using it. Tanoshi looked scared when they began hoisting her up. She glanced at the small block on the top of the mast, probably realizing she'd crash down against the deck if her weight popped the squeaking wheel out its holder.

The boat was rocking, and the unsteady motion was amplified at the top of the mast. Sometimes Tanoshi swung out far from the mast, and then, like a pendulum, she slammed back against the wood.

"It's really wild up there," said one of the sailors who'd been keeping lookout. "We've been taking turns, because no one can take the dizzying motion for long."

I watched Tanoshi slam into the mast again. She had trouble keeping her backside on the seat and almost slipped off the thin plank. We held our breath until she'd awkwardly regained her position and got one arm around the mast. Watching her struggle, I realized Tanoshi, without her magic, was a klutz. She'd grown up imbued with power. It'd never let her stumble or fall. In the past, she'd never made a misstep, stubbed a toe, or knocked over a cup.

When necessary, she could move like lightening with the precision of a machine. Once, just after her tenth birthday, an assassin from Takamatsu threw a spear at her back. When the weapon was just inches from her body, she whipped around and caught it in midair. After a red flash and an ear-hurting crack, black char and molten bronze fell to the ground. Her assailant then turned green, grew a long tongue, hopped away and his family needed to keep him restrained for the next few years so he didn't poison himself by eating flies. Now, it hurt to see my beloved sister, throwing up her breakfast while clinging to the gyrating mast.

"Lower her back to the deck," Sato shouted. "Before she falls."

"I'm all right," shouted Tanoshi. "Just give me a chance to get used to this. I have to try."

She didn't look all right. Her backside looked as if it could slip off the skinny plank any second. If she didn't have one arm wrapped around the mast, I'm sure she'd be dangling from the safety rope and screaming in pain as it cut into her. After a few nerve-racking minutes, Tanoshi appeared to settle down and began staring at the horizon. It soon became obvious she wasn't feeling anything. Eventually, she called down to Maki and asked her to turn the boat around slowly, perhaps with one side of her head pressed against the wooden mast, it created a dead spot for her.

Two revolutions later, after some breath-holding moments when the *Kaze* was sideways to the waves and rocked wildly, we all admitted the idea, while good in theory, wasn't going to work. "Let's bring her down before she falls," said Maki. "The poor girl's taken enough of a beating for one day."

Just as the sailors began loosening the end of hoisting rope, Tanoshi shouted for them to stop. Rather hesitantly, she raised one arm and pointed at the horizon. We turned to look, but saw nothing.

"Can you see land?" Maki called to her.

Tanoshi shook her head. "I feel something calling to me from that direction," she shouted. "We should go towards it."

Airi was already at her map. "We'll have to sail across the waves and not with them to our aft," she said. "From the position of the sun, I figure she wants us to go north. The bay is on the east side of our land, so I expected her to indicate a more westerly course."

Maki studied the map lines Airi had drawn. "If we head north, it'll have us beam on to the prevailing seas and rocking like crazy," she said. "Tanoshi could never withstand the beating she'd receive."

"The land has to be west of here," Sato insisted. "It can't be anyplace else. If we turn north, we'll not get close enough to see the mountains."

I looked up at Tanoshi who continued clutching the mast with all of her strength. She looked sick. Just how sure was she?

Maki turned to me and echoed my thoughts. "Do you think she can feel anything? Perhaps she's afraid to let us down? Could she be guessing because she can't accept being powerless?"

A few days ago, if Tanoshi had said, "go that way," I wouldn't have hesitated. But how did anyone cope with having part of what they considered themselves ripped away? Maybe she really was guessing, hoping her strength hadn't quite left her.

"One night's storm couldn't blow us that far away from our island," Sato slammed his hand against the map. "We must keep the wind behind us. When the weather clears we'll see the mountains. If we go north, who knows where we'll end up, and we're out of drinking water. This is not the time to trust a powerless witch who can't accept her weakness."

I stared at him, then noticed Airi looked ready to slap him. If Sato wanted to marry the prettiest girl in Kyoto, he needed to understand Airi would not tolerate anyone putting Tanoshi down. But his outburst made up my mind.

"We'll follow Tanoshi's lead," I said. "I know my sister. She would never put our lives in danger if she wasn't sure. She says that's the direction we must go, so that's our new heading."

Maki looked at me and nodded. "Bring Tanoshi down," she said before turning to her crew. "We'll put up our remaining canvas and I'll navigate by the waves. Tanoshi will be our compass, but she only needs to go up the mast from time to time to check our heading." Maki walked away to direct her crew, leaving Airi, me and a frustrated-looking Sato on the wheel deck.

Once back on the deck, Tanoshi couldn't stand. Airi and I kept a tight hold of her as we helped her back to the cabin. I wanted to say, "are you really sure?" But Airi was praising her for enduring the beating from the mast. I decided that having placed my faith in her ability, I'd not show doubt.

"The land was hard to detect. It's a long way off," Tanoshi volunteered as she took her sword from my hands and pressed it to her chest. "Many miaru. I don't understand how we could have traveled so far in just one night."

"And not in the direction we expected," Airi said. "There must be an explanation." She sat down and stared at her hand-drawn map. I was tucking Tanoshi into bed when Airi cursed. "Blast! There must be some powerful currents in this ocean, we must have become caught in one during the storm and it carried us far south, toward the pole. We're not west of our land, if we'd kept the waves to our aft we would have sailed right past it."

We both turned and looked at sleeping Tanoshi who still clutched her sword to her chest. I realized that even weakened, her power had saved us again.

"We're not saved yet," Airi said. "In a world of mostly ocean, there must be some extremely powerful currents. It might look as if the wind is pushing us through the water at five miaru an hour, but an underwater current could be shoving us back at the same rate or even more. With no landmarks to reference against, we have no way of telling if we're getting closer to home or not."

I nodded. Even knowing the direction of the land might not be enough if we were caught in an overpowering current. We might not be able to overcome an opposing current because the damaged *Kaze* only carried half the sails Maki had intended for it. "Those sails we spread out to catch rain," I said. "We need to canalize parts of the ship and use the wood to get more canvas aloft. We need to catch every bit of wind we can. Let's go and explain it to Maki."

Airi stared at her map. "Perhaps, in a while, Tanoshi can tell if we're getting closer to land," she said. "No matter what, we're going to be very thirsty before we get out of this mess."

Maki understood as soon as we explained our fears, as she'd learned about sailboats fighting opposing currents on her world. She agreed our best option was rigging every sail we could. Her one bit of encouraging information was that, as a catamaran, the *Kaze* didn't have as deep a draft as a single-hull sailing vessel, which let it skim the surface, providing some protection from underwater currents.

It hurt to rip out the ship's timbers, but we worked all afternoon and eventually had some shabby, makeshift rigging holding more canvas. I managed to convince myself we were moving faster through the water. Tanoshi went up the mast several times, and although she could confirm our heading, she wasn't able to tell if we were getting closer to land.

CHAPTER 7

After four days everyone suffered from dehydration. Maki dispersed the remaining water and fresh fruit as fairly as she could, although she begged Tanoshi, who spent so much time aloft, to take extra. But my sister refused to be treated differently. I'd built a hoisting chair, which held her more securely, and she insisted I include holder for her half-katana so it too could go aloft with her. However, hanging in that contraption ten meters above the rocking deck remained an arduous task. It hadn't rained, but the heavy sea fog prevented us from seeing more than a miaru or getting a proper look at the sky.

Tanoshi did confirm whatever called out to her from beyond the fog now felt closer. Sato claimed she was obviously guessing as the direction she wanted us to sail often changed. Airi said without a compass or any references other than the wind stirring up waves, it was more likely they were the ones changing. We no longer ran parallel to the wind, but now needed to tack into it. This meant Tanoshi needed more time up the mast to keep Maki informed of our true course as we zigzagged along.

The wind picked up during the night, and the resulting larger and confused waves made it impossible to hold course without Tanoshi's continuous guidance. She pushed herself to the edge of exhaustion, forcing me to step in and refuse to let her spend the entire night being battered in the cold wind.

"I must do it," she insisted. "We're in this mess because of me. Give me a minute, and I'll go back." Then she stumbled against the ship's rail and only my fast reactions stopped her from collapsing to the deck.

She looked helpless in my arms, this could not continue. "I'm wondering, now we're closer to home, if it's possible for you to get a bearing from down here on the deck. Why don't you give it a try?"

She nodded and asked me to take her forward where it might be easier to detect whatever called out to her. It wasn't easy to get my exhausted sister forward, and if I hadn't been holding her she would have gone overboard. As we inched our way along the rail, I could feel the cold wind increasing. I guessed it'd shifted once again, and if that were true, we were lost without Tanoshi's guidance.

Once at the bow, she stared at the misty ocean for several minutes before shaking her head. "I'm sorry, I think I can start to feel something, but then the boat dips or a wave splashes up and it's gone. I guess it's back up the mast for me."

"You need to rest. You can't continue like this. I'll tell Maki to bring down the sails and we'll try to hold position until morning."

Tanoshi looked at me. "Everyone's in danger, no one's had a drink in four days and now we have no fruit left. Many of the wives remain below. Poor Fumiko and Kanon are unable to stand. We must find land before some of us die."

I held her close, feeling her shivering in my arms. She'd pushed herself beyond what she could take, and now faced a night in the icy wind on top of a gyrating mast. "Rest first," I insisted. "I can't have you falling asleep up there." I knew she was in dire straits when she didn't protest.

"This stronger wind," Airi said, after running over to me. "It's thinning the mist." She pointed upward. "Look at that glow in the sky. It could only be our moon." I looked where she pointed. Yes, one small patch of the sky appeared brighter.

"One last time," I said to Tanoshi. "Get us one last fix and then Airi can navigate by the moon. Do you think you can do it?"

"One more time," muttered Tanoshi, "and then I can sleep." She turned to walk toward the hoisting chair, and I moved quickly and stopped her from falling. She was exhausted. I didn't know where she found the strength to stay upright.

It pushed her beyond her limits, but Tanoshi got us our fix. Airi scribbled some figures on her map and had Maki change course. Soon, my sister was back on the deck and I carried her below. Before I reached the cabin, she'd fallen asleep in my arms.

The wind continued to thin the fog, and before long we

could see the moon. Airi needed to remain on deck and keep recalculating our heading as the moon changed its relative position as it moved across the sky. I saw Sato staring at Airi, and I wondered if he was realizing what a super-intelligent and beautiful woman he'd let slip away. Well, I had no sympathy for him. He had no reason to call Tanoshi's integrity into question.

* * * *

The sun appeared on the horizon at dawn, the first time we'd seen it in four days. After the morning mist cleared, we saw a dark streak on the horizon. The sight sent renewed energy to our tired and thirsty crew. With all possible sails catching the wind, we surged through the water, everyone speculating on how long it would take to reach home. Both Maki and Sato expressed doubts. They'd expected to see the tall mountains in the land of the giants appearing above the horizon. They feared the dark streak in the distance was just the tops of those mountains, and we were still several days from reaching land.

But, as the day wore on, our telescopes revealed the green of a forest on gently rolling hills, and no sign of those high mountains. Sato insisted it wasn't our homeland, but another island.

"No way," I said. "The Moon Goddess assured my dad there was only one small continent on this planet and angels don't lie. Plus, if there were any more land masses, we wouldn't have fifty meter tides every day."

"But those mountains are over ten thousand meters high," Sato shouted. "They should be visible for many miaru. The storm can't have swept us that far in just one night."

"I understand," Airi said. "The storm didn't carry us out to sea, but swept us southward, toward the planet's southern pole. That would explain why it's so cold. What we're looking at is the southernmost part of our continent instead of its western shore where we left. A mostly ocean planet would create powerful currents via the corellas effect. We've been swept quite a distance, but we're south of our island and without Tanoshi's help we would have sailed past it. In fact, I bet we have never been far from land, it was always just north of us. But we were trapped in such a powerful current that, despite the wind moving us in one direction, the current opposed us. I bet we've been only inching our way toward home."

I looked at Airi with renewed awe. "You've remembered everything my dad explained about planets, tides and ocean currents, haven't you?"

"This is the kind of thing your dad used to teach on Earth," Airi said. "Of course, he taught me everything he knew. Haruko, what did you think I was doing on those days when you were in your shop building machines?"

Maki put her hand on my shoulder. "Airi has no equal, Haruko. You should know that. Anyway, we're definitely getting closer. Let's hope we can quickly find a source of fresh water. In case we can't get the *Kaze* close to shore, I'm having the crew ready the pilot boat and put one of the water casks on it."

I looked at the water barrel some sailors were bringing up from the hold. "If Tanoshi goes ashore, her powers will return. That'll be a big help in getting us home."

"Getting water is our priority," Sato said. "We can worry about the witch after that's accomplished."

Airi saw me making a fist. Quickly, she shouted we were both going below to get some rest and to wake us when we were closer to shore. I realized how tired I was and didn't protest. But, Maki's second in command or not, I was going to explain to Sato, no one ever insulted my sister.

* * * *

Late afternoon, the three of us came on deck and discovered the *Kaze* hove too, a few miaru from a sandy beach. Maki came over to us. "This is a shallow area, there's only five meters under the keel. Those waves between us and the shoreline are breaking on a reef. I don't dare bring us in any closer."

"Are we stuck out here?" I asked.

"See that small river entering the sea?" She pointed to a spot down the beach. "It will have carried sediment into the sea, which will choke the reef. Chances are there will be a gap. Hopefully, our pilot boat can get to the shore, and we can refill a barrel from the river."

"It'll be dark soon," I said.

"Sato says he'll risk it, dark or not." Maki indicated the little pilot boat bobbing alongside. Sato and one of the big water barrels occupied almost all the boat's center area. "Sato's volunteered to take Tanoshi ashore where she can regain her power."

"If he fails," Airi said, "we'll all die of dehydration. We only have one little boat."

Maki nodded. "Fumiko and Kanon are unconscious," she said quietly. "They are young and frail; the lack of water hit them hard. If we wait until morning, it will cost them their lives."

I saw the pain on Maki's face. This was what it meant to be a leader. Should she risk everyone's life to save those girls, or let them die to give the rest of us a better chance? For a second, I was glad I wasn't the one making the decision, but then realized once I became king, I'd need to make similar choices.

That reminded me of Kenshirou and Aunt Chie's endless leadership lessons. A leader needed to think about all of his people, and he needed to think long-term, not about what felt good at the moment. A proper leader took the pain of choosing between bad and worse onto himself.

"There's only an hour left before we lose the light," I said to Maki. "And we're not in position to launch the pilot boat. In fact, doing so means bringing the *Kaze* close to the uncharted reef in fading light. As darkness falls, how will Sato navigate to shore even if there is a place where the water is deep enough? Should he reach the beach, who's to say a hungry bear or some other large animal won't charge out of the forest? Just because we don't see any wal-rus here, doesn't mean they never use this beach."

I looked at Maki's one working eye, tears came from it and ran down her cheek. Yes, she knew she needed to wait until morning, but the idea of being responsible for the deaths of those girls was too much for her. She was torn between doing what was necessary and what her heart demanded. In the past, I'd always considered my pirate Aunt a strong, imposing, and slightly scary woman, but now, I realized I'd grown a full head taller than her.

"We are going to put out to sea and get some distance between us and this lee shore," I yelled so her crew could hear. "With first light, we'll return and I'll go ashore to bring back water. This is the only plan which gives us a chance of survival. If there was any other way, I would fully embrace it. As your future king, I will take the pain this decision causes upon my shoulders. As horrible as it sounds, this is my decree."

Maki looked at me, perhaps surprised I'd played the monarchy card. But then she fell into my arms and gave me a hug. After a few seconds, she released me, turned to her crew and began giving orders to bring the *Kaze* about so we could head to deeper water.

Tanoshi, Airi and I moved to the corner of the wheel deck as it looked like the crew didn't want to be near us. No one spoke, but I noticed Maki send the husbands of Fumiko and Kanon below to sit with their wives. I hoped the crew understood, but the hardness of it meant they didn't want to voice their approval.

Airi rested her head on my breast. "You did good," she whispered. "Maki needs the trust of her crew. You taking the responsibility allowed her to avoid being the one who put those girls' lives in danger."

"No one will look at me," I said. "They think I'm a monster."

"No," Tanoshi said. "Everyone's suffering from thirst. Most hardly have the energy to move. They're just struggling to do their job and not think about water."

"How are you doing," I asked her. "You've done far more than anyone. I'm amazed you can still stand."

"Oddly, I feel far better than I did earlier," Tanoshi said. "I believe just getting close to the land has revived me. Still, I'd give everything for a small cup of water."

The three of us sat next to the rail and watched the sun sink toward the horizon as the *Kaze* sailed toward deeper water. Like the rest of the crew, we didn't speak as our parched throats hurt. But unexpectedly, Tanoshi jumped to her feet and looked out to the water ahead. "There," she whispered. "There's something coming up on our starboard side, I can feel it."

I staggered upright and looked where she pointed. I couldn't see anything but gently rolling waves. Tanoshi pressed close and had me sight down her arm. Yes, when the waves moved past it, a slight discontinuity revealed a lump tossing in the swells. I thought it appeared like the back of a dead wal-rus. It made sense to see a few carcasses, as this ocean teamed with life.

Tanoshi clutched her half-katana to her chest, "Go toward it," she said.

I didn't hesitate but went over to the two sailors at the ship's wheel and told them I needed to change course. I guess I kinda pushed them out of the way, but they were so weak I think they appreciated a break. Maki must have been dozing as we'd almost reached the mysterious object before she made her way to the wheel deck.

"What's going on?" she asked in a hoarse voice.

"Tanoshi sees something in the water. It's coming up on the starboard side." Maki went over to the rail.

I saw Sato, moving slowly, come to join her. "I don't see anything," he said. "Just waves."

"It's ice," Airi shouted and pointed. "It's hard to spot because it's clear and looks the same as the water around it. It's a good half a meter across. We've got to get it aboard."

Maki shouted to have the sails lowered. The sailors moved quickly. The excitement spreading as each learned of the fantastic discovery.

"Why would we want to bring a hunk of frozen seawater on board?" Sato asked. "It's cold enough here. What good will a hunk of ice do?"

Myself, Airi and Maki turned to stare at him. Maki shook her head and went down to organize the sailors who were breaking out a fishing net to haul the ice onto the low aft catch deck. I spent a few minutes thinking about Sato. Why didn't he know freezing water separated salt from ice? The other sailors understood something that basic. Since we lived in a climate with long cold winters, I would have thought him more familiar with ice. Maybe he was a recent immigrant from Takamatsu? I'd have to ask Maki later. While Kyoto was too big to know every inhabitant, it seemed odd I'd never run into him before. He was larger than most pixies, strong and personable enough so Maki had made him her second in command. I saw my aunt from time to time. Sato and I should have met at some point. Had Maki promoted him right after he'd applied to join her river rats? Knowing how carefully Maki trained her crews, that seemed unlikely.

It was a good-sized hunk of crystal-clear ice. I estimated it'd provide half a barrel of water. Sailors started wiping it down to remove the clinging sea water, while others rigged a rack which could hold hot embers to facilitate melting. Cups and chisels were spread out on the deck in anticipation of the treasure to come. Maki made sure everyone knew to only sip the water slowly until their bodies could adjust. Naturally, their husbands would rush the first cups to Fumiko and Kanon.

Tanoshi told me she could feel two other ice chunks in the distance, but as the whole boat was now occupied, we decided not to make an issue of it. "I expect there are others floating around, enough to fill our casks," I said. "But, when you got close to the land, a little of your power returned. If you were to step onto the shore, I bet it would all come back. Having you at full power will make our journey home safer. It'll be a long journey, and we'll need to hug the shore to find our way. I'll tell Maki of the other ice chunks and explain my plan to her. Tomorrow morning, we'll take the pilot boat and get water from the river, just like we planned."

"Thank you," she said and smiled. "To be myself again. You don't know how much I've longed for it."

* * * *

Despite knowing there was more ice available, Maki agreed to keep it a secret. Dawn found the *Kaze* slowly making its way to the shoreline. Sediment from the river made the water shallower than we anticipated, making us anchor several miaru offshore. "Sorry," Maki said. "I don't dare get closer to the reef with this wind. You'll have quite a distance to cover. Sato knows how to sail the pilot boat, so I'm putting you in his hands." She handed me a heavy lump of gold with a line attached. "This is to check the depth. Haruko, you'll have to sit in the bow and use it to make sure you're not about to run aground."

Airi removed her bear-claw and gold necklace, and, along with her notebooks and precious slide rule, handed them to Maki for safekeeping. In return, Maki opened a long wooden box and removed the large bore rifle I'd made for her. "Just in case a bear comes out of the woods," she handed it, and a box of six big shells, to Sato. "Keep it dry and don't waste my ammunition, it's hard to make."

I pointed to my katana. "I've killed bears with this," I told Sato. "If we do tangle with a bear, be careful not to shoot me. My Uncle Taro taught me how to move around fast and randomly to confuse the animals."

Sato nodded. "I'm going to put the rifle in the aft locker to keep it dry. We'll be bouncing over dangerous breaking waves near the shore. We could be in for a wild ride. No doubt it'll get bumpy and wet. Why don't you keep your swords safe in the box too? That way there's no chance of you losing them overboard. There's not much room to maneuver, especially with the big water barrel taking up most of the space. The swords will be a hindrance if you're tossed around."

I hated being without my swords, but Sato had a point and it wasn't like I was much of a sailor. I stowed my katana and the half-katana that went with it. Airi sighed and reluctantly placed her half-katana in the locker besides mine. Tanoshi looked really upset, but after I assured her it'd only be out of her hands for a few minutes, she placed it alongside the three others. I told Sato we'd retrieve them as soon as we reached quieter waters near the beach.

Maki's little pilot boat was slow. She'd told me, on her planet this was a common design for moving goods. It held a single sail on a mast placed forward, which was counterbalanced by a heavy keel and rudder assembly aft. The sail's boom wasn't horizontal but rigged to swivel against the mainmast like a V. The design's advantage was its exposed cargo area. With the sail installed high, people could occupy the center area without worrying about a swinging boom over their heads. Sato had the sail at its minimum setting, so even with the strong aft wind, we moved slowly toward the shore, lurching up and down as the rolling waves passed beneath us.

There was just enough room between the mast and the bow for me to kneel and use the sounding weight. Sato insisted I keep checking, even though the water exceeded the five-meter-long rope attached to the gold weight. The tide was high, but the ocean rollers broke over the reef. As we got closer, it became easier to see gaps around the area where the river emptied into the sea.

"We'll head for that opening," Sato pointed. "Haruko, keep me informed of the depth, and Tanoshi and Airi can each take a side and watch for obstacles to make sure we're not getting close to any underwater reef protrusions. It might be tight, but if we all pay close attention to our tasks, we can make it. Just trust me to steer the boat."

Well, he might be a twit, but it sounded as if he knew what he was doing, so I didn't object to his abrupt orders. However, the gap in the reef looked plenty wide to me, over twenty meters at least. He didn't need to be so pompous. I tossed the sounding weight, with all the line played out, it didn't touch anything. No doubt the current coming from the river scoured the bottom and kept the gap deep.

We sailed down the wide channel for several minutes. I'd decided this was easier than I expected when Airi shouted my name. I spun and saw Sato was no longer steering the boat. Instead he had Maki's rifle pointed at Tanoshi, and he'd stuck my unsheathed katana upright in the deck next to him.

I shouted "what the hell?" when Airi leaped and placed her body in front of Tanoshi's, her arms spread wide in a protective gesture.

Sato laughed. "What are you doing, silly girl," he said.

"You designed this gun to kill bears. You know its bullet will pass right through you and still kill the witch."

"Why? Why would you want to kill Tanoshi?" Airi paused and then said quietly, "are you from Takamatsu?"

I didn't move. There was a mast and a big water barrel blocking my way, and with Sato's finger on the trigger of the big rifle, I feared any sudden move would result in my sister and Airi's death. I could only hope Airi would keep him talking while I stealthily reeled in the sounding weight.

"Of course I'm from Takamatsu," he said. "I've taken an oath to kill the evil witch who killed my beloved aunt, Oki Nami. I expected it to be difficult, and I was prepared to die, but right now, before she regains her power, is an opportunity I cannot pass up. The she-devil should thank me; this is quicker than dying of thirst."

"You!" shouted Airi. "You knocked the bungs out of the water barrels during the storm. Didn't you?"

Sato grinned. "I broke the compass and tossed its needle overboard too." I told you I was ready to die. Haruko's father used off-world magic to poison our queen's mind and he holds her hostage in the hovel you call a city. The evil he brought to our world could have been undone years ago if that witch sitting behind you wasn't protecting him. But she's helpless now. This is my moment. For countless generations, the noble families will remember my sacrifice."

"Tell me," Airi said. "How did you get captain Maki to accept you into her crew? Why does she trust you so much?"

"You are a clever one, aren't you," said Sato. "But you forget Takamatsu has witches too, many loyal and trustworthy witches even if they lack the power of your she-devil. One accompanied me to your city and confused the simple brain of the ugly off-world strumpet you call a captain. Ha, the fool actually believes I'm her best sailor and I want to command a boat of my own. A noble like me, a mere sailboat captain? The sheer lunacy makes me laugh."

Airi nodded to a point just behind Sato. "If you'd tried to become a better captain, you'd know to pay more attention. A big wal-rus is charging the boat, it could easily overturn us."

"Don't be stupid..." he began, but he just had to turn and glance behind him. If he'd spent more time in Kyoto, he'd have heard some of my dad's Earth stories and wouldn't have fallen for such a simple trick. But, in the half-second while his attention was distracted, a heavy hunk of gold slammed into his chest with all the force I could muster. It sent him reeling backward and over the transom. His finger did manage to pull the rifle's trigger, but by then it was pointing at the sky and the weapon's recoil sent the stock into his face just before he plunged into the sea.

As quickly as I could, I scrambled over the water barrel. Before I could get aft, Airi had my katana in her hand and was watching Sato struggling in the water behind us. He'd let the rifle sink and was trying to survive.

"He's not going to fight anymore, you knocked him hard," Airi said and sighed. "I suppose we'd best haul his ass back on board before he drowns. Tanoshi, hand Haruko the boathook, I think we can still reach the idiot."

But the boat had sailed on, leaving the panicking Sato behind. We three non-sailors struggled to circle the boat around so we could get close enough to reach him. Alas, it was not an elegantly done maneuver. We couldn't slow the boat with the wind pushing us toward the beach, so Airi folded the V sail into its closed position. I used the oars to inch us back to Sato. At least the fool was smart enough to shed his clothes so they didn't drag him down while he swam toward us. Finally, I got the boathook close and he managed to grab the end.

Before we let him board, I made sure he knew we were armed. I wore my long katana once again in its sheath, and Airi and Tanoshi each had their weapons secure in their belts. I regretted losing Maki's rifle, as they were so hard to make. But with it gone, exhausted Sato, naked and unarmed, didn't pose much of a threat. I was sure the gold weight had cracked a rib or two when he lay on the bottom of the boat moaning and gasping for air.

"We still need to get to the shore," I said. "Sato, you're going to have to tell me how to control this thing, it keeps turning sideways to the beach." I looked over the side and realized we were only a few meters from a jagged reef and moving toward it. I rammed the rudder hard over, but it didn't change our direction any.

"You need some sail up," gasped Sato. "Without any sails catching the wind you're just drifting."

"Airi," I shouted. "Do that thing you did with the sails when we were trying to get the boat to turn around."

We'd grown accustomed to the rolling waves, which rhythmically moved us up and down by a meter or so. We were dropping down after one such wave when there was a loud crack. A long shaft, like a stone sword, had rammed through the hull, seawater shot through the damaged planks.

Airi shouted, "What the hell is that?" The shaft snapped and tumbled onto the deck to lie at her feet. She was bending to pick it up when the next wave lifted us. This time, when we came down, at least two other stone swords pierced our hull, one long enough to knock the empty water barrel out of the boat.

I looked over the side. "There are more," I said. "It looks like someone made thousands of swords and tossed them into a jumbled pile. The waves are slamming us against them. The boat's going to be torn to shreds."

"Get aft," Airi shouted, "stand on the raised locker. That's the safest place." In a confused hustle, the three of us managed to crowd onto the little ledge.

Tanoshi bent over and grabbed Sato's arm. "Stand up, you fool. Your feet are a smaller target than your backside."

Just then a sword rammed through the deck alongside Sato. He reached up and grabbed Tanoshi's offered hand and yanked her down toward the deadly spike. Both Airi and I grabbed for my sister, but we were off-balance. As we tumbled downward, I knew Sato had won. The spike would go right through Tanoshi's breast.

CHAPTER 8

A red flash engulfed us, accompanied by a loud crack. When I opened my eyes, the three of us were tumbling though a misty place with no up or down. My panic subsided when I felt Tanoshi and Airi clinging to me.

"Don't let go," Airi shouted. "Remember your Dad's stories, we mustn't get separated."

My confused brain started to understand. Somehow, we were in the no-place between worlds. The one my dad had told us about after he'd been transported to Earth and back. Curiosity got the best of me and I looked around. This mist wasn't like the fog we'd encountered while on the boat; it gave no hint of movement. It felt more like things simply lost detail the farther away they were. To my left, I made out our poor battered boat, surrounded by bits of shattered wood. They appeared to drift aimlessly, but rotated slightly. On my right, I could just see Sato, now a dark, indistinct figure fading into the mist. I remembered what had happened to my Dad when he'd become separated in this place and drew my sisters close to me. And yes, as Dad reported, time didn't seem to have meaning. There was an odd feeling that either seconds or years had passed since the red flash.

Then, a gut-wrenching drop into water. I gasped from the cold shock before the three of us plunged downward, sinking into a green ocean. After the initial disorientation, I saw bright sunlight flashing on a rippled surface and realized that way was up. Airi was already tugging me in that direction, but Tanoshi lay limp on my arm. My head broke the surface, and I gasped for the sweet air while lifting my sister's head above the water. She coughed, water spewed from her mouth, but she made no effort to swim or tread water. I held her up, while the weight of our soaking clothes and the heavy swords we wore threatened to drag us under.

I was wondering how I could remove the belt holding my katana and keep Tanoshi's head above the waves at the same time when Airi shouted. "Over here. It's the boat."

Tanoshi made no attempt to swim. I held her with one

hand and rather clumsily kicked and paddled toward the wooden pilot boat. Battered and broken, it'd landed upside down, but the hull remained far enough above the surface to allow Airi and me to shove Tanoshi's limp body onto it. As the half-destroyed boat wasn't stable, we remained in the water and held onto the wood to make sure Tanoshi didn't slide off. When she threw up some water, I heard Airi say, "Thank the Goddess."

Tanoshi moved her head. I think she tried to say something but only coughed and lay panting against the hull. The initial fright over, I tried to make sense of what had happened. My sister had done magic again. Before the red flash, we were close to land. She must have reached down into herself and drawn on whatever power she could muster. To save us, she'd thrust us into the nowhere place and we'd ended up here. But calling on such power, especially in her weakened state, had left her exhausted and barely alive.

"Where do you think we are?" I asked Airi. "This water feels warm, and these waves are low and gentle. We've gone a long distance."

Airi looked around. "I think," she said after a few minutes, "this could be the Earth your dad came from. You know he's unable to go into the sea because his proper place in the cosmos is Earth. If he enters the ocean, which overrides the magic of the land, he'll be drawn back to it. You and Tanoshi have his blood, so you also have a connection to Earth. It would explain how Tanoshi could perform such a feat with her limited power. Still, it must have drained everything out of her. Your sister always amazes me."

"Except, we ended up in the middle of an ocean. Our troubles aren't over and Tanoshi is too exhausted to help."

"Problem," agreed Airi. "At least the boat came with us, but the hull has holes in it, so there's no way we can turn it over and use it to sail to land." She pointed to something sticking out of the aft end. "What's that?"

Airi swam to the stern. "It's one of those stone swords," she said. "I guess the boat ripped this one out of the reef. It looks like there's a clump of clams stuck to its back end." Airi hung on to the boat and studied the odd thing lodged in the boat's transom. "I understand. What looks like a long stone sword is actually half of an elongated clam shell. One of the clams in the center of this clump grew it and the other clams surrounding the sword-maker clam are supplying it with food and minerals so it can grow its sharp shell longer and longer."

"I give up, why would clams do something like that?"

"Food for all. If one clam grows a sword, then any fish or wal-rus or anything else that's swept across the reef during a powerful tide could be hurt or killed when they're slammed against it. The blood and tissue in the water then becomes food for the other clams. They're working together to increase their food supply."

"You're saying we were attacked by killer clams. If we get out of this, that's going to be hard to explain and not get laughed at."

"Well, it explains why there were no wal-rus around. They've learned to stay away from the clams."

The sun climbed higher in the sky while Airi and I hung onto the side of the boat. Warm water or not, both of us started feeling chilled. Tanoshi began to recover, but we refused to let her take a turn in the water. At least this sea was calm. Occasionally, a gently rolling wave lifted us half a meter or so, and we used the small elevation to scan the horizon.

"I think I see something," I shouted. "But I can't be sure."

"Where?" Tanoshi waited while I pointed. Then carefully, on the wobbly hull, she got to her knees. Finally she confirmed something was out there and it might be heading toward us. We waited and eventually Airi and I could see it. Tanoshi said she'd risk standing and waving when it got closer.

She didn't need to stand. It looked as if it was coming right at us. As it drew closer, I could see more detail. It was definitely an Earth boat. Dad had told us about them. No sails above the shiny black hull, and the short stubby mast only held a round ball and a fat stick that rotated. It looked big; several times the size of the *Kaze*. It wasn't a catamaran but a single hull with a sharp bow, which sliced though the waves creating white wings of water on each side. It wasn't moving especially fast, maybe the speed of the *Kaze* in moderate wind. We decided it would pass around a hundred meters away. Fortunately, a sailor stood in the bow. He waved before running into one of those house-like structures on the deck. I hoped he'd get the boat to stop.

It didn't slow down, but speeded up and changed course to head directly toward us.

"They're going to ram us!" Airi gasped.

"Swim," I shouted and started to help Tanoshi back into the water. She remained frozen and looking confused and frightened. I suspected she was trying to draw on her magic and getting nothing. "Quick," I shouted. "Into the water, I'll help you."

I glanced at the oncoming boat. Those waves from the bow looked like giant white wings. As it came closer, from my position it appeared enormous; the black hull with its deep red trim gave it a terrifying appearance. I realized, even if it swerved and went roaring past us, we'd be battered by the huge waves it produced.

At the last moment the boat did turn enough to miss us. It tilted over so far I guess someone had shoved the tiller against its stops. But those black sides came frightening close. We could feel the engines vibrating the water. Waves, terrifyingly high from our perspective, raced toward us. "Hold your breath," I shouted as a wall of water came at us.

The first wave slammed into us. At least we were far enough from the pilot boat that when it flipped we weren't hit. We heard a resounding crack come from the passing vessel. It sounded as if something large and metallic had broken. Several other waves followed the first and we swallowed water before the sea settled down again. I notice the big black boat wasn't plowing through the water as before. A large wave, which had been created in its wake, surged forward and caused the boat's aft to rise several feet.

I had problems of my own. Without the boat for support, my waterlogged clothes and heavy sword made it hard to keep my head above the water and hold onto Tanoshi. Airi saw me struggling to unbuckle my belt. "Don't let your sword go," she shouted. "These guys are not our friends." She pointed to our pilot boat. With it upright again, although swamped to the gunwales, we could see the mast sticking up. It gave us a direction and the three of us paddled toward it. I think Airi and I were on the verge of passing out when we finally got our hands on the wood.

"Still got your sword?" Airi asked between pants. I nodded and assumed both she and Tanoshi still had their weapons. We couldn't draw them while floating in the sea, but if those cretins tried to take us prisoner, we wouldn't be helpless. I was able to reach up and check the aft locker on the pilot boat, but its lid had been torn away, and my half-katana, which I'd left in it, was missing.

The big boat remained around two hundred meters away. Smoke shot from two pipes in its transom, and I could hear roaring from what I assumed were engines. I concentrated on keeping Tanoshi's head above the water. She was in a really bad way, and if those guys fixed their boat and sailed away, I doubted my sister could survive. I hadn't noticed it before, but Tanoshi's skin had a faint blue glow. In fact, where my arm held her body, it too glowed blue. It didn't hurt, in fact it felt rather warm and comfortable.

"There are blue sparkles all over my body," Airi said. "They seem to be making me lighter, even without trying, my head stays above the water."

I was about to agree the same thing seemed to be happening to myself and Tanoshi when I saw a huge hatch in the rear of the black boat opening. "What's going on with that boat?"

Airi looked over to the boat. "I think they're putting a small boat into the water. We need help. Let's hope they intend picking us up. But be wary, don't trust them."

A gaudily painted open boat, about the size of our pilot boat, came over. It didn't have a sail. I could hear the roaring of a propulsion engine. Despite my misgivings, I was rather excited to see a working internal combustion engine, which my dad had told me about. The boat moved slowly. The single guy on board waved to us, and turned the boat around to approach us stern first.

"He's got black hair," Airi said. "If this is Earth, then our green hair is going to stand out. If anyone asks, shrug it off and don't go into detail about where we're from. People here don't believe in magic."

Now the craft was closer, I saw they'd designed the boat to make it easy for people to board it from the water. Sticking out from the transom, right at water level, was a wide ledge which held a short metal ladder that the man flipped into the water. He gestured for us to use it to climb aboard.

"Are you proper healthy?" he shouted in English and then added. "Sorry, I mean are you all right? Can you get aboard on your own?"

"I'll go first," Airi said. "Then you can push Tanoshi up the ladder." She looked at me. "The guy's just a kid about our age. If he tries anything, I have my half-katana."

"Watch out for a handgun. Remember, they can be quite small." Airi nodded and swam over to the ladder. I wondered if the guy noticed her blue glow.

The guy helped Airi climb aboard. He seemed genuinely concerned when he saw me helping limp Tanoshi over to the boat. He turned his back on Airi and knelt on the ledge. Ignoring that Airi had her hand on the hilt of her weapon, he called to me. "Let me get my hands under her armpits. I'll pull her up while you push."

Tanoshi was able to get her feet on the ladder. Between the three of us, we were able to get her onto the ledge. Airi helped her over the transom. I wasted no time in scrambling aboard. There were white leather seats facing the boat's rear, and I helped Tanoshi over to one.

"Oh shit," the guy said. "You guys look really sick. Sumimasen. I mean, I'm so sorry. Did you swallow water from our wake?"

"We were in the water for a long time," I said as I wiped the wet hair from Tanoshi's face. "She's exhausted and we're cold." Fortunately, once we'd left the water the blue glow had abruptly ended. Maybe the guy hadn't noticed. He didn't seem to care about our swords.

"You really look cold!" The guy tilted back one of the seats to reveal a small compartment. "There's a bunch of towels in one of these lockers. Let me find them." He opened several other compartments as if he wasn't familiar with the boat until he came to one holding large colorfully patterned sheets of expensive cotton cloth. Removing the excess water from our arms and hair helped, but our wet leather clothes remained uncomfortable.

"There are blankets and hot food on the *Cardiac Bypass*," he said. "I'll take us there." He went over to a station with a wheel and some gauges. I gathered that was where this craft was controlled. Airi sat, looking exhausted, next to Tanoshi. I went over to them and started rubbing Airi's arms to get the circulation back.

"The kid looks harmless, and he didn't comment on how we look, but I don't know what we'll face on the big boat," I spoke in our language. "They did deliberately try to run into us. I might need you to back me up if things get difficult." Airi nodded and said she'd be ready.

I was surprised at the noise created by the boat's engine, even though it was muffled beneath its cowling. Steam engines are way quieter. Of course, I couldn't imagine building a steam engine small enough to fit on a little boat like this. Anyway, internal combustion devices are extremely powerful. We raced over to the big boat in less than a minute.

I didn't have to wonder how we were going to get off this little boat and onto the larger one. The huge hatch in the stern of the larger vessel remained rotated down into the sea. A kind of rail with rollers extended beyond the hatch, protruding into the water. The kid made several passes at the rail, apparently trying to get the two boats lined up. A guy standing in the hatchway kept calling out instructions and waiving him off when he didn't get it right.

Airi looked at me. "I don't think the boy has commanded one of these no-sail boats before. He doesn't seem very good at it."

I nodded, glad we could communicate in a language no

one else could understand. If there were problems, private communication would help. Eventually, the kid got it lined up close enough, and shoved a leaver on the side of the boat forward. The engine roared and we bounced back and forth as we shot up the ramp. One of the helpers secured a hook to the front of our boat and waved to the kid to shut off the engine. A cable pulled us all the way in. Behind us, I heard a loud hissing as the big hatch slowly rose into its closed position. The little boat was secured in a mini-dry dock in the enclosed metal cavern. Our boat sat lower than the walkways around the dry dock, so one of the helpers placed a metal ladder down, giving us a way to climb up to the dock's floor. This place didn't have windows, but it was made bright with glowing glass balls attached to the ceiling and walls. Actually seeing electric lights in operation was a strange experience.

We had no time to enjoy the novelty as five men came down a metal stairway. None of them looked happy.

"They're exhausted and suffering from the cold," said the kid who'd rescued us as he climbed up to the main floor. "We need blankets and something hot to drink."

"Then go get them," snapped the one in front. He wore a dark blue jacket with white trousers and a rather unfunctional peaked hat with gold braid. "Damn, we need this like we need another broken transmission." He turned to one of the men behind him who wore a more reasonable outfit and no silly hat. "Go find Doc Bryce and ask him what the hell he wants us to do with these clowns." He paused before shouting and pointed at our rescuer who was almost out the door. "Someone keep an eye on the brat, he's done enough damage."

We were still on the little boat's deck. Tanoshi hadn't made any attempt to stand and Airi stood next to her, keeping guard. I decided I'd best get off the boat. The men were on the higher floor and I didn't like being at a disadvantage. I climbed up to the metal deck and noticed Airi following me.

With Airi at my side I guessed I'd best start a dialog with these men who stood staring at us. "I am the Prince of the Kingdom of the Jeweled Moon." I began, doing my best to speak English clearly. "May we have the pleasure of exchanging names?"

"Freaking crazies," Blue Jacket turned to one of the men behind him. "We don't have time for these idiots. Go drag the black bitch up here. We'll put them in the aft cabin and the Doc can decide what to do with them after the ceremony."

The man moved as if he intended going down the ladder to get Tanoshi. Airi blocked his way. "She needs warm clothes and food. You are not treating stranded travelers with proper respect."

The man raised his arm as if to strike Airi. I grabbed his shoulder, used one of my dad's simple throws, and sent him tumbling over to the bulkhead. The leader, who was standing in front of me, reached beneath his jacket and pulled out what had to be a handgun, although it wasn't a revolver like my dad's. I yanked my sword out of its scabbard. Airi, who was closer to him, slammed the back of her half-katana against his wrist. The man yelped just before the gun clattered against the metal flooring. By then I held the sharp side of my katana against his neck.

"Be thankful she only used the back of her blade," I said. "Otherwise you'd have lost your hand." I shouted so they could all hear. "We know what projectile weapons look like. If anyone else displays one, I will kill all of you. This is not negotiable."

"You crazy punk," shouted an especially large man as he came toward me. "If you think you're tough—"

"Stand down!" shouted a man from the doorway. "He really can kill all of you. Don't doubt it for a second." He wore what looked like a black blanket or a large shawl decorated with red patterns, which looked like a child's drawing of a five-pointed star. The men remained still while the robed man made his way over to me. "Son," he said quietly. "You have my word you are safe. No one is foolish enough to attack you. Please, both of you, put your swords away. The Captain knows to behave himself."

I paused, thinking I couldn't maintain this standoff much longer. These guys didn't realize how exhausted we were. I suspected Airi remained standing on sheer force of will.

"I will place my trust in your word," I said. "Although the strange reception we have received will cause me to remain cautious." I slid my katana back into its sheath and saw Airi slowly doing the same.

"Thank you." The robed man and turned to his comrades. "There has been a change in plans. We will not be performing the ceremony tonight. You may go back to your duties." After the men left the dock carven, he turned back to me. "So, young man who knows what projectile weapons look like, those are very strange runes carved into your sword. I was amazed at how brightly they glowed. Do they have special powers?"

I almost said, "Hu?" before realizing he was referring to the names of my family etched into the side of my katana and filled with gold. Since the names were carved using the outdated and ancient script, which only Aunt Kenshirou knew how to write, I suppose they did look a bit magical. Since my mother and Tanoshi had done the work, and both of them held magical power, there was a possibility they actually were more than just names. At the time, they'd said it was just to make the katana recognizable as belonging to the future king.

I was saved from responding by the kid returning with a tray holding several packages and large cups of a steaming black liquid. For a second, I saw anger flash across the robed guy's face. Then he smiled and put his arm around the kid. "This is my beloved first-born son, Lawrence," he said. "He's brought you simple refreshment. Take your time, and when you're done, Lawrence will show you to his cabin where you can rest before dinner." Abruptly, the man turned and left the cavern.

I'll be the first to admit I wasn't good with English. Before today, it was just a game the three of us played with my father, but I found the robed guy's way of talking odd. Perhaps he was mimicking me, but his strange attention to my sword made me suspect he knew we weren't from this planet. Besides, he hadn't given me his name, only his son's. Even I knew how, in the world of magic, knowing a person's name gave power over them.

We sat alongside Tanoshi and ate quickly. Lawrence didn't object when we asked him to first sample the things he called cookies and take a sip of the liquid identified as coffee. The over-sweet food wafers revived us and Tanoshi said she could move again. Our new friend offered to lead us to where we could rest.

"Our clothes are wet and cold," Airi said. "Do you have anything we could wear while they dry out?"

"Oh, so sorry. Of course you're freezing. There's a bathroom with a shower on the main floor. You can use it to get warmed up while I hunt up something dry for you."

We followed Lawrence out of the docking cavern and into the main part of the ship. It was, as I expected, richly decorated; polished wood floors, and paneled walls with amazingly realistic paintings of various boats. Other than the strange paintings, and narrowness of the hallway, I could have been in my Takamatsu palace. Our guide led us up a ship's ladder to a higher deck. Actually, it was a stairway and I suspected it annoyed Airi to see good interior space wasted. But then, when we entered the bathroom, we realized efficient use of interior space was not the priority of whoever designed this craft. The three of us stood staring and confused by the huge room.

"I believe," Airi said. "Various pipes deliver either hot or cold water, but I don't see any valves." She turned to Lawrence and spoke in English. "This is a bit strange to us," she said. "Would you mind showing us how everything works?"

I think the kid was starting to understand we were different, because he just nodded and started giving detailed instructions of the fixtures. Airi kept nodding and paid close attention. I guessed, if we ever got home, our house would undergo some major renovations. Tanoshi loved the shower and seemed fascinated that just by turning one knob back and forth she could change the overhead spray from cold to hot. She set the spray as warm as she could stand and stood under it. Airi joined her and they started disrobing each other, not an easy task with soaking-wet leather outfits. This seemed to disturb Lawrence and he spluttered he needed to go find some dry clothing for us. I told him I'd appreciate it and began loosening my clothes. I wanted to get under the warm water also.

After we were reasonably warmed up, Lawrence opened the door dragging a box with wheels on the bottom and a handle extending from the top. He saw the three of us standing at the sinks and froze, staring at us. Then he quickly shoved the box into the room and half-closed the door.

"I. . .I'm so sorry," he sputtered speaking through the small gap left by the mostly closed door. "My dad has gone back to his room, and I can't get any cooperation from the crew. All I have are the clothes I brought with me when I came on board. They're still in this suitcase. These are just guy clothes, I'm sorry."

"You can come in," Airi said. "We're just trying to save our outfits by rinsing out the seawater and wiping down our swords to prevent the salt from hurting them."

Lawrence edged his way a few centimeters through the doorway. He pushed the box thing toward me while making a show of looking at the wall. Airi looked at me and shrugged.

Tanoshi hung her head and in our own language whispered. "We went through hell getting here, and I still can't find a guy who wants to admire my body. Are all the guys in the universe jerks?"

"It might be he's just trying to be proper. Dad said the people on Earth are more hung up about nudity than we are."

"Please turn around," Airi said. "I don't like talking to someone when I can't see their face."

"I should leave and let you dress," Lawrence said as he edged toward the door. "I'm sorry if my clothes are too small for your prince."

Airi laughed. "Well, come here and help me dress. Then I'll go have a chat with the big guy we saw earlier. I bet he'll loan Haruko some of his things if I ask real nice." She picked up her sword.

"Haruko?" Lawrence said. "Is that your prince's name?"

I realized with all the confusion we'd never exchanged

names. "Yes, I'm called Haruko. The pretty girl with the long black hair is my beloved sister, Tanoshi. The cute little one is Airi, she's like a sister to me as well as being my closest friend and confidant."

Lawrence, still refusing to turn around, spoke quietly. "Those sound like Japanese names."

I looked at Tanoshi and Airi. I think we were surprised he'd figured out our ancestry and also at the confirmation this really was the Earth our father had come from. I was wondering if it was wise to confirm his suspicions when he spoke again.

"My dad insists on calling me Lawrence," the boy said. "But the name I really go by is Kenji. I've lived in Japan most of my life and only arrived in America yesterday. You weren't speaking the same language I know, but I did understand some of your words and the way you sound makes me homesick."

"Kenji is a common name in our land," I admitted. "Now, will you turn around and tell us what's going on with this crazy boat?"

Kenji turned. Kenji stood staring at the three of us. His face became an impressive shade of red. He stood transfixed, and I worried he'd forgotten to breath. He took several steps back and retreated toward the door. "Oh my God," he gasped. "I shouldn't be here, please forgive me."

I grabbed his arm before he could run. "You must have seen naked girls before. Stop making such a big deal of it."

"You have green hair and pointed ears," he managed to gasp. "That's not human. And Tanoshi. . .ah, well." He paused before turning to me. "Is she a Goddess? I've never seen such perfect beauty, even in the movies."

Airi came over to him and grabbed his other arm. "You saw us when you rescued us, and you've been helping us all along, you must have noticed our hair and ears before this."

"No, you both had blond hair and I didn't see anything odd about your ears." He turned to Tanoshi. "Were you doing something so I wouldn't notice how beautiful you are?"

"The way you see us changed after you learned our names?" Airi asked. "None of the others on this boat indicated there was something different about the way we look. To them, we must have appeared as normal Earth Humans."

"We must be careful never to reveal our true names again," Tanoshi said. "And Kenji," she went over, put an arm around him and pulled the frightened guy to her chest. "Can I count on you to keep our little secret?"

The way he went wide-eyed made me think the kid had never experienced naked breasts pressed against him before. After a stunned silence, he uttered something unintelligible, but at least managed to nod. I thought Tanoshi acted a bit over-friendly, but this was the first time anyone outside of her family had complemented her on her appearance. Back home, those who didn't want her dead, kept their distance or interacted with stiff formality.

"You said there were clothes inside this. . . sut'kas," Airi pushed it on its little wheels. Please show us how it opens."

A nervous looking Kenji tried to pull away from Tanoshi, but my sister kept one arm around him and watched carefully as he moved a tab which made the case open. Some clothes fell to the floor. My sisters picked them up and discovered three identical black trousers, four white shirts and some cotton underwear and socks. I thought the selection rather limited considering the sut'kas could have held three or four times that amount. The trousers more or less fit Tanoshi. Airi needed to bunch them up around her waist and, after asking Kenji, use her katana to remove the lower part of the legs so they wouldn't drag on the floor. I think Kenji was intimidated because his thin white shirts did little to conceal the girl's wet breasts. Alas, nothing in the box would fit me.

"I grabbed the blanket from my bed," Kenji yanked a brown sheet of cloth from a separate compartment on the side of the sut'kas. "You could put it over your shoulders."

Well, it was better than nothing. I draped it around me and held it in place with my sword belt. The girls arranged their new clothes to their liking and made both Kenji and myself compliment them on how cute they looked in Earth-guy clothes. Kenji muttered that, with their breasts clearly visible, they might get into trouble if they appeared in public. Tanoshi just laughed and said she was recovered enough but still hungry and could use some more food and drink. She asked Kenji to take us to the food preparation area.

Tanoshi seemed really taken with her new friend. I had to remind her to put on the belt with her half-katana before we left the room. Kenji put our damp leather outfits in his sut'kas, saying he didn't want any of the other men on the boat stealing them. He paused after picking up one of Tanoshi's knee high snake skin boots and touching one of its many buttons.

"Is this real gold?" he pointed to a button.

I laughed. "Oh, yeah. Girls like to decorate their outfits with buttons. They do look better than laces, don't they?"

Kenji turned to me. "Don't let anyone else get a close look at them," he said. "Especially the guys on this boat." He shoved them into his sut'kas.

"Kenji," Tanoshi put her arm around him. "We were in the water for a long time and we need food and rest." He nodded and led us out into the hallway. Well, Tanoshi was definitely making a new friend. I just hoped she wasn't overdoing it. The kid already looked as if he worshiped her.

The galley was more functional than the opulent bathing room. Kenji opened a shiny metal door and from its cold interior, produced various preserved meats, cheeses, bread and butter. The meats and cheeses were bland, the tasteless bread was pasty and the butter, while it looked correct, was really sub-par. But we were hungry and ate ravenously. At least the water, which came in thin, soft, transparent bottles, was cold and refreshing.

While we ate, four of the crew, their clothes stained with grease, entered the galley. "Shit," said the large man who'd threatened me earlier and pointed at Kenji. "We're down in the cramped engine compartment busting our balls trying to fix the damn transmissions you wrecked, and you're sitting here stuffing your fat face. I should cram that sandwich down your girly throat, you worthless piece of shit."

Tanoshi stood. "You insulted my friend," she said. "Such a transgression is going to cost you. Remove your outer garments and put them on the table."

"You dumb black bitch, just who do you think—" He stopped talking when he saw both Airi and I stand with our hands on our sword hilts. "Shit," he said. "We've got work to do if we're ever going to get this worthless tub moving again." He looked at Tanoshi. "The Doc says we must leave you alone, but I'll remember you." The men shoved each other in their haste to get out of the galley.

"There's more strangeness on this boat than just advanced technology," Airi said in our language. "We must remain cautious, and. . ." she turned to face me, but her eyes flickered toward Kenji. "We must not assume everyone is our friend, even if they act that way."

"I agree," I said then turned to Tanoshi. "Were you trying to use magic on that guy?"

"I was angry enough to give it a shot," she admitted. "But I guess my power hasn't returned. He didn't act much like a frog when he left, did he?"

"You're still exhausted from getting us to this crazy world," I assured her. "It'll come back soon."

"I hope so, a witch without her power is pretty pathetic. I almost got you into a fight. I'll be more careful in the future."

Kenji looked at Tanoshi. "I understood a little of what you said. Are you really majo—a witch?"

The three of us looked at each other. We'd forgotten he spoke real Japanese, the language of our ancestors. Apparently, majo meant witch in both languages. My heart sank as I realized Tanoshi had just lost the first friend she'd ever made. Everyone was afraid of witches, especially those who could casually talk about turning people into frogs. I wondered if I should explain Tanoshi only turned people green and made them think they were frogs. But I realized it wouldn't matter. Real witches were terrifying.

Tanoshi looked at him and spoke quietly. "Yes. It's true. I'm a witch. The most powerful one our world has ever seen, if it comes down to it."

Kenji stood staring at her for a long minute. "Wow!" he exclaimed. "This is really neat. I bet I'm the first guy on Earth to make friends with a real, honest to God, witch. This is just great!"

"You're not afraid of her?" asked Airi.

"Why would I be afraid of someone as neat as Tanoshi? I think she's fantastic."

"I can hurt people with my power," Tanoshi said. "Most people find me scary."

Kenji looked at her. "In this world anyone can hurt others, if they're that kind of person. You saw the gun the captain carried. Here, people don't have to get close to kill you. What matters is the kind of person you are. I know you're not the type who hurts others without a reason. I want to be your friend."

Tanoshi gave the boy a long hug. I think she considered kissing him, but caught herself. Even saliva from Tanoshi could trigger the yokubo change. That would really complicate our lives.

Kenji's father, the man the crew called Doc, entered the galley. He glanced at his son before turning to me. "I realize you've had a bad time of it, but I can't have you threatening my crew with your swords. I understand you don't want to part with them, so I must ask you to remain in a cabin until we return to Florida. It shouldn't take too long, the men assure me they'll have both transmissions repaired soon. We should be back in Saint Petersburg before sunrise tomorrow. Then we can go our separate ways. Is this acceptable to you?"

The three of us looked at each other. We were tired, so arguing didn't seem productive. Besides, we knew how dangerous guns could be and this would keep us away from the crew. I told him I found it acceptable. Doc, addressing Kenji as Lawrence, told him to take us to his cabin, then turned and left the room.

On the way to Kenji's cabin, I asked him why his dad called him Lawrence.

"Because it's hard for my mother to pronounce." He didn't offer any explanation. Airi looked at me and shook her head. I gathered I shouldn't pry. Kenji led the way but remained silent.

After experiencing the opulent bathroom and the large, well-equipped galley, I almost commented on the plain and utilitarian appearance of Kenji's cabin. A tiny metal washbasin with a connected elimination receptacle occupied a corner of the room, starkly contrasting with the shiny glazed ceramic and gold fixtures in the large bathroom. While such an arrangement might be adequate for one person, we would be hard pressed to endure even one night in such cramped quarters. I was considering demanding better accommodations when Tanoshi staggered over to the small bed and collapsed onto it. Airi wasted no time in joining her.

"You can have the chair," said Kenji. "I didn't spend the day swimming in the gulf, so I can make do with the floor."

"I don't trust this crew," I said. "I'll sit with my back to the door. I'll wake if anyone tries to enter." I unsheathed my katana and, after settling, placed it on my lap. "I still haven't learned why this boat almost ran us down when we were in the water, or the strange attitude this crew has toward us. If I wasn't exhausted, I'd go have a long talk with your father and demand some answers."

"I don't know either," Kenji said. "This is just my second day in America, and nothing has made sense. My dad explained how he'd arranged this trip some months ago and wanted me to come with him, but he'd caught a bad cold and needed to stay in his cabin. I haven't had a chance to say anything to him beyond hello since getting off the airplane."

He stayed silent for a minute. "I can't explain what the Captain was thinking. Right from the time I came onboard, no one was friendly. With my dad sick in his cabin, I just hung out at the rail watching the water go by. Then I spotted your upturned boat and ran and told the Captain we'd have to stop and rescue you. He swore and turned the boat toward you and shoved the throttles forward. I started shouting. He shouted back and ordered me below. That's when I shoved him away from the wheel and turned it as hard as I could. The captain's a big guy; he yanked the wheel from my hands. So I grabbed both throttles and rammed them into full reverse. I guess you're not supposed to do that. There was this big crack and the propellers stopped turning. They said I'd broken the transmissions."

He shook his head. "The captain started cursing, but before he could hit me, my dad came on deck. After he learned there were people in the water, he told me to take the ski boat and rescue them."

I didn't know what to think. These people seemed crazy and dangerous. I didn't know enough about Earth to understand the strange relationship between Kenji's father and the rest of the crew. Who was in charge? Anyway, the story made me put more trust in Kenji, and with tiredness threatening to overcome me, I decided to think about it later and get some rest.

* * * *

A roaring, accompanied by the room vibrating, woke me. I was panting, gasping for air. The room felt hot and stuffy. My head throbbed as if I'd drunk too much beer. I staggered to my feet noticing how everyone else remained unconscious. "Wake up, wake up," I shouted while shaking Tanoshi and Airi.

After they sluggishly sat up on the bed, I managed to rouse Kenji. "They must have fixed the engines," he muttered. "It sounds like we're underway again."

Kenji shook his head. "God, it's stuffy, is the air vent closed?" Walking unsteadily, he went to a small grill near the ceiling. "There isn't any air coming out. We're running out of oxygen. Quick, open the door."

The door didn't budge. Kenji tired some tricks with the levers, finally admitting the room had been locked from the outside. I looked at the metal door, for the first time noticing how closely it fitted against its jamb. The only explanation was they'd designed this room to be airtight.

Kenji went across the room to the hull side of the cabin and examined one of the two, small round windows. "This porthole is sealed shut," he said. "In fact, it's not designed to be opened and the glass looks to be at least two centimeters thick." By the time he'd stopped talking, I was breathing heavily and still felt as if I wasn't getting enough air.

I turned to Airi and Tanoshi. "Someone is trying to

suffocate us. We're prisoners in here."

CHAPTER 9

While Kenji banged on the door and called for help, the three of us examined the room. The cabin walls, which appeared at first glance to be wood, turned out to be a thin paper-like substance stuck to solid metal. We ripped up the floor and found the pretend-wood planks were a thin veneer over metal flooring. I repeatedly attacked the porthole glass with the hilt of my sword, but it wasn't like any glass I'd ever encountered and Kenji told me it was an unbreakable plastic.

"This room is a prison cell." Kenji sat down on the edge of the bed. "Without an air supply, it turns into death chamber. They—my father—intends to murder us."

"But why?" Airi asked. "They don't know us, and we planned to be out of their lives tomorrow morning? It doesn't make sense."

I nodded, unable to think of any reason people, who we didn't know, would want us dead.

"It's our swords," Tanoshi said. "I felt something dark about the man wearing the silly robes. He saw the words on the side of Haruko's sword glowing. He knows they hold magic power and he wants them for himself, and he's smart enough to know he could never take them by force."

"My sword has magic power?" I asked.

Airi sighed. "Haruko dear, you kill bears with that thing. Didn't you ever wonder why it was so easy? Everyone else is terrified of fearsome, two meter tall animals with vicious claws and teeth. Tanoshi and your mother both worked together to infuse your sword with protective magic. Remember, since the very first, a queen has ruled Takamatsu. As a male and heir to the kingdom, you have enemies. Most of the nobles are horrified by the thought of a man ascending to the throne. Yes, those marks they etched onto the side of the blade are not really names. They're enchantments to give it great strength and speed."

"Oh," I said.

"Let's get out of here," Airi said. "We're in the rear of the boat and I believe the back wall of this cabin butts against the big holding chamber where they dock the small boat. The metal feels cold, there's even condensate on it. So, that wall, and the one which is part of the ship's hull, are made from thick metal. The wall with the heavy door feels cool to the touch, meaning it's made strong, as most imprisoned people would try to batter down its door. But the last wall" she pointed. "I held my hand against it and could feel the metal start to warm, indicating it might look strong, but the metal is thin."

"Right then," I said. "Let's start hacking at it."

"Use my half-katana," Airi thrust her sword at me. "It holds the power to protect the monarch. Plus, being shorter, it will be easier to ram though the wall."

I took her weapon, reared back and shoved its sharp point at the wall. The sword shot through the metal all the way to the hilt with less resistance than stabbing a bear. I needed to pull it back a bit. "It's soft metal," I said. "Look, it's hardly a millimeter thick. I wonder how they are able to roll steel so thin?"

"Hurry!" Airi smacked her hand against her forehead.

With my palm against the black of Airi's blade, I shoved the sword to the floor. The metal separated easily, with a sound similar to the device which opened the lid on Kenji's sut'kas. Two down strokes and one across the top let me fold the flimsy metal to the floor and form a doorway. Behind the metal we encountered a soft white foam Kenji called insulation. Once I ripped it away, we came to the backside of the wall of the next cabin. It wasn't real wood, just a five-millimeter thick piece of something made from compressed sawdust which had already collapsed from my blade's cuts. We scrambled through the opening. The fresh air hit my lungs like the aroma of newly-brewed beer.

"Wait!" Shouted Kenji who'd remained behind. "Don't forget the suitcase. Your gold is valuable." He passed the sut'kas through the opening. I didn't like the idea of getting into a fight clad in only a loose blanket. Everyone waited until I'd dressed in my proper clothes. They remained damp and cold, but the familiar leather felt comforting. I was myself again. Airi and Tanoshi put on their boots so they wouldn't be barefoot.

"We'll take the ski boat," Kenji said while we dressed. "We can't be two hundred kilometers from land. It should get us back to Florida."

My dad had decided a thousand meters would be around two of our miaru, even though we hadn't got around to accurately defining our larger units of length. I thought four hundred miaru a long distance for a little boat, but I had no idea of the range of an internal combustion engine.

The door to this cabin wasn't locked. I opened it and peered into the hallway where the noise coming from of the engines was louder. Our luck held, the narrow hallway was empty. Kenji knew the way to the boat-dock cavern, and we followed him.

One man, holding a rifle and inhaling smoke from a burning white stick, was the only occupant of the docking cavern. He didn't look very alert, and I fear I approached him too casually. He swung his weapon around faster than I expected, and although my sword knocked it to the side, a shot shattered the silence.

"We're taking the little boat," with my blade against his neck, I yanked the rifle from his hands and handed it to Kenji. "Open the big hatch and help us get it into the water." I shouted at the man. A few drops of drawn blood convinced him to nod in agreement.

Kenji held the rifle. "I've never fired a gun before, but I think I can use it to guard the hallway until you get the ski boat into the water. Once the hatch is down, unhook the winch cable attached to the front, then shove the hull backward. Don't forget to put my suitcase on board."

Airi, holding her half-katana, took over watching the man at the controls of the big hatch. As it opened, blue, foul-smelling smoke from the engine's exhaust swirled into the cabin, and the noise was deafening. I guessed this hatch was not supposed to be opened when the boat was in motion.

The slow moving hatch was almost all the way open when some crewmembers charged down the hallway. Kenji fired the gun over their heads. None came through the door.

"I heard them say there're going to get a machinegun," Kenji shouted. "We gotta get out of here before that happens."

I got Tanoshi into the little boat and tossed my sword sheath and the sut'kas in after her. When Airi turned toward me, the crewman did something to stop the hatch from moving. It still tilted upward enough to prevent the boat from sliding down the rail and into the sea. The man tried to grab Airi. I leaped. For a second, my sword hung in the air as I realized I was about to kill another human. The man cringed, shouting, and holding up his hands in surrender.

"Make the hatch open!" I shouted, but he collapsed to his knees screaming, "No, No!"

I turned to Airi. "Did you see which valve he closed?"

"He hit an electric button on the panel," she pointed. "But I didn't catch which one. Everything here uses electricity." I nodded, we knew about electricity, but our steam-driven world hadn't had time to develop it. Even if we could read English, the control panel would still be indecipherable to us. I looked at the big hatch, frozen in its halfway-down position. The choking blue smoke was now dense enough to make me feel dizzy.

"Look," I said. "Electricity may run the pumps, but those are hydraulic cylinders doing the lifting."

Airi went over to the hatch. "Yes, they are hydraulic. Those I understand."

Tanoshi screamed. Airi and I whipped around to see the fool crewman held a handgun pointed at me. Right at me. All I could see was the big round hole and the guy sighting along the top of the weapon. He wouldn't miss at this distance.

Just as the gun fired, a red streak slammed into his chest. I'm sure the bullet brushed the hair on top of my head before continuing out of the half-open hatch. The fool flipped backward, doing a somersault, before he lay still with hilt of Tanoshi's sword sticking from his chest. I had no idea she could throw her sword with such accuracy or power.

Airi looked at me. "Sever those hydraulic lines, do it quickly, we've got to get out of here."

I understood, and after a few slashes, high-pressure oil shot across the room. While I did that, Tanoshi helped pull Airi over the transom. The big hatch sagged downward, but it'd not reached an angle where we could get the little boat into the water.

"Get my katana," Tanoshi shouted. "That man must not have it."

As I ran toward the dead guy, the rapid crack, crack, crack of a machinegun sent bullets through the open door and bouncing around the cavern. For some reason, the bullets went high, a few bouncing off the ceiling and others going out the hatch opening. Kenji ducked back behind the doorjamb, and remained frozen, his eyes wide, his hands shaking.

"Get in the boat," I shouted. He didn't move. I couldn't leave him to die. I ran over, slammed the door closed, picked up the kid and tossed him into the bow of the boat. The severed hydraulics had let the hatch collapse, and the boat began sliding backward into the water.

With a crash, the door opened and, led by a guy holding the machinegun, the thugs charged into the cavern. The machinegun guy saw me and pointed the weapon in my direction. This was just like fighting a bear—move and confuse. In the instant before he pulled the trigger, I leaped to the side, my feet used the steel hull to propel me across the gap, and my katana slammed down on his weapon. My sword went right though, severing the gun into two pieces.

"Haruko!" Tanoshi screamed. "Get in the boat, jump."

I looked. The little boat had slid off the rails, and the forward motion of the big boat was about to leave it behind. With the gap increasing quickly, I ran and leaped, tossing my katana into the boat while in the air. A good move, as I splattered into the water, fortunately close enough to grab the little cable connector, which stuck out of the boat's prow.

As I made my way to the little boat's rear, one guy on the big boat shot at us with a handgun, but with his boat bouncing over the waves, and range increasing, none of the bullets came close.

Kenji was at the boat's controls, and I could hear its

internal combustion engine making an odd grinding sound. Then, with a loud bang, the engine began roaring the same way as it had earlier. As I scrambled over the transom, white water appeared at our wake, the boat turned sharply and then accelerated, its prow lifting into the air.

"The yacht isn't fast enough to catch this one," Kenji shouted over the noise. "But I dropped the rifle. I want to get us out of range before they find it. Everyone stay down."

I crawled over to Tanoshi. "I didn't get your sword. It's still on the big boat."

She nodded. "It might not be too bad. Unless that man can find a way to corrupt it, it'll not be much use to him."

"Still, it holds magic power," I said. "And judging by the way it streaked across the cavern, quite a bit of magic power."

"I've been feeding power into it for several years," Tanoshi said. "It's very strong. When we were on the *Kaze*, without any power of my own, I couldn't tap into it until we were close to the land. It used a lot saving us from the stone swords, but there must be quite a bit left. Anyway, if we can get my feet on land, my real powers will return. Then I'll take it back. It would not be good for it to remain on this world after I used it to kill. Such an act hurts both me and the sword."

I put my arms around her, and assured her there'd been no other choice. But I could see the hurt in her eyes.

The boat's engine became quieter. Kenji said we were far enough away, and he was reducing speed. I looked back and saw the big boat turning and guessed it intended following us. Kenji gave Airi a lesson in driving a powerboat. It was simple to operate. She only needed to learn how to control the speed. Kenji explained how this craft, which he called a ski boat, could go very fast, but at a slower speed, it would go farther before running out of fuel. However, if we went too slowly, it wouldn't go as far. He needed to find a speed that would give us the greatest distance. There was a compass just above the control wheel, and Kenji said if we kept heading east, we would run into the Florida coastline.

After traveling for some distance, I thought it a good time

to question Kenji and try to understand this craziness. "Was the man in the black robe really your father?" I asked.

"I think so, but I don't know anymore. Everything has been crazy. I honestly don't know what to think."

"Tell us everything," Tanoshi said. "Start from the beginning. It is important we understand."

Kenji remained silent for over a minute. "Where to begin? Yes, the man in the black robe claims he's my father, but I know little about him. I know he's rich. But I guess that's obvious from the size of the boat he owns. He's a doctor, my mother told me that, but he doesn't practice anymore as he owns several clinics and part of a private hospital. He has other investments. I know he's made it onto those super-rich guy lists."

"You said you lived in Japan," Airi said. "He and your mother don't live together?"

"He'd divorced my mother before I could walk." He smiled. "That's a good place to start the story. This is what my mother told me. When he was younger, my dad toured Japan and met my mother. She was still in high school, and didn't speak more than a smattering of English. She admitted she wasn't a great student and the two of them could barely communicate. A poor orphan high school girl with limited prospects, and a rich American doctor who called her cute. When he proposed, my mother saw it as her big chance and accepted. They moved to America and I came along nine months later.

"By then, Mother spoke better English. She'd also learned what a miserly, mean spirited, and abusive man he was. As she'd turned into a mother, and was no longer a mysterious oriental cutie, he wanted to end the relationship. The divorce paid for us to return to Japan and gave her a small stipend to live on. It was minimal at the time, and as inflation took its toll, not enough for us to get by. For most of my school years, I worked part-time jobs to help with the expenses."

"Wow," Airi reached over and put her hand on his shoulder. "Your dad sounds like snake-shit. Why did you come back to America to meet him?"

"Schools in Japan are intense. Between having after-school jobs and being a bullied half, I never did well with my studies. Certainly, there was no chance of me getting into a Japanese university."

Tanoshi interrupted. "What's a half?"

"That's the name school kids call those who're not full blooded Japanese. It's an insult. I didn't have friends while in school, no one wanted anything to do with me. Although, I suppose having to rush to a job right after classes added to my isolation. One time, hoping to make a friend, I joined the kendo club after discovering the faculty intended shutting it down for lack of members. I thought they'd appreciate another guy. However, once I'd learned the basics, the more advanced kids used it as a way to bat me around. The club president thought it funny. Eventually, I had to quit."

"What's kendo?" I asked.

"It's a sport like sword fighting with wooden swords and lots of padding. There are strict rules on what you can do. If you don't follow those rules, you can really hurt your opponent."

"I know what you mean," I thought of training with my Uncle Taro. We'd used wooden swords too, but a monument's lost concentration always resulted in a bruise. My hand rested on the hilt of my katana, it was now part of me. The pain had been worth the price.

Kenji continued his story. "After I finished high school and every university I'd applied to rejected me, my mother received a letter from my father. He said I could attend a school over here. He promised to arrange everything and even paid for a tutor to improve my English before I came over."

"You really speak English well," Tanoshi said. "You're much better at it than us."

"My father said he had everything arranged. Supposedly, I'm enrolled, and I start classes at the University of South Florida next week. He asked me to come over early, so we could get to know each other. But when I got off the plane, I was met by the boat's Captain. He said my dad was sick with a cold, but he'd planned this trip some time ago and we'd get together once he felt better."

"And then he was willing to kill you just to get our swords," I said. "It still doesn't make any sense."

"The way the crew of the *Cardiac Bypass* acted toward me before we picked you up, didn't make sense either," Kenji said. "Even while attending a Japanese high school, I'd never faced such open hostility. I'd expected the crew to act politely to the owner's son, but they went out of their way to ignore me. That's how come I'd was standing at the rail looking at the water when we came close to you."

"The Captain tried to run us down," I added. "There is something evil about that boat. What did you call it, the *Cardiac Bypass*. Does the name have meaning?"

"It's an expensive medical procedure. My mother told me my dad was a heart doctor before he became so rich he didn't see patients anymore. Still, the foundation of his wealth comes from the cardiac clinics he owns. I guess he thinks the name is clever."

Tanoshi went rigid. I think she was holding her breath. Then she spoke quietly. "Kenji, what is your father's name?"

"Oh sorry, I guess I never did tell you. Everyone on board called him Doc, but his name is Jack Bryce."

It was my turn to gasp. I looked at Tanoshi.

"It's the interconnected web of magic," she said. "I suppose that's why we dropped into the water where we did."

"How could you know of my father?" asked Kenji.

"Your father tried to murder our dad just to save the little bit of money it'd take to scrap an old worn-out boat," I explained. "He would have succeeded in killing him, except the Moon Goddess transported him to our world at the last second."

"Now Jack Bryce, the cardiac surgeon, is fabulously wealthy," Tanoshi said. "He made a deal with the evil one."

"Why would you think that?" Kenji looked confused.

Tanoshi explained. "There are rules governing the spirit world. When the Moon Goddess saved our father, it gave the evil one an opening to act in your world. Evil could offer a deal to the man who'd tried to kill the one the angel had saved."

Kenji hung his head. "You're saying my father sold his soul for wealth and prestige. What does that make me? I carry his blood."

"It makes you our friend," Airi said. "Blood means nothing; it's the person that counts. You've already proved you're not greedy like your father. You told us how the gold trimmings on our clothes are worth a great amount of money in your world. When we reach shore, those bits will give us food and shelter until Tanoshi gets her power back and we figure out a way to get home."

* * * *

We could see the blue haze of land on the horizon when the ski boat ran out of fuel. It was frustrating to be so close but dead in the water. One drawback to internal combustion engines is they require a specific fuel. You can't just break up bits of the boat and burn them to make steam. The open boat had no cover, letting the merciless afternoon sun beat down on us. We had no water or food and sitting around thinking about how thirsty we were made it worse.

Tanoshi sat up and looked at Airi. "Quick," she said. "We must take our proper clothes out of Kenji's sut'kas and put them on. I feel it's important."

No one argues with a witch's intuition. Airi and Tanoshi stripped and donned their cold, damp leather outfits. No sooner had they finished than we spotted another boat. It moved fast, so it wasn't the *Cardiac Bypass* but a good-sized white boat with a high prow and a large, low aft deck. There was a cabin in the center with a second control station on top of it, and above that a metal framework, which held yet a third station, just large enough for one man.

"It's a sport fishing boat," Kenji explained. "See those outrigger poles and the fancy fighting chair on the back deck. I'm going to wave my shirt. Maybe they'll come and see if we need help."

The boat did slow down and approach us. Four shirtless men on the aft deck stood staring at us while drinking something from bright-red containers. They waited until the man, who was up in the high tower, made his way down to the deck. "What's the problem," he shouted.

Kenji explained how we'd run out of fuel. "You got a radio? Call Sea-Tow." Came the reply. He then turned to the other men and said something that made them laugh.

"We don't have a radio," Kenji shouted.

The man who'd talked with us shook his head, let out an audible sigh and said something about tourists. "OK, I'll call it in for you. Just sit tight, they'll get to you in an hour or so." He turned and walked toward the lower cabin.

"Please," Tanoshi shouted. "We have no water, could you give us some?"

The man, who I suppose was a captain, turned and came over to his ship's rail. "What were you kids thinking, coming way out here in a little bow rider without fuel or supplies? You're lucky the gulf is calm today. Anyway, I got water bottles, they're two bucks each."

One of the men holding a red drink container laughed. "They're just kids, cut them some slack," he said to the captain. "You made three thousand bucks today, and we only caught one damn tarpon." Even at this distance I could see the man giving the captain a hard stare.

"OK," shouted the captain, "give me a second, I'm coming alongside." Despite its size, the big boat could maneuver deftly. A few minutes later the men on deck tossed lines to us. We secured the two boats together, and the man who'd spoken up for us passed over clear bottles filled with cold water. As we drank, the four men crowded the rail and it was obvious they were staring at Tanoshi and Airi.

"What's your names?" A shorter, fatter man asked Airi.

I panicked, knowing it might be bad if they identified themselves, even if they didn't use their real names. Our green hair and pointed ears would make them wonder about us.

Kenji came to the rescue. "This is May, and the dark-haired beauty is Judy," he shouted a little too loudly.

The man gave Kenji an annoyed look. But then Airi, now May, thanked him for the water and said she'd never seen a tarpon before, and could she and Judy come onto their boat and see it.

"Sure, why not," said the man who'd given us water. "It's always nice to have pretty girls on board." He held out his hand and helped Airi over the transom. Two of the other guys jostled one another trying to be the one who helped Tanoshi. No one commented when Kenji and I followed them onto the big boat. The men told us their names, John was the man who'd acted in our behalf and his companions were, Richard, Bill, and Harvey. Kenji told them his name and identified me as Matt. That spooked me as Matt was what they called my father while he lived on Earth. I couldn't remember telling Kenji that.

The fish, the tarpon, lay in a locker surrounded by ice chips. By the way the men had talked I'd expected something larger. This one was barely a meter in length. Airi was careful to praise it anyway and she was told Richard had spent an hour in the fighting chair catching it. I was impressed that neither Airi nor Tanoshi burst out laughing. One of our sushi-tunas was at least twice as big, and no one strapped themselves into a fancy chair to catch one.

"They must be really good eating," Airi said.

"Oh, I've heard they don't taste that great," Richard replied. "Tarpon are sport fish. I'm going to mount this baby."

"What does he mean by mount?" A wide-eyed Tanoshi asked me in our language.

I paused; Earth customs couldn't be that different from our own. But catching fish and not eating it didn't make sense either. I thought of an acceptable response. "Maybe he means he's giving it to the poor, remember Dad telling us how Earth was a lot like Takamatsu with rich and poor people."

"It doesn't sound like you are from around here," the man called Richard said. "And those leather outfits don't look comfortable in this heat." He pointed to my katana. "Are you carrying a real weapon?" I looked at him. Of the four of them, his heavy build and thick arms made him appear the most formidable. I noticed he carefully kept some distance between us. I got the feeling he knew about fighting.

Tanoshi turned and smiled at him. "We're from Japan,"

she said. "We're just visiting your country. I guess we must look a little different."

He smiled back. "Japanese, you say." He looked confused for a few seconds then shook his head and turned to me. "Anyway, I should warn you not to carry a sword in public. I wouldn't want to see you get into trouble."

"We're cosplayers," said Kenji. "That's why they're wearing leather outfits. The swords aren't real, they're just painted wood. We were attending a convention in Saint Petersburg and took a little time out to have a boat ride. I guess we kinda messed up."

"Oh, I've heard of cosplay," Harvey said. "It's big in Japan. I didn't know it was catching on over here."

"Yeah," John said. "These kids aren't out to hurt anyone. Really dumb coming out this far in a little boat with no supplies, but we were all young and stupid once." He waved the captain over and they talked quietly. The captain shook his head a couple of times until John took a small booklet from his back pocket, wrote something on the top page, tour it out and handed it to the captain.

"OK," John said. "Our captain has agreed to tow your boat back to Johns Pass. There's a fuel dock just beyond the bridge. You can ride with us till we get there."

We thanked him, Airi and Tanoshi giving him, and the captain, deep bows of appreciation. While the captain rigged extra ropes to the ski boat—he intended securing it to the side of the fishing boat rather than towing it behind. John invited us to sample the contents of those red drinking containers.

"It's beer," Kenji whispered. "You open the can like this." There was a little ring on top of the container, and when pulled upward it ripped open a small hole in the unbelievably thin metal. Airi and Tanoshi copied the trick and we had our first taste of Earth beer.

"This is really good beer," Airi said and Tanoshi agreed after she'd downed most of the can. Bill and John pointed out there were more in the 'cooler' and we could have as many as we wanted. I wondered if the men thought they could get the girls drunk. I smiled, thinking this beer, while tasty and refreshing, wasn't nearly as strong as the stuff we'd been drinking all our lives.

The conversation got awkward when the men started asking about Japan. Plus, it was obvious they didn't like Kenji answering their questions. The beer might not have been strong, but after a couple, Airi and Tanoshi had trouble keeping their made-up answers straight.

Airi asked if there was an elimination container on board, and after some laughter at our poor English, learned what she wanted was called a 'head' and it was inside the lower cabin. Both she and Tanoshi hustled to the head, no doubt glad to take a break from answering questions they didn't understand.

When the girls returned, Airi smiled and spoke quickly. "Part of cosplay is singing," she said. "Would you like to hear some Japanese songs?" I'm always amazed at Airi's intelligence. If they were singing, they wouldn't need to answer questions. Of course, the men, who'd tried keeping up with the girl's beer intake, agreed.

Singing was a fundamental part of our lives. Songs and music filled our evenings and when performing routine tasks. In fact, Airi started out with a planting song, one the women sang as they moved rhythmically down the newly-hoed fields inserting seeds at regular intervals. I found the top of the 'cooler' made a different sound depending on where it was hit, and could provide a background beat.

We knew many songs by heart. It was easy to let one flow into the other. Airi and Tanoshi even did some duets. The biggest hit came when we three did our distorted version of the Earth Grapevine song, which had been so important to Tanoshi's witch mother. It was a long song, and after it'd finished I saw our boat entering a channel and we were heading toward the land.

"This song is special," Tanoshi said. "I feel the need to sing it before the sun goes down."

Tanoshi had a melodious voice with an amazing range, and even singing a capella she displayed richness and depth. I'd always assumed she'd enhanced her singing ability by using her magic, but it seems I was wrong, or at least that part of her power remained. The song sounded just as sad and beautiful as it always did. The song told of the lives lost through the ages. It spoke of the accidents, the diseases. It included the brave soldiers who'd died keeping the grain fields safe from Kyodia monsters. It touched on the grief the newcomers to our world held, knowing the destruction of their planet had ended the lives of many innocents. There was a lot of underlying sadness in our little world, and this song was our way of never forgetting those who'd paid the price so we could live our lives.

As she sang, I understood this was her way of apologizing to that foolish man on the *Cardiac Bypass* who she'd killed. Even though she sang in our language, when she finished, I saw tears in the men's eyes. For a long time, no one spoke, no one moved. Finally, the captain left the wheel, came over to John and returned that little bit of paper.

CHAPTER 10

We had some luck after tying the ski boat to the fuel dock at Johns Pass. Apparently, the fishing boat needed to travel to some other berth, where the men had parked their vehicles. With the sun almost at the horizon, the captain didn't give them time to question us about Kenji's nebulous statement about some friends coming to take care of things.

The men at the dock wanted money. Kenji explained how his dad, Doctor Jack Bryce, owned the boat and he'd come and take care of everything. After some bickering, the men moved the ski boat to a side dock to await payment.

While we'd all used the head on the fishing boat, after the many beers, moving made me realize there was still a need I'd better address. I guessed the girls had the same problem and asked Kenji if he knew the local customs about such matters.

"Most places like this have what they call restrooms," he said. "My English coach told me that much. Let me look around." After a minute, Kenji steered us to some doors on the side of the building and told the girls to go inside. Then he needed to stop Airi from opening the door with the simple block outline of a nude person and go through the door depicting a man wearing a kilt. Earth is a confusing place.

"Your outfits might be almost passable on a vacation beach," Kenji said as we relived ourselves into some smelly ceramic containers in the other 'restroom'. "Remember, if anyone asks, you're from Japan and here for a cosplay convention. However, we need to do something about your swords. Richard was right. The police will stop you if they see them."

In the end we stuffed my sword and its scabbard down a leg of one of his extra trousers and bundled some of his other clothes around everything, enabling me to wear it on my back. His suitcase, I could now pronounce the word properly, was large enough so a small cut in the top allowed us to jamb Airi's half-katana and Tanoshi's empty sheath inside. Thus prepared, we left the fuel dock and went to get real land beneath our feet.

Tanoshi ran to a place near the water where she saw some rocks and sand. She got down on her knees and pressed her hands against the ground. After a minute, Airi asked her if she could feel anything.

"No, nothing. I suppose I need to give my power more time to recover. It's been so long, I shouldn't expect it to return quickly. At least we're on land again, that's the main thing."

"They may have built this dock area using fill," Kenji said. "It's not real land that nature made. Let's walk back toward the sea. The ground there might be better for your needs."

Heading down a small road toward the ocean, we came to a brightly lit building with many land vehicles in front of it. Kenji identified it as a restaurant, a place that served food in exchange for money. "Too bad we don't have money," I said. "Other than the beer, we haven't eaten anything since yesterday."

"I'm hungry too," Kenji agreed. "I do have a little Japanese money. I wonder if this place will take it? Stay here, I'll go ask." Kenji took some brightly colored bits of paper from a pocket in his suitcase and walked toward the restaurant.

I sat on the rear of one of the land vehicles. "We shouldn't have drunk so much beer without food," I said. "I'm starving and a bit light-headed. If they don't take Kenji's money, do you think they'll barter for a bit of gold?" Airi and Tanoshi both sat with me on the vehicle's rear and admitted they too felt tired and not as sober as they should be.

"Hey! What do you jerks think you're doing? Get away from my car." A large man stormed toward us. Another man, slightly smaller, ran behind him. Two women in fancy dresses and illogical shoes that made them walk funny brought up the rear. The man shouted some things I assumed weren't complimentary.

I got to my feet, Airi and Tanoshi did too, but Tanoshi stumbled and thumped against the vehicle's metal as she regained her balance. The man began screaming, using words I didn't understand. Before I could respond, he reached beneath his jacket, produced a pistol similar to the one carried by the captain, and pointed it at me. My sword remained wrapped up. I leaped left, sprang off the rear of another parked vehicle and slammed into the guy from the side, forcing his gun arm up as we collided. I heard the gun make a loud clunk, but it didn't fire. Then he was on the ground and I'd pried the weapon from his hand. About this time, everyone around us began screaming.

Kenji came running over and pulled me from the man. He took the pistol from my hand, did something which made the stack of bullets fall from the handle, tossed them under the vehicle, and gave the unloaded weapon back to the guy, while saying we didn't want trouble. The man didn't take defeat gracefully and continued his tirade. He pointed at Tanoshi and, I assume, accused her of damaging his property. But he shouted and spoke so quickly I couldn't follow his English. Then he screeched several words I'd never heard before.

Everyone went quiet. In the hush, the guy's friend went over to him. "Larry, let it go. Don't get nailed for a hate crime. Be cool, dozens of people heard what you said and your MG isn't even scratched. Let's just leave."

The man got to his feet, while muttering about 'special privilege.'

"We gotta get out of here before he retrieves his ammo," Kenji said. "Let's move." Airi grabbed Tanoshi's arm, and the four of us hustled down the road toward the ocean. No one stopped us, but I felt as if the crowd was staring at our backs. Once we were a good distance away, Kenji said he'd dropped his Japanese money when running back to us and now we were broke.

Kenji knew nothing of this place, but he guessed there might be a dark spot around the base of the big bridge we'd passed beneath when coming in. At the edge of the bridge we discovered a small beach. We'd lucked out; this side of the bridge was far quieter and darker than the other, which was close to many brightly illuminated stores and dozens of people wandering around them. I found the intensity of the many-colored lights, the noise and the raucous music overwhelming and was glad we weren't closer.

Out of ideas, we sat on the sand and watched the low waves surging against the shoreline. With the sun below the horizon, even this tropical climate felt cold. I feared it'd be a tough night sleeping on an exposed beach.

While this area wasn't as boisterous as the other side of the bridge, I spotted a few couples, holding hands, walking along the sand. A mirau down the beach numerous lights illuminated several buildings and Kenji said they were hotels—places where visitors came to enjoy the beach. He didn't know much about American laws, but feared the area in front of the hotels could only be used by those who'd paid the hotel for the privilege. While he admitted he wasn't sure, none of us wanted to risk gun carrying police confiscating my katana.

"I'm sorry," Kenji said. "I know very little about this country. It's different from my home. I never expected to come here, and didn't want to, because I was always resentful about the way my father had abandoned my mother. But I couldn't pass up the opportunity to get an education. Foolishly, I even believed he might want to make things right with her. I crammed for six months improving my English, but I didn't learn much about the culture."

"Are you sure there are people who will give us money for our gold?" Airi asked.

"There's a problem. Many things look like gold but aren't," Kenji explained. "The only people who'll take your nuggets and give you money are those who have the facilities to make tests so they're sure you're not offering them something fake. We need to find a gold dealer, but I don't know how it works here."

* * * *

The night grew darker and most people left. Down the beach, in the brighter area in front of a hotel, some remained on the sand. Two people, holding hands, strolled out of the bright area and walked in our direction. They often stopped to stare at the water, and kissed each other before continuing. It was pretty obvious they were lovers.

"If they come any closer they're going to spot us," Kenji said. "Remember, the word is cosplay, and we're in town for a convention."

"Look," Airi said. "They're both women. And they act lovingly toward each other. They must be part wives from a family like ours."

"You might be right," Tanoshi agreed. "They may be more understanding than those people near the restaurant. Perhaps they could tell us where we could find shelter." Tanoshi turned to me. "You and Kenji stay here. Airi and I will see if they are friendly." Before either of us could protest, the girls began walking toward the strangers.

I unwrapped the hilt of my sword, just in case these crazy Earth people carried tiny pistols. After a minute it looked as if the newcomers were willing to listen to Tanoshi's story. I couldn't hear the conversation, but they talked amiably. After a while, Airi handed one of them a gold button which she'd cut from her boot. The woman carefully inspected it before handing it back while shaking her head.

"I think I understand," Kenji whispered. "Look, let's go meet them, but make sure they know you are Tanoshi's brother. And perhaps you could you convince Airi to pretend I'm her brother. I'll explain later."

Since the two women didn't seem dangerous, I rewrapped my sword. They didn't appear as happy to see us as they had with Tanoshi and Airi, but they didn't turn around and leave.

"You're from Japan and you've got yourselves stranded on this beach with no American money," the taller woman said. "That doesn't make sense. . ." The woman looked at Tanoshi and after staring at her face, said, "Well, we can offer you a meal. Come back to the hotel with us, there's an outside bar that serves hamburgers and such. I'll treat you."

As we walked along the beach, we exchanged names. Kenji intervened to give us fake names; Natsuko, Kazue and me as Takeo. They introduced themselves with American-type names. Michelle wore a dress and was the smaller of the two. Her long hair almost reached her waist. Frankie wore trousers and stood a head taller. Her deep brown hair was only shoulder length. She seemed to really like Tanoshi and after learning I was her brother, insisted they walk together. Frankie asked Tanoshi about Japan, and primed by our time with the guys on the boat, she was able to lie without help from Kenji. Frankie said she often watched Japanese DVDs and was especially fond of a type called yuri.

"Oh, me also," said Tanoshi who was in full, act like you know what you're talking about mode. "I just love yuri, it's my favorite." Frankie put her arm on Tanoshi's shoulders and pulled her closer. Michelle laughed and grabbed Airi's arm.

It appeared the hotel did allow non-guests on their part of the beach, at least when accompanied by paying guests. Everything was so far from our understanding I fear the three of us just stood staring at the bright lights—brighter than daylight even, and milling crowds of laughing people. Kenji came to our rescue and directed us to a wooden table. We sat, looking confused and overwhelmed, until Michelle brought us drinks. She held one of those super thin soft glass mugs containing beer for herself, but the drinks she gave us were brown and far too sweet. I almost spit my first sip out.

I raised my eyebrows and looked at Kenji. "The drinking age for alcoholic beverages is twenty-one. If you look young, they need to see some identification," he whispered.

That was disappointing, right then I could have used another beer or three. Obviously, living in such a confusing place with no identification or ability to read signs was going to be difficult. Without Kenji we'd be in real trouble. But this was only his second day away from Japan; no doubt he had his own trouble understating this culture.

Michelle sat next to Airi. "Kazue, you speak English with just the cutest accent and the way you mispronounce most words is adorable," she began. "I've never been able to learn a foreign language. Tell me more about Japan, do you live in Tokyo?"

Airi was saved from making up more lies because a group of guys with musical instruments chose that moment to shatter the night. They were really loud. I'd no idea anything could produce so much noise. Perhaps they were playing a song, but the volume was intense, the painful discordance swamped the individual notes. Tanoshi and Airi covered their ears.

"Make it stop," Tanoshi shouted in our language. "Please, make it stop!"

And it stopped.

I turned; the guys were bent over on their hands and knees vomiting onto the raised platform that held their instruments.

Michelle sighed. "Bunch of stupid druggies," she muttered and stood. "Well, I guess we'd best go help." She turned to Tanoshi, "I'm a nurse and Frankie's a doctor. It looks like we're needed."

We sat, watching like everyone else, as our new friends tended to the sickened boys. After a few minutes, several men in uniforms, pushing a mobile bed, arrived and took over the care of the kids who now sat, looking better but embarrassed, next to their instruments. It turned out the kids could walk, and the new men led them away.

Frankie came over. "The paramedics are taking them to a hospital for monitoring," she said. "The kids admitted they'd downed some illegals just before they came on stage. Their vitals were steady. They're not in any danger. Just another case of bad drugs."

I wondered if Kenji understood what she'd said. Apparently the guys were all right and, since two workers were cleaning the dais, I assumed the excitement was over.

A young girl in a short, unmarried-maiden short, dress came over holding plates of food accompanied by an older, overweight man also carrying food. "I appreciate you stepping up to help those kids," the man said as he placed the plates on the table. "This is on the house, just ask Teresa here, if you want anything else." He then shook Frankie's hand and once again thanked her for her help. Kenji asked Teresa to bring us glasses of water. He was a smart kid; I was impressed how he remembered the small details.

The sandwiches were illogically thick. Their height exceeded my jaw's ability to expand. We watched our American friends and learned the knack of squishing them down and taking small nibbles from the side. I liked the variety of vegetables they held. The cheese, while bland, was decent enough. But the main ingredient was cow meat. I'd been forced to sample it a couple of times on my trips to Takamatsu, where they slaughtered cows for food. Tanoshi and Airi had never tasted it, as the few cows in Kyoto were kept for making cheese. Their bodies only became leather and such after they died of old age. With our abundance of different vegetables, along with fishes, snakes, and chickens, we saw no reason to eat unpleasant-tasting cow meat. Fortunately, Tanoshi and Airi were hungry enough to get the burgers down without comment, although they finished their fried potato sticks first which, I admit, were just as good as the ones we made.

While we ate, Frankie and Michelle told us about the hospital where they worked, which was in a place called Philadelphia, and they were flying back there early the next morning. It got complicated when Frankie asked Airi about her mother's specialty.

"She just helps people when they're sick or hurt," Airi said.

"Oh, she's a GP," Frankie nodded and that seemed to settle the issue.

Michelle remarked the other people in the bar were upset, as they'd come to hear the band, which, for some unfathomable reason, was famous. The man who'd given us the free food was going from table to table explaining the problem, apologizing and trying to get people to stay and eat his food anyway.

When he came to our table, Kenji stood and pointed at us. "You've noticed the odd outfits my people are wearing. I'm their manager. In Japan, they are famous singers, and they're over here as the main attraction at a cosplay convention. Since we're not going anyplace tonight, would you like them to step up and provide some entertainment?"

The man nodded and he and Kenji had a quick discussion. I didn't catch what they said, but Kenji smiled and shook hands with the man.

Kenji rested his hand on my shoulder. "Here's the deal. He's willing to let you use the equipment. If you get up on the platform and sing like you did on the boat, you can keep any tips you make. Sound like a plan?"

"Just for singing like we do most every evening?" Airi said.

Kenji looked at Tanoshi. "Just don't sing the sad song again, these people want to have a fun evening." He led us to the platform and gave Tanoshi and Airi black sticks with a cloth covered round knob on the end. "This is a microphone," he whispered. "Just sing in a normal voice, it'll make you louder." He then went over to an electronic device and started adjusting its knobs. I was glad we'd met Kenji. Not only did he think fast, but he knew all sorts of obscure things.

There was a drum set. It appeared almost identical to the one my dad had made for me, except this one was not made from wood and leather and had a third, midrange drum and double cymbals. I picked up the sticks and found them well-balanced. I mentally thanked my Aunt Chie.

Everyone in Kyoto played a musical instrument, and most could sing as well. Music was how we passed most evenings before the adults left to have sex. I preferred the flute, because it blended with Tanoshi's exceptional voice well. However, Aunt Chie, who pretty much ran everything so my mother didn't have to bother with politics, encouraged me to take up the drum as well.

"You're going to be their king," she'd explained. "By adopting the drum, you can provide a background beat for everyone else. It will connect you to your people. Everyone will remember how the king of all the world joined them in their song. It will make you part of their lives and they'll support you."

Aunt Chie was right. When I saw how much it pleased people when I accompanied them, I devoted myself to becoming a better drummer. My dad, working from memory, designed and built an Earth-like set for me.

Kenji grabbed one of the microphone things. It did amplify his voice as he introduced us. "My friends are over here from Japan. They're on a tour promoting the big anime hit, 'The witches of Eden' and they're made up as the show's main characters. For your enjoyment, they're going to sing some songs from the show, and some of Japan's latest hits." He pointed to each of us in turn starting with Tanoshi. "Let's give a warm welcome to Natsuko, and Kazue with Takeo on the drums."

Perhaps the crowd was drunk, but they cheered and clapped, and a few of the guys whistled when Tanoshi and Airi waved to them.

Tanoshi and Airi started with some simple ditties the little kids in the colony liked to sing. It gave me a chance to get the feel of this new rig. The thinner heads gave a lighter sound, but with three mids, two cymbals and one foot activated base, I found I could really express myself.

The people seemed to enjoy our music, even if it was in a language they'd never heard before and never would again. They clapped and cheered after each number and got excited when the girls, in their short dresses and wildly flowing long hair, danced around the platform.

After a dozen songs, Tanoshi turned to me. "You ready to do grapevine?"

I flipped the drumsticks and knew I'd mastered this set. "I'm ready," I smiled. "Let's go for it."

Grapevine was one of the few songs we knew in English. Well, almost English, the years of repetition in our land had not been kind to its original pronunciation. When we began, the crowd cheered and many joined Tanoshi and Airi in dancing around. The middle part was my specialty, my chance to show what an unaccompanied drummer could do with an especially nice drum set. I got into the music and let the rhythm carry me. When my solo ended, I noticed everyone was standing, staring at me. Then they started clapping and cheering. It got so confusing that Tanoshi and Airi never did get to do their end bit.

Kenji came onto the platform and said he hoped they'd enjoyed our show. He placed an empty beer glass on the front of the platform and stood back. To my surprise, people surged forward and began putting paper money into it. Then they wanted to stand next to us and hold out a little box-like device that flashed after they'd extended their arm. Others had a friend hold the box while several of them crowded around us. Since the money was piling up in the glass, we went along with whatever these crazy people wanted.

After the last girl got, what I heard her say was a 'cool selfie,' with me, Kenji picked up the money. After a minute, he told me we'd made almost seventy dollars. I assumed he meant we'd eat tomorrow.

I asked Kenji about the flashing boxes. He explained they recorded our image so it could be seen later. Several tables still held people continuing to drink and eat, and Kenji spotted one of the girls who'd recorded my image. He went over to her and asked if we could see the 'picture' she'd taken. The girl was happy to oblige and took out her box. After fiddling with it for a few seconds she gave it to Kenji who held it up for me to see.

There I was, a perfect likeness in a detail no artist could accomplish, complete with green hair and pointed ears. Kenji slid his finger across the screen and revealed more scenes of our performance. Airi's green hair and ears were obvious. At least Tanoshi could pass as a brown-skinned Earth person with long, and especially thick, black hair.

"These boxes record our true selves," I whispered to Kenji. "What are they?"

"Well, this one is a Smartphone. Some of the other's used regular cameras. Both types capture an image so it can be seen later. I left my phone in Japan, because it doesn't work with the American system."

"Everyone can see our green hair and pointed ears when they look at their phones."

"Yeah," said the girl as she took her Smartphone back. "When we saw you sitting there in your dyed hair and fake ears, I told Nancy you were entertainers. I'm glad I got to see your act, it was great."

I looked at Kenji, using fake names or not, it appeared everyone could now see we were different.

I walked over to Tanoshi and Airi and told them what had happened. Tanoshi nodded and said it was because the last of her transport magic was fading.

Frankie and Michelle came over to us. "You have some money now," Frankie handed Tanoshi one of those little boxes. "You can use my phone. Call a cab to take you back to your friends on the mainland."

My sister stared at the incomprehensible device before offering it to Kenji. "Can you work it?"

Frankie stared at Tanoshi, "It's a Samsung phone. You should... Natsuko, you must be exhausted. All that dancing around after a long day stranded on a beach." She turned to Michelle. "We do have a double room. You think maybe? It's just for one night and these kids really look as if they could use a bed."

"Why not?" Michelle said. "We can't just abandon too cute girls at this time of night. But the boys will have to sleep on the floor."

We quickly agreed and followed our new friends to their hotel room. I kept thinking about her casual reference to the mainland. If we weren't standing on real land, could it be the reason Tanoshi's power wouldn't return.

The elevator was intimidating. We knew the principle so none of us freaked when it jerked upward. The hotel room was small, but it held two large beds. Since we'd always slept close together, just one of those beds would be fine for the four of us. But, not wanting to offend our benefactors, I didn't suggest it. Besides, I doubted Kenji could sleep pressed against a naked Tanoshi.

"Natsuko, you use the shower first," Frankie said to Tanoshi.

"Thank you," Tanoshi started stripping and Airi began removing her outfit also. "Are you going to join us?"

Michelle started giggling.

"Oh, that's right, you're Japanese," Frankie said. "You like bathing together. Will the boys wait in the hallway?"

Rather hurriedly, Michelle pushed the pair of us out of the room. But not before Kenji got another look at Tanoshi's breasts. Once again, his face turned an impressive shade of red.

"In the shower, it will be obvious Airi's pointed ears aren't fake," Kenji said as we settled on the floor with our backs to the closed door.

I nodded. "We might have to tell them who we really are. They seem like nice people who could handle the truth. You didn't freak when you learned Tanoshi is a witch from another planet."

"I'm Japanese and grew up watching anime. Those shows have witches and kids from other planets all the time. It's pretty much the standard. I guess I was primed to accept you. An American doctor and a nurse will have a more scientific outlook. They'll consider witches and magic transport too silly to accept. But they do seem like decent people. I still can't get over how easily they decided to let strangers sleep in their hotel room. Not many people would have done such a dangerous thing."

"You're right, we can't count on people being this helpful to us all the time. Somehow we have to get Tanoshi's power back so she can return us to our own time and place. I remember Frankie talking about going over to the mainland. Does that mean this is not real land? Could it be what you called 'fill' before? If so, it could be the reason her magic isn't returning."

Kenji thought for a minute. "This area is too big. I believe it's what's called a barrier island. I know a little about geology because that's what I intended studying at the university. A barrier island forms a little way offshore from the mainland, after the sea currents create big sand bars, which rise above the water line. This is not continental rock beneath us, it's a pile of sand washed up by the sea."

"And people build big hotels on a sand pile?"

"There must be enough money in it to make it worth the risk. I don't understand Americans either."

"We need to find a way to the mainland tomorrow. Getting Tanoshi standing on real land might be the only chance we have of going home."

"Any chance I could go with you," Kenji whispered. "I'm stranded here. My wallet and passport are in the safe on my dad's boat. I can't get back to Japan even if I had the money for a ticket. I'm afraid to go look for my father. The man tried to kill me. My own father. We weren't close, but what happened on the boat doesn't make sense." I saw a tear fall from his cheek. He shook his head, "Well, I should assume he's not going to get me into school now."

I put my arm around his shoulders. "I'm sorry," I said. "We've been worrying about our own problems and forgetting what you have been going through. In the last couple of days, your whole life has fallen apart. Your own father has turned against you. I can't imagine how much it hurts even if you didn't really know him. Let's just say we're in this together. Don't forget, Tanoshi is a powerful witch. Some of the things she can do amaze even me. If there's any way to take you with us, I know she'll find it."

"Thanks, I'd risk anything to stay with you guys. Can you tell me about your world?"

"Everything here looks scary to us because we don't have electricity. Compared with this world we're primitive. For you it would be like stepping back in time—far back in time. Think of all the modern things you enjoy and take for granted. Could you live without them?"

"I could do that," Kenji said. "Smartphones and the internet are way overrated."

"Think about it carefully," I said. "Our little city, just a colony really, endures months of freezing weather during winter. Almost half of our yearly labor consists of stockpiling enough coal so our homes remain tolerable through the cold months. We expect every male who can, to spend several weeks working in one of the mines. To us, iron is a thousand times more valuable than gold because making it means someone has to dig out the ore, the coal and the limestone, before we even get to the blast furnace part. We work hard, all day, every day."

"You didn't become such a good drummer working in a coal mine. Tanoshi and Airi have perfect, well-practiced, singing voices and know lots of songs by heart. Tell me the rest."

Kenji was smart, I'll give him that. But I'd played up the

negative side because I felt sure Tanoshi couldn't get him to our world even with her powers restored. Everyone belonged in the land of their birth. At the moment of death, occasionally, transport became possible. The Moon Goddess had brought my dad to our planet just before he drowned, but even with her spiritual power, it'd been hard for her. Out in the ocean and separated from the land where we belonged, we'd been transported here, but Tanoshi and I carried our father's blood and had a connection to this place. Airi's connection to the moon goddess' world and Tanoshi's power might get us back, but I doubted we could drag Earth-born Kenji with us.

Kenji, noticing my silence, spoke again. "For all its faults, your world sounds a thousand times better than what I've got here. Even if I could find my way back to Japan, the life I face is bleak. My mother lives in poverty and my lousy school grades will never get me a decent job. I'll work some shit manual labor job and I'll never have a chance of a future. Over here, my so-called father tried to kill me. I'm not sure what he'll do if he ever finds me, but I can guess such an important man would go to great lengths to prevent anyone finding out he tried to murder his own child. Haruko, if there's any way at all, I want to go with you."

"We owe you," I said. "Without your help we wouldn't have any chance at surviving in this crazy place." We sat for a few minutes. "It's not all work back home," I admitted. "We have many no-work festivals. My mother has decreed that each day, as evening approaches, those who can, stop and spend time relaxing. We sing and play music, some tell stories. In the warm months we play sports, soccer is my favorite. Wintertime, we have indoor games, some of our own and some Earth games like checkers, and dominoes—I'll admit no one has ever beaten Airi at chess."

"Your world sounds perfect."

I laughed. "Nothing is ever that good. I'll save the bad parts for later. Just know we ended up in your world because we almost died in ours." We sat silently until Airi opened the door and told us we could come in. The soft floor covering had an unpleasant smell, but Kenji and I were so tired we slept through the night.

CHAPTER 11

We got to ride in a car. The speed was dizzying, and the way other cars whipped around us going even faster frightened the three of us. Even Frankie swore after one car swerved in front of us and then rapidly decelerated. She needed to stop so quickly we were rammed against the front seats as the wheels screeched in protest.

The rental-style car, which seemed to be a smaller than most other vehicles, squished the four of us in the rear seat. Tanoshi sat on Kenji's lap and Airi was on mine, although she insisted on turning around so often to see everything Michelle had to admonish her to quite squirming before she broke the front seat supports. It was really cramped as we'd put on our 'cosplay' clothes, both to make our swords seem natural and to continue the fiction the rest of our troupe expected our return.

Frankie had offered to take us to our hotel on the mainland, where we could rejoin our friends. After a little thought, Kenji said "Hilton." Fortunately, when Frankie checked her Smartphone, there really was a place called Hilton on the mainland. She said they'd just have time to get us there before they needed to drive to the airport.

After we pulled up to the Hilton's ornate door, we scrambled out of the car and stood massaging our legs. Frankie said they needed to leave if they were going to make their flight, but Airi stopped Michelle before she got back in the vehicle.

"Look," Airi said. "I don't want you to leave thinking we tried to trick you back on the beach when I offered to sell you this." She handed Michelle the button. "When you have a chance, take it to a gold buyer and see what he offers for it."

After they drove away, Kenji said we should move before anyone from the Hilton questioned us. He told me all the money we had would not even get us a meal at such a luxury place. We made our way to the street, and Kenji directed us toward some tall buildings in the distance.

"We need to get you dressed more normally," he said.

"Hopefully, when you're wearing regular clothes, we can find someone who'll direct us to a place where we can spend the night. Look for big buildings with a cross near the top." He made a figure with his fingers. "They are called churches and they might be willing to tell us where we could get help."

We walked for a miaru or so, each of us taking turns pulling Kenji's now battered suitcase. We came to a street Kenji identified as Central Avenue. With so many brightly decorated shops lining both sides of the road, we agreed it had to be the town's main road. We found a shop displaying clothes in the window, but once inside, Kenji said they were expensive clothes for rich tourists. After an apology to the proprietor, we hustled back onto the street.

"We're in the wrong area again," Kenji said. "These shops are for tourists. I doubt we'll find any store selling cheap clothes or one willing to buy your gold. We need to talk to someone who knows the city and can direct us to places used by locals."

We walked along the road, Kenji explaining what he knew about America, shops and anything else that caught our attention. After missing breakfast, we felt hungry and the enticing aroma from one small store made us break our resolve to find a cheap place.

The food was plentiful and delicious. After Tanoshi marveled at the size of the eggs on her plate, I explained to Kenji how my father had discovered our chicken-birds living in the wild back when Tanoshi was a year old. We did eat the bird's eggs, but they were tiny compared with these. We were discussing my dad's breeding program when the waitress placed the bill for our food on the table. Kenji didn't look happy, and as we watched him counting the money to satisfy the waitress, we realized, unless we could sell our gold, we'd soon be going hungry.

The waitress' screeching lecture about 'tipping' left us all embarrassed and depressed. Once back out on the street, we walked quickly down the sidewalk. At least we hadn't made things worse by asking the disagreeable woman for help.

"Look," Kenji pointed at a store with necklaces and other

sparkling jewelry in the window. "That sign says they buy gold and unwanted jewelry. Just what we need."

We had a short discussion. Agreeing, after our misunderstanding at the restaurant, we should be careful with what might be our only means of survival, Tanoshi cut one button from her boot and gave it to Kenji. The young woman who greeted us became hesitant on learning we wanted to sell rather than buy, and after looking at the button made a call on her Smartphone. We were asked to wait until an older man came out of the back room.

The tests he made were long and extensive. He even used a tiny drill to obtain samples from deep inside the metal. He finally announced it was pure twenty-four karat gold. After some fiddling with his phone, said he'd give us one thousand, eight hundred and twenty-six dollars.

"Cash?" Kenji asked.

"Of course not. We don't carry that kind of cash in the store. I'll issue you a business check. Take it to your bank and they'll give you cash if you really want to carry it around."

"We don't have a bank in this country," Kenji admitted.

"You'll need to open an account. It should be easy enough with this check and some ID. They probably won't release the whole amount until the check clears. But you'll get your money soon enough."

The four of us looked at each other. With no IDs, our one hope wouldn't work. Why did everything in this country need to be so complicated?

"Look," Kenji said to the man. "We really need some cash today. How much can you give us in spending money? We're willing to take a loss."

The man looked at Kenji before shaking his head. "We're a legitimate business. We don't accept stolen items. I though it odd to see pure gold in such a crude state when you came in. If you're looking for a fence, this isn't it. I don't know what you melted down, but I want no part of dealing with you. You should leave or I'm calling the cops." He pushed Tanoshi's button across the counter and waited for Kenji to retrieve it.

Back on the street we looked at each other. "Now what?"

Airi asked.

"That was a fancy place," Kenji said. "We'll need to find a less reputable outfit who'll give us cash money. It could be dangerous doing business with such people, and they won't give us even half of what it's worth. I guess our first task is to get out of this tourist area. Let's keep waking. The stores don't look quite so gaudy farther along this road."

A new problem arouse as we walked away from the tourist area. Our outfits and appearance became more noticeable. Several times I saw people staring at us. Then, a small girl dressed in black and wearing a tall black hat, which looked like an upturned cone with a wide brim, came over and asked me if I was an elf.

I remembered my dad's story of meeting his first wife, Sachi, for the first time. He'd thought her an elf after seeing her pointed ears and green hair. But after realizing she was the prettiest and cutest girl he'd ever met, decided the word pixie suited her better, as Earth fantasy-lore said they were more loveable than elves.

I smiled and said, "Actually, we're pixies. I hope that isn't a problem for you."

The girl put her hands on her hips. "Pixies are small," she announced. "Everyone knows that!"

Damn, a smart-ass kid. Well, while I knew little about Earth myths, my dad had said they were made-up stories. I decided to play along. "Pixies can be any size they want. You can tell we're not elves because pixie girls are much prettier." I pointed to Airi.

The girl looked at Airi and nodded. "Maybe," she said. "But I think you're elves. Anyway, my mom will know for sure. She's a witch."

I think we all gasped. After a moment of silence, Tanoshi spoke. "I'd like to meet your mother. Does she live around here?"

The girl smiled. "Mother's shop is just down this road. I'll take you there. She sells lots of neat things, you'll love it. Follow me."

The girl led us some distance down a side street. Here, the

buildings looked older and less carefully maintained. Some walls had odd patterns and words splashed haphazardly across them. I unwrapped the hilt of my sword. Kenji slid over to my side. "It's all right. They do this in Japan too. The kid's job is enticing people to come to a shop located in a less noticeable place."

The shop had an unpainted wood door and above it hung a wood sign depicting a lady in a black dress holding a stick. From the end of her stick emerged a shower of golden five-pointed stars. Oddly, instead of being random, all of the painted stars had the same orientation. Like Jack Bryce's robe, one star-point was aimed at the ground.

"I think it's a tourist place for people who like to play at being witches," Kenji explained. "It's sort of a game—like cosplay."

My eyes took a minute to adjust to the shop's dark interior, although my nose was well entertained by a variety of strong and unusual smells. The only ones I recognized were wood and leather. The store appeared crammed with every sort of odd item. The first thing I noticed was an array of those black cone hats in various sizes. One wall held hundreds of unlit candles in every shape and color, although most appeared versions of black.

Kenji nudged me. "That's a stuffed crocodile," he pointed at a huge lizard-like animal hanging from the ceiling. "I've never seen one before."

"Mother, customers!" the kid shouted.

A beaded curtain rustled and a tall woman wearing a black dress and an excessively tall cone hat, emerged. She held one of those sticks similar to the one on the sign.

"Penelope, dear. Who have you brought into my den of Earthly delights?" she spoke in a husky voice while waving her stick in the air. "Are they true Wicca or just innocent tourists curious to learn the mysteries of nature?"

The kid sighed. If this was how her mother greeted customers it had to get old. "Neither," she said. "They claim to be pixies, but they look like elves to me. They were wandering around looking confused."

"Are you a witch?" Tanoshi said. I could tell by her voice my sister was getting annoyed. I agreed, this seemed like a pointless game we didn't have the time or money to play.

"Look at the hat," said the woman in a less deep voice.

"Why?"

"It's a witch's hat, dear. That's how people know I'm a witch."

"Oh," Tanoshi said. "I just turn a few people into frogs and let the word get around." OK, my sister was in full, this-is-stupid mode. I think we were remembering there weren't any real witches on Earth. My dad had assured us this was a world where science ruled. Kenji was right; this daft woman was playing a silly tourist game.

The woman moved close to Tanoshi and then took several quick steps back. "Oh" she gasped. "You emit such power. You're not some silly Wicca! You are truly one of us."

I looked at Airi. Could there really be witches on Earth? But if Tanoshi held power, why hadn't her abilities returned? As none of us responded, the cone-hat witch continued. "Yes, with such power, I'm sure the master sent you to me. There are few of us left." She looked closely at Airi and myself, almost as if noticing us for the first time. "I see, these are your familiars. Were they once animals, or did you bespell pitiful and weak humans?"

Tanoshi laughed. "My friends were never pitiful and weak." She pointed to me, "When he walks into the woods, the bears run away."

"Enchanting a strong human requires great power; you must be a favorite of the master." She pointed to the bead-curtain doorway and removed her cone hat. "My name is Lucida." She threw her hat down. "You don't need these to look at these silly tourist trappings, come inside."

Tanoshi followed the strange woman, and we followed Tanoshi. Beyond the curtain the decorations changed. We saw burning candles, jars of herbs, and a wall holding leather-bound books in neat racks. I felt more relaxed after spotting pictures of woodland scenes and animal statues in every available spot. There were even a few potted plants. Anyone who liked nature couldn't be all bad.

I noticed Tanoshi edging close to one of the lit candles. She casually placed her hand over the flame but quickly withdrew it. I understood, she'd been checking to see if her fire-control magic had returned. Going by her quick withdrawal, the flame had been able to burn her.

"I keep this back room for the Wicca," the woman said. "Just the usual earth-spells and crystal junk they go for, but we all need to pay our bills." She went over to the far wall where there were shelves holding a variety of books. To the side protruded a candle holder without a candle. She twisted the holder until we heard a loud click. She pushed on the shelves holding the books, and the whole thing swung inward like a door. "This is my secret chamber. Come inside"

We entered a dimly lit room. It wasn't large, but we could stand without crowding one another. However, I found the smell unpleasant, like meat that had gone off or perhaps that coppery blood smell you have to endure while gutting a seal. It made me nauseous. In the dim flickering light of a few candles, the room seemed almost bare, although the walls were painted with odd words and what I guessed were distorted pictures of animals.

"You can feel the power," the hat-witch said to Tanoshi. "Can't you?"

"Other than the smell, this room does feel different," Tanoshi said. "It's not like any other place I've been in your city." I caught the slight smile on Airi's face; she could tell by Tanoshi's tone she was indulging this strange woman, waiting to see if the hat-witch gave any indication of real magic power.

"And now!" with a dramatic sweep of her hand, the witch pulled back a curtain on the far wall. Behind it was a dais holding the stature of a handsome man with horns, oversized genitals and the legs and feet of some unknown animal. Around the base of the stature lay all sorts of odd items, I recognized bottles, jars, bones, and coins, but the jumbled mess held other things I couldn't place. "Behold the master," shouted the hat-witch. "He who grants your deepest desires."

She did something and a strong overhead light displayed the stature in all its illogical glory.

We stood silent until Kenji said in a whisper, "that's a stature of the devil."

That confused me. I remained silent, until the hat-witch spoke. "Lucifer, king of the entire underworld! The most beautiful one." From my dad's adventures I knew who Lucifer was. Now I understood—this silly woman worshiped evil.

"The statue is a little wrong," Tanoshi shook her head. "Lucifer has a rather prominent scar across his cheek. Trust me on this."

"What?" shouted the hat-witch. "Lucifer is the most beautiful of all the spirits. He cannot be marred in any way!"

"The real Lucifer is mean and a liar," Tanoshi said. "It'll go badly for you if you are fool enough to fall for his enticements. I've seen what he does to those who give themselves to him. It is not a pretty sight. The scar he carries is his reminder not to mess with those who can see though his lies."

The hat-witch staggered backward until stopped by the statue's dais. "You!" she spat. "Are you saying you hurt my beloved master? Be careful of your boasts, fool. The master's revenge is terrible."

"Actually, it was my father who gave him the scar. I've only killed his minions. I see you are beyond help, we will leave. Just be glad you're not a true witch, for that alone protects you from your folly." Tanoshi turned. "The woman deludes herself. She does not emit real power. We are wasting our time here. Let us leave."

We filed out, passing through the Wicca room and entering the front of the store where the child waited. "Is mother all right?" the child asked.

"We didn't see any items that interested us," Kenji said. "But you have a fascinating store."

A screech made me spin around. Crashing through the bead-doorway, the hat-witch rushed toward Tanoshi. Using both hands, she held a sword above her head, preparing to slash it down on my sister. I dove, sending the woman sprawling into a table of candles. Only after the hit did I realize I'd overreacted. The woman's fighting ability was nonexistent. Airi could have disarmed her with less drama. I pried the sword from her hands and helped her to her feet. "I hope you're not bruised, but you shouldn't do things like that," I said quietly. "You could get hurt."

The hat-witch spat at me and followed it up with a string of curses, all of which were new to me. As she ranted, I looked at her weapon. Out of amazement, I turned to Kenji.

"Look at this thing! It's completely illogical. The weight is in this wide top end. Its improper balance will make the blade slower than one twice its length. Plus it puts the sweet spot on the shaft's weakest place. And what's with these curved mini-blades protruding around the base? They would only hinder the user when fighting."

"It's a fantasy sword," Kenji said. "Copied from some movie I suppose. Movies don't have anything to do with real life."

"I'm sorry," I said to the kid, who looked about to cry. "Your mother might have a few bruises, but I feared she might hurt my sister." I put the worthless sword down on a table out of reach of the hat-witch.

The woman looked at the sword, then at me, and screeched we'd all regret the day we crossed her path. She finished her tirade by screaming we would die horribly.

The kid tugged on my arm. "She doesn't mean it. Please don't call the police. If they come here again, they'll take her to a hospital. When she takes her medication, she's not like this."

"Are you going to be all right if we leave?" asked Airi.

"We'll be fine. I'll close the shop and let her rest. This happens sometimes."

Tanoshi pulled on my arm. "Let's go," she whispered.

"That was a very dark place," Tanoshi said once we were back on the street. "The poor woman might not have any witch powers, but I could smell death in the air around her. I thought I might be sick."

"She was sick in the head," Kenji said. "I saw dead

pigeons around the base of the statue. That must have been what you smelled. People with mental problems can convince themselves of any crazy thing. I guess she truly believes she's a witch, and is acting out things from movies and books about witches. I feel sorry for the kid, she must know there's something wrong with her mother but doesn't know what to do to help her."

Kenji continued. "The kid should be in school. That she's staying home helping her mother is a bad sign. With her mother's craziness, this store can't be making money. It's got to be hard for her. I bet the girl's sacrificing her education trying to keep her mother out of a mental institution."

In Kyoto children came first. With our low birth-rate, we considered every child special. To abuse a kid was inexcusable.

"I wonder if there is some way we can help the child?" Airi asked. "Her mother's fascination with evil will eventually turn on her."

I agreed, but first we needed to find shelter and a way to turn our gold into money. "Our options are limited right now. Remember this place. When we can, we'll come back and try to help the little girl." We looked around at the shabby buildings. It seemed only the central road catered to tourists. On this side road many stores appeared empty, and several had large sheets of wood covering their windows.

Kenji pointed. "We should go that way. It'll get us out of the tourist area, where we might find people and stores better suited to our needs. See that elevated roadway? I bet near it we won't find fancy tourist shops. We might even find a pawn shop willing to buy your gold."

That sounded encouraging. We walked for several hours, reaching what Kenji called the old city. Along the way we met others, some would stop and talk, but often they were confused in the head and couldn't answer questions coherently. One man managed to give us directions to a pawn shop. Considering the neighborhood, we assumed this shop wouldn't be as picky as the jewelry store. Kenji again warned us not to expect much money for our gold.

We found the store, and it did look far different from the jewelry store. There was a metal latticework protecting the window displays which were filled with different objects. Other than the jewelry, most of them I couldn't identify.

"We shouldn't expect to get much from a place like this," Kenji said as we entered. "Let's only offer one button and see what we get."

After we allowed the man to cut the button in half to run a chemical test on the interior, we got one hundred and ten dollars. Back on the street, we commiserated and Kenji taught us a new phrase; 'Ripped-off.' At least now we would eat and get some less-conspicuous outfits from a used clothing store.

Young Kenji wasn't as used to walking all day as we were, so Airi was pulling his suitcase when four guys, each riding a loud two-wheeled vehicle, rode onto the sidewalk and forced us into the roadway where they surrounded us. They wore black leather jackets with red words and the image of a chicken-bird on the back. When they were sure we had no escape paths, they revved up their engines repeatedly, the loud sound hurting my ears. They had those burning cigarette things in their mouths, and deliberately flicked them at our faces. These cigarettes were bigger, fatter and smelled differently from those we'd encountered at the beach.

When the engines shut off we could hear them laughing and shouting. They had a rapid way of speaking, and used words I didn't understand. Still, it was obvious they weren't friendly. While all that was going on I'd unwrapped the hilt of my sword. When one of them tried to grab the suitcase away from Airi, I drew the blade and shouted, "Stop."

There followed a moment of silence, presumably a long sword wasn't a common sight in a culture with guns. I faced the guy harassing Airi, and missed the one behind me, who rode the biggest vehicle, pulling out a pistol. Before I turned, he'd grabbed Tanoshi and held the barrel to her head. His shouts sounded garbled, but it was easy to deduce he was ordering me to drop my weapon. With my sister in such danger, I had no choice but to obey.

The smallest guy in the group picked up my sword. This

guy spoke more clearly, shouting, "Remember Pearl Harbor." I didn't understand the reference, but I could see it upset Kenji. The guy appeared taken with my sword, and began swinging it around while shouting "Look, I'm a Samurai." I remembered Tanoshi admitting she'd put magic in my sword. I don't think it liked its new owner.

One of his swings came dangerously close to cutting his buddy. Even I understood the cry, "Watch it" and "cut it out!" but the idiot swung the sword even more energetically. Everyone backed away, his friends shouting commands that went unheeded. The leader stumbled as he tried to avoid the swinging blade. Tanoshi took her chance, shoved the guy, and dove to the ground. The fool with the sword, shouting "Kamikaze attack," made a complete circle as he swung the weapon with outstretched arms—just as the leader staggered forward from Tanoshi's shove. Reflexively, he put his arm and the sword sliced thorough it.

We stood staring at the severed arm. Blood shot upward from the stump. His hand, still holding the gun, clattered to the ground. The leader, a look of amazement on his face, slumped to his knees.

In that half-second when the sword wielder stood staring at what he'd done, I moved. A pincher blow to both kidneys, and I grabbed the dropped sword before it reached the ground. A kick sent the sword-fool into one of the vehicles and he knocked it over, both crashing to the pavement. I spun, ready to attack any who looked about to produce a weapon.

"Don't kill them all," Airi screamed, no doubt to let those fools know their death was a real possibility.

"On the ground! All of you," I slashed the sword so it slit the tip of one guy's nose, did a fast sidestep, like when fighting a bear, and sliced off one vehicle's shiny handlebar. They all rushed to comply.

"We should save…Stumpy," Tanoshi pointed at the guy holding his bleeding arm. "A death could be a problem for us, and he's losing blood."

Airi was already removing one of the thin leather strips she used to tie her jerkin shut. "I need a stick or something," she said. "A tourniquet will need to be really tight." I looked around; sticks were not common on an urban road. Airi picked up the pistol which lay next to her. "It's bigger, but similar to the one the guy had at the restaurant," she said. "The bullets are in the handle. If I push the right leaver—ah that's it." From the gun's handle the black holder for the bullets shot out and hit the pavement. "Now it's unloaded, I can use this."

Expertly, Airi applied the tourniquet and by twisting the leather using the gun as a leaver, she stopped the blood from flowing. The guy didn't protest or resist while she worked. I assumed he was in shock.

"Here," Airi said to the guy. "Hold this tight. If one of your friends can use their Smartphone, the paramedics should come." The guy didn't respond. "Look," she shouted, grabbing his remaining hand and putting on the gun. "You must hold this steady or it'll spin around and let your blood start flowing again." She shoved his hand hard against the gun.

The gun fired. The bullet splattered against the road, ricocheted and tore a fist-sized hole a two-wheeled vehicle's fuel tank. Everyone jumped, especially me who'd seen Airi remove the bullet holder from the weapon. Apparently one shot had remained in the gun, and it made my heart skip as I realized how often it'd been pointed at Airi as she'd twisted it around to tighten the tourniquet.

Fuel ran from the tank's ragged hole, and flowed toward one of those smoldering cigarette ends. A sudden whoosh, and flames shot toward the bike. The flames climbed the fountain of spilling fuel and immediately the bike was engulfed.

"Run!" shouted Kenji. "Everybody run for it, the bike's going to blow!"

Stumpy's buddies saw the flames and took off. I grabbed Airi's patient and pulled him to his feet. In his stupor, he allowed me to drag him away from the inferno. Airi, who never seemed to lose her cool, grabbed Kenji's suitcase and pulled her own half-katana from it. My dad had explained how hydrocarbon fuels could explode if mixed with sufficient oxygen, but I had no idea what would be a safe distance.

The whole street went red. Airi, behind me, remained close to the explosion. I dropped Stumpy and spun around. Airi held her short sword with both hands. She held it upright, the sharp edge facing the inferno. The blast was being sheered apart and forced to go around her. Like a boat plowing through waves, we were in a sheltered zone created by her sword. After the blast, the flames subsided and the bike blazed like a bonfire, although the smoke was much blacker than a wood fire.

Kenji broke my paralysis. "We've got to get out of here. The police will arrive any second. Leave the wounded guy for them. If they catch us, they'll confiscate your swords."

I left Stumpy on the pavement, grabbed the suitcase and the four of us began running down the road.

CHAPTER 12

We took shelter in an abandoned building. It'd been a crazy escape. But for some reason, none of the numerous police vehicles, sirens blaring and lights flashing, noticed us as we ran from the fire. Kenji steered us into a narrow road he called an alley, and half way down a weed-overgrown path we discovered the back of a dilapidated building with its windows boarded up. A much abused door, secured with a chain, gave us entrance after one blow from Airi's short sword.

This building must have been a store in better days. I saw rusted metal racks and debris covering the floor. Lying around were old boxes, bottles, and paper wrappers in abundance. Against one wall, a soot stain revealed where someone had lit a fire on a metal rack yanked from a shelf.

Kenji put his hand up. "Stop. Watch where you put your feet. Druggies have been using this building, and they leave broken bottles and used hypodermic needles around."

After a couple of, 'what do you mean' questions, Kenji explained how some people used thin hollow needles to inject poisons into their body to make them feel good for a few minutes. The needles they discarded were small, exceedingly sharp and might penetrate our shoes, possibly giving us a disease. Both Airi and I looked at Tanoshi, if she couldn't get us out of this crazy hell-hole, we would never survive in a world this insane.

Using the tip of my katana, I cleared a safe path over to a room which must have been the front of the store. Away from the light entering from the open rear door, it became hard to see anything. I could just make out wide boards covering broken-out front windows. Fortunately, the boards didn't join well, letting a little light through the cracks. I noticed Tanoshi doing that thing with her fingers to create a light ball, but she gave up when nothing happened. Making mini fireballs was her easiest magic. My earliest memory was of lying in my cot and laughing at the pretty balls Tanoshi created to swirl around my head. That she could no longer perform such a simple trick had to crush her spirit.

Since the room was stuffy and bad-smelling as well as dark, I used my sword to expand two of the cracks between the boards to the width of a hand. Sunlight and fresh air came through the gaps. Here, the litter was less intense, and a couple of scruffy bedrolls hinted how others had sheltered here and had kept the floor cleaner. Kenji pointed to several metal signs nailed to the walls and explained they threatened to arrest anyone found using this place.

"That might be to our advantage," Kenji said. "The building's owner is trying to keep street people out. This might be a good place to hang out until the police stop looking for us."

After checking for hazards, we sat on the floor and discussed this new problem. "We should assume the police rounded up those bikers," Kenji said. "Rest assured, they'll claim we attacked them for no reason. Your clothing and appearance is unique, all the officers in the area will have your description. They'll be searching for us."

"After it gets dark, let's make a run for it," I said before remembering how in an electrified society, darkness wasn't nearly as absolute as it was on our world.

Kenji shook his head. "I don't know about the police in America, but in Japan, our police pride themselves on never making a false arrest. They find a way to pin something on almost everyone they bring in, deserved or not. I'm sure having swords is reason enough for the police to take us into custody, even if those guys admit they attacked us. Which, I doubt they will."

We hunkered down, listening to the irritating sounds of police vehicles. I wondered what we should do if they found us. I asked Tanoshi for her opinion.

She stared at the floor. "If we lose another sword, I doubt we can get home. I was counting on the magic contained in the swords to break us out of this place. Your mother and I infused them with all the power we could to protect you. I thought once my power returned, I could tap into the sword's need to see you safe and use it to break our false bond to this world."

Would I need to kill a policeman to keep my sword? Could I kill someone who was only doing their job? "We'll just have to hide here and pray to the Moon Goddess no one finds us."

The long afternoon wore on. Once, some people, possibly policemen, came to the back door which we'd left open, but after a short discussion about 'filthy druggies and their needles," they'd left without investigating further.

In the stifling heat we felt weak from thirst. Despite the expensive breakfast, my body insisted more food would now be appropriate. Even Tanoshi and Airi's stomach's let out an occasional growl. Kenji put on the last shirt from his suitcase and said once it was dark, he'd sneak out and try to buy us food and water with our remaining money. Then later, in the dead of night, if everything seemed quiet, we'd try to get as much distance from this area as we could.

Kenji left after dark, and we spent two difficult hours waiting for his return. Just as our fears were becoming unbearable, he arrived carrying a paper bucket-like container holding what he called fried chicken. We were hungry, the coated meat tasted great, although the bottles of water were even more welcome. With our energy somewhat restored, we tried to come up with a plan.

"There were a couple of guys at the fast food joint who were pretty talkative," Kenji said. "I've learned there is a big road called thirty-fourth street some distance from here and it has shops the locals use. In fact, there are a couple of places which sell cheap used clothing. It's a busy area and if we can get you dressed into something less noticeable, we can hold out. Of course, it'll mean selling more of your gold to some pawnbroker for next to nothing. However, the people who buy used clothing won't be rich. Perhaps we can find one with a bank account, and for a cut of the profit, they might help us get a better price for your gold. It's a chance anyway."

"That sounds good to me," I said. "In the early hours of the morning, we'll make a run for this thirtyfur place."

"I saw a lot of cop cars patrolling the streets," Kenji said. "They were everywhere. And if they see anyone running, they're bound to investigate. It's best to go slow and sneak from one hiding spot to the next. It could be difficult. I fear there's every chance they'll catch us."

"I can't kill a policeman," I said. "It's not like they are bad guys. They're only trying to keep people safe. If any of them stops us, we'll have to give up. I know we'll lose our swords, but perhaps we could get them back after they hear our story. Some people might believe us. Kenji believes us. He's never once called us crazy."

Kenji looked down. "Truthfully, if I hadn't picked you out of the ocean myself, I never would have believed you came from another planet. Of course I'm trying to help you. My father tried to kill me and left me stranded in America with no money, identification or way to get home. But I think, if I just met you on the street, and hadn't seen for myself the power in your swords, there'd be no way I could accept you came from another world. Even for a Japanese boy who spent his youth watching anime, it's just too far out."

"I understand," Airi said. "Even though our father told us about this place, I could never have believed the things science can do if I hadn't seen them with my own eyes. Still, the Goddess might yet help us. She knows if we can't get Tanoshi home, everyone in Kyoto will become slaves."

A dazzling light turned the dark room into day. Our blinded eyes saw nothing but the round disk of a white, miniature sun. Reflexively, I drew my sword, but had no idea who, or what, I faced.

"All right," said a voice behind the light. "I was just starting to believe you weren't crazies, but what does a major city in Japan have to do with some guys who claim to be from another planet?" There was a pause. "And Matt, please put down your sword. You just said you'd never kill a police officer."

I took a step back. "My dad's here?"

"Oh" Tanoshi stood. "It's Richard from the boat that brought us to land. Remember, Kenji gave us fake names when we thought it'd keep us from being recognized."

"Oh yeah," I muttered and lowered my sword.

"Kids, me and the guys have been searching for you. What

have you gotten yourselves into?"

"Richard, are you a police officer?" asked Airi.

"Yes, but I'm not on duty." Richard pointed his light at the ceiling so it stopped blinding us. "When me and the guys got back to our cars, none of us could understand why we'd left you stranded at the fuel dock. It was as if we were sleepwalking or something. After driving to the station, I checked, there isn't anything remotely like a cosplay convention going on either here or in Tampa. Then a report came in saying some strangely dressed kids with swords had cut off some fool's hand and trashed a biker gang. I guess, just by the way you moved, I knew your sword wasn't a wooden prop. But I have a hard time believing a major city like Kyoto, could be in any danger of being enslaved."

"They're not talking about the city in Japan," Kenji said. "It's the name they gave to their village. They really are from another world and are desperately trying to get back home."

"And I take it your spaceship crash landed here?"

"How did you find us?" Airi asked, no doubt to divert the question.

"Oh," Richard said. "Easy police work. Knowing you were stranded, I had the guys go to every fast food joint in this area. The kids behind the counter learned they could earn an easy twenty if any strangely dressed people or Asian types came in. All they had to do was call my cell and keep you talking for as long as they could. I got the call, and made it to the chicken joint just in time to see you heading down the street. Kenji, you need to be more street savvy. You never even noticed a car without lights creeping along only half a block behind you."

"It's been a long day," Kenji muttered.

"Anyway," Richard said. "You need to get out of here. There's a bulletin out for dangerous perps carrying swords. Your story isn't going to wash with any cops who don't know you. Shit, I'm not even sure I believe half of what I heard myself. But anyone who can sing like you..." he looked at Tanoshi. "Never mind, my van is in the alley. I'll take you to my apartment and we'll sort out everything there." He pointed to the rear door. "Oh, and don't make any sudden moves around Bruno. He's a K9."

I had no idea of what he was talking about, but I couldn't turn down the chance to get out of this stiffing room. We'd cope with whatever technological insanity a Bruno was when we met it. The things you learn. A van meant a vehicle twice the size of a rental car. As we approached it, I heard a click and the van's interior lit up, along with smaller lights glowing around the vehicle's edges.

"Nice wheels," Kenji said. "Is that what Americans call a minivan?"

Richard nodded. "It's old, but I need it for Bruno, besides, it's the only thing I got to keep after the divorce. Anyway, remain still after I let Bruno out. Let him get a sniff of you. If he knows you're my friend, he won't hurt you."

That didn't sound good, and I saw Airi grip the hilt of her sword, just like me.

A Bruno was a large fury animal with a long jaw filled with teeth similar to a bear's, only smaller. I tried to remember if my dad had told us anything about such Earth animals.

"Oh," shouted Tanoshi. "Isn't he cute?" She got down on her knees and spread her arms. The Bruno yelped and ran toward her. As I drew my sword, and Richard shouted "Bruno, down boy!" the beast reached Tanoshi and started licking her face as she laughed and hugged it.

It took us a second to realize the Bruno wasn't attacking Tanoshi, but welcoming her as a friend. We stood, looking confused, until the animal lay on its back with its paws in the air so Tanoshi could rub its belly.

"He is not supposed to do that," Richard whispered. "Two years of training went into making sure he wouldn't do that. Five years on the force, and he's never done anything remotely like that. Shit, among the downtown dealers, he's known as the hound from hell. Just what kind of person is Judy?"

"She's a witch," Airi said. "It can take some getting used to. And her name is Tanoshi."

"Ah," Richard said. "Somehow Tanoshi seems more

appropriate. Anyway, will you help me separate them? We've got to get out of here before any uniforms show up."

Eventually, we, along with Tanoshi's new friend, squeezed into the minivan. Kenji explained Bruno was a dog—an animal Earth people kept as a pet. Bruno was an especially large breed called a German Sheppard, which was trained to help the police in their duties. Richard added Bruno was fast, and had already chased down seven fleeing suspects. By the way he talked, I could tell Richard had a lot of affection for Bruno. I hoped Tanoshi hadn't upset their relationship. The dog now had his head on her lap and was having her scratch behind his ears.

Richard controlled his van with one hand while he talked on his Smartphone. We rapidly approached an intersection with a red light hanging above it. Richard slammed on the brakes, causing the wheels to squeal and we slid to a stop just before entering the crossroad where another car sped past, narrowly missing the front of the van.

"Sorry," Richard said. "My bad. But I needed to let the other guys know I'd found you. After skipping out of work and spending the day searching for you, they really wanted to come over tonight. I managed to convince them to wait until morning. They have wives, and after the screwing over I got, I convinced them they shouldn't bring any stray girls as pretty as you two home. Unfortunately, my place is kind of a dump. What, between alimony and child support, I live cheap."

I looked out the window and watched the crazy lights of an electric society flash by. I hadn't understood half of what Richard said, maybe Kenji could explain it when we were alone.

"You know it's odd," Richard said quietly. I wasn't sure if he was talking to us or himself. "John arranged the fishing trip to cheer me up after the divorce. If I hadn't been down, we never would have been out there to rescue you. It's scary to think I came so close to never meeting the most wonderful girl in the world."

We drove off the brightly lit roads and onto some darker side streets with large trees whose branches dripped with long tendrils of moss. Set back from the street I could see the lighted windows of houses. After a few abrupt turns we approached a largish house with many vehicles parked on the street in front of it.

Richard pulled tight behind a green van. "See those stairs on the side of the garage," he pointed. "They'll take you up to my digs. Don't run or anything, the main building is a boardinghouse and some of my neighbors can be snoopy. I don't want the manager finding out about you being in my place."

We walked single file up creaking wooden stairs. Richard opened the door and explained he wanted us inside before he turned on the light. The light revealed a room with a couch and a television larger than the one in the hotel room. Everywhere I saw empty bottles and bits of crumpled paper, some in the shape of boxes, some similar to the container which had held the fried chicken.

"Sorry about the trash," Richard said. "I'll clean the place up. The bathroom's behind that door. There's only one bedroom. I guess we'll let the girls use it and we guys will make do with the floor and couch in here." He grabbed a container and started tossing empty bottles into it. "Maybe tomorrow, John can find us some better digs. But I have to admit, right now my bank account's almost empty. There's little I can do."

"You have a bank account?" Airi turned toward him. "You can take a check to them and they'll give you spending money?"

"I guess so, but I doubt they'll take a check issued on another planet."

"We have these," Airi held out one of her buttons. "I understand they're considered valuable on Earth."

"They're solid gold," Kenji said. "Their buttons are pure twenty-four carat." He then told Richard of our experience with the gold buyer and the pawn man.

Richard looked at the buttons on the girl's boots and clothing and said, in the morning, as soon as the stores opened, he'd get us all the spendable cash we needed.

CHAPTER 13

I got to sleep between Airi and Tanoshi. Airi explained to Richard I was her world's future monarch. As my official protector, no way would she let me out of her sight. Richard just nodded and took it in stride. I think he'd reached strangeness overload. So the three of us got the bedroom, while Richard and Kenji made do with the couch and chair in the other room. Bruno, of course, curled up at the foot of the bed, which I suppose was his usual spot.

The bed was softer than I was used to, and elevated. I wondered if they needed to prevent insects from crawling off the floor and bothering people in the night. Maybe I should explain how we'd solved the problem by keeping food areas and sleeping areas separate and instituting a rigorous cleaning regime.

I was starting to doze when Airi sat up. "We should talk," she poked me in the ribs. "Bruno's a police dog and trained not to be friendly with strangers. His reaction to Tanoshi got me thinking. From what your dad told us, this is a world where people are cautious around strangers. Yet Richard and his boating buddies went out of their way to help us, they even skipped out on doing their jobs today. Remember how Frankie and Michelle allowed four complete strangers to share their hotel room? And Kenji, even though he has reason to help us, is begging to stay with us no matter what. I don't think he could stand being separated from Tanoshi."

"When you look at it like that, I agree we've been lucky. Many of the people we've met have been remarkably decent. But that guy at the first restaurant, the crazy pretend-witch, and those fools on the bikes were just the opposite."

"The witch had given herself to evil. Those bike fools, and the gun-guy at the restaurant, were disreputable people who attacked before talking to us. All the naturally decent people we've encountered are surprisingly willing to help. I'm not sure it's because of luck. Tanoshi's ability to manipulate objects and play with fire is unique. All other witches just make people see or believe things. Like the one who caused

Maki to make Sato her first mate even though she'd just met him."

Airi shook Tanoshi awake. "Have you been using your power to make the people we meet like and trust us?"

Tanoshi sat up before shaking her head. "I've been desperately trying to get my fire magic back. I've not given any thought to persuasion magic. After I made those guys green and convinced they were frogs, I swore off doing stuff like that. It feels wrong to mess with a person's mind."

I patted Tanoshi's arm. "Yet Bruno, a dog trained not to be friendly with anyone except Richard, went wild with affection the moment he saw you. Animals are much more in touch with magic than humans. I'm thinking your persuasion magic has strengthened. You're affecting those around you without being aware of it."

"My thought too," Airi said. "It would explain why Michelle and Frankie took us in. While we were showering, they both admitted they didn't like, or trust, men at all. Michelle even seemed confused by her own actions. And then, those guys from the boat spent the day and evening searching for us and checking every fast food joint around."

"I sang the deep love song on the boat," Tanoshi said while hugging herself. "There's a lot of emotion in music, especially that song. If the persuasion part of my power really was working without me knowing it, they might be more than just concerned with my well being."

"They probably are in love with you," Airi sighed. "They're married to other women and this world doesn't allow part-wives. When they turn up tomorrow, things could get difficult."

Tanoshi stared across the room before speaking. "Perhaps my persuasion power has increased, but my fire magic hasn't come back. I'm still a witch, but this might be how witches are on Earth." She turned to me. "I can't get us home without my fire magic."

We sat on the bed in the darkness. No one spoke as we digested this frightening concept. "Let's not jump to conclusions," I said to Tanoshi. "Remember how it took you time to recover your power after blasting through rocks while we were building the road around the mountain. After you brought down that huge cliff in the bay, we knew it'd take longer for your power to recover. I'm sure your fire magic will return. It just won't happen quickly in this place." Tanoshi agreed, but her hesitant voice betrayed her doubt.

"Anyway," Tanoshi said, "tomorrow when those other men show up, I'll try to reduce their affection for me and send them home to their wives. It'll be a good test to see if I really do have enhanced persuasive power."

We agreed to sleep and the familiarity of lying between Airi and Tanoshi finally let me relax. I slept well until the first light woke me. Oddly, both Kenji and Richard complained it was too early, but they both became alert after Airi and Tanoshi walked out of the bedroom to get to the bathroom. We'd forgotten how Earth men had a problem seeing naked females. Still, it got us up and functioning without wasting any precious daylight.

Unfortunately, it turned out very little happened around dawn. It was something of an insight to realize how an electric society, with its ability to hold back the night with artificial lights, now wasted several hours of natural light in the morning. Good working hours when cool, refreshing air made even the heaviest jobs lighter.

Richard went out and brought us a breakfast from a 'fast food joint.' The buns with eggs and preserved meat were tolerable, but those things he called pancakes were inedible. I had no idea how anyone could stand such intense sweetness. I almost gagged while watching Richard devour all four servings.

We were discussing the need to buy food we could eat; primarily vegetables, nuts, beer and fish; no cow meat and nothing sweet, when the other men from the boat arrived. They almost knocked me over as they crowded around Tanoshi. Listening to the confused things they said and pleaded, it was obvious they were becharmed. Even Bruno became upset with these interlopers, and ignored Richard's orders to 'stand down.'

"Et, tu, Bruno?" Airi said. This had me confused until I remembered one of my dad's campfire stories. Airi never forgot anything.

Possibly by using some of her power, Tanoshi eventually got the four men, and their dog, to sit lined up on the couch. I took Kenji back into the bedroom and told him to stay there and not listen until I came to get him.

Speaking slowly and clearly, Tanoshi began explaining how she thought they were wonderful strong men, capable of overcoming any obstacle with their iron-like character. Then she said how she was proud to become a sister to them, and such a relationship was special to her. There was a little grumbling and confused looks, but she turned to praising their wives and children and how the love between a man, his wife and their family was far stronger than anything the world could throw at them. Soon the men nodded and tears began flowing. She spoke some more, but it was obvious she now had four caring brothers and one faithful dog, and not a bunch of jealous lovers.

The crisis past. With it, came the knowledge, while Tanoshi remained a witch, she was not the same witch. Unless her other side emerged, we were never going to see our families again.

The men were now cooperative, especially after Airi gave them an edited version of how we came from another planet and were stranded here. I suspect Tanoshi's power let them accept the story without question or freaking out. John, the lawyer, took several of our gold buttons and said he'd get us a good price for them. He even promised to buy some Earth clothes for us. Harvey knew of a boater's supply shop that sold travel cases for fishing rods, and explained these would serve to hold our swords while we were outside without drawing undue attention. After learning we disliked cow meat and preferred fish, Bill said he'd go to a wholesale dock he knew and get us an ample supply.

"I tried to get another day off," Richard said. "But Bruno and I need to get down to the station today, or I'll be in trouble. I'll show you how to use my television. It'll let you learn about our world. Sorry, but I only get basic channels. I can't afford cable."

Bruno left with Richard only because Tanoshi insisted. When we were alone, Tanoshi came over and spoke in our language. "I'll need to do the same thing to Kenji" she said. "But. . . I should practice and get a better feel for using this increased power. I—ha, don't want to hurt him."

I understood. She might have enthralled Kenji, but he was the first boy, other than me, to ever suggest she was loveable. What he felt for her could be the beginnings of true love, and she wasn't going to jeopardize such a prize by using magic to change his mind.

* * * *

I found television's stupidity painful to watch. If it wasn't for our need to improve our English, we never would have been able to endure it. Kenji said daytime television was the worst, but in the evening the stations put on better shows and some had interesting stories. He lamented Richard didn't have a device called a DVD player, but after we got money, he'd buy one as he wanted Tanoshi to see the Japanese anime shows about witches.

We were feeling upbeat until the midday news show came on and exposed the truth about what a horrible world this was. Airi pressed against Tanoshi. "You'll get your power back. I just know you will," she whispered. "We won't have to live here much longer."

Over the afternoon, Tanoshi's three new brothers turned up bearing gifts. John brought us a selection of clothes, most of which sort-of fit. When he handed Kenji an envelope containing money, he explained it was an advance. "I got several thousand dollars for those three gold nuggets, but the check needs to clear. Meanwhile, this should tide you over. I'll produce an accounting when I bring you the rest of your money."

"He's definitely a lawyer," Kenji whispered.

Harvey's fishing pole holders did conceal our swords and he'd thought to buy a hat and shirt with pictures of fish on them. The shirt had English words I was told said, "Fishing is my Life." Such a sentiment seemed illogically extreme, and I wondered what kind of person would wear such an idiotic slogan if he wasn't carrying a sword in the long thin case.

Bill's gifts were the most immediately appreciated. Along with what he called a 'cooler' filled with fish, he'd thought to buy many different kinds of vegetables. I recognized various peppers, squash, carrots, tomatoes and potatoes. I was surprised by their size and unblemished appearance. My dad had brought some Earth vegetables to our world, but in the intervening years we'd bred them for taste. Now ours were smaller and appeared less perfect. I suspected the growers here followed the opposite plan.

Kenji was teaching Airi how to use an electric cooker and we all anticipated the first proper meal we'd had in many days when Richard and Bruno came home.

"The place reeks of cooking fish," Richard said. "Shut off the AC and open a window."

He had a point. A blue haze hung heavy in the small, closed-off room. While we'd grown up with the smell of cooking fish, in this concentration it became rather oppressive. The city of Takamatsu, where our ancestors had lived for countless generations, was nestled in the warm, dry, rain-shadow of high mountains. There'd been no reason for them to develop indoor cooking. When my father founded Kyoto, with its cold rain and snow, roofed kitchens became a necessity. But our inherited preference for outdoor cooking, and the risk of a kitchen fire destroying a whole house, created a compromise. Our kitchens abutted the main house through a short walkway that could be torn down in an emergency. They also sported Dad's technological marvel: the chimney and fume hood, which sent smoke and most cooking smells high into the air.

The open door and windows drew out some of the smoke. Richard entered. Wordlessly, he sank down on the couch. "Got a beer?" he muttered.

Tanoshi brought him a beer. "I'm sorry we made the place smell," she began. "None of us are very good at cooking, and the electric cooker isn't like a cast-iron coal burning stove."

"Oh, it's OK, I know the room's small and not really designed for cooking. I'm just upset with my ex-wife."

"What happed?" Tanoshi sat down next to him. "Did you go see her?"

"Yeah, I should have stayed away, but I couldn't stop thinking how I really love her and I can't stand being separated from my kids. Foolishly, I took her a dozen roses and some chocolates and tried to talk to her about us getting back together. She didn't exactly throw me out, but she made it clear she doesn't want to see me except when I pick up Jill and Adam for visitation."

I could see Tanoshi biting her lip. She stared at the floor for several minutes while Richard finished his beer. She put her hand on his forehead. I feared she intended to confess she'd manipulated his feelings. Instead I saw that sly smile she got when thinking of some crazy stunt. "You're a good man, Richard," she said. "Tell me, when do you next get to see your children?"

"Saturday afternoon, but I'm not sure I can wait that long."

"Saturday it is then. We'll come with you and make it a party." She looked into his eyes.

"Oh, that sounds like a really good idea."

* * * *

Saturday turned out to be three days away. Through watching the television and incessant questioning of Kenji, we'd used the time to learn more about Earth than just the names of the days of the week. Kenji bought a laptop computer with our new riches, and Airi was actually freaked by the things it could do. I suspect, if she'd been able to read English, she'd have demanded one for herself. In the evenings, Richard took us shopping and we now wore better clothes. However, I worried the sight of Airi and Tanoshi wearing miniskirts and tight blouses drew too much attention to us. Although, between that distraction and Tanoshi's mind power, no one noticed the fishing pole container slung over my shoulder. I'm not even sure they noticed me.

Richard's family home was several miles away on a road with numerous, variously painted, but similar, one-story houses separated by five meters. He stopped in front of a blue house with dark blue trim around the windows. I saw a small white car, the same size as Michelle's rental car, parked on a cement slab in front of the house.

"Charlotte's home at least," Richard said. "Last time she was out shopping with the kids and didn't get them back until late. I only got to see them for a little while before their dinner."

I saw Tanoshi nod; no doubt this was going to be a test of her ability to manipulate people's emotions. When Richard got out of the van, Tanoshi moved quickly, ran around the vehicle, grabbed his arm and pulled it around her waist. Thus joined, she and Richard approached the front door.

The door slammed open before the two of them reached it. A slightly overweight woman with short hair, stood with her hands on her hips staring at them. She tossed a burning cigarette to the ground. "Who the hell is that!" she screeched. "I'm not letting my children around some underage black floozy."

"Pleased to meet you, Charlotte," Tanoshi used her calmest voice. "Rest assured, I'm older than I look. Richard has told me so much about his wonderful children I just had to come and meet them."

The woman stared at Tanoshi for what seemed like an eternity, her lips frozen into a scowl. "What could you possibly see in an old fart like Richard?" She finally said. "You could get any guy you wanted."

"Richard is special," Tanoshi said. "He's such a wonderful man. I'm lucky I found him before some other woman snatched him up."

"Richard? The only thing he cares about is that damn dog," Charlotte replied.

"He's so handsome," Tanoshi continued. "Warm, loving, and kind. He loves his children so much. To find a man both strong and masculine yet capable of such intense affection is rare. It made me really happy to find out he was available."

I could hear the lilt in Tanoshi's voice, she'd aimed those words right at Charlotte's soul. I saw confusion, jealousy and finally regret flashing across her face. But from some inner recess she seemed to rally and shook her head. "You're fucking crazy, bitch. I'll give you some free advice, don't think he's goanna be your sugar daddy. Shit, he was late with my child support last month. I'd have been better off if that bullet had killed him. Then I'd have his life insurance."

I could see the look of surprise on Tanoshi's face. Next to me Airi whispered, "What a horrible woman. She doesn't deserve a man like Richard."

Tanoshi appeared at a loss. That her persuasion magic could fail after her previous successes must have shaken her confidence. Richard broke the awkward silence.

"Are the kids ready to go?"

"Adam hasn't finished his homework. His teachers called me twice this week about him acting up in class. He's grounded until he gets his homework done."

"The divorce agreement gives me visitation rights," Richard said. "This is the third time you've played this game. I need to see my kids."

"So take me to court, if you can afford it," snapped the woman. "But I'll bring up your late child support payments. Since you're dating an underage black whore, maybe I'll get your visitation rights revoked. Plus, I'll get internal affairs on your ass." She turned around, reentered the house and slammed the door.

"She's still the same," Richard said. "It never changes."

After staring at the house, Richard wiped his eyes, turned and walked back to his van, we followed.

"Your friend John is a lawyer," Kenji said after we were seated in the vehicle. "Can't he help you? You have the right to see your own children."

"John does real estate and property management. Divorce is way out of his expertise. Actually, he did recommend the firm I used. But, they were a top rated outfit and as I didn't have much money, they fobbed me off onto one of their new hires. Even John said the guy did a shit job."

"Then John owes you a favor," Airi said. "Tell him you need a larger apartment. Something with more bedrooms. We can afford to help you pay part of it." I looked at Airi, obviously she'd learned a lot about this world in the past four days.

I didn't talk to Tanoshi about her failed plan until later when the three of us were alone and could talk in our own language. "I know you could have forced that woman," I said. "Why did you back off?"

"Her underlying nature wouldn't have changed. Richard deserves better. Forcing people against their nature, well, it feels wrong. Now I've grown up, I've only done it to those fools who tried to kill me. Richard and his buddies, they are fundamentally decent people who care about others. That's why my song affected them. Unless I push it, persuasion power has a lot to do with what kind of person they are. Remember, my song didn't affect that captain who didn't want to give stranded boaters a little water. I'll sit with Richard and let him see his ex-wife as he really knows her. But he will always miss his children, I won't change that."

We discussed Richard's problem without thinking of any clever ideas. I thought with our gold, Richard might be able to get a better lawyer involved, but Airi pointed out how we didn't know how long we might be stuck in this world. We needed to allocate our resources carefully. A larger apartment would be cost more, and it wasn't as if we could get jobs.

Airi had a point; between the laptop, food and clothes, we'd already spent almost all of what John had given us. This world was expensive.

CHAPTER 14

Tanoshi sat with Richard and listened to the story of his failed marriage. She had her arm around his shoulder, and I knew she was gently removing the compulsion she'd given him to love that horrible woman. Airi got out our leather outfits, cut off the remaining gold buttons and put them in a cardboard box. Tomorrow, she'd give them to John and have him turn them into Earth money. She felt, since we'd offered to pay some of the rent, we needed to know how long it might last. Kenji made us a passable fish dinner. In the evening we ate, drank more beer than was prudent and after the television began another depressing late-night news show highlighting all that was insane with this world, we went to bed.

I was sleeping when Tanoshi shook me. "Fire," she shouted. "It's close, its calling to me."

"Hu?" I managed to say as I sat up. My movement disturbed Airi, and she moved more alertly than me.

"I hear something crackling," Airi said. "It sounds like it's below us." Just as the three of us got to our feet, Bruno started barking.

"Get Kenji and Richard," Tanoshi shouted. "The fire is growing fast and its close."

Even with my shaking and Bruno's barking, it proved hard to wake Richard, who'd handled his depression with too much beer. By the time I had him out of bed, I could smell smoke and feel the wood floor vibrating. Airi ordered us outside. Richard tried to turn on the lights, but nothing happened. The door had a double lock and a bolt securing it, and in the dark, he fumbled to find the right key.

Opening the door sent a wall of evil-smelling smoke into our faces. Behind us, over by the kitchen stove, a jet of crackling flame blew floorboards upward making the room glow red. By now, the noise was so loud we needed to shout, not easy with smoke burning the throat.

"Onto the porch, it's the only exit." Richard pushed Tanoshi and me out the door, but Airi ducked under his arm and ran back inside. I looked at the steps leading to the ground. At their base, yellow-red flames shot into the air creating an impassable wall of fire. I saw Tanoshi spreading her hands out in the hope her fire magic had returned. Nothing happened and the fire began to sweep up the wooden stairs toward us. I looked over the side of the porch, thinking the few meters to the ground wouldn't be a difficult drop and discovered the ground coated with a liquid that burned with bright yellow flames.

"That's fuel oil," Richard shouted. "We can't jump. It's slippery and if we fall, the oil will get on us. We're trapped. Someone is trying to kill us."

A coughing Airi staggered out of the smoke-filled room. Soot covered her naked body, but she held our two swords. "Get us down to the ground." She handed me my katana. I understood, we stood on the only place free of the liquid fueling this inferno. We couldn't jump, but the boards beneath our feet would protect us from the flames.

Two stout wood posts rising from the soil below supported the porch. While the base of these posts was being consumed by the fire around them, they wouldn't burn through before the heat and smoke killed us. I drew my blade, held my breath, leaned over the side of the porch, and separated the porch deck from those support posts. The porch tilted, but didn't fall.

"The wall," Airi shouted. "There's another support beam attached to the house wall. Cut us free of it."

I understood. They'd added these outside stairs to this garage when they'd turned the upper floor into a separate apartment. This little porch, necessary to reach the apartment door, was supported by those two outer beams and a horizontal beam attached to the wall. Quickly, I sliced through all the porch boards along the wall edge and structure began collapsing. Because the stairs remained connected to the rear of the porch, it couldn't fall straight down, but was pushed forward by the stairs like a connecting rod shoving a piston.

To prevent us from hitting the ground too hard, I rammed my katana into the side of the garage with one hand and held onto the front of the porch floor with the other. My sword ripped through the wood with a loud tearing sound, but the trick checked our descending speed. No one was hurt when everything hit the ground, right on the edge of the fuel-oil's inferno. Coughing and choking, we ran for fresh air and safety.

Once clear of the fire, Tanoshi sank to the ground. We rushed over to her. "It's gone," she whispered. "I thought when I needed it most, there'd be a little something, some fire magic, but, there was nothing."

Airi knelt at her side and hugged her but didn't speak. I didn't know what to say, my sister was hurting in ways I couldn't even imagine. Her fire magic was as much a part of her as her arms and legs. Fire magic let her manipulate real objects. I think we'd expected it to come through in a time of need. But even facing death, it hadn't responded. I didn't know if she could survive such disappointment.

Screaming sirens and flashing lights forced us back into the here and now. Flames from the burning building now leaped into the air and dozens of official vehicles came to a screeching halt on the street. As the fire threatened to spread to the boardinghouse, evacuating those residents became the priority. This was helpful, many people on the street, in various night dresses, made us less conspicuous. With remarkable efficiency, men in heavy coats used powerful water hoses to spray the side of the threatened building. The garage and Richard's apartment were considered lost and received less attention. When it collapsed on itself, huge flames and burning debris shot into the air, causing panic among those trying to contain the problem.

In the confusion, we were ignored. Richard said he knew those responding to the emergency and went to talk with them. Soon, he returned holding several blankets. Apparently, even in an emergency, Earth men had a problem seeing naked women. Still, it gave Airi and me a way to hide our weapons, the only things we'd managed to save. Richard went back and talked with those in charge. After a long conversation, one of them loaned him a Smartphone so he could call John the lawyer.

"They don't know you were in my apartment," Richard

explained as he led us away from the craziness. "They know Bruno is a K9 and they're letting me get him out of the confusion. I'll need to go back and answer more questions. It's considered a crime scene, although the building owner stowed paint and other flammables in the lower part of the garage. There'll be a full investigation, but right now the Fire Marshal assumes that was the cause. Still, it was fuel oil dumped on the stairs and under the deck. My supervisor thinks someone set the fire to trap me inside."

"Who could have done such a thing?" Airi asked.

Richard paused before responding. "I've helped arrest a lot of people, and Bruno leaves a few scars if they tangle with him. These hoods serve a little time in jail, and then they're back on the street. I suppose one of them held a grudge. Maybe it was for the best I wasn't living at home with my kids."

"Do you think someone was after us," Tanoshi said. "We're stranded here because at home they want me dead."

"Few people know you're on Earth," Richard replied. "My friends would never betray you. If the government did learn you were space aliens, they'd want to capture you alive. For sure, they'd want to know where you hid your spacecraft. That's the plot of a dozen movies."

Airi and I exchanged looks. Where were Richard's ideas coming from? We'd always avoided explaining anything to him about how we'd reached Earth. We stood silently until John drove up in a large vehicle Richard called an SUV. Kenji got in the front, we three and Bruno squeezed into the rear seats.

"I think your persuasion power is greater than you realize," Airi whispered in our language to Tanoshi as John drove away from the fire scene. "Richard is making up stuff he understands to avoid asking us difficult questions."

"Did you notice," I said. "How we stood around naked and holding swords while all those police and fire fighter people ran around, yet no one noticed us? You know how Earth guys are about seeing naked women, and the police should have freaked when they saw my katana. It was as if we were invisible until Richard brought us these blankets. Tanoshi, your power is so strong its protecting us without you being aware of it."

"We will need your ability to survive," Airi said. "We lost everything in the fire, not only our clothes and Kenji's computer, but our gold too. Tanoshi, I know you don't like using persuasion power, but it's our one asset. Think of it this way, everyone in Kyoto needs you to return or they'll end up as slaves. To help them, you might have to be more forceful about having people here help us."

Tanoshi shook her head. "But I have no fire magic. None at all, and without fire magic we're not going home."

"It's not completely gone," I insisted. "Remember, you sensed the garage fire before it was noticeable. The liquid burned super fast, but your early warning saved us. If we'd delayed just another minute we never would have survived. It was your connection to fire that saved us. I think, because persuasion magic is strong on this Earth, it's pushing down your fire magic. But, if we knew more about how magic here works, we should be able to bring your real power back."

"That silly hat-witch," Airi said. "It's time we went back and insist she tell us what she knows. She might give us some clues, or at least a place to start searching."

"All right," Tanoshi whispered. "I'll do it. It's for the people of Kyoto."

* * * *

"We grow sugar beets at home," I explained. "But not many and it's a lot of work to extract and process the juice. We use sugar very minimally. I'm sorry, but this syrup is far too sweet for us. But the pancakes and bacon taste just fine without it."

Andrea looked at me and laughed. "Well, I guess you really are aliens from another planet. But you're not Hollywood aliens. You girls are so pretty you'd intimidate any movie starlet and your brother looks like he could model for the cover of a romance novel."

John's wife, Andrea, had welcomed us to her home last night. She was a tall, thin woman whose breasts, while hidden by a tight brown sweater, appeared too large for her body shape. I'm sure, by Earth standards, with her long brown hair and deep blue eyes, she was quite attractive. Even at this early morning hour, her face showed signs of careful makeup and she wore both a necklace and earrings made with a shiny green stone. She had a wide smile and laughed easily. Richard had told us, of all of his friends, John had no children. Women on Earth didn't have our low fertility problem, and despite the makeup, I thought she might be middle-aged, odd they remained childless.

When we'd arrived at John's house and Andrea had seen soot-blackened, naked Tanoshi and Airi, shivering beneath thin blankets, she'd forgone any explanations in order to hustle the two of them into a bathroom, while ordering her husband to take care of 'the boys'. After that, she ran around preparing the 'guest bedroom' and finding suitable night clothes for us. She'd been so intent on finding those outfits, and turning a couch into a bed, we agreed not to make an issue of our usual sleeping arrangements or how my sibling and I never bothered with nightclothes.

Come morning, after the smell of fried bacon wakened me, we learned she'd spent hours finding clothes that more or less fit us. So, as it was important to Earth people, none of us would be naked.

"With my big meeting this afternoon, I really need to get to the office," said a tired-looking John. "Will you be all right until I get home? Richard spent the night at a friend's place. He might come here, but maybe not as he doesn't want anyone to know about you. Besides, he's got his hands full. The fire destroyed his driver's license and all his papers. Fortunately, he's got buddies at the station house ready to help him, but even for a cop, state bureaucracy can be a bear."

I looked at Kenji, there were many things I needed him to explain.

"They'll be fine with me," Andrea said. "I'll take them shopping for some proper clothes after the stores open."

Andrea kissed her husband while we attacked the rest of the bacon-covered pancakes. She returned and sat at the end of the table. "So Kenji," she began. "John said you're from Japan, but you've lost your passport, money and identification. There's a Japanese consulate in Miami. They could issue you another passport. I'm sure they'll contact your family in Japan and get you airfare to go home."

"I'm afraid my mother doesn't have enough money for my airfare," Kenji said.

Andrea poured herself another cup of coffee. "Well, how about your brother, can't he help you?"

"I...I don't have a brother," Kenji's face looked red.

"Oh, I'm sorry, I just assumed. I guess I remembered wrong then. When I was in college I took a course on Japanese culture because I planned to get a job at the state department. Of course, that was before I met John."

"You remembered correctly. Kenji does mean second son. That's not my real name. My mother registered me in school as Kenji because she thought if the other kids believed I had an older brother, they wouldn't bully me for being a half. It didn't make any difference, but I prefer that name over the one on my birth certificate."

"What's your real name?" Andrea paused. "Oh, I'm being pushy. You don't have to tell me if you'd rather not."

"That's all right. The name on my birth certificate is Lawrence Bryce. You might have heard of my father, he lives around here; Doctor Jack Bryce."

Andrea slammed her coffee cup down. "You're kidding me. The Jack Bryce. He's richer than God. He could buy you a thousand tickets home with his pocket change."

"Except, if he finds me, he'll have me killed. He's already tried once."

The sound of chair legs scraping across the wood floor made us jump as Andrea shot to her feet. She looked at Kenji, then at me, then she walked over to the sink and stood staring out of the window. When the silence became too long, I thought I should say something.

"Do you know Kenji's father?"

Andrea turned. "I'm the local coordinator of the committee to get Jack Bryce elected governor in two years. I've met him in person, I've shaken his hand. He's the most charismatic man I've ever met. His policies, well, he's exactly the kind of politician this state desperately needs. He's pro-business. He'll do away with the thousands of stupid rules and all the environmental regulation crap holding this state back. He'll create jobs for thousands of people. He'll clamp down on the schools and get rid the worthless teachers by testing the students to see if they're learning anything. Florida needs this man. He's our hope for the future."

She turned and looked at Kenji, the scorn, the hate in her eyes obvious to us. "Now you come along with some trumped-up accusation about him trying to kill you? Are you insane, or did you take money to repeat this slander?"

We sat there, the woman's pancakes going cold on our plates, as we tried to come to grips with this new development. Was she going to throw us out? Would she demand these clothes back first?

Tanoshi broke the silence. "Tell me," she said. "When you shook Mister Bryce's hand, did he stare into your eyes for what seemed like a long time?"

Andrea turned and looked at Tanoshi. The two women stared at each other. "It's all right," Tanoshi said. "I understand. Why don't we go sit on the couch in the other room?" As if in a trance, Andrea followed Tanoshi out of the kitchen.

"I guess Tanoshi's not the only person with persuasion magic," Airi said. "Kenji, Your dad is more dangerous than we thought. He has real magic power. I suppose the evil one gave it to him after the Moon Goddess deprived him of his kill by bringing Haruko's dad to our world. That man is a strong adversity."

Kenji looked at the table. "Do you think he, or one of his goons, set fire to the apartment to kill me, so I wouldn't talk and ruin his political career?"

Airi rubbed her chin. "No," she said. "He wouldn't risk damaging our swords. He has Tanoshi's sword and enough magic to feel the power it holds. Now he'll want mine and Haruko's. With the three swords he could subvert their power to his own ends. They'd make him invincible; he must know that. I suspect he's using his resources to find us. Getting our two other swords will be the only thing that matters to him."

Oh great, I thought. Not only is there a fire bug trying to kill us, but we have a guy with unlimited funds, resources and even magic power hunting us down.

"If it wasn't one of Richard's enemies who set the fire," Airi said. "Then it was the hat-witch. She knows we're in town and she's sworn revenge. While she's not much of a witch, she could have cast a spell to locate us."

* * * *

Later that day, a tired Richard came by, picked up Bruno, and they both hustled off to work. Andrea, dressed in a different outfit, announce we were going shopping, so we got to ride in yet another kind of vehicle. This one Andrea called a 'beamer' and it was far more luxurious than any of the others. I'm sure the seats were real, expertly-tanned and dyed leather. Polished wood trimmings surrounded a mini television in the dashboard, which, when it wasn't showing the road behind us, offered numerous choices for anyone who could read English. A gentle stream of cool air from numerous ports kept us comfortable even under the Florida sun.

Kenji sat between Tanoshi and Airi in the backseat. Tanoshi had her arm around his shoulders and was teaching him various words in our language. It had to be hard for him, as many Japanese words and syntax were close, but not identical to ours. Still, bolstered by the belief we wanted him to come to our world with us, he made a concerted effort.

I sat alongside Andrea, who drove erratically as she regaled me with an angry tirade against Jack Bryce. She couldn't get over him using magic to turn her into a monster who cared only for the rich and was willing to shift the burdens of society onto its poorest citizens. She had nothing but good things to say about Tanoshi who'd freed her from the horrible man's lies. I had to respect Tanoshi's persuasion power. Andrea now believed her current opinions represented her true self. She didn't suspect Tanoshi had used a counter-magic on her. Well, what did I know, perhaps caring for others really was her true self, and by holding to that ideal and living a decent life, she'd find favor in the eyes of the High God. Still, it gave me an insight of the ways the rich and powerful abused others. This was truly an insane world.

Our first stop was a used clothing store where we exchanged our ill-fitting, inappropriate clothes for less conspicuous outfits. Andrea said we could now enter a proper store without raising suspicion, and she'd take us to 'the mall' where we could get more stylish outfits. I thought the ones we now wore were perfectly fine, but Andrea seemed to be enjoying herself so we didn't protest. Going to the used clothes store had been useful, as, by remaining close to Tanoshi, Airi and I discovered no one noticed our swords. This new power my sister possessed was truly impressive.

The little television in the beamer's dash gave Andrea directions to the hat-witch's store, which, in the local vernacular, was 'downtown.' We pulled over to the side on the main road, and I told Andrea and Kenji to stay in the beamer before we went to question the witch. I didn't want Andrea to watch Tanoshi's persuasion magic at work and start to wonder about her own changed state of mind. However, Kenji insisted on going with us, and Andrea said she wasn't going to be left alone. I sighed and we got out of the vehicle. The five of us walked down the side street toward the store. I didn't see the little girl and hoped her mother had finally allowed her to go to school.

CHAPTER 15

Before we opened the door to the hat witch's store, I mentally reviewed the layout. The large room off the street entrance held the pretend witchy things she sold to tourists. Beyond a beaded doorway she had a smaller room with goods for Wiccans. At the rear of that room, a secret door gave access to the alcove containing a statue of something from the evil regions.

Kenji said the sign said 'closed,' but when he tried the handle, the door opened. A wave of unpleasant odors rolled out; rotting food, urine, and perhaps something more sinister. Airi reminded me Earth witches made potions to give them power. It smelled as if our witch had recently brewed something especially nasty. Trying to ignore the stench, I made sure my sword was loose in its sheath, moved Kenji out of the way and entered the dim room. Looking around, it appeared the witch hadn't had any recent customers and wasn't making any effort to lure them in. Dust and dirt covered the floor, along with numerous items which had fallen from various displays. The stack of pointed cone hats lay strewn over one side of the floor.

"Something's wrong," said Airi who'd followed me. "This place carries the odor of death. Perhaps the witch has died and no one discovered her body."

"Let me find a light switch," Kenji pushed past me. I turned and saw, despite the smell, all of us had entered the store, Andrea holding a piece of cloth to her nose. Kenji found some switches and I heard them make a clunk but no lights came on. "Power's off," he muttered. "Maybe a fuse has blown."

Tanoshi pointed. "Go through the beaded curtain. I feel something strange coming from there."

I nodded and put my hand on the hilt of my sword. "Airi and I will go first." Airi put up her hand to tell the others to stay back and we entered the dark second room. I couldn't see anything. "Let's grab some candles," I said to Airi. "We need more light."

"Don't bother," came a voice from the darkness. "I'll give you the light you need." After a flash, hundreds of candles began lighting themselves. Each one ignited the one next to it in a chain reaching around the room. They were all black with green tinted flames. In the corner stood the hat-witch, her distorted features appeared ghastly in the strange light. Other than her stupid hat, she wore tattered clothes covered with stains and dark splotches. I think one of her breasts was exposed, but covered with so much grime, it was hard to be sure.

"He said you'd escaped my flames," the witch spoke in a crackled voice. "I've been waiting for you." She pointed at Tanoshi. "Come closer if you want to learn about real magic. It's not all silly candles, crystals and dancing around naked."

Tanoshi started to push past us. Both Airi and I put out an arm to stop her. "Who is this he, you spoke about?" I said. "Tell us, who told you about us?"

She cackled again. Perhaps it was an Earth-witch thing like the stupid hats, but I found it annoying. "So strong with your sword of power," she said. "Let's see how brave you are without it." She thrust her arms forward, her hands releasing a powder that bloomed into large, green-sparkling cloud.

Reflexively, I held my breath, but could feel the dust settling on my body, burning my eyes making every inch of exposed skin itch. The dust congealed around our swords, no doubt attracted by the power they held. I saw my sword hilt glow green as it fought the attacking magic. The three of us tried to step back, but collided with Kenji and Andrea who stood behind us. As we sorted ourselves out, I heard the witch screaming. "Now my beauties, they are yours."

I looked back and, with my blurred eyes, saw the door to the third room, the one with the obscene statue, opening. Two large males staggered out. They moved as if every movement needed planning so their stiff joints could handle the motion. Both held their mouths wide open, viscous goop dripped from the teeth. As they moved into the light, I saw they were bare-chested, with a large five-pointed star carved into their skin. From the center of the star a wooden stake protruded, and by its position I knew it penetrated their hearts.

"They're already dead," I shouted, forgetting the need to hold my breath. I suppose we all felt the taste of blood and offal.

"They're zombies," shouted Kenji. "Oh my god, they're zombies. Don't let them bite you! Get out of here, get back on the street." All of us squeezed through the beaded opening and into the main room. Andrea screamed and went to her knees while holding her head in her hands.

Dead guys walking around were called zombies and everyone knew about them. Why, if Earth-magic could make such atrocities, did people claim there was no magic here? Anyway, considering how slowly they moved, I decided to get the others outside and then cut these things to bits. Without a head or legs, they'd not be a threat. Airi, always one step ahead of me, was already trying to open the street door.

"It's locked," shouted Airi. "Let me..." she grabbed her sword's hilt, no doubt to cut her way through. I saw her struggle with the blade. For some reason, she didn't seem to be able to get it out of its scabbard. With panic rising in my chest, I tried drawing my own katana and discovered it too wouldn't come free. I ripped the scabbard from my belt, and with all my strength, tried withdrawing the blade from its sheath, but try as I might, they would not come apart. By now, the slowly moving monsters were through the opening.

Using two hands, I swung the heavy sheath at the head of the nearest zombie and heard the satisfying crack of a shattering skull. The thing fell back, flopping to the floor, its head now distorted into an impossible shape. The other monster tried to use my distraction to attack from the side, but a swift karate kick snapped one of its knees and sent it tumbling to the floor. "Ok," I gasped, "now let's get the door open."

Kenji shouted and pointed. Slowly, both zombies rose to their feet. I heard their broken bones cracking as they moved. I charged, no matter what, there had to be a limit to how much damaged they could absorb. Hitting them was easy. Time after time, I sent them to the ground with shattered bones. Soon their skulls became distorted lumps holding glistening teeth. Yet, after each blow they recovered, and as their leg and arm bones became more fragmented, they rose and moved more quickly. Several times I needed to use my enhanced speed to avoid those goo-dripping teeth. From the corner of the room, where Airi guarded the others, Kenji kept calling to me to beware the teeth, apparently just one bite from a zombie would result in my death.

Over and over, even with my sheathed sword, I inflicted what would normally be killing damage. They seemed impervious to such attacks, and as the fight drew long and repetitive, I felt myself tiring. I'd tried destroying their jaws and teeth, but even quicker than other body parts, those bits returned to normal. Between ducks and blows I looked for the hat-witch, but she'd retreated to the other room. I didn't dare follow and let these monsters get past my guard and reach my sisters. My strategy involved continuously kicking or beating them back to the rear of the now-destroyed room.

How long could I keep this up? Even when fighting a bear, I'd never before fought this ferociously for so long. My arms began to feel as heavy as iron and I know my speed at dogging the monsters slowed. Several times those sharp teeth almost found their mark.

I believe, as I fought, Airi and Tanoshi worked on either breaking down the door or smashing through the front window. Even Kenji helped. By either magic or the strength of Earth construction, they weren't having any luck.

A hard blow sent both of my attackers to the rear of the room, and in that moment, while their bodies reconstructed themselves, I staggered back to Airi and Tanoshi. "I need an idea," I panted. "This isn't working. I can't keep it up much longer. Give me a plan, any plan."

"Hold still for a second," Tanoshi held out her arms toward the zombies as they began their relentless stagger across the room. "The power," she gasped. "It comes from a piece of wood embedded in their hearts. Remove the wood and they will become truly dead."

I rather wished I'd know that when the end of the stakes

had protruded from their chests. In the ensuing fight, those bits had worked their way deep into the blood-coated chest cavity. Now they weren't even visible.

"Use my half-katana," Airi said. "The sheath is smaller. It'll be easier to pry the wood out of them with it. Just don't get yourself bitten!"

I nodded and made the exchange. Don't let them bite you. Easy advice, but I'd need to get close and personal to work those stakes out of their chest. I called up some reserve strength and charged the monsters. At the last second, I leaped into the air and slammed my feet into their stomachs, sending them tumbling to the back of the room.

I dove at the nearest zombie, landed on its chest and used my elbow to knock its head back while I rammed the end of Airi's sheath into its chest. The thing started to twist and buck, but I could feel the end of the sheath rubbing against something hard. We struggled, it trying to get its teeth close to my arm, me trying to work the sheath through its viscera and pop the wood up far enough to reach.

Finally, the top of blood soaked wood appeared above the goo surrounding it. I dropped the sheath and was reaching for the stake when the other zombie dove at me, those terrible teeth aimed right at my face.

A crash. Kenji slammed into the attacking zombie and shoved it to the side, the two of them tumbling together giving me the half second I needed to yank out the damn bit of wood. The thing beneath me went limp. But Kenji was now entwined with a monster which only needed to find a bit of his body to bite. Forgetting the sheath, I dove and managed to grab the zombie's head and force it away from Kenji's face. I was exhausted and the thing was strong. I could hardly hang onto the pulped cranium because it felt like holding wet bread dough. It squirmed to free itself, bits of flesh sliding beneath my fingers, constantly forcing me to change my grip.

"Quick!" I shouted. "Dig into the chest, find the stake and get it out. You must do it. I can't hold on for long."

The next second, as wide-eyed Kenji stared at me, felt like the longest second of my life.

"Do it," Tanoshi shouted. "Save my brother."

Kenji's hand rammed into the zombie's bloody chest. It squirmed, fought, those teeth chattering as it felt the nearness of a victim. And then, at last, it went limp and Kenji held that small, wooden stake in his trebling hand.

"Thanks," I gasped. "You did it."

He only nodded and I needed to help him stand.

With my arm around Kenji, I looked at Tanoshi. I'd never seen her this angry before. "The witch is in the other room," she snarled. "Now we'll get some answers."

After leaving Kenji with the still terrified Andrea, who refused to budge from her corner, we cautiously entered the rear room. The witch didn't attack us with her dust. After determining she wasn't in this second room, we assumed she'd retreated into the back area with the statue. Before we opened the door I tried drawing my katana again. This time I was able to pull it almost all the way out, but too tired to make much effort, I let it snap back.

"Her magic is weakening," Tanoshi said. "She's exhausted too."

Good to know, but I was pretty spent myself. Airi, sensing my weakness, unlatched the door, kicked it open and jumped back. No cloud of dust pursued her, but the stench that permeated the building rolled out and made me gag. In the back of the room, a single light shone on the statue, which now appeared red, no doubt with blood.

Carefully, we eased toward the doorway. Airi froze. "Oh Goddess, it's the child," she shouted. "It's the little child." I pushed forward and looked where she pointed. There, on the floor beneath the statue, lay the girl we'd met on the street, although it was hard to recognize her as her ripped-open chest left her in a pool of blood and gore. We stood in silent horror. To deliberately kill a child went against everything we believed. No one, in the history of Kyoto, had ever intentionally hurt a child. Here, one had been cruelly murdered.

"This is what it means to embrace evil," Tanoshi whispered. "This is what it wants from me."

It brought home the constant struggle Tanoshi endured. Her fire witch power was always calling out to her to embrace its evil origins. This was why she walked when she could fly, smiled when insulted, and did a thousand other things the hard, human way when her magic could make any chore disappear.

Tanoshi pointed at the cowering hat-witch. "You stupid fool, what terrible price you paid for a pointless moment of power. Your daughter is dead, your minions have failed, and your home is destroyed. What hollow lie did you believe?"

The hat-which held a curved dagger, probably the one she'd used on her daughter. The woman looked at Tanoshi and then back to the girl's corpse. "Penelope," she muttered. "Penelope, what have I done? Oh God, forgive me." She turned the dagger around, and before any of us could react, thrust it deep into her chest. I guess it hurt more than she'd expected, because she screeched, almost standing as she reared back, her arms flailing, before dropping to the floor. The three of us stood staring, not sure of what we should do.

Finally, Tanoshi spoke quietly. "At the very end, the evil one thinks it funny to let his victims realize the true horror of their deeds." She turned to me. "We'll not learn anything more here, but someone used this weak woman's stupidity and gave her great power to kill us."

I nodded. We had an enemy and it looked as if he had the same magic as Tanoshi when she had full use of her fire powers. And he wanted us dead.

We backed out of the statue room and found Kenji. "Andrea's freaking," he shouted. "I don't think she's going to hold it together much longer. We need to get out of here, someone might call the cops and there are two dead bodies that would be impossible to explain." I hustled him toward the front of the store before he saw the horror in the back room. Two zombies were enough for anyone. Fortunately, with the hat-witch dead, I could draw my blade and the wood door shattered easily.

Andrea was incapable of driving. We'd been lucky just to coax her out of the store on her own power. It fell to Kenji, who'd never driven and didn't have a license, to take us home. He assured us he understood the principles and could manage, even if Americans did drive on the wrong side of the road.

Tanoshi sat next to Andrea in the backseat, and I could hear my sister whispering we'd only been attacked by robbers. No doubt Andrea would soon have a more normal explanation to ease her mind. Plus, having Kenji drive speeded her recovery. The jerky stops and starts, the sudden swerves to get out of the way of other cars and the constant blaring of horns directed at us made her realize her beautiful beamer might be in danger. After a badly executed turn, which had us bouncing across a sidewalk, she insisted on taking over before we had an accident or drew a cop's attention and had to explain why Kenji and I were covered in blood.

We did make it home without incident. Andrea immediately left to go to her bedroom and talk to a Mister Valium. I assumed it was something done with a Smartphone. The four of us retreated to our room to clean up and try to formulate a plan. Kenji insisted his father was behind it, and I was inclined to agree. Tanoshi didn't think he possessed sufficient power even if he did posses one of our swords. We hadn't come up with any ideas when Richard and Bruno arrived.

"The whole department, including the media, is going wild," he began. "They're saying some crazy woman downtown, who sold Wicca supplies, went off her rocker. She bludgeoned two homeless guys to death, killed her daughter and then committed suicide. It'll be all over tonight's news. It might even make the national news." He looked at me. "You wouldn't happen to know something about it, would you?"

"We were talking about leaving to live on our own," I replied. "It's getting dangerous for you to be around us."

"Yeah, I thought so." He looked at Tanoshi. "John and Andrea, they're what I call yuppies. They're not going to handle anything spooky or dangerous. I'll talk to John when he gets home. He's a real-estate lawyer and should be able to find us a place."

"You'll come with us?" Airi asked.

"Bruno would bite me if I didn't. We serve and protect. It's painted on the side of my cruiser. Besides, if any suspicion for today's debacle falls on you, I can give you a warning. Now, you want to tell me what happened?"

Even after all that had happened, talking about magic doing the impossible wasn't easy. Richard couldn't get his head around the idea of real zombies.

"But you know about zombies," I said. "Kenji recognized them right away. You even have a name for them. They're part your world and they are magic."

"No," Richard said. "Yes, they're in movies and books, but they don't exist in real life. Right now there happen to be a lot of movies with zombies in them, but that's just make-believe."

"I understand," interrupted Tanoshi. "The evil one lacks creativity. He can't think of anything new. He, or anyone who's given themselves to him, can only copy ideas from humans who have a connection to the creator. People thought up zombies, so they are now part of evil's arsenal. But it still doesn't tell us who's behind this."

"It has to be my father," Kenji said. "He has one of your swords, and he'll do anything to get the others. Knowing you would need to learn about magic on Earth, he must have made his people check everyplace that sold witchy stuff. After he learned of our encounter with the stupid woman and she'd failed at trying to get revenge and kill us, he guessed we would return to confront her."

"What we saw today was full-on magic power," Tanoshi said. "Only evil could have provided her with such power. It would take a strong compulsion to force a woman to murder her own child."

I agreed with Tanoshi, but we'd been watching Earth news every day. Over and over, we'd seen stories of people hurting and killing others. Murder is common, and people here killed family members quite often.

"In the movies, they call male witches warlocks," Richard said. "Just saying."

CHAPTER 16

I really liked our new home. It had three bedrooms and two rooms for washing, although only one had a tub big enough so we could sit together and soak. Kenji saw the well-designed kitchen and promised to make many Japanese-style meals. Tanoshi loved the fenced-in backyard where she and Bruno could play after he came home from his K9 job. It was in a quiet neighborhood, but even so the place had an alarm which would alert us if anyone tried to break in.

We had Tanoshi to thank for this luxury. Andrea's distress at the witch's store attack had faded to a half-confused memory, which she considered no big deal, when her Husband, John, came home from his law firm. What concerned her most was John failing to get offered a partnership.

It took many questions before we understood. John had made a deal with a big luxury apartment complex being constructed near the waterfront. Apparently, John's deal meant anyone who wanted to live there would need to do business with his firm. He explained it would create a large revenue stream. He and Andrea had expected he'd land a partnership and an increase in salary. That failure concerned both of them far more than Andrea's little 'attempted mugging.'

As Andrea and John consoled themselves with alcoholic beverages, Tanoshi stood and told them she could solve John's problem. All she needed to do was meet the people who'd made the bad decision. I suppose, if Tanoshi hadn't already been working her magic, they never would have agreed. The next day Tanoshi, dressed in one of Andrea's 'business suits' and me in a heavy coat to hide my sword, entered the over-plush offices of one of Saint Petersburg's top law firms.

Tanoshi used her power to its maximum. I think everyone in the building believed she was the most wonderful person they'd ever encountered. The top partners came over to shake her hand, and in doing so spent several seconds staring into her dark eyes. The next day John, the newest partner in the firm, had a corner office, a big raise and what he called an impressive bonus.

John quickly bought this fully-furnished house, ostensibly as a rental property, but we were to live there as house sitters until he could find suitable renters. It'd all happened so fast I knew Tanoshi's power had been hard at work.

The next week passed quietly. We spent much of our time watching television to improve our English and gain a better understanding of this world. Kenji bought a new laptop. He and Tanoshi spent hours researching articles on witches. Unfortunately, Kenji encountered so much made-up silliness that anything real remained hidden under the garbage.

Between reading articles to Tanoshi, Airi also demanded his time. He read articles on chemistry, physics, and early steam technology to her. Airi claimed her steam-injector design was superior to the ones once used on Earth locomotives. However, she was impressed after finding the diagrams of the stationary Corliss engines which employed a rotary valve arrangement to make better use of the expanding steam. She assured me these engines would be much more efficient but would require machining to tighter tolerances than the slide valves we currently used. Now, with my new high-accuracy metal lathe, we could build an engine that used far less precious coal.

All this verbal interaction helped Kenji learn our version of Japanese. Richard, who spent most of the time at his police work, always came home exhausted and made no attempt to understand our language. That was a relief. Even if Tanoshi regained all of her power, we knew it'd be hard for her to drag Kenji from this world, taking another person would be beyond her ability. Besides, Richard had children who he'd never leave.

Between reading to Tanoshi and Airi, Kenji used his computer to learn what he could about his father's businesses, his numerous houses and the possible location of his boat. "He's hiding," Kenji said. "He must be afraid to face Tanoshi head on. I doubt he'll be in any of his houses. He'll stay hidden until his people find us."

"Let's take the fight to him," Airi said. "We'll do

something to draw him out. Sitting around waiting for him to discover where we are could get us killed."

I agreed but couldn't think of any way we could do anything. "The man's super rich," I mused. "He can go anywhere and hide anyplace. How can we get at someone like that?"

"The man loves money," said Airi. "He sold his soul to get more of it. All we need to do is make him lose some."

We sat around trying to think of a way we could use his weakness to our advantage. I agreed in principle, but nothing came to mind. I feared we'd have to wait for him to attack us.

"I'm not a hacker," Kenji said. "But I know a bit about computers and their biggest weakness is a real person needs to know the passwords to use the system. With those passwords, you can really make someone's life miserable." He turned to Tanoshi. "After seeing what you did with John's bosses, I'm wondering if you could have someone tell you something and then forget they told you, or even forget they ever met you?"

"I don't know," Tanoshi rubbed her chin. "It might be possible, but I'd need to practice before I went someplace where they could report me to Kenji's father."

* * * *

"Do you believe in God?"

The man wearing the odd collar stared into Tanoshi's eyes as he considered his reply. My sister wanted to try her new skill on someone highly educated and used to being in command. This guy headed a huge church that attracted many hundreds of parishioners, and Richard said he was considered one of the most respected, and intelligent, men in the city.

Tanoshi found it easy to get our neighbors to spill all about their sexual escapades, or reveal the password to their home Wi-Fi networks. She didn't think confusing their weak minds any big feat. Today, she'd decided to tackle someone with the willpower to resist her.

"No, it's all bullshit. Preaching is an easy job, a couple of hours on a Sunday morning spouting some crap I ripped off the internet and coming in for the occasional high-paying funeral or wedding gig. The rest of the time is my own. Great job if you can tolerate all the perfume-reeking widows. Sure beats going nine to five in some office and getting an ulcer from the boss."

I almost gasped and I saw Airi turn her head and cough like she'd swallowed something the wrong way. Intelligent and respected? The man had spilled his deepest secrets with less resistance than the eighty-year old gal who'd described some strange sexual things she did with her husband.

Since Tanoshi had initially been raised by a real Goddess, disbelief wasn't an option for her. I feared she was going to make him confess in front of his congregation. I could see her stiffen and knew her anger was about to explode. Fortunately, Airi put her hand on Tanoshi's shoulder.

"Make him write it down and sign it. Then make him forget everything. That's the test we're here to perform. Remember the Moon Goddess assured us the High God never cares about belief or worship. His only concern is how we treat others and how we learn and grow. We'll just go away and let him be really, really shocked after he dies. I bet the High God gets a chuckle out of meeting people like him."

Tanoshi sighed and I saw her shoulders relax. "All right, we'll do the test, but I feel bad for those people he's deceiving."

After Tanoshi got his password to the church's computer network, and Kenji added it to the list he kept, we left the hypocrite to his life of luxury and ever-growing karmic debt. After returning to Richard and his minivan, we sat outside the church building while Kenji used his laptop to see if the preacher-man's Wi-Fi password worked.

"Yeah, it got me right in," Kenji said. "And this is interesting. It seems by using his password, I can access an E partition that wouldn't show up for anyone logging on using a different password. Let's see what it contains."

Since he was in the back of the vehicle, we couldn't see the screen as his fingers worked the keyboard. "Holy shit," he shouted. "It's all porn. Thousands and thousands of all kinds."

"What's porn?" Said Airi as Kenji typed. The laptop's speakers let out a scream that sounded like someone being tortured.

"Damn!" Kenji slammed the lid of his laptop shut. "I could have lived my whole life without seeing that." He looked at Richard. "It's the kind of porn that gets you arrested in Japan. Maybe here too, can we do anything about it?"

"What's Porn?" Airi shouted this time.

"I'll explain it to Haruko later," Richard said. "Then he can tell you. There are many different kinds of porn, but some can make you lose faith in the human species. It seems our preacher-man is not a nice person."

"Can we report him?" asked Kenji.

Richard shook his head. "Not without admitting we found out illegally. We'd be in more trouble than he would be. Besides, guys like that are always caught. If he's using the black web and downloading snuff films, he's embezzling funds to pay for it. The guys in the vice squad told me the heavy duty crap costs a fortune, and that's how they catch most perps. Maybe I can tip some people off and work it from that angle."

"Wait a week or so," Tanoshi said. "If we need money, we now know who we can force to give it to us without feeling guilty afterward."

"Yeah," Airi said. "That would be just. In fact, let's go back. Remember John telling us about an expensive restaurant on the beach with the best fish in town. I wouldn't mind going there tonight." She turned to Tanoshi and they both smiled before getting out of the minivan.

The preacher-man showed us a hidden suitcase stuffed with bills of every denomination. He called it his emergency stash and handed Tanoshi five thousand dollars. She told him to go take a nap and forget everything. On our way back to the minivan, she whispered it was nice we'd discovered our own bank account.

* * * *

Perhaps the grouper wasn't great by our standards, but Kenji and Richard thought it excellent and I remembered Earth's oceans were almost fished out, while ours teamed with an endless variety. I loved the wine, which Richard explained cost as much as he made in a week. With Tanoshi's power making the servers extra attentive and oblivious to our age and the swords Airi and I carried, we lingered over the best meal we'd eaten since coming to this world.

Relaxed by the wine, Richard told us about his divorce. His wife hated his profession and they'd never enjoyed a trouble-free marriage. She was not a dog person and often raged at having a dangerous animal around her children. Their marriage came apart after he'd leaped in front of Bruno to save him from a drug dealer's attack and taken a bullet in the leg.

"She raised holy hell because I'd almost died protecting a dog," he explained. "But Bruno has saved my butt many times. We've formed a bond I can't explain. Actually, Bruno's old for a K9. I give him pills for his arthritis every morning. The department wanted to retire him a year ago, but I know he couldn't stand being separated from me all day."

"Your wife divorced you because of your injuries?" Airi asked.

"Not right away, I was laid up with rehab and such. I guess having me around the house made her decide to file the papers. It must be a cop thing, there's a lot of divorced guys in the department. We're sort of separated from the rest of society. How do you regard cops on your world?"

I paused, wondering how I could explain it in a way that wouldn't offend him, or scare Kenji and make him reconsider coming to our world. Tanoshi just came right out and told him the truth.

"In Takamatsu, the army does what you call policing," she began. "But in Kyoto, we've never organized anything similar. However, every young male spends time in the protection squad before he gets married."

"Protection squad?"

"It gives our boys a chance to meet different girls, and the girls a chance to evaluate them. It's useful as there are many dangers around our young colony, including poisonous snakes that sometimes make it past the defenses. The boys carry weapons and escort people when they go beyond the built-up area. Mostly, they protect the workers out in the vegetable fields."

"You teach responsibility right from the start," Richard said. "No teenagers without prospects and too much time on their hands. I wish we could institute something like that around here."

After the meal, somewhat unsteadily from the wine, we walked out of the restaurant and onto the adjoining beach. The sun was low over the gulf, the blue of the western sky starting to show traces of orange and yellow. This area was quiet, but others walked along the beach, couples waiting for the coming sunset and listening to the crashing waves as they hissed across the wet sand.

"If we were home," I said. "We'd shed clothes and swim, but Earth people have this hang up about nudity."

"You get real naked women," Kenji sighed. "We get pathetic two-dimensional images. You're much more advanced."

Airi turned to Tanoshi. "You wanted to try a difficult test," she said. "What do you think? Could you make everyone on this beach ignore us or believe we're wearing bathing suits? You'd have to extend your influence for quite a distance."

"Now that would be a test," Tanoshi laughed. "I'm game, if you don't mind making a mad dash for the minivan should someone see the truth."

Airi laughed. "All right, let's strip."

Those bottles of wine did taste good, but I think they were stronger than we realized. I just hoped the alcohol hadn't reduced Tanoshi's persuasion ability. Both Richard and Kenji said they'd remain on the beach to guard our stuff. I understood; these guys hadn't spent their lives around women who enjoyed having guys admiring them. Anyway, now my clouded brain thought about it, I couldn't leave my sword unguarded. In fact, I wasn't sure being separated from my weapon was a good idea. But the chance to frolic in the water with Airi, like we did when we were kids, was just too good to pass up. I promised myself I'd just go out a little way and keep a close watch on the beach. Besides, I could move really fast when I needed to.

"I thought you said you'd look like you were wearing a bathing suit," Kenji stammered after Tanoshi removed her clothes.

"You and Richard are family," she replied. "You get to see the real us." My sister looked happy. Kenji looked like he was holding his breath. She went over and kissed him on the cheek. I understood, she wanted him to get used to seeing her naked so he'd relent and come soak with us during our evening bath. Dating an Earth guy, with all their hang-ups, wasn't easy. I wondered how Earth girls managed it.

The water felt warm, and the waves were the right size to splash without knocking you off balance. Tanoshi and Airi waded out until they encountered a drop-off that had them plunge up to their waists. "Oh, there's a deep spot right here," Airi said. "But just a little way out the waves are breaking on a sandbar. It must be shallow again. Let's swim out to it."

I saw two cute bottoms break the surface as they both dove into the deeper water, racing each other the few meters to the sandbar. I hesitated, not sure if I should follow. The water had sobered me a little, and now, even though Richard and Kenji were protecting it, the idea of getting far from my sword didn't feel like a good idea.

Airi and Tanoshi reached the sandbar and stood. The shallow water only reached Airi's knees. She waved to me. "Come on slowpoke, just beyond this point the water's the right depth for swimming."

I sure hoped Tanoshi's magic was working, because to me it looked as if there were two beautiful and naked women standing with only their lower legs hidden by water. The sun wasn't at the horizon, so the light remained bright enough to make out some attractive details. I looked back at the beach; no one pointed. I guessed my sister's magic did work.

Just a couple of minutes, I thought, then I'll come right back. I dove, intending to slide across the deep spot underwater. It took longer to get to the sandbar than seemed logical. I reached the bar and looked back, wondering if the distance had been greater than I expected. But there was the beach, just where it should be, yet it'd taken four strokes to cross a short distance, which shouldn't have needed two.

Tanoshi and Airi had waded over to the ocean side of the sandbar and were now up to their waists. I noticed a blue glow in the water around Airi, and felt gut-wrenching terror. How, How could I have forgotten something so important? "Stop!" I screamed. "Come back." They dove into the deeper water on the ocean side of the sandbar. I watched Airi moving under the water, swimming out to where the depth was over her head, her position obvious by an ever-increasing blue glow. When her head broke the surface, her face was covered with sparking blue dots. Tanoshi, next to her, also glowed, but not with the same intensity.

I turned toward the beach and shouted with all my strength. "Kenji, Richard, we need you. Come into the water and grab us, we're in danger." I didn't have time to explain as I was already plowing across the sandbar to reach Airi, who made a great effort to swim toward me, but her hands passed through the water, barely causing a ripple.

Tanoshi too, must have remembered the danger, and although glowing blue herself, dove toward Airi before she was transported back to the world of her birth. At least Tanoshi and I, with our father's Earth genes, were not being affected as quickly as Airi, who didn't belong in this world. But, if we didn't get our feet on solid ground soon, we too would end up in the nowhere place before making a random landing on an almost all ocean world.

Tanoshi and I reached Airi at the same time. Both of us hugged her as close to our bodies as possible. The blue glow evened itself out, decreasing Airi's and making us glow brighter. The surrounding water felt warm, no longer able to suck the heat from our fading bodies, and instead of letting us sink, it pushed us upward. As our connection to this world faded, we became less dense.

"Can you touch bottom," Tanoshi gasped. "The magic I used to send us here has worn off. We must reconnect with the land."

I tried, but the water wasn't going to let anything as light as me anywhere near the bottom. I grabbed Airi's legs and used them to push myself under, raising her higher in the process. At one point, my toes scraped the sand, but the fleeting contact was quickly lost and I bobbed back to the surface.

"Again!" Tanoshi shouted. "For a second I felt denser and could move us a bit. The sandbar is close, we can make it."

I lacked her confidence. Every second we remained suspended in the ocean, the blue glow increased and with it our ability to remain in this world. I tried, using all my strength, but the water would not let me sink far enough. Gasping for air, I broke the surface and shook my head.

It couldn't end like this. I took another breath and shoved myself under. The blue glow let me see the bottom. It appeared close, but despite my best efforts, I could not get down far enough. My foot hovered a fraction from the sand, but even stretching every muscle in my leg, it didn't quite make it. My lungs began to burn from lack of oxygen. Then a ripple went through my body and for a second I felt heavier. My big toe scraped across the sand, and the glow around my foot faded. My lungs bursting, I shoved my foot down and felt my weight increasing.

Tanoshi must have felt the change and used her increase in density to push against the water. Shoes appeared on the sand next to me. Kenji had reached us. Once he grabbed Tanoshi, the blue sparkles began fading. Making sure I didn't let go of Airi, I broke the surface and gasped a lungful of sweet, refreshing air.

Kenji pulled us onto the sandbar. "You were on fire!" he gasped. "Electric sparks were all around you."

"You saved us," Tanoshi said. "But we have to remain touching until we can get back to the beach. Hold onto my arm and don't let go." The four of us stood on the shallow sandbar and let the sparkles fade. Richard had only come as far as the beach side drop off. Now we appeared less terrifying, he splashed across the deep spot and joined us. With two Earth people anchoring us to this world, the blue went away. Holding one another tightly, we paddled back to the beach.

We sat panting on the sand and Tanoshi explained what had happed to Kenji and Richard. "We were almost transported back to our own world," she began. "The oceans on all the worlds are the same, and people belong on the world of their birth. When we were in the ocean and not touching the land—"

"What's going on? Why are you bare-ass?" Two large men approached us. I looked around and realized a crowd was gathering. Attracted by the blue light and the naked girls, people now ran toward us from up and down the beach.

"This is a family beach," shouted the other man. "Skinny dipping is a crime."

Others began to push closer. I saw the flash of Smartphones. I looked to Tanoshi, hoping she wasn't too exhausted and could make these people forget what they were seeing. Before I could say anything, Airi screamed and pointed. Farther up the beach, where we'd left our clothes and our swords, several guys were picking through our belongings. Already one of them was inspecting my katana and another held Airi's short blade.

"Stop!" I shouted as I got to my feet. "Leave that stuff alone." I tried to push past the two guys. The larger one grabbed my arm and yanked me back. The other guy lurched and got his hand around my other arm.

"You can wait here for the cops," the big guy shouted. "Damn pervert. Waving your dick around for all to see, there are kids on this beach."

I tried to push free of these idiots while shouting thieves were stealing our possessions. This only made the men hang onto me more tenaciously. They were both strong, and other than doing serious bodily harm, I wasn't going to get free. I wasn't sure if the other guys had actually taken our swords or were just looking because there were many people blocking my vision.

"I'm a police officer," Richard shouted. "Let him go, right now." I hadn't heard Richard's cop voice before, it was quite commanding and the two guys did pause and loosen their grip.

"Let's see your badge," said the larger man. "I saw you

swimming with these clowns."

"They're running away," Airi shouted. I knew what she meant, and these fools had delayed me long enough. My knee slammed into the groin of the larger man as the other guy got an elbow in the stomach. They both grunted and let me break free. Shouts of "grab him!" and, "don't let him get away," came from the crowd. Many were laughing like this was some sort of entertainment. At least four guys tackled me at the same time and I went down.

A red flash and the screaming started. The fools holding me down reared up, holding their heads. Others in the crowd either went to their knees or staggered backward. Obviously Tanoshi had recovered enough to use her magic. The anger-driven blast also affected Kenji and Richard, and both ended up on the sand.

I stood, perhaps a little unsteadily. At the top of the beach, four guys were jumping over the low wall separating the beach sand from the restaurant's parking lot. One held my sheathed katana high, like the prize in a game. No doubt, another of them had Airi's short blade. Maneuvering around the collapsed bodies, I started after them.

They had a good lead and the dry sand slowed me. By the time I'd reached the parking lot's hard surface, the thieves were in a car and its tires squealed as it headed for the main road, a cloud of blue smoke shot from its exhaust pipe. I ran harder, desperate to get a better look at the vehicle before it sped away.

Amidst screeching brakes and blowing horns, the thieves' car cut into traffic. Initially other cars blocked them as the traffic slowed and stopped, no doubt their drivers confused by such a rash maneuver. It gave me the few seconds I needed to race across the parking lot. By shattering the rear light of a parked car, the thieves' car broke free of the blockage and, with a great cloud of smoke, roared down the highway, the back of their car swerving like the rear of a fish. By then, I was only fifteen meters behind.

It was an easy car to follow. Its bright red paint and lack of a top made it distinct. Its license plate wasn't white with green letters like most car's, but was dark blue with white letters. I knew if I could get close enough to memorize the shape of those letters, Richard might be able to find the miscreants. All I needed to do was run a little faster. As they needed to swerve around slower cars, they weren't pulling far ahead.

Run faster, I told myself as the consequences of losing those blades came to me. We could never get home without them. Without Tanoshi, Takamatsu would overrun Kyoto, enslave its people, kill my father and make my mother a puppet in the city's palace. Here, Kenji's father would find us, and with no defense, he'd take his revenge. We would die.

Airi would die.

I ran as I'd never run before. Soon, my bare feet felt numb as they pounded against the roadway. Sometimes, other moving cars got between me and my quarry. That helped, a leap, a few steps across the roof and a leap back to the ground gave me a speed boost as the vehicle I'd run over, screeched and swerved behind me.

I could see the thieves' faces. Three of them were looking back at me. They were shouting, no doubt telling the driver to go faster. I had them now; several cars waiting at a red light blocked the road in front of them. When they stopped to avoid ramming those vehicles, they were mine.

The red car again swerved into the lane designated for oncoming traffic, but this time, instead of straightening out and speeding through the intersection as I expected, it spun. Its tires squealed and made black streaks of rubber on the pavement as the car went completely around, its rear crashing over the sidewalk and into a store's wall. The guys inside screamed while smashing against one another and the car's sides. The engine made a loud bang and smoke came from under the hood.

I was on them. Anger boiling, I didn't hold back as much as I should. I'm ashamed to admit all four kids—teenagers, received a thrashing which included broken bones, cracked ribs and smashed noses. I calmed down only after I held those two precious swords in my hands. Once again a crowd had formed, and I, displaying the thing no Earth male was ever supposed to reveal, was the center of some astonished looks. I could hear police sirens approaching, but with so many cars stopped in the intersection, it delayed their arrival. That gave me the minute I needed to push through the crowd and start running back toward the beach, and my one chance of avoiding arrest: Tanoshi.

CHAPTER 17

I woke in the bed back at our house. My feet hurt and looking down, discovered them wrapped in thick bandages. Airi and Tanoshi sat at my bedside. I had a vague recollection of running back toward the beach, some people pointed, but the growing darkness was my ally, and soon Richard's minivan screeched to a halt and both Airi and Tanoshi ran out to grab me. I guess I passed out.

"Don't get out of bed," Airi said. "Your feet are cut up." Airi explained I'd slept for over a day. During that time, Richard and Tanoshi paid a visit to his doctor and returned with powerful Earth antibiotic creams, which prevented my battered feet from becoming infected. She also told me Tanoshi had regained a little of her fire-witch power and had used it to speed my healing.

"Your power is returning?" I said to Tanoshi. "That's the best news ever."

"Not much, and I don't think it's going to improve until we can recover my sword." She paused. "Well, let me explain. Back when we were in the ocean and losing our connection to this land, the Earth magic, which I now understand is all about persuasion, faded. That let me feel my own power, it's still there, but blocked. I managed to grab a little. Remember when I helped you reach down and touch the sand? Anyway, now that I'm back on land, it's blocked again. Although, I seem to be able to pry out a little, around the edges, so to speak."

"You think your sword can help you break the block?"

Tanoshi nodded, "Your mother and I infused each of the three swords with different powers. Airi's sword is to protect our world's monarch. Like your katana, it can cut through metal.

"My sword is different. The hilt contains earth from our world and a little of a dress the Goddess once wore. The idea was for it to help Kyoto grow and protect it from danger. It contains the most magic. Actually, after I first experienced magic exhaustion after blasting through rocks, I decided to add to its power, creating a reserve I could call on if needed.

That's why I risked blasting away the cliff. I thought I'd be able to draw on the sword's reserve afterward. Unfortunately, once my power was completely drained, I couldn't tap into its magic at all. It only opened up when we got near the beach and were in danger from the killer clams. I used its power then, but it still contains more and anyone with enough magic could break the seal. It's the sword we need to get back."

They'd given my two swords power without telling me. I was about to ask what other magic Tanoshi and my mother had given my katana, when Kenji and Richard entered the room.

"You outran a sports car!" Kenji shouted. "I'm still not believing it."

"First time anyone blew past the speed limit without using a car," Richard said. "Damn, I wish I had radar on you. Anyway, I managed to get a peek at the accident report. You did have a little advantage. Those kids were cruising in an antique sixty-five Ford Mustang. Beautiful car, but their father used it for display at rallies, and had only restored the body. Plus, suspensions have come a long way since sixty-five. Those old rear-drive cars don't handle the same as modern ones. The kid couldn't handle it, that's why he spun out."

"How are those guys doing," I had to ask.

"Ah," Richard said. "Well, they'll recover. Two are already home from the hospital. Because of the accident, it isn't clear what happened. The witnesses gave different accounts. The media has freaked out about a mysterious, naked green-haired guy running down Beach Drive and leaping over and past moving cars. There are a couple of blurry images from surveillance cameras, but your face isn't recognizable. Some stories have linked you to the unexplained lightning strike, which knocked out people on the beach and fried their electronics. There's so much confusion, no two people can give the same account. One old gal swears Elvis came out of the sea."

I was wondering what an Elvis was when Kenji spoke. "We should assume my father figured out you were behind it. He'll have people putting the clues together to find us."

"When Haruko is able to walk," Airi said. "We should move again."

"Where would we go?" I asked. "Everything about this world is confusing to us. At least we know a little about this city and here we have Richard and Kenji to help us."

"We shouldn't put Richard in any more danger," Tanoshi said. "He has a family."

Richard shook his head. "I'm not going anywhere, we're in this together. You said thousands of people would be killed or enslaved if you don't get home. I'm a cop, it's my job to stop stuff like that from happening. Besides, you need me. I'm the only one who can keep an eye on the guys in department and warn you if they learn anything that might lead them to you. The craziness at the beach and Haruko running down the road and leaping over cars remains an open investigation. It isn't over yet. Tanoshi might need to come down to the station and work her magic on the detectives. Anyway, Bruno would bite me if I took him away from Tanoshi."

Realizing he had much to lose and nothing to gain by helping us, we repeatedly thanked Richard. Tanoshi hugged Kenji. "You were brave to reach into the blue fire and grab me," she whispered. "I know it looked like we were engulfed in lightning. You risked death to save me." Kenji turned red. Really red. I guess the two of them were getting serious, but we'd not told him of the consequences of sex with Tanoshi. The Goddess' curse might sound attractive to a teenage Earth boy, but before committing, we should tell him about all the duties of those in an extended family and what they accepted in order to protect one another.

In the evening, Tanoshi and Airi went for their bath and I couldn't accompany them. There was too big a risk of infection if I soaked my feet in bathwater. I hated being sick. Probably due to all the magic users in our house, I'd never been laid up before. Nor was I good at lying in bed. From my earliest recollections, I'd worked from sunrise to sunset, often pounding metal in the foundry or racing through the forest to stop some dumb bear from hurting people. To add to my distress, Kenji pointed out I wasn't burning what he called calories. I needed to eat less or risk getting fat and sluggish. A third of my usual intake might have been enough, but I'd never felt so hungry. I think I inspected the bottom of my feet every hour in the hopes the cuts had healed. Airi assured me my wounds were making a speedy recovery. It sure didn't feel that way.

That night, as the three of us lay in our bed, I quizzed them on what magic they'd placed on my katana. There was a long silence before Airi spoke.

"Nothing you haven't already experienced," she spoke hesitantly. "Your sword moves fast, follows your need, remains sharp and strikes with enhanced power. Your mother did it to help you stay alive. Actually, what made the biggest difference was my father giving you his magical speed. We preformed the ceremony when you were three years old, after an assassin squad from Takamatsu threw spears at you. Fortunately, Tanoshi was close so none hit you."

"That must have been when you turned them green and made them think they were frogs," I said to Tanoshi. "I always thought they'd targeted you."

"Back then they didn't understand my power," Tanoshi explained. "They thought that without the evil knife, I was no stronger than any of the other witches in Takamatsu. What really scared them was the thought of a male on the throne. They feared breaking the chain which reached all the way back to our first ancestor."

"I always knew it would be a problem. But I thought we'd sorted it out after I agreed to marry a girl from the Clothmaker family."

Airi put her hand on her forehead. "Sometimes you can be a little slow in the uptake, Haruko. She only agreed because every girl in Takamatsu wants to marry you. You're prime husband material. Besides being our future king, you're handsome, smart, bigger and stronger than anyone else, and have this strange hobby of chasing down marauding bears. Anyway, the Clothmakers expect that while they'll let you be king in name, their first daughter will be our real monarch and, in time, her daughter the future queen. That's why there haven't been any more attacks on you. However, they know of Tanoshi's real power and they want her gone so she can't upset their plans."

"You...you think I'd make a good husband?" I said to Airi. We looked at each other. I think we both turned a bit red.

"All right," Tanoshi said. "What we need to do is find out where Kenji's father is hiding and take back my sword. That's our priority. I'm going to disrupt his companies and make him lose money to draw him out. We'll probably have to fight, so we'll need Haruko's feet healed. Let's lay low for a few more days."

* * * *

Between the Earth medicine and Tanoshi's trickle of power, over the next four days my feet returned to normal, although the pink, fresh skin lacked calluses. Richard and Tanoshi bought me some soft shoes called sneakers, which proved to be just what I needed. While in the store, Tanoshi found leather coats and pants and insisted on buying a set for all of us. She even bought a large black-leather overcoat for me to hide my katana. I have to admit I liked these tough work clothes. They would provide as good protection as the leather outfits I wore back home. Richard said they made us look like a biker gang.

Apparently, leather clothes in the quality Tanoshi had found were expensive, depleting our money supply. To replenish it, we needed to visit our bank—the pathetic pornfool who kept a suitcase full of cash hidden in his office. As the man happily counted out another three thousand dollars, Kenji noticed a gun in the suitcase and asked Tanoshi to make the man give it to him.

Richard was none too happy with Kenji's new weapon, saying guns were dangerous in the hands of the inexperienced. Especially this forty-five automatic, which possessed a strong kick and required skill to use effectively. We postponed our raid on the medical centers so Richard could take Kenji to a gun range and have him practice. That evening Tanoshi needed to use her healing power on Kenji's sore wrist as he could barely move his hand.

We didn't waste the added time. There was much we needed to learn, ideas to make our lives easier after we returned home. Airi wanted to absorb as much Earth technology as she could and made Kenji read article after article on his laptop. I found learning about this world depressing. Wars, constant wars. Kenji said there were always wars someplace on Earth, and had been through all of history. I found the brutality overwhelming, especially that committed by armed soldiers against helpless civilians. Discovering such atrocities continued even to this day was the hardest to understand.

Learning about how people, over and over, followed and praised those who led them into such misery confused me. I almost told Richard how my father had visited a world not much worse than this one, which the High God had judged unworthy of continuing. But, knowing Richard couldn't come with us, I said nothing, I wasn't the High God and didn't know enough to make pronouncements on the state of this place.

That evening, as I luxuriated in the first bath I'd enjoyed with Airi and Tanoshi since cutting up my feet, I told them of what I'd learned about this world's endless cruelty.

"There's plenty of magic in this world," Tanoshi said. "But no one recognizes it. Because I'm a witch, here, I'm able to bend people to my will with an enhanced power of persuasion, because this type is common on Earth. Many Earth-people can tap into this power, they call it charisma, and it makes the weak-willed follow those they see as leaders. Like our stupid porn-loving preacher. His power prevents his followers from seeing him as the shallow, self-serving fool he is."

"I think you're right," I agreed. "Kenji told me about some of the recent Earth wars and from what he said, usually just one man, who somehow convinced others to follow him, started them. He told me his county, Japan, is across a narrow sea from another land which is ruled by a horrid man who keeps his people in poverty and starvation and prevents them from learning about the outside world. He gets away with it because he controls an army of over a million. A million men support this evil man even though they watch their own families starving and being worked to death."

"Magic power used for evil," Tanoshi said. "We must find our way home. For those of us on the Moon Goddess' world, this is our hell."

"It's time to put our plan into action," Airi agreed. "Although I like learning about Earth technology, we've stayed long enough."

After our bath, we learned Kenji had rented some DVDs called documentaries. These were more useful than the story-movies he usually brought home. The first one was on astronomy and gave us wonderful insights into how a world was formed. It confirmed my dad's claim the universe was nearly four billion years old. No one had believed him, but since his science helped in many other ways, no one argued about it.

"Our father was a high school teacher," I told Kenji. "He knows something about many different things, but admitted he doesn't have a deep understanding of any one subject. Many of these ideas are new to me."

Kenji picked up the DVD case. "There's been a lot of progress during the last few years. I bet they didn't know some of this stuff when your Dad taught school. Much of what we now know comes from the Hubble orbiting telescope. It's made some fantastic discoveries in the last few years."

"So many stars, so many possible worlds," Tanoshi said. "This is why people follow fools like the preacher man. They can't get their minds around a God able to create such an unbelievable universe. They want a little God who they can control, not one so vast and overwhelming he can create this huge and complex universe, and yet make it possible for his children to understand every detail."

"Mostly, they refuse to believe in any god," Kenji said. "For astronomers, that's common. Don't forget, everything can be explained by science. Before I met you I ignored the question. I actually planned to study astronomy when I was in high school. But, because I had to work several jobs, my grades were never great. In the end I admitted I was too weak in math to handle astronomy courses. When I came over here, I planned majoring in Geology, but I guess that's not going to happen now."

The three of us looked at Kenji. We'd forgotten the suffering he was going through. He'd lost his future, his own father wanted to kill him, and now his only chance of survival lay with three strange people who claimed to have magic. I suspected only his attraction to Tanoshi kept him from complete despair.

My sister put her arm around him. "You're a part of my family now," she said. "You have a future. Not the one you expected, but it'll always be interesting and fun."

Richard had no interest in watching documentaries and, since he couldn't watch sports on our one television, read the newspaper he'd brought home, a habit he'd begun to keep tabs on any stories about the green-haired man who could outrun cars. He clicked off the television and we turned to him. "There's an ad in the personals section that might be about you," he said.

He read: *To the mysterious dark beauty who sings like an angel in Japanese. You and your talented green-haired friends are missing a very important button. We'll be outside your hotel every evening until we find you. We desperately need to meet with you again. We can't live without you anymore. Please come, Michelle and Frankie.*

I looked at Tanoshi and Airi. Airi shook her head. "That's us all right. And there are enough hints that Kenji's dad will figure it out if he sees it."

"Well, he won't know what hotel they are referring to," Kenji said. "Only Michelle and Frankie know which hotel we pretended to stay at."

Richard laid the newspaper on the table. "The ad has been running for over a week. I'll bet they put it in other newspapers too. They might have even put up posters in the area where they left you."

That didn't sound good. Kenji's dad had many people working for him and his whole life now revolved around getting his hands on our swords. He could have lookouts stationed at every hotel in town. "Why?" I asked. "Why would Michelle and Frankie do something like this? They had good lives in their own city and we only met them for one night. I'm sure they were surprised when the button turned out to be gold, but going to such great lengths to return it doesn't make sense. Airi gave it to them as a gift."

"It's not about the button," Airi said quietly. "Back then, after we'd first arrived here, Tanoshi's persuasion magic was working even though she didn't know it. We were desperate and needed them to like us. Remember how easy it was for Tanoshi to persuade them to let us spend the night in their hotel room. We even bathed with them. If they've quit their jobs and are spending all their money looking for Tanoshi, they must be in love with her. They don't understand they feel that way because of magic."

Kenji and Richard looked at each other. I didn't have to guess what they were thinking. Kenji especially, he was in love with Tanoshi, and now he must realize he felt that way because Tanoshi wanted him to. Richard looked around the house. The nice house we'd contrived to get him. He at least, had come out ahead. Maybe he wouldn't hate us. Kenji clicked on the DVD player again, but none of us resumed watching the show.

"We'll have to go met them," Tanoshi finally said, "even if it turns out to be a trap. I didn't mean to make them care for me. I should put things right." She turned to Kenji. "Let's go for a little walk."

After they returned, Kenji went to his own room without saying anything. Tanoshi said she didn't feel like taking a bath, and retreated to our bed. She tried not to show it, but I think she was crying, at least on the inside.

CHAPTER 18

The letter was written in Japanese, which only Kenji could read. It confirmed our worst fear. Michelle and Frankie were prisoners, and they would die unless we handed over our swords. The letter told us to go to a place called the west end of The Fort Desoto beach at midnight when the moon was full. Kenji said he thought that was soon, but would look it up when we got home.

Richard, in his full policeman uniform, continued trying to pry more information from the guy who'd been sitting outside the downtown Hilton holding the letter. He knew nothing, just a homeless guy who'd earned a hundred dollars to wait each night for us to turn up. Whoever had given him the letter had never revealed his face or name. When it became obvious the man couldn't tell us more, we let him leave.

"It's odd the letter didn't warn you not to call the police," Richard said. "That's usually the case with ransom notes. If they're not afraid of the police, they must feel confident."

"Dad has many goons working for him," Kenji said. "He must have a plan in mind. It probably involves a lot of guys with guns."

Richard thought for a minute. "The police have firepower too. While I can't tell them about you, I could claim I got a tip drugs were coming in. If I take Tanoshi to the station and have her persuade my captain the info is legitimate, the department could assemble a strike force."

As we drove home, we refined Richard's idea. Since the meeting was on a beach, it made sense Kenji's dad's boat, the big *Cardiac Arrest*, would be waiting offshore and he'd send a smaller craft to meet us on the beach. Police helicopters could search the waters for the drug-runner's mother-ship while the police arrested anyone who came ashore. Richard thought it a good plan with a real possibility of success. He felt confident they'd release Michelle and Frankie unarmed, explaining that when the police surrounded the boat, no one would risk a death penalty by killing hostages.

I didn't think it'd be that easy. I doubted Kenji's father

would walk into such a simple trap. But I sat all the way home without raising any objections. It was hard to think about, but as a prince and future monarch, my responsibility was to recover Tanoshi's sword so we could get home. Like Aunt Chie said, a ruler made the hard choices and took the pain on himself. If it came to choosing between saving thousands of people on my world, or rescuing Michelle and Frankie, I'd have to sacrifice them.

The police in this world were powerful and competent. I'd put my trust in them and hope they'd come through. Kenji's father must know his money would not save him if he killed a police officer. Later, I'd talk with Tanoshi and Airi about creating a plan to get aboard Kenji's father's boat, and of course, developing a fall-back plan in case it all went wrong.

* * * *

After receiving the letter, we had four days to prepare. Because Tanoshi was so persuasive, the police involvement went out of control. We now had a major operation using swat teams from several districts and a helicopter from the coast guard. No way could we sneak past all those officers to confront Kenji's dad. Richard advised us to stay out of sight, as there was a real danger those excited cops would mistake us for the bad guys.

It'd seemed simple enough when we'd formulated the plan. Tanoshi took a Smartphone with a recording to Richard's police station. Several men, actually Richard's friends, could be heard discussing a drug shipment arriving from Columbia. They revealed the time, date and drop off-point. Tanoshi gave the police a sad tale of how she and her two friends were at the table next to the miscreants, and after realizing what was going on they'd begun recording the conversation. Tanoshi, having drunk too much beer, needed to rush to the bathroom, and when she returned she saw the drug dealers leading Michelle and Frankie away at gunpoint. As Tanoshi hid behind a table, she heard one of the men say these girls knew too much and they would be taken to the boat as hostages until the drop was complete.

Now to me, the story sounded like too many coincidences,

but after Tanoshi smiled and repeated it several times, none of the officers, all the way to their top people, questioned it. Richard thought it funny. "Yeah, Tanoshi's power is impressive, but this is the kind of thing these guys live for. A big drug bust, swat teams charging in, helicopters lighting up the water, flairs and flash-bangs shattering the night. God, this is what these guys dream about. They're all thinking about the awards, citations and television interviews as they stand in front of those bales of confiscated dope."

I wished we'd come up with a better idea. But now, with so many people involved, we'd just have to let it play out. Besides, we did have some tricks. Airi, working with Kenji, had formulated a clever rouse should the police raid fall apart. Whatever happened, Jack Bryce wanted to get his hands on our swords, and we needed to get Tanoshi's sword back. In the end, it would come down to a confrontation between us.

* * * *

Fort Desoto Beach was at the end of a long road and bridge structure, which led out into the ocean. Well, I called it the ocean until Richard explained we were looking at the gulf side of Tampa Bay. I told Richard it was a bit like the trail we'd built between our boat harbor and the seal hunting grounds near the salt cave. He told me seals were a protected species and people would take great offense if they learned I'd killed even one. I pointed to his gun belt. "What animal do you use for leather? Seals are all we have. Besides, there are millions of them. The males fight one another so their females have a spot to give birth. The few we take don't affect their numbers at all."

It was a pleasant ride. We headed out in the late afternoon and to our right, the setting sun turned the evening sky red and orange. While crossing the bridge portions, we drove past people fishing over the edge. It didn't look as if they were catching much, but perhaps, on such a pleasant evening, it didn't matter to them.

"It must be strange to fish for hours and not catch anything," Airi, staring out of the window, spoke. "For all we lack at home, in some ways we are fortunate." We talked about fishing, describing to Kenji and Richard the various types we caught and the names we'd given them. I guess we were trying not to think about the coming fight, and our slim chance of saving Michele and Frankie. Even Bruno, sitting on Tanoshi's lap, could feel the tension and remained quiet, occasionally licking Tanoshi's face.

We rode in Richard's minivan. The police vehicles taking part in this raid were unmarked, so those supposed criminals would not realize how many police were in the area. As civilians, they refused to let us take part in the operation, but Richard, with a little help from Tanoshi, convinced them we should be close so Tanoshi could identify the hostages. That meant we were going to the site early and would remain in the minivan, which Richard would park outside the dangerous area.

Just what was Jack Bryce's plan? Did he know we three could not enter the ocean? Was that why he'd picked this spot? We'd considered these questions many times, including what would the police do when no drug dealers showed up. Still, it made sense Jack would send a boat with goons to make the trade. Hopefully, they would be carrying weapons, which would give the police the arrests they needed. I doubted he'd have the *Cardiac Arrest* any place close. And that would be where we'd find Tanoshi's sword.

We arrived at a good-sized parking lot made for people using the beach. Late in the day, many cars began leaving, but some people remained on the sand, watching the last of a spectacular red sunset. We walked over and joined them.

"I've never seen sunsets as colorful as this," I told Kenji. "Of course, we live in a mountainous area and don't see the sun reach the horizon, but even when I was at the ocean, the sky didn't put on such an impressive display."

"Lucky you," Kenji said. "That means your atmosphere is clean. Pollution causes our red sunsets. The soot particles absorb the blue light leaving only the red rays. Even if it's pretty, its a sign of an atmosphere in trouble."

"There's so much here we could learn," Airi said. "As soon as we get Tanoshi's sword back, we'll have to leave, but part of me would like to stay and learn more."

We watched until the sun dropped below the horizon. There was no green flash marking the end. I wondered if I should ask Kenji about the missing green flash, but perhaps he'd never heard of it. Despite the similarities, our worlds were different. Still, I wondered if there was a scientific reason the tip of our sun flashed green just before it disappeared below the horizon.

Tanoshi threw a stick for Bruno until he tired, then we headed back to the minivan and the long, nervous, wait until midnight. I noticed other cars and vans pulling into the lot. The police were assembling. Most parked closer to the beach, leaving us, at the far end of the lot, alone. I didn't know if the police had arranged to keep the streetlights out, but this area, far from any city, was soon dark, only a reddish full moon rising in the eastern sky providing light.

Five people and a large dog didn't fit well in the minivan. Even with its AC running full blast, the warm humid evening made us uncomfortable. Our leather outfits were over-warm, and I knew Richard suffered the most as he wore a heavy vest designed to protect against bullets. We'd brought bottles of water, but with several hours to wait, we'd finished them and there was a rather smelly puddle around the left rear tire. Richard felt concerned for Bruno and explained dogs were especially vulnerable to heat prostration.

"I'm going to walk over to the other guys," Richard said, "and get more water. Just hang tight for a minute."

"Take Bruno," Tanoshi said. "A dip in the ocean will cool him off."

Richard nodded, held up the leash and Bruno scrambled out of the vehicle. We watched the two of them walk toward the beach area. I wished I could follow, my legs felt cramped from sitting. My feet, although supposedly healed, itched enough to make me grit my teeth.

Just as Richard and Bruno reached the far end of the parking lot, a police car pulled up alongside us. I was surprised, as I understood they'd only use unmarked vehicles, but this one had regular markings on the sides and a light bar across the top. The doors opened and two uniformed officers stepped out and approached our minivan from both sides. The policeman nearest my window motioned for me to lower it.

"We're here with officer—" I stopped. There, in the dim light, stood someone I never expected to see again. As my mouth opened in surprise, Sato pointed the barrel of a gun at my face.

"This is a machine gun," Sato shouted. "It's a lot more advanced than that piece of junk Airi designed. If I pull the trigger, dozens of bullets will splatter your brains all over the car. This is Earth, here science rules, and this gun can kill all of you." While he spoke, the guy on the other side of the car smashed the window and pointed his weapon at Tanoshi and Airi. A second squad car pulled up and three armed goons, dressed as officers, rushed to aid Sato. Jack Brice had sprung his trap, and we'd walked into it.

"You don't have to die," Sato said. "We only want your swords. Hand them over, and you can go free and make good lives for yourselves on this world. Believe me, this place is a damn sight better than the primitive hovel we came from. I'm doing you a favor."

Five of them, and while they had guns, over by the water armed officers waited to pounce. These guys didn't want to get into a fight they would lose. On the downside, we'd die first. "If we give you our swords will you free Michelle and Frankie?"

"Uh? Mich. . . Oh sure, no problem. Once he has your swords those bitches are no use to Mister Bryce."

Even I could tell he lied. I wondered if Michelle and Frankie were still alive. Bryce had sold his soul for power. He wouldn't leave anyone around who could cause problems.

"Quit stalling and hand over the swords." Sato looked around, no doubt worried a real policeman might come over to investigate.

"I'll give you both swords," I said. "But first, I want to see our friends alive. You'll have to take us to them."

"Just give me the damn swords," Sato snarled. "Or I'll blow your brains out right now."

"Shoot your weapons and you'll get into a gunfight with the hundred police officers over there," I pointed. "Even if you were lucky enough to escape with our swords, it wouldn't do you any good. Tanoshi put a spell on them. They cannot be removed from their sheaths. It was something she learned from an Earth witch. I'm sure you know who I mean. When we see our friends alive, Tanoshi will release the spell and you can have the swords in return for everyone's freedom. Do we have a deal?"

"Bullshit," Sato said. "That spell takes a lot of power to cast. Mister Bryce needed to make the stupid bitch sacrifice her own daughter to get the power necessary."

"You know Tanoshi isn't like any other witch. Once she felt the spell, she understood it and made it far stronger." I smiled. "Here, if you don't believe me, try it yourself." I handed him my sword. Sato looked at the heavy wooden sheath and studied its gold runes and the symbols of the royal family. He'd seen it enough on the boat and after a minute accepted it as legitimate. He tried to draw the blade and stopped after realizing it wasn't coming out.

Sato motioned to one of the goons. A really big guy, much bigger than me, with arms as large as tree trunks came around the minivan. Sato smiled and handed him the sheath. "OK, Zeek, there's a limit to any spell's power. You can break it."

Zeek was strong, in truth, watching him strain made me worry he might succeed. But Earth epoxy's proved as strong as Kenji had said, and after a few minutes, the panting goon shook his head. One of the other men said they needed to leave before some cop came over.

"Shit," Sato said. "Ok, we'll take them with us. Mister Bryce can sort this mess out."

The goons dragged us out of the minivan. One of the goons saw Kenji's gun and took it from him. They had what Richard called handcuffs, and each of us had our wrists connected by metal links. Once they were confident we couldn't fight, they shoved us into the rear of the squad car. It had a cage arrangement preventing us from reaching the front seats and the four of us barely fit in the rear. As a goon put the handcuffs on her, Sato grabbed Airi's half-katana and I saw the anger on his face when he learned it too, would not let itself be drawn.

Sato got into the front next to the driver, our two weapons on his lap. The other police car followed as we drove out of the parking lot. We awkwardly shifted our bodies in the cramped space, and I worried Sato might notice how we gave Tanoshi extra room so the real swords strapped to her back wouldn't poke us. At least her persuasion magic worked on Sato. When we'd made this plan, none of us expected to meet someone from our world.

I shouted to distract him. "Sato. How come you speak English? You know more of their idioms and phrases than we do?"

"I'm special," he responded. "You bastards thought you'd killed me by sending me into the nowhere place. But this great, beautiful, God rescued me. It felt like he opened a door in my head, and I remembered how to speak English. I can speak it far better than the squeaky trash you use in that hovel you call home."

I remembered Tanoshi saying this planet was the hell for those of us under the Moon Goddess' care.

"Sato," Airi said. "This god you met, did he have a scar on his face?"

"He was beautiful beyond words," Sato replied. "The little scar added to his beauty, it told of being who would fight and suffer to protect those he loved."

We fell silent. It wasn't a god who'd saved Sato. It was the Evil One. It was our father who'd given him the scar. As my father was under the protection of the angel Mike, no doubt Lucifer intended extracting his revenge on Tanoshi and me. I didn't reply, fearing if Tanoshi became upset she might let her magic waver and Sato would see the real swords. After a few minutes, the cars drove onto the sand at the far end of the Fort Desoto Park. The moonlight revealed a long thin boat in the shallows lying parallel to the beach. Two men holding machine guns stood guard.

With multiple guns pointed at us, Sato pushed us across

the shallow water and made us scramble up a ladder and onto the boat's rear deck. A few minutes later, three huge engines roared to life and we headed out to sea. I was grateful the boat had been close to the shore. We'd only gotten our legs wet and the blue glow hadn't revealed itself.

The three engines were loud, making talking pointless. On each of the engine covers was the number three hundred. I assumed that meant horsepower, a silly unit. I did a bit of mental math to convert it into the proper units my Dad used. It came out to a staggering six hundred kilowatts for the three of them. It was depressing to think this one boat held more power than all the steam engines I'd ever built.

The boat headed away from the land. None of us liked being on a small boat just a few centimeters from the ocean. Sato looked relaxed and confident. It occurred to me he didn't know if he fell into the sea, he'd return to the world of his birth—probably in the middle of some endless ocean. I hoped we could use his ignorance to our advantage.

Once we got into deep water, the boat crashed into the waves, bouncing and sending great spays far into the air. Earth technology was impressive, and I understood why they'd made this boat long compared to its width. It could cut through choppy water at high speed. In fact, I was sure we went as fast as a car on land. Maki the Pirate would love a boat like this one. Of course, the noise from those three engines gave me a headache. Steam engines were a thousand times quieter; none of us had endured anything this loud before.

I think the racket got to Sato. He motioned for us to retreat down into a small cabin just in front of the cockpit. Sato was careful to have one of his goons, carrying a machine gun, enter the cabin with us. The boatbuilders must have understood the noise problem, because once Sato closed the hatch it muffled the engine sounds.

Sato spoke in our language. "Look," he began. "All Mister Bryce wants is your swords. He has nothing against you personally. Rather than fighting, why don't you release the magic, and I'll turn this boat around and take you back to shore." He looked at Tanoshi. "I know I tried to kill you, but back then I was under orders. None of that applies anymore. This is our new home. We're all stuck here and the intrigues of our former pathetic little world no longer concern us. This is a wonderful planet, better in every way from that primitive dump. When the god opened my mind, I knew this was the place where I belonged. All I'm asking is for you to think about the great lives you could have here, and it'll only cost you those swords, which mean nothing to you anymore."

He looked at Tanoshi. "There are lots of people in this country with brown skin like yours, guys who might actually find you attractive. This is the only world where you could get yourself a husband."

I considered grabbing for one of the real swords and removing Sato's head. But the handcuffs and the armed goon made me hesitate. Kenji put his hand on Tanoshi's arm. "Baka," he said and pointed at Sato. Apparently, Kenji had been able to follow the conversation a little. Baka was Japanese for idiot, but not a word used our language. We'd learned it while discussing the greedy preacher-man.

Tanoshi laughed. "Kenji needs to meet with his father. They have issues to settle. And you, Sato, you might want to reconsider your relationship with a man who could order his own son killed."

Sato switched to English and turned to Kenji. "Mister Bryce never wanted to hurt you. When you tried to kill his servants, they had to defend themselves. He's willing to forget the incident and pay your way through school as he first intended."

Kenji held up his hands. "After he removes these handcuffs, I'll trust him."

"You're missing the big picture." Sato continued speaking in English. "The great god sent me here to help Mister Bryce. He's a wonderful and intelligent man who wants to make this world a better place. He knows, with the magic in your swords, he can accomplish his goal. Once he becomes the President of this county, he'll have the power to make real changes and unshackle corporations from pointless regulations so they can provide a world of plenty for everyone. The god says he can save this planet from its own stupidity. He needs the power in your swords to get elected. That's the reason I was sent to help him."

We remained silent. I debated whether it was worth arguing. Sato had bought into the evil one's lies, and a Takamatsu noble would never change his mind. I was saved from making a reply when the hatch leading to the cockpit opened and one of the goons shouted Mister Bryce was on the radio. Sato almost tripped as he scurried back to the cockpit. Since Bryce hadn't called Sato on a Smartphone, I deduced we were far out to sea, beyond what Kenji called the towers.

Tanoshi pleaded with the goon who'd remained in the cabin, saying she desperately needed to use the bathroom. The man shrugged and kicked open a door in front of the cabin. Thanking him profusely, Tanoshi eased herself into the small enclosure. After a few minutes she reemerged and I saw light glint from the cutting edge of our swords. Tanoshi had removed the tape.

Having sacrificed our sheaths to fool Sato, it left the sharp edge of our swords exposed. Kenji suggested using a black tape to provide a little protection from accidental cuts while Tanoshi wore them on her back. I'd decided the tape was thin enough so, if the weapon needed to be used in a hurry, the blade would cut through it. Of course, my sword would be more effective with the tape removed.

There was no sword inside the sheath Sato held. To make the weight the same, Richard took me to a hardware store and bought several lengths of soft steel. As those straight bars wouldn't fit into our curved sheaths, I'd needed to do a little reshaping.

Last week, while I worked, Kenji told me how army officers still wore swords as a sign of their rank. He said guns and bombs made swords obsolete, meaning few modern swords could withstand combat. He told me how wars here were fought. His story of the war between his country and this one fascinated me the most. I found it hard to imagine battles of such ferocity using weapons far advanced from ours. When he told me about the atomic bomb which had ended the fighting, I needed to stop work and sit on the ground while my brain absorbed the horror of dropping such a monstrosity on innocent civilians.

"If such bombs exist," I said to Kenji, "and your father is in the grips of the evil one, perhaps Lucifer's plan is to have such weapons used again."

"The ones they dropped on Japan are small by today's standards," Kenji said. "Today, they build hydrogen bombs which are many times more powerful. They say, if a full-scale war ever broke out and all the bombs were exploded, it'd end life on Earth."

I stood for several minutes, watching the heat rise from the briquettes in the forge, which Kenji and I had built from a bar-b-q grill and a blower from a car-parts store. "It might not be only my world that is in danger," I said quietly. "The evil one has formed a complex plan. He intends destroying both our worlds."

All we had to combat his plan were two steel bars sealed into fancy wooden sheaths with epoxy.

CHAPTER 19

A little after dawn, the speedboat reached Jack Bryce's *Cardiac Arrest*. It looked as if he'd made only temporary repairs to the rear boat-loading-hatch, which we'd left dangling after our escape. I spotted two steel cables wrapped around the outside of the hatch to hold it in the closed position. It made me wonder if Bryce was as rich as everyone claimed.

A set of stairs secured to the side of the outer hull led down from the main deck to the water. Since we had limited use of our hands, I appreciated not having to scramble up a ladder. Once on the big boat's deck, I looked around and could not see another boat or any land. Actually, I was impressed how Earth technology could let two boats find each other in the middle of a vast sea. There was no time to gawk, the gunmen told us to stand against the aft rail and wait for Doc Bryce. Other than the goons standing guard, the rest ignored us as they needed to secure the speedboat for towing and get the main vessel underway. I heard the word 'Mexico' repeated several times and Kenji whispered we were heading to another country.

We waited for a long time. I suppose Sato needed to give Bryce a report and explain why he'd brought the four of us instead of just the two swords. No one said anything about Michelle and Frankie; more evidence they were no longer alive.

"I can feel Bryce trying to use the magic in my sword to break what he thinks is the spell sealing the others in their sheaths," Tanoshi whispered. "Get ready, he'll be storming up here soon."

"It's odd he hasn't discovered its not magic," I whispered back.

"He's locked into thinking its magic power," Airi said. "After giving the hat-witch the spell to seal our blades, it prevents his mind from considering any other explanation."

To help hide the swords on Tanoshi's back. Airi and I took up positions on either side of her with Kenji in front. When the fight started, we'd need to grab our weapons and slash through one another's handcuff chains. I was hoping Tanoshi's persuasion magic could confuse the gun goons long enough so we could get our weapons.

After what seemed like hours, Bryce came up a stairway and onto the deck. He wore the same odd cloak with the silly symbols as last time. "Stop this foolishness and release the blades," he shouted. "You can't escape. Your only hope is to cooperate with me."

"Hi dad," Kenji said. "Good to see you too."

"Lawrence," he shouted. "Get away from the witch. I'll only tell you once."

"We came to conduct a deal," I said. "Bring out our friends, and we'll release the magic binding the swords."

The man stared at me. "You're in no position to bargain. Your witch can't protect you from bullets."

"If you kill us," I shot back, "you'll never gain the power in the swords. If any of us die, the binding spell cannot be broken. Why are you reluctant to let us see Michelle and Frankie? It's a simple request."

I could see a vein in the man's neck throbbing. His anger and frustration appeared ready to explode. Finally, he took several deep breaths. "Those women aren't on board. They're…in a hotel room back in Saint Petersburg. After you break the spell, I'll order them released."

Kenji spoke. "Then let us speak with them. I know you have a satellite link."

Bryce did not respond. It was time to accept our friends were dead. Even after hearing about all the wars on Earth, I still found it frightening to come face to face with such depravity.

Bryce spat on the deck. "No spell is unbreakable. I know the price the stupid witch paid to bind your swords, as I gave her the incantations. I can undo your spell with an equal sacrifice. This is your last chance, release the swords, or I'll do it the hard way and use your own weapons to kill you."

On a whispered order, one of the gun goons dragged Kenji to the side. I thought Bryce still retained a shred of humanity and didn't want to kill his son, when he spoke.

"Take him, and the others, down to the hidden room. I'll let them see the consequences of their stubbornness." He turned to the guy holding a pistol to Kenji's head. "Don't kill him. I need him alive for the ceremony." He started to walk away, but then turned. "Shit! What did I tell you about that room? The sides are metal. No guns without silencers. Do I have to think of everything? I value my hearing even if you don't."

Bryce and Sato left. There was a delay as the goons retrieved some other guns. One guy kept his machinegun aimed at us, as the others exchanged theirs for pistols with long barrels that had a cumbersome attachment on the end. Obviously, this was to muffle the noise. I'd helped build several steam engine boilers, and knew how loud the inside a metal container could be. My dad was really fanatical about everyone wearing ear and eye protection when doing anything in our shop.

With the fat gun barrels pressed against our backs, they led us down to the lower mechanical part of the boat. We eased our way between two rumbling diesel engines, which I would have loved to have stopped and examined, especially after noticing they weren't identical. Besides being mismatched, they looked old and dirty, as if they'd seen long service before being installed on this boat. The prod of a gun against my back returned me to reality and I was forced toward a bulkhead and into a compartment with an even narrower walkway down its center. This involved some rearranging as we could only pass between what had to be fuel tanks single file. Each of us ended up with a gun goon behind us, and I guessed Tanoshi was using her persuasion power to its maximum to stop the guy pressing his gun against her leather jacket from noticing the swords beneath it.

The final door, which looked like a hatch in a large fuel tank, led to Bryce's hidden room. With all the black candles and odd designs on the walls, it appeared disturbingly like the hat-witch's sacrifice room. However, this altar was larger and placed in the center. The four goons who'd forced us through the hatch made us line up against the wall in front of the opening we'd just entered. They took up positions on either side of the altar with their pistols aimed at us. This way they could shoot at us without the danger of hitting one another. I wondered about the power of their weapons, if they were too powerful, the metal walls and ceiling would cause the bullets to ricochet dangerously.

There was only one electric light on the curved ceiling. Bryce lit multiple candles. As the room brightened, I saw leather straps dangling from the altar.

"Bring Lawrence forward," Bryce commanded. He looked at his son. "Well boy, this isn't what I'd planned, but those swords will give me far more power than what I'd obtain from a simple sacrifice. You're proving more valuable than I'd expected. You should feel grateful. You get to pay me back for all the money I spent supporting you."

"The pittance you sent my mother didn't even cover our food costs," Kenji shouted. "You miserable cheap, murdering son of a bitch, I'll see you dead and in hell where you belong."

"Stupid half-breed," snarled Bryce. "You're the one who's going to hell today."

I was about to grab for my sword when Airi put her hand on my arm. "Not yet," she whispered in our language. "Wait."

It was hard to watch them manhandle Kenji onto the table and secure his arms, legs and torso with leather straps. Every part of me wanted to grab my sword, but Airi was never wrong. If she said wait, then I had to follow her lead. However, when Bryce ripped open Kenji's shirt and drew a five-pointed star over his heart by dribbling hot candle wax, I came as close to losing it as I'd ever been. Kenji tried not to cry out, but his curses sounded pained throughout the ordeal. My fists were so tight, a fingernail drew blood from my palm.

"Just a little longer," Airi whispered. "Get ready."

Bryce put several large and impractical red-stoned rings on his fingers, and on his head he placed a miniature pointed hat, with bits flopping down around his ears. Sato donned a robe with similar markings and then placed our two fake sheathed swords on either side of Kenji, securing them to his body with multiple red ropes. Bryce went to the back of the room to a closet with doors that looked like gold. After a saying some weird sounding words that weren't English or Japanese, he pressed a series of buttons on a device like a telephone's keypad and the doors opened. Beneath the gold shell, they were steel and at least two centimeters thick.

Very carefully, Bryce reached in and removed Tanoshi's sword from the cabinet.

The sword.

The sword that could send us home. Now I understood, Airi knew we needed to wait for him to open the cabinet. Even my katana might not cut through such a thick hardened-steel door.

Airi turned to me. "Prince, you may now kill those who would put your people in danger."

Tanoshi shouted in our language. It was just something about their lack of bathroom expertise, but I'm sure it sounded scary to the gun goons as she sent them a wave of confusion It gave Airi and me the seconds we needed to grab our weapons from beneath her jacket. Airi swung the half-katana and severed my handcuff chains. Quickly, I did the same for her and Tanoshi.

The goons remained unresponsive, but one had his gun leveled at Tanoshi. I rushed across the room and rammed my sword through his heart. He slumped to the ground, dragging my sword down with him. It took a good second to yank the blade from his body, giving Bryce and Sato a chance to retreat to the back of the room. I became aware of the problem. In such confined quarters, I should have grabbed the shorter blade. Katina's were slashing weapons. Inside this fake fuel tank, with its low ceiling, I'd hit something if I tried using my long blade for anything but stabbing.

The other goons began recovering from Tanoshi's confusion magic. Well, just two as one now had a neck artery spurting blood from Airi's weapon. The last goons, no doubt seasoned professionals, had recovered their wits. Guns they'd held casually came up, and both had a clear line of fire at Tanoshi. I leaped, sending one slamming into the table holding

Kenji. The goon's gun fired. Even the muffled retort sounded loud in the metal room. The bullet went over Tanoshi, who'd flattened herself against the deck, and ricocheted twice against the steel walls. I dove across the table and rammed my sword to its hilt through a goon before he got his weapon aimed at me, leaving my sword trapped in his chest.

The last goon, who'd taken the shot, remained fixated on killing Tanoshi. I saw him turning his weapon as she rolled to the side. Abandoning my trapped sword, I leaped just as every candle, and the overhead light, went out. With no windows, the room became completely black. I landed on the goon just as he pulled the trigger and managed to shove his arm to the side. I thought the gun's muzzle flash looked as if it pointed away from Tanoshi, but I didn't know if my sister had been hit or not. Using my weight to hold the goon down, I got my hands around his head and twisted. He stopped moving.

"Anyone hurt?" I shouted. Kenji's scream stopped me from hearing a reply. As I got to my feet, diffuse light entered the room from the rear, behind the gold cabinet. A second door! Bryce and Sato were escaping. I looked to the dead goon, who should have had my katana sticking out of him, but the weapon was gone. Bryce now had two of our swords.

Airi rushed to the table and begin using her blade to cut Kenji free. I didn't wait, without a sword, I charged through the small hatch Bryce had left open, and ran up a narrow, steep staircase.

The stairs ended at another small hatch which opened on the most elaborate bedroom I'd encountered on this world. I supposed this was where Bryce slept. The fleeing Bryce and Sato had left a heavy chair, which must normally hide this opening, toppled to the side. I saw the main door to the cabin and charged out onto an adjoining elevated deck.

Running up an outside stairway from the main deck, came Zeek, the big goon who'd almost pulled the iron bar from my sheath despite the epoxy. He held a thick round club like those I'd seen used on the television sports game Richard liked to watch. He smiled when he saw me, no doubt confident his club would be enough.

I smiled back. Yeah, he was much bigger than me, but so were bears. I doubted anyone had told him how fast I could move. If I survived this day, I'd have Uncle Taro to thank. Of course, it would help if I had a weapon.

He swung the club as if he aimed for my feet. I almost jumped to let it pass under me but I saw his eyes flicker to my chest. I lurched back just in time as he jerked the stick up to waist height. The man knew a trick or two. I collided hard against the port rail, and had to leap to the side to avoid a follow-up blow.

Another attack and another barely avoided blow. He kept the club moving, it looked like a blur, giving me no way to get past his defense. No doubt, he intended getting me cornered with no place to dodge. I jumped around the little deck trying to prevent him from backing me up against a rail. I needed to do something. This upper deck adjoining the bedroom wasn't large. It was only a matter of time until he forced me into a spot where I couldn't avoid his blow.

He pointed to the rail, laughed and shouted I could easily escape if I wanted. Did he want me to jump overboard? I doubted he knew of my vulnerability to the ocean. But the boat was miles from land. The sicko thought it'd be amusing to watch me drown.

I obliged the goon and rushed for the rail. True to my guess, he didn't follow and paused to watch. My hands on the varnished wood rail let me control my body as I somersaulted over it. A quick reverse in the air let me land facing the deck. Instead of my feet continuing toward the water, I brought them in so they'd hit deck's outer edge. With my knees fully bent, I was positioned for a standing jump. I gave it all I had and reached the top of the fancy cabin. The goon stood motionless below me, still wondering why I hadn't plunged down into the water. Just as he started to turn, I leaped and sent us both crashing to the deck.

My speed paid off. I moved first and got onto his back. I'd never performed a choke hold with any force before, but my dad had insisted I learn it, 'just in case.' This was that case. The guy was strong. He dropped the club and tried pulling my arm away from his neck. His fingers dug into my flesh as we rolled around the deck. He had size, weight and a gym-toned body. I had a lifetime of pounding iron, pulling plows and swinging a pick at a coal face. I could feel his hands weakening as the lack of oxygen shut down his brain. His legs lost their power and we finally stopped rolling around.

The man stiffened and went limp. "OK," Airi said. "You can let go of him now." I looked up. She wiped the guy's blood from her sword. "Hiroshi," she said. "You don't have to do everything yourself. All you needed to do was draw him away from the door so I could attack from behind. With all your jumping around, I couldn't find an opening that didn't put you in danger."

"Bryce...my sword." I gasped as I staggered to my feet. "Must stop him." Behind Airi, a bare chested Tanoshi stood with her arm around Kenji, holding him up. He had Tanoshi's cotton undershirt tied around his chest. I could see blood oozing from beneath it.

"Kenji!" I shouted.

"He'll survive," Airi said. "The cut is shallow. I think Bryce aimed for his neck, but in his hurry and the darkness, he missed and just sliced across his chest."

Tanoshi explained. "He knew if he compromised the sword with a murder, it'd make it easy to subvert its power."

Airi handed me her half-katana. "Go find Bryce and end this."

The fancy bedroom was on the boat's uppermost deck. Airi and I charged down the stairs to the main deck. I peered over the rail above where the external staircase led to the water and saw the speedboat with Bryce, Sato and several other men on it. Shots rang out and bullets splattered against the side of the boat. We jumped back from the rail and dove to the deck.

"He's getting away," shouted Airi, who lay on the deck alongside me. The speedboat's three engines roared to life and with a great spray of water, it shot away, taking Bryce and our swords with it. I thought they intended leaving us behind, but after a hundred meters the engines stopped and the boat's prow dropped back into the water. Then, very slowly, it came back toward us. Three men with rifles stood near its bow, and I saw a forth armed goon the cockpit. We retreated inside the rear cabin.

Sato shouted to us in our language. "Hiroshi, we're not going to shoot you. We want to trade. If you agree to give Mister Bryce the last sword, he'll let you live. We'll take you back to Saint Petersburg. You have my word. Mister Bryce doesn't want any more killing, he just wants the sword. You know now he has two swords, there is no way you can return home. Take him up on his deal and make good lives for yourselves in this wonderful world. It's far better than where you were before."

"Does he really think we're that stupid?" Airi muttered. She patted me on the shoulder. "Speak in English and remind him we have guns now. Bryce has only four goons left, if they try to come on board, they are going to die." She handed me one of those pistols with the muffled barrel. "I'll go pick up the other guns those guys dropped," she whispered.

She shouted to Tanoshi and Kenji who'd remained on the upper deck and asked Kenji if he could pilot the boat.

"I think so," Kenji replied. "It has a GPS. I can get us back to Saint Petersburg. I'll go up to the control bridge and I'll see what I can do."

Since we were alone on the big boat, our position didn't seem so bad. Bryce had made a tactical error leaving the ship. Part of me wondered why he'd done it. Surely, since he and Sato still had four gun goons, they couldn't be that afraid of me.

Sato started shouting again. "You don't understand. There are bombs onboard. We can sink the boat at any time. But you don't need to die. All Mister Bryce wants is the last sword."

Even I didn't need Airi to tell me that was a bluff. "Sink a big expensive boat like this," I shouted. "No one is that stupid. Besides, the sword would be lost too. Then no one would have it."

There was a delay as Bryce and Sato had a conversation. I wondered what stupid story they would come up with. I looked around. Despite his wound and with Tanoshi's help, Kenji had made it to the control bridge. Hopefully, he could get us back to land. Kenji was proving to be a tough kid. I hoped he and Tanoshi could work out their problems.

Sato began shouting again. "This is your last chance to hand over the sword and get a free ride back to land," he said. "Mister Bryce would prefer to handle this the easy way, but he has this GPS location and we're over the continental shelf. The water is shallow enough for salvagers to recover the sword. Since that would use up the profit he plans to make by sinking the *Cardiac Arrest*, he's willing to make a deal. You don't need to die today, just a little cooperation and you can have a great life."

Well, it was a good story. I suppose Earth technology could record a position on the ocean. But making a profit by sinking an expensive boat didn't sound realistic. I decided to call his bluff and told him there was no way we would ever give him the sword, and they could follow us back to land if they wanted.

"Is that your final answer?" Sato shouted.

"Unless Bryce wants to return the swords he stole, that's my answer."

To my surprise, the speedboat's three engines came to life and it roared away at what looked like its top speed. I hadn't expected the standoff to end this quickly. I sat wondering what I'd missed. Then, as I was making my way up to the control bridge to see if Kenji could turn the boat toward land, the bombs went off.

There were three explosions down in the lower part of the vessel. They weren't loud, but the deck shuddered and the windows either cracked or shattered. "Airi!" I shouted. Was she down below looking for guns and near the blasts? I turned and ran to Bryce's fancy bedroom. The little hatch leading to his secret room remained open. If Airi had gone down there to pick up those dropped pistols, she could be in trouble.

I rushed down, cursing as I tripped on the narrow stairs. There was no light in the special room, other than what came down the stairway. Between the darkness, and the eye-watering stench, I almost missed her as she lay slumped in the far corner.

I rushed over, calling her name, almost going headfirst into the wall when I tripped on the buckled floor. I picked her up. Her clothes dripped with a foul smelling liquid. I panicked as I realized it was the boat's fuel. It didn't smell like the gasoline Richard used in his minivan. It was the less explosive kind, like what had been used to start the fire at Richard's old apartment. I saw a glowing three-centimeter gap between the bulkhead door to the tank compartment and the bomb-distorted floor. Through that opening fuel flowed into this room. I looked at my feet and discovered it sloshing against my sneakers. Any second, the fire on the other side of the battered door would spread to the liquid in here.

Airi remained unresponsive. I'd need to carry her up the narrow, one person wide, staircase. After trying several ways to fit the two of us into the narrow passage, I ended up walking backward and dragging her by her armpits. Just as I reached Bryce's bedroom, light, heat and smoke came pouring out of the hatch, revealing the fuel in the hidden room had ignited. I dragged Airi out to the small deck attached to the bedroom and kicked Zeek's body over to the rail. As I ripped those fuel-drenched clothes from Airi, I saw the blood running down her face and assumed she'd hit her head on the steel walls when those bombs exploded. I felt her legs, fearing a bone may have broken when the steel bottom of the converted fuel tank bucked from the bomb planted beneath it. Fortunately, her legs seemed intact. Perhaps being small and light had saved her. She'd just been bounced into the air when the floor had sprung upward beneath her feet.

I'd finished removing her soaked clothes when Tanoshi and Kenji came down from the control bridge. Kenji looked pale and I saw a large red streak beneath the makeshift bandage on his chest. Tanoshi had her arm around his waist, and it looked like she was the only thing keeping him upright.

"What happened to Airi?" Tanoshi shouted.

"She was inside the steel room when the bombs went off. I think she was tossed and struck her head. She's still breathing, but she took a bad hit." As I removed my fuel-soaked sneakers, which stung my sensitive feet, I explained about the spilled fuel flooding the room and why I'd needed to remove her clothes.

"Make sure there's no diesel in her mouth," Kenji said. "That stuff is deadly if it gets into the lungs."

Airi's mouth didn't seem contaminated, and while I was checking she began regaining consciousness. We encouraged her to cough, and it did seem her lungs remained clear. A small blessing, except the flames shooting from the boat's aft section were now five meters high and the black-oily smoke reached far into the sky. I carried Airi, and we made our way toward the bow, the only smoke-free area left.

"I have bad news," despite his injury, Kenji spoke clearly, if slowly. "I found the box on the bridge for holding life jackets empty." He pointed to the rail. "See that hook. It's supposed to hold a life ring ready to throw if anyone falls overboard. There are several around the boat. Someone has removed all the rings. They rigged the boat to burn and sink and made sure anyone left on board had no chance for survival."

I looked at the empty life ring holder. "If we jump into the water, we'll need to hold onto objects from this world, or risk transportation back to our own planet where we'll land randomly in the vast ocean." We looked around, here in the bow, there was nothing lose and everything around us appeared to be made of metal. I heard a crack and saw flames roaring out of the buckled rear deck. We moved away from the expanding fire and found ourselves trapped near the anchor hoist protruding from the prow. Smoke swirled around us making it hard to breath.

"The top of the side rail is made of wood," Tanoshi shouted. "Chop out some pieces. They'll be better than nothing."

I hacked at the rail with the half-katana. Most of the rail was painted steel, and a bar ran along the underside of the wood, which was only there for appearances. It took an inordinate amount of time just separating two half-meter lengths of wood from the steel rail. The sword had done a lot of cutting through metal, and even with its magic enhancement, it was losing its edge. The smoke billowed around us, and the heat from the roaring flames blistered my skin. "That's the best I can do," I said. "We'll have to jump and take our chances. Let's hope Kenji can anchor us to this world."

The four of us, holding one another as tightly as we could, jumped into the sea. At least it took us away from the smoke and flames. I don't think we could have survived for another minute. The bits of wood and Kenji helped. I didn't see any blue sparkles on our bodies as we kicked and bobbed our way away from the blazing boat. The black smoke now rose high into the air, a distress beacon for any nearby boats. Maybe we'd get lucky.

Even if we weren't transported, how long could we tread water? Those bits of rail provided only minimal flotation. The cold water revived Airi and after she stopped coughing, she looked around. "Our world will call us home soon," she muttered. "Look at my feet."

Yes, her feet appeared blue beneath the water. "Let's shift," I said. "Airi is in the most danger. She should be closest to Kenji." Tanoshi agreed but before she could move another, larger, bomb went off inside the *Cardiac Arrest*. Not only was it loud, but we felt the pressure wave just before a real wave crashed over our heads.

Kenji was weak from loss of blood, but he opened his eyes. "That one was to sink the boat," he gasped. "Dad's making sure there won't be any evidence."

The *Cardiac Arrest* listed to port and began going down by the stern. The bomb must have blown out a huge hole, because it upended and rapidly slid under. The noise was unbelievable, things inside broke up while the fire hissed and crackled as the sea engulfed it. We were a distance from the boat, but not out of danger as fuel rose to the surface and continued burning on top of the water. The flaming slick spread out, threatening to reach us.

"Hold onto my belt," I shouted and maneuvered so they

could get a grip. I began swimming from the inferno, putting everything I had into the effort and pulling the others with me. The blue sparkles increased, making us all, except Kenji, less dense. It made it easier to pull them along, but I remembered it would also make my hands less effective when interacting with this world's water. Soon, they'd just pass through the sea like ghosts.

Except it didn't seem to be happening. Each of my strokes shoved against the water and moved me just like swimming in the river at home. The burning fuel slick came close, but I kept us ahead of it until it reached its maximum spread.

We weren't out of danger. Kenji appeared white and lethargic. Blood still came from Airi's head wound. Between the two of them, if this world had fish that were attracted to blood in the water, we'd soon have another problem. All three of us had blue sparkles around our legs. Airi even had them on her back. If she wasn't holding Kenji tightly, she would have already left us.

Although our reduced density and the two chunks of rail kept our heads above the water, I doubted we'd last much longer. Other boats should have seen the great smoke plume rising into the air, but this was Earth. People here seemed far less concerned with the fate of others. Would anyone take the time to come and investigate? And could they reach us before we drowned or were attacked by fish?

"You need to let me go," Airi said in a whisper. "I'm not of this place. The ocean is trying to send me home. Even Kenji is starting to glow because I'm holding him. If I let go, his connection to this place might be strong enough to keep you both here."

"Don't say things like that," I shouted. "If you died, I couldn't go on living. If we live or die, we'll do it together. Don't forget we still have the third sword, Bryce will come back to claim it any minute now."

As the fuel slick thinned, the flames died down. Soon the blaze concentrated on a small area above where the boat sank. When the rolling waves lifted me high enough, I saw the flames came from various floating objects. "Look," I shouted.

"There's stuff floating. Things from this world. They'll prevent us from being transported home."

"They are way over there," Tanoshi said. "You might not make it. Your legs and ass already have sparkles. You know how once your hands start to fade, it's impossible to swim though the water..." she didn't finish.

"I need to try. If we don't do something we can't make it." I took one piece of the rail and tucked it beneath my shirt hoping it would keep me connected to this world long enough to reach the flotsam. As I swam away, both Tanoshi and Airi began crying.

Oddly, I moved quickly. My hands bit into the water and propelled me like they normally did. In fact, the more distance I put between the others and myself, the faster I moved. I risked a quick glance and saw my whole body, except the bit where the wooden rail pressed against my chest, appeared almost transparent. Then I saw my hands. They weren't blue and remained solid. Of course, I still wore those metal handcuff rings. Metal made on Earth. They stopped my hands from being affected by the blue. With the rest of me sliding through the water with little resistance, I raced toward the remnants of the sunken boat with the speed of a tuna.

I dove underwater when I reached the fire, and coming up from below, grabbed one of those circular rings floating on the surface. I yanked it under to put out the flames, and found it buoyant. There were several. Obviously, they'd been hidden someplace and had popped up after the boat went under. With two of them around my body, I made a slower return to the others as surrounded by the Earth material I was no longer friction free.

Once Kenji wore a floatation ring, we didn't have to work to keep him afloat. Airi's ring didn't completely stop her blue, but did reduced most of it. Tanoshi and I had the bits of rail and by holding on to Kenji, we were safe from the transport danger. Now our main worry was the fish who'd be attracted to blood in the water.

Five minutes later the first of the blood-hungry fish arrived. I could see its dorsal fin breaking the water's surface as it circled us. I estimated it to be over two meters in length. "I think it's wondering if we taste good," I said. "If it makes a run for us, I'll smack it with the hunk of rail."

"I can see two others coming toward us," Airi said. "They look really big."

"I'm going to try persuasion magic," Tanoshi said. "I'll project the feeling that we don't taste good. I don't know if that kind of magic works on fish, but I'll try my best."

The fish didn't attack, but they didn't leave and circled us at a distance, occasionally coming within ten meters before deciding we were not the meal they were looking for. I could see Tanoshi straining as she kept up her 'not good to eat' barrier and I feared her exhaustion would eventually let it falter. A couple of times, one of the big fish charged straight at us, and I could feel the increased wave of revulsion Tanoshi sent out to persuade it to change its mind. Airi began having dry heaves, and I didn't feel all that great myself. Once Tanoshi learned a new trick, she got very good at using it. But magic was exhausting and, after fifteen minutes, as Kenji began turning white from blood loss, Tanoshi began gasping and used my arm to keep her head above the water.

For all our efforts, it looked like Bryce had won. I suppose there was a small chance if we let go of the Earth material holding us here, the nowhere place might deposit us close enough to the land on our world to survive. Not very likely, but perhaps a better death than being eaten by these fish. I suggested the idea to Airi, but she insisted we hold out until the very last second. She felt Bryce would make another try for the last sword to avoid the cost of mounting a salvage operation.

When I first saw the boat, I assumed it was Bryce returning. As it came closer, it proved to be a battered and rusted fishing boat with large nets hanging from multiple masts. The big fish kept their distance from the vessel after a man on board used a rifle to shoot one of them. Then, several scruffy-looking men, who wore yellow rubber suits, hauled us over the transom and our ordeal was over.

CHAPTER 20

"Bryce's boat continued sending out distress signals until it went under." Richard sat on the couch and tried to explain the craziness. "After it sank, an automatic EPIRB rose to the surface and sent out a homing signal. That area of the gulf is called the Florida middle grounds. There are always fishing vessels around. Before the *Cardiac Arrest* went under, three different boats, and a coast guard helicopter, were racing to the scene."

I'd never forget the helicopter hovering over the fishing boat and lowering a stretcher for Kenji. Earth technology amazed me. Since Kenji had lost so much blood, the coast guard gave him plasma on the helicopter. Then, once at a hospital, he'd received two units of donated blood. I know this because Airi insisted on learning every detail, probably with the hopes we could adopt similar procedures at home.

Kenji remained in the hospital, although Richard expected his release tomorrow or the next day. However, he was no longer our Kenji. He was once again Lawrence Bryce, and the Japanese consulate would soon replace his passport, which they believed had gone down with the boat. Richard explained how American customs agents recorded identifying data on everyone entering the country, and since Kenji remained unconscious, some clever detective work had revealed his identity.

Once informed, Kenji's father became the very pinnacle of a concerned parent. He promised to take care of any hospital bills and was making arrangements for his beloved son to return to his mother. It was only the most pressing of business problems preventing him from rushing back from Mexico to be at his son's side. But he'd assured the media there was no one more important in his life than his son and heir, Lawrence. It had to be the evil one's work, as without even showing his face, Jack Bryce had ended up, like Earth people said, smelling like a rose.

"I can't believe he sank his expensive boat," I said. "We know the man's fanatical about money. It doesn't make sense."

"He might not have had much of a choice," Richard explained. "I don't think the *Cardiac Arrest* could have returned to an American port after he'd built a secret room in a fake fuel tank. Boats, which have traveled overseas, need to clear customs when they dock. The agents are always on the lookout for people smuggling drugs. He'd have a hard time explaining a hidden devil worshiping shrine, and if it got out, he could kiss his political career goodbye."

"But to sacrifice so much money," I said. "Could it be we don't understand him?"

Richard shook his head. "With insurance, I doubt he lost much, maybe he even made a profit since he had it built overseas. I've heard of a scam where a cheaply built boat is given a false invoice, allowing it to be insured for more than it cost. It's an old scam. I'm surprised he managed to get it past today's insurance companies."

I looked at Tanoshi, such a trick would be easy for her, and Bryce did have magical ability. I remembered those old mismatched engines. Yes, Bryce had built the boat with the intention of sinking it.

"I understand," Airi turned to Richard. "On your planet, people obtain magic power by making a blood sacrifice to the evil one, the bigger the sacrifice, the greater the power received. Remember the pathetic hat-witch who killed her own daughter. I believe Bryce built the boat to sacrifice his son in a way that could never be traced back to him. He thought it would give him the power to enter politics despite his questionable business career. Kenji told us how his father was once called before a legal tribunal and pretended he knew nothing of the ways his company tricked the government into paying for medical procedures that were never done."

"It's called pleading the fifth," Richard explained. "It was in the papers a few years ago. They couldn't prove his involvement, so his company paid a fine and that was the end of it."

"At least he doesn't have the third sword," I said. "I doubt he'll do anything until he obtains it. If necessary, I'll carry it into the ocean so he can never get his hands on it."

Tanoshi spoke for the first time. "Don't sacrifice yourself too quickly. Airi's half-katana is the weakest of the three. It's just so she can defend you. Bryce has the two powerful swords. Sato might know how to use your long sword to break the seal on my sword."

"Oh shit," I said, glad I'd learned a few Earth swear words.

Airi interrupted. "We need to get Haruko another katana, a good one. He's fast and an expert swordsman. Even an Earth sword would be deadly in his hands."

"You know," Richard said. "The army confiscated many Japanese swords after the war and brought them to this country. It's still a sore point between our countries as most are now in the hands of private collectors. The ancient handmade ones fetch fantastic prices and the collectors have an online community where they trade with one another. We could find out who they are."

Airi smiled. "Since they were taken without permission, I'm going to invoke my ancestry and take one back."

That evening, Richard worked the computer to find collectors rich enough to own better-made Japanese swords. Myself, Tanoshi and Airi discussed ways we might take the fight to Bryce rather than waiting for him to break the seal on Tanoshi's sword and strike first. We agreed, once Kenji returned, we would leave this house, go into hiding and use stolen passwords to disrupt Bryce's companies. Possibly, we could even get him into trouble with the government again. At some point he'd need to return. Tanoshi felt confident her persuasion power would be enough to get us past any guards. This plan wasn't much, but at least we were doing something.

Tanoshi gave us a little good news. While we were in the water and in danger from the circling fish, she'd drawn on all the power she could muster to keep them at bay. While doing this, the ocean allowed her to once again feel her suppressed fire magic, and that contact had strengthened her fire ability by another fraction. She did admit it'd come at a cost, because as her true power increased, it reduced some of this world's heightened persuasion magic. She displayed her regained ability by putting her fingers together and creating a small fireball, about the size of a bean seed. We were happy to see her fire magic returning, but after a discussion, we agreed, right now her persuasion magic would help us the most.

Three days later, when Kenji came home from the hospital, everything changed. He didn't come alone, but brought with him five men wearing dark suits and, most amazing of all—Sato. I couldn't believe he had the nerve to walk through our door, but there he was, wearing a dark Earth suit with a red tie over a shiny blue shirt, polished shoes and an illogically tall hat, which hid his pointed ears. He'd cut his green hair short and dyed it black.

"Don't get upset," Sato shouted. "I'm not here to fight. I'm here to save all of us."

"These guys are lawyers," Kenji pointed to the suits. "My dad wants me back in his life, and he's made out a will making me his sole heir. It's all forgive and forget."

"This is quite unusual," said one of the suits. "I'm Victor White, Esquire. I'm a partner in the firm of White, Strunk, and Potter, one of the premier firms in the Bay area. We've handled Mister Bryce's affairs for many years, but this is the first time he's made out a will. In fact, it's an iron-clad non-revocable will, which means it can never be changed or challenged. It leaves everything he owns to this gentleman," he pointed. "Lawrence Bryce."

"Can we believe this?" I said.

"I was told," continued Whitesquire, "there would be some skepticism and Lawrence and his friends would need assurance of our credentials." He handed me a card. "Take your time, do all the research you want. Also note we have pre-filed this will and testament with the state. Nothing can change it now. In the event of Jack Bryce's passing, all his assets, which are notable, go to Master Lawrence."

Richard took the card from my hand. "I'll have Jack check and see if the will really is filed. I know of this law firm. If these guys are who they say they are, I would trust them."

"You are welcome to come by our offices," Whitesquire

said. "We have nothing to hide."

"We'll be sure to do that," I said, "but perhaps you could speak with my sister for a moment."

As Tanoshi looked into the lawyer's eyes and grilled him about the deal, Sato approached Airi and me. "I understand you need to check everything out," he said. "Let me explain the reason Mister Bryce is doing this."

"You're not noted for your honesty," I muttered.

Sato laughed. "Ain't that the truth? I know you have no reason to trust me. That's why the lawyers are here." He led me to the back of the room and spoke in our language. "If you hear the reason, you'll agree it makes sense. You see, Mister Bryce intends entering politics. They do politics differently on this world. Now it's known he has a son, it's necessary he appear to be a loving father. If Lawrence was to end up dead, even the suspicion of Bryce's involvement would derail his plans. Since he doesn't care what happens to his money once he's gone, this is his way of healing the rift between them and assuring himself of cooperation. Lawrence can continue his paid-for university education just like he'd planned, and he'll receive a stipend after he graduates. His only duty will be to publicly maintain a positive attitude toward his father as Mister Bryce pursues his political career."

He turned to me. "Rather than continue with our unproductive antagonism, and risk a fight, which could attract attention, it'd be best if you went back to your own world. You know, with the two swords, it's now within Mister Bryce's power to open the gateway. However, if you should choose to remain here, there will be money and identification provided for you to make good lives in America. Perhaps the four of us could discuss these ideas privately and in more detail." He turned and glanced at the lawyers.

"Your words sound sweet," I said. "But Bryce murdered Michele and Frankie. I have no reason to trust someone who can kill so easily. In fact I—"

"Bryce didn't kill them," interrupted Sato. "He was upset and angry when it happened. It was totally against his orders. Even if you'd never showed up, he intended to pay them off and release them. You understand he was stuck many miaru away on the boat and not there in person, and the men he hired weren't the best. Those women overpowered them and almost escaped. One of the fools gunned them down. After that, they needed to hide the bodies. It was a complete disaster. As a Prince, I'm sure you know how it's hard to get competent underlings. We've all experienced it."

I'd never had problems getting people's cooperation. If I talked to them and explained my reasons, they'd always been eager to do their share. But Sato was a Takamatsu noble; I suspect he treated people differently. Tanoshi and Airi came over to us.

"They are who they say they are," Tanoshi began. "Bryce's will, which leaves everything to Kenji, is real and cannot be changed."

Sato nodded. "It's Mister Bryce's hope we can get past the unfortunate events of the last few weeks. With his plan you can go back to your own world. Once back there, Tanoshi will regain her true power. You can forge new swords and rule Takamatsu. I intend to remain in this wonderful modern society as Mister Bryce's confidant, so I care nothing of that world. Such an outcome would be the best for all of us."

Airi shook her head. "I suppose the one condition to this generosity is us giving you the last sword?"

Sato nodded. "I know surrendering your only bargaining item will make you uneasy, but Mister Bryce can open the gate between worlds with just the two powerful swords he now controls. You can hold onto your sword right up to the moment the transfer begins, and you're convinced he is not tricking you. He truly wants to resolve this without any more trouble." He turned to Tanoshi. "Look into my eyes and you will know I speak truthfully."

The lawyers appeared uncomfortable with us speaking in our language. Mister Whitesquere came over and said they needed to leave. Sato said he'd give us time to think over the offer and would call us in a few days.

* * * *

After the lawyers and Sato left, the five of us sat around

trying to understand what had happened. Although first, Airi and Tanoshi needed to see Kenji's scar and grill him on his recovery. Once again, Earth technology had healed in five days what would have taken weeks on our world. Despite the red scar on his chest, Kenji claimed to feel just like he normally did.

I told them of Sato's offer, and Tanoshi confirmed everyone told the truth as they knew it, although Sato may have had the power to hide things from her. Richard said he'd have John check on Bryce's will, but given the law firm's reputation, it was most likely valid. Somehow, it seemed like the fight was over and we had a way home.

I saw Tanoshi looking at Kenji and I'm sure there was a tear in the corner of her eye. She'd stopped the boy from loving her, but the idea of leaving him hurt her more deeply than she'd ever admit.

"I suppose," Airi said. "Our chances of getting our swords back from Bryce and his elite goon army are impossible. If we want to return home, his offer might be our only choice. However, we need to be sure he can really get us back to Kyoto, and not just dump us randomly on the planet. We can do that much without his help."

"Good point," I agreed. "Tanoshi's half-katana contains the link to the land, but we'll need to make sure Bryce knows how to activate it."

"Are you really thinking of going home," Kenji said, "without me?"

We remained silent. Did Kenji still want to go with us and give up a life of luxury in a modern world for our primitive, work every day if you want to survive, existence?

Richard gave voice to our thoughts. "You stand to inherit several billion dollars," he told Kenji. "There are banks who'll loan you money now, just based on you future worth. If you stay, you'll never again want for anything. You could live a life only a few ever get to experience. Think of what being a multi-billionaire means. You could travel the world and enjoy the best of everything."

"We have an obligation to return," Airi said. "Remember,

we told you what would happen if Tanoshi couldn't get home? Many lives will be lost."

"Then go!" Shouted Kenji. "Just go already." He stood and stormed to the bedroom, slamming the door behind him. We turned and looked at Tanoshi.

"I really did take away his compulsion to love me," she said quietly. "I know I did. He only thinks of me as a friend. I made sure of it."

Why did Kenji feel so strongly about us leaving? We'd explained how the people of Kyoto would suffer if Tanoshi wasn't there to protect them. Could it be that he still loved her? That was good, but also bad as there was no way Mister Bryce would send him to our world with us.

Richard broke the silence. "I understand. If it wasn't for my children, I'd beg to follow you also. Your society might be primitive, but you're not caught up in a death spiral of consumerism led by the greedy and the shallow. In your world you work together, everything you do has value to your society and your children. Here, our lives are superficial, our efforts to create a decent world constantly thwarted by the rich and greedy. Religions try to force others to follow their illogical teachings by either laws, murder, torture or blatant destruction."

He sat on the couch and looked at his feet. "I'm a policeman. Every day I deal with society's broken rejects. Most have no real education, no way of pulling themselves up. Yet they see entertainers, athletes and corporate money men wallowing in their obscene greed. Men like Bryce have rigged the system. For those on society's underside there is no opportunity. This is a country which spends many times more on jails than it does on education. Shit, even education is rigged by the elite and their political stooges. Kids come out of collage owing bankers ten years or more of their lives, they're just like indentured servants." He turned to me, "don't you see, for a few days Kenji believed he could have the life humans were meant to live. Even becoming one of the moneyed elite isn't enough to make up for losing such a dream."

It was Airi who spoke next. "We've all felt it. For all the wonderful things we experienced in this world, we would do anything to get home. I know, if we remain here much longer, we'll go crazy. Perhaps that's why we jumped at Sato's offer."

She stopped talking, looked at me, and then at Tanoshi. "OH Shit!" She shouted. "That son of a snake. Sato used persuasion magic on us."

I looked at Airi as the truth dawned on me. "Why was I ready to trust him? Why? He's revealed his true intentions at every chance."

"We were vulnerable because we wanted to go home so much," Tanoshi said. "He used that feeling to blind us to words we would normally have seen through. He used a subtle persuasion, so I wouldn't detect it."

"Yes," I agreed, "now we must think clearly. The evil one saved Sato's life, gave him magic power and sent him to help Mister Bryce. Satan never does anything to be nice. There must be a dark reason."

Tanoshi jumped up and ran to the bedroom after Kenji. I guess she explained everything because after a few minutes, Kenji rejoined us. His eyes appeared red. Tanoshi might believe she'd made him stop loving her, but I think Kenji's feelings came from a magic stronger than hers.

"I'm starting to put it together," Airi said after they joined us. "Bryce already had a connection to the evil one, from when our Moon Goddess broke the rules and saved Haruko's father. Bryce used that connection to become immensely wealthy."

"He used his magic power to become a dark witch in this world," I said.

"Warlock," corrected Kenji.

"Anyway," Airi continued. "Having lured Kenji onto the boat, Bryce was in the hidden room preparing for a sacrifice which would give him even greater power when we turned up and Kenji brought us onboard, disrupting his plans. Sometime later, I suppose after we'd escaped, the evil one sent Sato to him. Sato told Bryce about our swords, and how, if he possessed them, he'd gain more power than even sacrificing his son. Power enough to become the president of this country. He's been coaching Bryce since then and giving him spells to increase his ability."

Airi's theory made sense. "The real question is what does Satan hope to gain by using Bryce and Sato?" I mused. "It certainly isn't to give them good lives. The evil one hates humans, and especially those who are stupid enough to serve him."

Airi had the answer. "Bryce believes the power in our swords can make him become the president of this country. Having achieved wealth, he now wants power. For some reason the evil one intends granting him his wish."

Richard spoke up. "Such a man would be a disaster. We had a self-centered, egotistical idiot in power a few years ago. He got us into some pointless wars costing thousands of lives and gave us an enormous national debt. The country is still dealing with the aftermath of that debacle."

I remembered my conversation with Kenji. "The evil one intends to trigger a nuclear war, and will use Bryce to start it. That's why he saved Sato from the nowhere place and sent him here."

"Damn," Richard swore, "what have we gotten ourselves into? We're in way over our heads. Bryce is a billionaire with a private army of mercenaries and has magical powers."

"He doesn't have the third sword," I said. "I doubt he'll do anything until he obtains it. If necessary, I'll carry it into the ocean so he can never get his hands on it."

Tanoshi laid her hand on my arm. "Don't sacrifice yourself too quickly. Airi's half-katana is the weakest of the three. It's just for defense of the monarchy. Bryce has the two powerful swords. Sato can use your long sword to break the seal on my sword giving Bryce access to its immense power."

"Well, we will not be taking Sato up on his offer." I said.

"However, that might be the only way we can get close to Bryce and our swords," Airi said. "Right now, the man's in this country called Mexico. Unless he comes here, we have no chance."

Tanoshi made a suggestion. "Kenji and I could disrupt his

companies," she said. "That might bring him back. Perhaps I could work my way up to the important people in his organization and use them to create havoc."

Kenji took a small card from his pocket. "That reminds me. While I was in the hospital, my dad sent his personal physician to examine me. The regular hospital staff were really impressed because I rated such attention. One of the nurses explained how that doctor only treats my father. He has no other patients. The man did a thorough job. He looked me over from head to toe and ordered dozens of tests and even expensive MRI exams." He handed me the card. "This is his address and number. He told me to call him if I started feeling sick."

"A doctor who only cares for only one patient?" Airi gasped. "How could a healer withhold his talents so basely?"

Richard took the card from me. "It's common for rich people. Maybe Bryce has health issues he doesn't want anyone to know about."

"Even so, it'll work for us," Tanoshi said. "Kenji can pretend to feel sick. That will give us time to plan and get Haruko another sword before we confront Bryce."

CHAPTER 21

We caught a break. Sato called to say Bryce had divined he could draw more power from our swords on the night of the full moon, in three Earth weeks. It gave us time and Kenji didn't need to claim sickness. We did argue about the location. Bryce wanted to hold the ceremony at one of his estates, but Tanoshi told him the swords gained strength when near the sea. As Bryce didn't fully understand the swords, he believed her and we settled on going back to Fort Desoto beach. Not the best choice, but at least we wouldn't be inside the walls of a guarded compound.

Richard did locate a collector of Japanese swords who lived in Tampa and learned the man owned a katana costing many thousands of dollars. Tanoshi got us in to meet him and after looking into her eyes, he agreed the old piece of junk was only worth a couple of hundred bucks. However, the second I touched the blade, a wave of terror went up and down my spine. My stomach heaved and I threw up on the man's floor. Tanoshi knocked the weapon from my hands and the horror ceased.

"It's evil," she shouted. "This sword has killed innocents." She didn't touch it, but held her hand over the blade. "Beheadings, hundreds of beheadings. They were kneeling on the ground, quivering and begging for mercy when this blade sliced through their necks. I don't believe it ever fought another sword, all it ever did was kill those who couldn't fight back."

"It must have belonged to an important shogun," Kenji said. "Back then, that was the way they lived. They condemned people for the most trivial of reasons, even for not bowing low enough when someone important walked past."

Naturally, the man didn't own another katana. In fact, he admitted how, after acquiring this blade, his fortunes had turned and he could no longer afford this hobby. He revealed the half-katana, which fit into the holder beneath his display blade, was just a modern copy bought to complete the set. He told us a sword and gun store in downtown Tampa would sell us as many modern copies as we wanted.

So that was where I got my new katana. They hadn't made it properly, with a hard, sharp cutting edge and a softer steel back for strength, but it'd been machined from a strong alloy so it wasn't as useless as I expected. When Airi saw the store's many half-katanas, which the owner called Wakizahi, she came up with an idea. We bought one for each of us, Kenji and Richard included. Now, knowing how we'd swapped swords and sheaths around before, when Bryce saw all five of us carrying both a pistol and a Wakizahi, he wouldn't know which sheath contained the one he needed. It might stop his men from shooting me on sight. Hopefully that, along with Tanoshi's hard-won, new surprise, would give us the edge we needed.

Airi and I carried fake pistols, toys that might pass a casual inspection. Without identification we couldn't buy real guns, and having Richard buy them for us could cause him to lose his job, or worse. Besides, we were trained to edge weapons, and that useful store had sold me a nice folding knife and a dagger I could strap to my lower leg. A little extra armament never hurt.

Airi didn't believe Bryce would resort to violence. A shootout with a police officer would put him at risk of ruining his political career. Since he'd first asked us to come to his estate, we didn't think he or Sato knew of our susceptibly to the ocean. But Bryce knew the swords held the power to send us back, or at least off this world. We hoped he'd resort to violence only after he realized our real aim was retrieving our swords.

* * * *

It might have been Bryce's doing, but the day before the rendezvous, Richard fell ill and paramedics needed rushed him to a hospital with a burst appendix. While he was expected to recover, he'd remain in bed for several days. We debated trying to postpone the meeting until the next full moon, but Airi feared given an extra month, Bryce might discover he already owned the most powerful swords and didn't need

Airi's. Kenji told us American policemen had dangerous jobs and every year some died at the hands of criminals. Given a month, Bryce could arrange for Richard's murder in a way that couldn't be traced back to him.

The next night, as a full moon rose in the east, Kenji drove us, with Bruno, down to Fort Desoto. Lacking Richard's protection, Kenji had exchanged his toy pistol for Richard's service weapon. I suspected borrowing an officer's gun without telling him could cause problems for him and told Kenji not to use it unless he was desperate.

As agreed, we met Bryce and Sato accompanied by three, of what I assumed were the best goons money could buy. Other than an altar placed near the water, and a house-on-wheels called an RV, parked a few meters away, the place appeared deserted. I assumed Bryce had used magic to keep outsiders away, making a point about how strong he'd become. When we'd expected Richard to accompany us, Bryce had agreed to the limit of five people each. His group now outnumbered us by one, but we had Bruno, and the old police dog was no pushover.

We'd expected trickery, and Tanoshi detected ten goons hiding in the brush behind the beach. The month's delay had paid off, giving Tanoshi the time she needed. She'd risked death by repeatedly going into the ocean and having Kenji drag her back to land at the last second. Each time the blue sparkles calling her home appeared, allowing her to regain another fraction of her fire magic power, although at the cost of reducing her Earth-enhanced persuasion ability. Each time, the blue appeared sooner and now she couldn't enter the sea without risking her life. The small power boost was all she was going to get.

"I'm glad you were smart enough not to try using confusion magic again," Bryce said to Tanoshi as we walked across the beach and into the light created by several powerful lamps on posts stuck in the sand. "I've cast a spell, your illusions can't fool us."

"We assumed you would," Tanoshi sighed. "It neutralizers my only power in this world, doesn't it? Other than starting a gunfight, we're at your mercy. Our question is, can we trust you to send us home?"

Bryce smiled. "Of course. It's to my advantage to get rid of you with as little fuss as possible. Since sending you home means there's no bodies to worry about, I have no need to shed blood tonight." He looked at me. "My only price is the sword you're wearing." He nodded and then saw all of us wore half-katanas. "Ah, your switching trick again. I get the feeling you don't trust me."

"When we see the portal opened, and know it is our land you're sending us to, then the third sword is yours." I said. Bryce looked at Sato and then at his three gun goons. Opening a portal to a specific place would be much harder than creating some random hole. We'd assumed he might consider violence. Bryce began rubbing the base of his ear. One of the gun goons whispered into his coat collar.

"I fear you'll discover those men beyond the beach have gone to sleep on the job," I said as pleasantly as I could. He looked at me. Even in the glaring artificial light, I could see his face appeared white. "It's time to stop the tricks and make good on our deal, or admit you don't have the power and we should leave."

Bryce spoke hesitantly, no doubt wondering how we'd neutralized his hidden forces and what magic we still possessed. "It will exhaust me, but I have enough power," he said. "Stand behind the altar. I'll put the swords on it and chant the spell. You'll see a portal to your world open. Once you're convinced of my sincerity, give me the last sword. The real one, please, I'll know if it's fake. Then you can walk through the portal and be whisked home, none the worse for your adventure. Once there, you can make yourselves new swords at your leisure."

He turned to his son. "Lawrence, in the RV I have the paperwork for you to attend the university. Now this unpleasantness is behind us, I'm hoping we can establish a father-son relationship. Once I start my push to become the Governor, I'd like it if you could accompany me on some of my campaign stops."

Bryce looked exhausted as he stumbled across the sand to the big RV. Because of the shadows cast by its headlights and those lights placed around the altar, it wasn't easy to tell, but I thought he looked thin and stooped beneath his silly magic-cloak. Magic was exhausting, and he'd been working with our swords for a month. If he wasn't in the best of health, it would make sense he'd try violence before attempting to open a portal. But that would alienate him even more from Kenji, which would interfere with his political ambitions. Still, I memorized where the goons stood and whispered to Tanoshi to remain alert.

Despite our agreement, another person got out of the RV. My hand went to my katana's hilt, but Kenji said it was Bryce's doctor. I looked carefully and saw the man was older and overweight. Not exactly a threat, and since it looked as if they were going to produce the swords, I let it pass.

One of the goons helped the two men pull a heavy case from a locker. Bryce leaned against the side of the vehicle as the doctor opened the lid and took out two swords. Finally, there they were. I looked to Tanoshi and Airi, making sure they were ready to move.

"No," Tanoshi said. "Something's not right. The swords feel. . .hollow."

Another sword switching trick? But Bryce couldn't open a portal without the real ones. If he thought he could survive a fight with us, he was more stupid than I expected. Acting as if all was normal, the doctor placed the swords on the altar. Bryce stood behind it and began chanting. After a minute, a mist formed above the water, about three meters from shore. Surely he didn't think we'd believe a mist was a portal. Creating a mist was one of the simplest types of magic, even I knew that.

A yellow light appeared in the center of the mist. It flickered several times, the yellow fading and more colors emerging. Then, there, in the center of the mist, appeared a building, and not just any building, but the Takamatsu royal palace. Its green copper roof, the yellow brick road leading to it, and the ornate gold gates bearing the seal of the monarchy were unmistakable. Odd it wasn't Kyoto, the city where I lived, but technically, while I'd not been there all that often, the palace was my home. I suppose the magic sought to send me there. I don't know how he'd done it, but Bryce really had opened a portal to our world. I did look carefully to make sure it wasn't like a television picture projected onto the mist, but the palace and the grounds around it had real detail and depth, as if we looked through a tunnel. The tunnel shifted a little, revealing some other buildings on the hillside before returning to the Palace. It appeared so real I knew it couldn't be a trick.

"Hurry," Bryce shouted. "I can't hold the portal open for long. You may emerge a few feet above the ground. I doubt it'll be a long drop, but Sato says Tanoshi can fly in your world. Just to be safe, why don't you hang onto her as you walk toward it?"

What should I do? We'd come here to get the swords back, but right in front of us was home. Just a dozen steps and the problems of this world would no longer concern us. Home; where we were needed to save my people. Who was I to decide the fate of this world? I belonged in the land beneath the Jeweled Moon.

But my swords, in the hands of a man like Bryce, would create untold suffering on this world. I was a prince. My job was to make the hard choices and take the suffering upon myself.

"Listen to the engine on the RV," Kenji said. "It's revved to the max." I turned and looked at him. What did a revved up engine have to do with anything?

"Electric power," Kenji whispered. "Something is using a hell of a lot of it." He looked around and then at the portal glowing over the water. "That's a hologram. Even though it's in three dimensions, it's a picture created by lasers. He's trying to fool us. There must be a small model of the building beneath the altar."

Right, Sato was from Takamatsu. He'd seen the royal palace every day and could easily describe it in enough detail to create a model that would fool me. "Fight time," I said in our language and touched Airi's arm. "First plan."

Leaving Bryce and Sato to Tanoshi, Airi and Kenji, I went after the gun goons. Three fast steps as I drew my katana and the first goon lost his head as I ran past. This modern sword didn't slice cleanly, and that slowed me down. The second goon's hand had reached his weapon. I flipped the sword to sever his gun hand, but failed to make a clean cut. A quick stomach kick sent the wounded guy tumbling before I went after the last one. He remained over by the RV, and had managed to draw and level his weapon at me. Just then a loud crack like a close lightning strike made him blink. Before his eyes were open again, I'd rammed the point of my sword through his ribcage.

Tanoshi had subdued Bryce and Sato. It took time to cast a spell and both of them failed against Tanoshi's new trick. Sato lay on the sand, Airi's sword pressed against his throat, his eyes were wide and I guessed he wouldn't even consider moving his lips in a way Airi might consider a threat. She yanked Sato's sidearm from its holster and tossed it into the sea.

Tanoshi, holding Bruno's collar to keep him from doing damage, stood over Bryce who sat holding his head. "What the hell did you do," he muttered. "That wasn't magic!"

"That was the power of the vacuum," Tanoshi said. "You have your son to thank for teaching it to me."

"Lawrence knows magic?"

"Kenji knows science. He told me there's a statically small chance all the air molecules in a room could suddenly move in the same direction and leave half the room without any air. It's not likely to happen, but it doesn't contradict any thermodynamic laws. Magic can change the odds. If every air molecule around your head moves in one direction, the vacuum created will cause other molecules to rush in with tremendous force." She smiled. "Being slammed on the head by an air hammer hurts, doesn't it?"

We'd forgotten the doctor. He was edging away, perhaps hoping to make a dash for safety. Kenji drew Richard's service pistol and shot at the ground near his feet. "Hold it," he shouted. "I don't think you're good enough to pry a slug out of your ass." The man stopped and turned with his hands up.

"Now," Tanoshi said. "Where are the real swords? Where have you hidden them?"

"My chest hurts," Bryce gasped. "It hurts real bad. Call an ambulance."

"First the swords," shouted Tanoshi.

"Those are your swords, Please, I'm dying. I need help."

"He's not lying," the doctor shouted. "He's very sick. Please let me help him."

"You're not half as sick as you're going to be if my hand slips off Bruno's collar," Tanoshi spoke in a low voice. "What's wrong with our swords? What did you do?"

Ignoring the danger, the doctor ran to Bryce. He held a small red bottle and sprayed something into his patient's mouth. Bryce shook his head and panted. Finally, he looked at Tanoshi. "I removed most of their magic. Sato told me how to do it. You're screwed; there is no way for you to get home now."

He didn't say more, but made a loud groan and collapsed to the sand. The doctor rolled him onto his back and, with both hands, began repeatedly shoving down on the center of Bryce's chest. Tanoshi looked at me and I shrugged. Who would have expected the man to just up and die?

Airi got it together first, she grabbed Sato's shirt, dragged him to his feet and stuck the point of her sword beneath his chin. "All right, start explaining. No lies. Tanoshi will know, and one more body on this beach won't make any difference."

I saw blood running down Airi's sword. Its tip now penetrated Sato's skin.

"Mister Bryce is dying of lung cancer," Sato squeaked until Airi pulled the sword back a little. "Plus his heart is weak. He's had what's called bypass surgery four times, and after the boat business, he had another event which almost killed him. He intended using the power in your swords to heal himself. But there wasn't enough magic for what he intended, so he spent a fortune setting this up to fool you into handing over the last sword without Tanoshi removing its power."

Airi shook her head. "No amount of magic could save someone that old and sick, even the smallest wounds require more than most witches control. What are you not telling me?"

Bruno, barking loudly, jerked against his collar. Tanoshi shouted and pointed behind me. I turned. The last goon, over by the RV, the one I'd only sliced through the wrist and kicked, held a gun in his good hand. He was pointing it towards us. Towards Airi? Without thinking I threw myself at her, desperate to shield her from the bullet. As I moved, the gun blasted and I heard a whiz as the projectile zipped past my head. Then Airi, Sato and I tumbled onto the sand in a confused heap.

"He was aiming at you, dummy!" Airi shouted. "Move. Like in a bear fight."

I wasted no time rolling away. Then I lurched to my feet and leaped left. When fighting a bear, never remain in one place for even half a second. Using all my speed, I lunged right and left. The gun goon was a seasoned pro. He got off two rapid shots, the blasts so close together they sounded like one. But I wasn't even close to where he aimed. Then my sword rammed through his chest. At the same time Bruno crashed into the man's body, his teeth snapping shut against the guy's throat. The old dog stopped moving and rolled onto his side, blood gushing from his throat. The man had stopped shooting at me to defend himself against the charging dog. Unfortunately, Bruno ran in a straight line, making himself an easy target. The old K9 police dog had sacrificed himself thinking he could save me.

Bruno's unnecessary death overwhelmed me and I stood with my sword buried in the man's chest. Dogs, loyal, lovable and brave, were special. We sure could use them on our world.

I heard a pop behind me and Tanoshi screamed. I turned to see the old doctor pointing a small device with wires leading to her chest. A Taser. Richard owned one, and said they used electricity to disable people. Tanoshi collapsed to the ground. Then, to my horror, I realized Sato had used my collision with Airi to pull a second gun from somewhere beneath his jacket.

He now held its barrel against Airi's temple.

"Don't anyone move," Sato screeched. "Stay where you are! Everyone, drop your weapons, do it now!"

Kenji hesitated before tossing his gun onto the sand. Reluctantly, I dropped my two blades and the toy pistol. Sato ordered Kenji to pick up my half-katana. I guess Sato's magic let him know it was the real one.

"If you want to leave," I said, "we won't stop you. Bryce is dead and we're trapped on this planet. There's nothing to be gained in continuing this fight, and a lot to be lost if Earth law enforcement finds us around these dead bodies."

The old doctor stood and backed away from Bryce's body. He'd left a syringe sticking out of the man's chest. The doctor turned to Sato. "He's still with us," he said quietly, "but we must hurry."

"You're as naive as ever, Haruko. It's not over. If you want to save Airi, pick up Mister Bryce and carry him to the RV. The doctor will tell you what to do." He turned to Kenji. "You," he shouted in English. "Go with them and keep that sword where I can see it."

I walked over to where Bryce lay on the sand but could only see Tanoshi. She'd fallen in a twisted lump, drool flowed from her mouth. She lay absolutely motionless, not even a flicker of life remained. Something inside me assured me she was really, completely, absolutely, dead. "You...you killed her," I shouted. "Why?" I just stood there staring at the impossible until I heard Airi screaming. I realized Sato was shouting for me to pick up Bryce.

Airi, with an Earth gun pressed against her temple, was in danger. Somehow I needed to fight past my horror and the pain in my heart. "All right," I muttered to Sato. "I'll do as you ask. But if Airi dies, you will too, never doubt it." I looked at the fat doctor. He was pointing a second Taser at me.

Sato laughed. "Electricity is the opposite of magic. Send a big enough jolt though a witch and it does for her. Primitives like you won't believe what electricity can do to your body."

Apparently Sato had done some research of his own. None

of us knew electricity was deadly to witches. Trying to see through my tear-filled eyes, I grabbed Bryce's limp body and tossed it over my shoulder. The fat doctor screamed at me to be careful. I blinked away my tears, pushed away my grief, and watched Sato. If his gun wavered from Airi's temple even a fraction, the son of a snake would end up with it up his rectum. I guess Sato knew it too. He kept a tight grip on Airi, so the two of them, very awkwardly, shuffled toward the RV, making Kenji and myself lead the way.

The inside of the RV wasn't like I expected. No beds, no kitchen, no comfortable seats. All signs of a home on wheels had been removed to turn it into a miniature hospital. In fact, the machines and devices along the walls appeared more advanced than those where Richard had gone for his surgery. In the room's center was not one, but two, narrow operating tables. They sat side by side and were connected by a clear plastic trough about the size of a head wide and a hand-width deep. Rather ominously, there were half-circle cutouts on the front edge of the rectangular trough right where someone lying on the table would rest his head. The sides around the cutouts each had rubber gaskets, hinting the trough could be filled with water with someone lying with his head in the contraption so only his mouth and nose would remain above the liquid.

Then nausea, like I'd experienced after picking up the collector's Japanese katana, hit. I staggered and almost dropped Bryce's body. Once again the doctor screamed at me to be careful. Over by one wall hung hundreds of bags, similar to those the hospital used to give Kenji blood. They were all filled, but the dark red liquid inside sparkled with tiny blue lights. I didn't have real magic power, but I could guess that was where Sato had moved the magic from our swords. That power, mixed with what must be human blood, had morphed into something truly sinister. Closer inspection revealed the tubes from the blood bags were connected together and rigged to fill the trough connecting the operating tables. This had to be how Bryce had planned to use our magic to cure himself of his fatal diseases.

"Lawrence," Sato shouted. "Place the sword in the sulcus." Kenji stared at him. "That's the plastic trough connecting the two gurneys, stupid." Kenji complied, the sword reached from one side to the other. Sato turned to me. "Lay Mister Bryce on the gurney," Sato pointed. "Place him so his neck rests in the cut-out and his head is in the trough and touching the sword's hilt."

The table Sato pointed at didn't have hold-down straps. The other table had many. This did not bode well for anyone who lay alongside Bryce with their head resting on the sword's sharp end. Slowly and carefully, as if I was trying to please the frantic doctor, I removed Bryce from my shoulder and held him around his chest. Then, in that moment when they thought I was cooperating, I shifted my grip, getting one arm around his chest and the other across his head. "I'll snap his neck," I shouted. "You know I can kill him in an instant, even if I'm shot." I looked at Sato. "Don't think for a second I'll let you live if Airi dies. You haven't seen half of what I can do, and how fast I can move when angry."

We stood for a long minute. No doubt each of us wondered how to end this standoff. I saw sweat dripping down Sato's face. He'd seen me kill the professional gun goons in the space of two heartbeats and as a Takamatsu noble he'd heard stories about my fighting ability. He must know the only thing keeping him alive was the gun he held against Airi. How long could the two of us face each other? Who'd tire first? All the while I was trying to cope with the ever-increasing nausea created by being close to those evil bags. A weakness spread from my chest into my arms and legs. My feet, which I thought had healed, began to burn as if I stood on hot iron. What terrible thing had they done to collect that blood?

"Whatever Bryce's plan was," I said quietly. "It's failed. Sato, you don't need to die for a stupid earth man. We're trapped on this planet. It's time we end this fight and go our separate ways."

Sato looked at me. To my surprise, I spotted a tear running down his cheek. "I can't, Haruko," he said in a whisper. "I'm here to help Mister Bryce become President. If I fail, I...Well,

I can't allow that to happen." He paused, and then stood taller. "I know you love Airi. I'll spare her life. I give you my word as a Takamatsu noble and the second son of the house of the Clothmakers. All I ask is for you to swear, as my Prince, you'll leave without fighting or interfering."

"And Kenji?"

"Lawrence stays here."

"Don't agree!" screamed Airi. "They plan to kill Kenji to save Bryce. You must not let them succeed, no matter the cost."

"That's stupid," I said. "Bryce is old, decrepit and eight ways to dead already. Even if they bring him back today, he won't live long enough to become president. We've watched enough television to know about Earth politics..." I looked at those bags of human blood, all set to pour their magical contents into the trough and over the magic sword reaching between the tables. I remembered Bryce's will. The will leaving everything he owned to young, healthy Kenji. I looked at Airi and knew she'd already figured it out.

"I'm sorry Sato," I said, still trying to hide how sick and disorientated I felt. By now I struggled to support Bryce's weight without showing signs of how much I was straining. "You know I can't let you go through with it. There are over six billion people on this planet, and if the corrupted soul of this man gains the power of the president, he'll kill them all. Look, I know the evil one who saved you from the nowhere place frightens you. But, even after all that's happened, if you choose to do the right thing, the High God will protect you from his anger."

"I was dammed before I entered that place," Sato said. "Nothing I do here will make my fate any worse. My only hope lies with making Mister Bryce this country's president. I know you can kill his old body, and maybe even me, but it'll cost you the life of the one you love."

While I'd been talking, the doctor had edged to one side. I realized the danger when Sato's eyes flickered toward him. I tried to turn, but vertigo made me stumble. As bile rose in my throat, for the first time in my life, my speed and agility had left me. As Bryce's body slid to the floor, the fat doctor leveled his Taser. I saw his lips forming a smile as he pulled the trigger.

Kenji dove between us. I heard the crackling from the horrid device. Kenji yelped as the electricity shot through his body, and having lost control, slammed into the wall. Before I could react, a gunshot, painfully loud in the metal RV, shattered my world.

Terrified, I turned, but Airi still lived. The bullet had gone wide and blasted through the thin RV's wall. Sato and I both looked toward the open doorway. Tanoshi peered over the threshold. She probably couldn't stand, and no way could she enter and endure the evil coming from the contaminated blood. Somehow, she'd crawled over and had been able to use the air-hammer trick to knock the gun away from Airi's head.

I knew everyone expected me to flash across the room and disarm Sato. I made my best effort, but slow as I was, it wouldn't have been enough if Airi hadn't grabbed Sato's gun hand and forced it down. When I reached him we grappled for control of the gun. Damn, he was strong, or maybe I was weak. I couldn't overcome him. If Sato hadn't been surprised by my ineptitude, he'd have turned his weapon on me. After a second, realizing he could win this fight, he forced me to the floor. Rolling top of me, he laughed, enjoying the moment, as he slowly overcame my resistance so the gun would point at my head.

"You're about to die," he whispered, "my stupid prince."

Airi smashed a heavy electronic box on his head. It shot sparks and smoke. From the front of the box, a stream of pink paper shot out while the machine's pens created numerous squiggly lines.

As I pushed Sato's limp body off me, I heard a clattering and saw the doctor on his hands and knees scrambling to reach the dropped pistol. Airi kicked him in the head while I got to my feet. I stomped on his hand but couldn't break a single bone. Still, forcing myself past my vertigo, I grabbed the gun before the fat doctor reached it.

I pointed the gun at the quivering doctor. "Get Kenji. .

.Lawrence. Treat him, if he dies you will too."

Actually, Kenji was already moving. As Richard had explained, Tasers weren't supposed to kill and apparently Kenji was strong enough to shake off its effects. Airi went over and helped him to his feet and the two of them made their way out of the RV. I staggered over to the trough and retrieved my short sword before grabbing the unconscious Sato by one leg and dragging him out into the sweet relief beyond the evil room. I took some delight as his head bounced off each step before his body slammed to the ground.

I knelt on the sand, panting, with the tip of my blade against Sato's chest for an inordinate amount of time. When I looked up, Tanoshi and Kenji remained locked in the most passionate of embraces. They might have pretended about not being in love, but their fright and reunion had put an end to such foolishness.

"How?" I gasped. "Tanoshi, I was sure you were dead. Sato said electricity would kill witches."

"It sure hurt," Tanoshi said. "But I knew if I moved Sato would shoot me. I used that trick of amplifying a desire, which he'd used on us, and cast an aura of dead around me. Since that was what he wanted, he believed it. He even thought the idea of electricity being deadly to witches was his idea. Fortunately, I'd had plenty of practice using that kind of persuasion while I was trying to stop those shark-fishes from thinking we were good to eat."

I laughed. Not a funny laugh, but one of overwhelming relief. My sister lived, and nothing else mattered.

"Haruko," Airi shouted. "It's not over. We're trapped on this planet and there are dead bodies, bags of human blood and all sorts of crap here. If we don't want to spend our lives in an Earth jail, we need to do something."

I'm glad Airi could keep things in perspective. I'd been thinking about a cold beer.

Airi went over to the fat doctor. "You said Bryce wasn't dead. You will keep him alive long enough to get to a hospital." The man hesitated until Airi whispered. "You know your life depends on it." The man repeatedly nodded and Airi pointed him toward the RV door. She then went over and dragged Kenji out of Tanoshi's arms. "Neither Tanoshi or Haruko can go into the vehicle again," she told him. "The place even gives me the creeps, and I'm not the least bit magical. But someone must collect those bags of blood and spill their contents into the sea."

"I'll do it," Kenji agreed. "But why do you want to save my father?"

"He can't die on this beach. He must die in a hospital to prevent suspicion falling on you. Please let the stupid doctor take care of him. You can beat on the stupid fool all you want afterward. In fact, tell him he's not to let Bryce regain consciousness, but to give him drugs so he stays asleep until the end. To make sure of his cooperation, tell him, if he fails, Tanoshi will hunt him down no matter how far he runs or how deep a hole he hides in."

Airi turned to me. "Sato's regained consciousness and is just pretending," she said. "Keep the blade against his neck while I talk with Tanoshi."

I looked at Sato. His ruse exposed, he opened his eyes. I picked up my modern katana and tossed it to him so its hilt lay against his hand. "If you want to try to escape or fight me, I'd be grateful. I don't like the idea of one of my nobles spending his life in an Earth jail." I backed up a couple of meters, stuck Airi's half-katana into the sand and sat down. "I'll wait for you to get on your feet," I added.

Sato smiled. "I'll stay right here, if you don't mind."

I shook my head and placed my hands in my lap. "What did you do to create such evil? I swear, being near those bags almost killed me."

"You don't want to know. Let's just say I used the blood of your friends to wash the magic out of your swords. I just wish I'd known how being close to those bags took away your strength. Properly set up, I could have won."

"Yes," I agreed, "I imagine you would have."

We waited. I expected him to try to fight or flee. He was, after all, a Takamatsu noble, and I thought he'd rather die with a sword in his hand than just meekly waiting for his death. Did he really think I'd let him live after what he'd done?

Airi returned. "Tanoshi has enough persuasion power to get those goons, which Bryce hid in the brush, to clean up everything and dispose of the bodies. She'll make them fear if any traces remain, they will be convicted of being accessories to multiple murders. When she gets through with them, they'll be so terrified they'll work without questioning it."

With so many bags, Kenji needed to make several trips. Each time he sliced open a bag, the blood flashed blue as it met the water, but the light quickly faded and only a dark stain remained in the sea. The three of us watched, knowing the blue light was our magic leaving this world. Magic that might have sent us home. In time, the last bag was drained. Kenji checked the load in Richard's gun and said he'd accompany the doctor and make sure Bryce made it to a hospital. Airi said she knew enough to drive the minivan, and we'd follow and pick him up.

Only one task remained.

I made Sato stand, pick up the Earth-made katana, and walk toward the ocean. I thought he'd run or turn to fight, but he just walked where I directed. "You murdered Michelle and Frankie," I said as the incoming waves splashed against his feet. "You know the penalty."

He turned and threw down the weapon I'd given him. "You can't kill a noble without a trial," he shouted in a high-pitched voice. "I was only following orders, and I'm entitled to a trial. "Who made you judge, jury and executioner?"

"I'm your prince. It's part of my job description." My blade flashed, and more blood stained the already polluted water.

I stared at the moon for a long time before I picked up the severed head and tossed it into the deeper water. A small blue light appeared in the waves and then faded. The blood-stained waves washed against my feet. This was one of those times I hated being a prince.

Airi pulled on my arm and I saw she held the two swords we'd come here to reclaim. "Bryce removed their magic, but a little of his evil remains in the iron. We can't use them, but they shouldn't remain in this world. Put them on Sato's body and throw everything into the sea. Having them rust away beneath the vast ocean of our planet is the best way to be rid of them."

My sword had served me well, and it hurt to see it and Tanoshi's weapon destroyed. But Airi was right. If anyone on this world found them, it could give the evil one an opening. I slid both of them beneath Sato's expensive leather belt, picked up his headless body and using all my strength, tossed it as far out to sea as I could.

Airi turned and looked at me. "Oh great. I wanted to see if his Earth clothes went with the body. Haruko, you don't need to overdo it every time."

We both stared out to sea. Finally, about a hundred meters away, a faint blue light glowed in the waves. After a few minutes it blinked out and all trace of Sato having walked on this world disappeared.

CHAPTER 22

We buried Bruno beneath the rear lawn and planted flowers over his grave. A little of Tanoshi's magic brought them into bloom and made the spot beautiful. After Richard came home from the hospital, he stood over the grave for a long time. We gave him privacy, so if he shed tears, no one would know.

On the evening of Richard's homecoming, Jack Bryce died without regaining consciousness. Two days later, everything went crazy. First, the lawyers came to drag our Kenji, their Lawrence, downtown. When he returned, he told us the lawyers claimed he'd be tied up with paperwork for many days as they worked through the vast extent of the estate. Unfortunately, and perhaps as a part of Bryce's plan, the media learned of Kenji's rags to super-riches story. The next day dozens of media people waited outside our door with elaborately technological vans parked on the street. Some fools even entered our backyard and trampled across Bruno's flower bed.

Late in the morning, the lawyers retuned and again hustled Kenji away. The media people followed. However, some remained, and after Richard left for his reduced duty desk assignment, they began knocking on our door. We hid in the back room.

After they finally gave up, a new problem arose. The girls arrived. Lots of them. Most carried flowers and placed them on our front stoop with stuffed animals and Japanese-style pottery containing burning incense. I needed to rush out and grab one overstuffed pot before it started a fire. While I couldn't read the notes, which I assumed where condolences on the loss of Kenji's father, I could tell each included a phone number and a photograph. Apparently, it wasn't quite true Earth girls were prudish about displaying some parts of their bodies.

That afternoon the telephone began ringing, and soft female voices asked to speak with poor Lawrence and assure him he wasn't alone in this strange country. Airi finally figured out how to disconnect the annoying device.

Richard eventually came home and, after gingerly stepping over the flowers and politely explaining to the remaining girls Lawrence wasn't expected to return, made it through the door. After listening to our sad tale, he handed me several newspapers. All showed pictures of Kenji on the front page. Richard read the accompanying stories, which told how a poor destitute Japanese boy stranded in America and living on the charity of a friendly police officer, had just inherited several billion dollars.

"Kenji's good looking," Richard said. "His confused appearance as the lawyers took him to their car must have made quite a few young women think he needed a loving companion. I believe that's the plot of many romance novels. Young, available, billionaires are rare. I suppose many local girls saw it as their big chance."

"Kenji loves Tanoshi," Airi shouted. "He wouldn't want anything to do with those . . . girls."

"Of course," Richard said, but he didn't say it with conviction. I knew enough about this world to know a person with that much money could have anything this society offered, including all the compliant women he wanted. When offered a life of luxury and pleasure, would Kenji stay true to Tanoshi, a no-nonsense witch from a primitive world? It didn't help that right then Richard received a call from Kenji, who couldn't get through on our phone, and learned the lawyers had put him up in a downtown hotel to keep him away from the media. Apparently, the legal issues of his inheritance were complicated and would take several weeks to sort out.

Days passed, and the note Richard pinned to our door eventually caused people to leave us alone. Richard bought us a Smartphone, which Kenji used to call us. He sounded happy, admitted the complications were far more complex than he could understand, and with the media dogging his every move, it'd be some time before he could risk meeting with us again. I wished he'd said something reassuring to Tanoshi. Maybe he hadn't learned of his sudden popularity with the opposite sex, or maybe he just assumed she'd trust him. After all, he was young and perhaps hadn't yet learned women needed the unspoken things spoken aloud.

After many phone calls, Richard went to see Kenji, who'd moved to a guarded high-rise apartment. Kenji explained his father had left detailed instructions for his estate, no doubt to provided continuing resources for a long political career. The lawyers were upset and uncooperative with Kenji's desire to sell the companies. He'd accomplished a little, but his major achievement was arranging for his mother to join him in America. Richard said we could meet her and Kenji when she arrived next week.

* * * *

Kenji called the day before his mother was to arrive. He explained he now had a better handle on his wealth and hoped he'd soon be able to live a normal life. While he couldn't risk returning to our house, we could go to an airport VIP lounge and meet him and his mother.

We arrived early. As friends of Kenji, a young lady in a crisp business suit escorted us to a fancy lounge where we could watch aircraft land. Airi soon had her nose pressed against the glass as she ogled the big flying machines. "We must get some identification," she said. "If we're going to live in this world, we must ride in an airplane."

Richard shook his head. "After Nine Eleven security became very tight. A fake ID might get you a drink in a bar, but it wouldn't be enough to get you past the TSA."

"We have time," Airi replied. "We'll find a way."

Yeah, we had time. I still couldn't accept we were going to live out our lives in this place. For all its technological glory, this was our hell. If you weren't born to the never-ending greed and pointless cruelty, the insanity became overbearingly obvious. I thought people here insensitive, their lives reduced to banality as they made war, murder and corruption their daily entertainment on electronic devices designed to insulate them from their fellow humans.

Plus, I worried Kenji would take his new-found wealth and leave us behind. Richard's policeman pay couldn't support us and his two kids. Just the craziness of these last few weeks had wiped out his savings. Tanoshi suggested we revisit the corrupt preacher man, but it turned out his perverted desires had become known and he now sat in jail awaiting trial for embezzlement and possessing child pornography.

The door to the lounge opened and two ladies entered. One appeared older with white streaks in her hair, she looked tired, confused and out of place in a dress that didn't quite fit. She wore a hat with too broad a rim and shiny red shoes, which looked new and made her walk as if her feet hurt. The other girl was young, pretty and dressed to accentuate her youthful curves. I knew what makeup was, and this girl was an expert at using it. No one could rival Airi's beauty, but this girl came closer than anyone else I'd met in this world.

The older woman bowed so low I feared she might topple forward and said something in real Japanese. Tanoshi knew a little from teaching Kenji our version, and was able to bow and make the correct response.

The young girl spoke in English. "Hello. I'm Kiki Komiya. This is Kenji's mother Ono. She's forgotten much of her English, so I few over with her to make sure she was safe. Is Kenji here?"

"Kenji hasn't arrived yet," Airi said. "They said your aircraft would not land for another hour. I expect he's on his way now."

Kiki looked at Airi, her pupils constricted to tiny dots and her pretty face no longer looked as attractive. "Are you Tanoshi?" Even I picked up on the hard edge to her voice.

"Sorry," Airi said. "We should introduce ourselves." Airi made the introductions and when Kiki learned Airi wasn't the girl Kenji had told his mother about, her countenance changed. She looked carefully at Tanoshi and once again became a cute, smiling Japanese girl. She muttered something I didn't catch, but it sounded like a laugh.

Kenji arrived and rushed to his mother. I almost didn't recognize him in his dark blue suit, shiny light red shirt and dark red tie. From his carefully trimmed hair, past the huge gold watch on his wrist, to his elegant leather shoes, he made even those fancy lawyers we'd met look shabby. After hugging his mother he greeted us and embraced Tanoshi.

Kiki rushed over and insisted on giving him a long hug. He sure had a confused look on his face. Everyone began talking at the same time. Eventually I learned Kenji and Kiki went to the same middle school, and she insisted they'd been close childhood friends. By the look on Kenji's face, I think this was news to him, although he did admit they'd known each other at school. He asked her about her career, and she told him she was more popular than ever and her latest music video was at the top of the Japanese charts. Richard whispered to me she was what was called a 'pop idol' and was famous enough to have appeared in American commercials. Since she'd managed to wedge herself between Kenji and Tanoshi, I didn't see this as having a good end.

Kenji wanted to take us to dinner, but his mother was exhausted from the long flight and we agreed he should take her home. Kiki explained she'd flown over just to accompany his mother, so Kenji offered her a ride in his limo. After they left, we stood in the lounge staring at the door and wondering what had happened. In time, Richard drove us home. No one spoke during the trip.

Kenji called late in the evening and apologized for the confusion at the airport. To make it up to us, he invited us to a fancy restaurant in Tampa the next night. He explained he wanted his mother and Tanoshi to get to know each other, which caused the gloom in our house to lift. Richard said this was a really fancy restaurant, took the next day off from work and, using borrowed money, bought us better outfits.

* * * *

Kenji, or one of his 'people', had reserved an entire room at the restaurant. The four of us, plus Kenji, his mother, and Kiki, sat around a large table. Kenji placed his mother and Tanoshi together so they could get to know each other, which left him at the other end of the table next to Kiki. Airi, Richard and I sat between them and we could not get a general conversation going that included all of us. The only time Kenji spoke just to us was when he handed Airi the gold button she'd given to Michelle. Apparently, Bryce believed it possessed the power to make people fond of him, and he'd kept it in a fancy container on his desk. I was glad we got it back. It, and Airi's sword, were all we had left from our home world.

The dinner was a disaster. This restaurant, judging by its elegant decor, the finest in the city, specialized in cow meat. Our inability to read English made us agree to have whatever Kenji ordered. After some tasty fried mushrooms and other dishes called 'appetizers', the main course arrived. Richard dug into the thick red steak with great gusto, claiming he'd never before tasted anything so delicious. The three of us stared at the bloody juice seeping from the not-especially-cooked cow muscle and wondered how we'd get through the evening. After saying it tasted as good as Japanese Kobe beef, Kiki leaned over and kissed Kenji on the cheek.

Kiki wore a body-hugging tiny black dress, which sparked with innumerable bits of light-reflecting glass. The dress only added to her flawless makeup, flowing black hair, full breasts, which threatened to pop out of their minimal covering, and expensive jewelry hanging from her ears, neck, wrists and ankles. She had to be the peak of what Earth men lusted after in a woman.

We however, wearing ill-fitting clothes from a discount store, looked like refugees from another planet. Which, I guess we were. I suppose we could have presented ourselves better, but Airi, chief protector of her prince, wouldn't go out in public without her sword and wore an overlong dress to help Tanoshi's weakened magic conceal the weapon. Tanoshi looked more stylish, but she'd found few clothes in her size, plus her brightly colored blouse and skirt weren't the best quality and in this place appeared tawdry. There had only been one suit coat that fit me and it was short in the sleeves and too tight across my shoulders. The coat's outside pockets were fake, so I'd put a large folding knife, a gift from Richard, in a small inside pouch where it bulged as if I carried a gun. I guess Richard, in his policeman's dress blues, was the only one of us who fit with the restaurant's elegant decor.

Communicating with Kenji's mother, Ono, wasn't easy.

Her English was weak, and our distorted version of Japanese only confused her. But her fondness for Tanoshi was obvious, and using what common words each of them knew, she managed to assure my sister Kiki had never been a real friend to Kenji. She'd been surprised when the pop star turned up asking to accompany her on the flight to America. I guess, on Earth, being a young, handsome billionaire had a strange effect on women. However, as the evening drew to a close, we were all aware of how few words we, and Tanoshi, had exchanged with Kenji.

On the way home, Richard showed us a check for nine thousand, nine hundred and ninety-nine dollars. "One dollar more and I would need to report it on my taxes," he explained. "But, this will cover our immediate needs, and Kenji promises to have something more permanent set up soon. The kid's all right, he knows how to look out for his friends."

His friends. I looked at Tanoshi. We thought she was more to him than a friend. But after a lifetime of poverty, acquiring an unimaginable amount of money had to mess with his mind. Now he had a pretty girl from his own world doting on him, a girl who'd be more than willing to teach him to enjoy every aspect of his new wealth.

"Kenji's a good person," Tanoshi said. "He saved our lives. We never could have survived without him. We owe him everything. The least we can do is support him and let him enjoy his new life. He deserves every bit of it." I put my arm around her and pulled her close. I couldn't think of any words of comfort. She whispered, perhaps more to herself than to me. "This is for the best. If we'd married, I'd have always feared his affection was just a result of my magic. At least, now I know I successfully removed the compulsion from his mind."

Poor Tanoshi, was having so much power a curse? It seemed to make it impossible for anyone other than her family to love her. How could she survive a lifetime of loneliness? "Airi and I will be at your side forever," I replied and got a small smile in return. Power, such as she controlled, stopped people from seeing you as a person. As the car drove through the night, I wondered if the High God suffered from the same problem.

* * * *

"We're only assuming the ocean's transport magic will deposit us randomly on our world," Airi said. "But it might not. There does seem to be subtle connections. We landed right in the path of the boat carrying Jack Bryce, the man who'd caused your father to come to our world. There's every chance we could drop into our ocean close enough to swim to shore."

We were sitting around the house with little to do. Richard, having recovered from his operation had returned to work. "Just walking into the ocean is big risk," I replied. "If we guess wrong, we die. But with the only other choice being living out our lives here, maybe it's a chance we should take. However, let's not rush the decision. We'll decide after considering our other options." I didn't say it, but I still hoped Kenji would come through and reunite with Tanoshi. It didn't look good. Yesterday, Kenji and Kiki flew across the country to Hollywood. It turned out one of the things Kenji inherited was a private jet complete with pilot. Kiki's agent had arranged for her to meet a big shot in the American film industry, and Kenji seemed willing to do anything she asked to help her career. Or maybe he just wanted to try out his personal jet. Anyway, they were gone and wouldn't be back for a week or more.

Three days later my fears were confirmed when Kenji called to say he and Kiki were flying to Japan with several producers to scout locations for a movie in which Kiki would play a major role. He explained he'd become a financial backer, and they'd list him as a co-producer in the movie's credits. He went on to say how exciting it was to meet famous people while attending Hollywood parties. Just before he hung up, he said he was sending us a debit card which we could use to buy anything we needed.

"He's buying us off," Airi said. "He's discovered a new life, one that doesn't include us. The money is so he doesn't feel guilty about abandoning us. It's time we made plans to get home. I'm convinced the magic won't let us drown."

"Not yet," Tanoshi said. "Let's wait until Kenji returns. He deserves a chance to know what being rich is like and then decide. Besides, I'd like some time to study the magic pulling us home. Perhaps I could learn enough to be sure of where we'd land."

I feared Tanoshi was unable to accept Kenji was lost her. "I agree we should wait," I said. "There's still a lot we don't know. Let's use the time to find out more. Besides ourselves, we now have two items from our world, Airi's sword and the gold button she gave to Michelle. I wouldn't want to lose the sword, but let's put the button in the ocean and see if it shows any sign of returning. It might give Tanoshi some insight."

They agreed and after Richard came home we asked him to take us to the nearby beach. Our first test was holding the button underwater and watching for any blue sparkles.

Tanoshi could no longer risk entering the ocean, so I waded out up to my knees, bent over and submerged my hand holding the button. At first, nothing happened; the button didn't even glow blue. I was about to stand and declare the test a failure when I noticed a milky glow in the water. A picture gradually formed. It wasn't distinct, like a hologram, more like shadows which faded if you looked too closely. I could still see the gentle ocean swells surging toward the sand and splashing against my legs, but deep inside the water, human figures moved.

It took me a minute to grasp what I was seeing, but as the detail increased, I could make out soldiers, dressed in Japanese-style armor attacking unarmed villages. They were killing the men and the forcing females into a huddled group. The scene changed to a more substantial town, and I watched those same women walking the streets and tending to their new masters. It was obvious they were now pregnant by the gold glow around their stomachs. None of them looked happy about it.

The water clouded and then a golden woman with wings was in front of those pregnant women and they appeared to be flying. They faded into the distance and I assumed the vision was over.

Before I could stand, a flash caught my eye and I saw a battered, Earth-style boat caught in a raging storm. Towering waves were ripping parts of it away. Its demise looked imminent. At the very front of the boat, something inside created a golden glow. The angel reappeared, and with what looked like a mighty strain, grabbed the glow and pulled it, along with the rest of the boat, out of the ocean. Then, like waking from a dream, I knew the vision was over.

I turned back toward the beach and saw Tanoshi and Airi holding each other and staring at me. "Haruko," Airi screamed. "Are you all right?"

"What happened," Tanoshi shouted.

I needed to rush to the shore before one of them ran into the sea to reach me. After a lot of confused talking over each other, I learned I'd remained still as a statue. I told them about my vision and pointed out it only showed the stories every kid in our land learned about the angel bringing the pregnant women to this planet. The second vision concerned our family history of the Moon Goddess rescuing my father so he could end slavery in Takamatsu. "I think it was a daydream," I admitted, "I didn't see anything I didn't already know. It's not like I have magic power or anything."

Airi sighed. "Haruko, you're our future monarch. Since the very first woman set foot on this world, the monarchy has possessed magic power. Of course you have it! Don't you remember how sick the evil blood made you? That was because your power reacted to it."

"Oh!" I managed to say. "But the vision didn't reveal any information we could use. It was just history." We walked in silence up the beach to Richard. I guess I'd always known I had a smattering of magic, certainly my speed testified to it. But I'd never thought of it as serious, nothing like Tanoshi's power.

"Why," Tanoshi said, "did Haruko see things he already knew. There must be a reason?"

"We're here," Airi replied. "Because when the Moon Goddess intervened in this world and saved your father, it gave evil an opening to also intervene and do something equivalent. He almost succeeded in having Jack Bryce destroy this world. Remember, spirits live under strict rules. If any spirit openly helped us, the evil one would be free to act also. Perhaps Haruko's vision contains a useful hint. Something less than an intervention, but helpful if we understood it. Haruko, explain what you saw again, don't leave anything out."

As Richard drove us home, I repeated the vision. Airi and Tanoshi often interrupted me for more detail. They took note of the gold glow coming from the front of my dad's boat. As they quizzed me, I remembered it'd looked as if the Goddess had grabbed the glow, rather than the sides of the boat, when she'd pulled it out of the storm.

Airi hugged me. "Yes, I understand. I remember your dad telling us how the trawler's forward cabin was crammed with every vegetable and fruit that market had available. Jack Bryce bought them to stop anyone discovering the bomb he'd hidden in the cabin. Plus, if anyone questioned him about the boat's unusual sinking, he'd have witnesses who could testify he'd intended making the voyage and only a kid's medical emergency caused him to remain behind."

"Of course," Tanoshi said. "The seeds from those vegetables and fruits are now the basis of our diets. It was those seeds, and their promise of future life, which helped the Goddess move my dad and his boat to our world."

Tanoshi and Airi began talking rapidly, and I was hard pressed to keep up. They'd realized it was the unborn babies the first women held that made it possible for the Moon Goddess to bring our ancestors to this planet. Later, she'd used all those seeds in the trawler to save my father. They decided life to come held a special magic—a need to survive, and such magic could help us return to our world, not in some random spot in the vast ocean, but in a place where they could survive and grow.

Airi put her hand on my shoulder. "The vision was telling us we need to carry as many seeds as possible. They will guide us to land, or at least close enough to land so we can swim ashore. Haruko, we're going home."

CHAPTER 23

While driving home, we convinced Richard to search the web and find out how to buy rubber tree seeds. On our world, we suffered from the lack of rubber. True, we grew a weed with a milky sap which, with some refining and treatment, gave us a little rubber-like substance. But my dad often lamented there'd been no rubber tree seeds on his boat, and our lack of rubber would always hold us back.

We wanted other seeds too. Leafy vegetables like lettuce, cabbage, broccoli and cauliflower. Although my dad had brought them, they'd not possessed seeds. Plus, some of the fruits on his boat, like bananas, were sterile hybrids. Although a few kernels from his ears of sweet corn sprouted, it turned out his table corn was created by a hybridization method and our crops reverted to what was called field corn, which was tough and not very sweet. While it produced good cornmeal and grits, it didn't make a tasty vegetable. Now, with all of Earth's seed bounty to choose from, it was hard to contain our excitement.

"Chocolate," Tanoshi insisted. "Be sure to get chocolate seeds. Everyone loves chocolate."

"They call the plant cacao," Richard explained. "I've heard raw cocoa is quite bitter. They have some strange way of treating it to make it palatable. You'll have to do some research."

"Richard's right," Airi said. "We need to take our time and find out everything about the seeds we choose, what kind of soil and climate they need, how they grow and if they are seasonal or perennial. There's a lot to learn. We shouldn't rush out and grab any old thing." She turned to Tanoshi. "Besides, Kenji will be back. We need to give him time to make sure of what he wants to do with his life."

I agreed with Airi. While it didn't look as if Kenji remained interested in coming to our world, I could see Tanoshi hadn't given up hope. We needed to give him every opportunity to come to his senses.

* * * *

Two weeks later, boxes began arriving daily. The pile in the spare bedroom now reached the ceiling, and Airi had filled several notebooks with details about cultivating the various seed varieties. She'd laughed after discovering cotton plants needed one hundred and eighty frost-free Earth days. "Our longer summers easily meet the requirement. We can grow plentiful cotton and free ourselves from the Clothmaker's yoke. Their trees could never compete with such a fast growing and productive bush."

I felt the excitement. Returning with a bounty of different seeds would change our world for the better. Soon, Kyoto and Takamatsu would become equal trading partners and the threat of war would end.

One of the stowed boxes contained four large backpacks to carry the seeds, Tanoshi insisting we continue assuming Kenji would come with us. Since we'd received few calls from him, I harbored doubts. Anyway, with all the different seeds and roots we'd obtained, we'd need more than four backpacks to take everything.

Kenji called while I was opening the boxes and repacking the seeds into thin plastic bags to protect them if we landed in the sea. Tanoshi and Airi were discussing whether we should take sugarcane. Tanoshi wanted a plentiful sugar supply for her chocolate dreams, Airi pointing out we already grew sugar beets. Taking cane would mean leaving other seeds behind as her research indicated we'd need both a variety of seed types and several large stem pieces called cultivars to establish a viable crop. Plus, too much sugar around would give everyone a desire for it, along with the dental and other health problems it'd created on Earth.

Kenji explained he and Kiki were returning to America. Now the lawyers had given him possession of Jack Bryce's huge house on the bay, he wanted to throw a party to celebrate the legal stuff being mostly over and Kiki landing a starring role in a major movie. We, along with Richard, John and Andrea, were invited. It sounded like he'd decided to stay on Earth, but Tanoshi announced she and Airi would buy clothes suitable for a party as this might be the last time Kenji could enjoy his wealth.

Andrea took us to an upscale store and using Kenji's card we spent lavishly. I finally got an Earth-suit that fit. Andrea found dresses for Tanoshi and Airi as revealing as the one Kiki wore at the first dinner. But that night, as Andrea taught Tanoshi to apply makeup and jewelry, I felt an overwhelming sadness. My sister wasn't giving up without a fight, but I feared the battle had been won by money. Once again my poor Tanoshi would end up alone.

Richard's old minivan looked out of place among the limousines and upscale cars parked beyond a tall iron gate. He found a spot a little distance from the other vehicles, and we walked toward a huge carved wooden door, which would have looked at home on the Clothmaker's estate. Torches burned on either side of the door, and as we approached, an elegantly dressed older man came out and asked for our names. As he checked them against a list, Richard whispered "Butler," after seeing my confused expression. Inside the door we met John escorting Andrea, who wore a long bedewed gown, a style rather different from those dresses she'd picked out for Tanoshi and Airi.

We discovered this wasn't a small affair. The high-ceilinged room beyond the front foyer held dozens of people, the men wore suits putting mine to shame, and their mates sparkled in long, flowing, floor-sweeping gowns. I recognized one of the lawyers who'd worked with Kenji. Andrea pointed to a man and said he was a big-time Hollywood actor. I noticed every woman wore a long dress—which meant Tanoshi and Airi were the only two in the room with short, sexy outfits suitable for an informal gathering. I guess Andrea, the yuppie, wasn't quite the friend we thought she was.

I looked around at the opulence. Beneath crystal chandeliers, long tables covered with lacy cloths held silver dishes of bite-sized food. Another table held dozens of liquor bottles and a man stationed behind the table shook a silver and glass container as he prepared some concoction for lady in a red and lace dress. On the other side of the room, three musicians played stringed instruments. As everyone talked loudly, I couldn't hear their music. I wondered how the musicians felt with everyone ignoring their efforts.

Kenji and Kiki stood together at the opposite end of the room near an oversized clock with a gold pendulum swinging back and forth to tick off the seconds. Two other couples surrounded them and they were laughing while having an animated discussion. Kenji, the billionaire entrepreneur, looked at ease in his tailored suit as he sipped from a crystal glass of red wine. Kiki, next to him, wore a black, floor-length gown that revealed much of her breasts, its front held up by a single strap across her shoulders. The strap had embedded a row of large, sparkling gems which flowed down the dress to accent where the dress parted to reveal the pink of a leg and upper thigh. Her black hair, arranged in an elaborate style, held a bejeweled pin with flashing gems, which matched those on her dress. Despite myself, I thought her attractive.

Kenji hadn't noticed we'd arrived. Airi grabbed Tanoshi's arm and pulled her to the side. "We don't seem to be dressed properly," Airi whispered. "Now what?"

Tanoshi looked around the room. "Either it'll make a big difference, or no difference," she said. "I'm finished playing games. Let's go meet Kenji."

Before we moved, Kenji's mother, Ono, hustled over to us. "Tanoshi-san," she gasped, sounding out of breath. "I be happy you here. I don't know people, this house." Using both hands, she grabbed Tanoshi's arm. Ono wore an excessively fancy dress with some large and rather gaudy jewelry. Both the dress and the jewelry gave me an uneasy feeling as if they didn't belong on a woman who'd done menial labor all her life.

She spoke to Tanoshi using both broken English and Japanese words. Tanoshi didn't appear to be having trouble understanding, and as I listened, the meanings seemed to form in my mind. Perhaps, as Airi insisted, I really did have a little magic.

Ono claimed Kiki was a bad influence on her son. While he'd been away he'd sent her several packages containing expensive dresses and jewelry, but in all that time, he'd only called once. He'd spoken for just a minute before saying he had something to do. Ono revealed Kiki had never been a friend to Kenji while they were in school. In fact, she'd been one of the instigators in harassing him about not being pureblood Japanese. His mother felt the young woman was only using him to get ahead in the movie business.

While Ono talked, I studied the other guests. I counted around twenty males with their companions. The guests differed from the many people wearing simple black and white outfits who brought drinks and bits of food on trays. I didn't like it and felt annoyed Kenji had hired them. In Kyoto, even my mother refused to have servants. The Moon Goddess decreed we should never have greater or lesser people.

Tanoshi shook her head when one of the servants offered us drinks and then said we should go meet Kenji. As she strode across the room, I noticed everyone hustling to get out of her way. Even on Earth, people instinctively knew to give ground to a pissed-off witch.

"Hello Kenji," she said, her voice flat and without emotion. "I see you've returned."

"Tanoshi," he stammered. "I'm so glad you could make it." The two of them stood staring at each other, the silence growing awkward until Kiki grabbed Kenji's arm.

"Kenji says you're a real witch," she said to Tanoshi with a grin on her face. "Are you going to turn me into a frog?"

"No point," Tanoshi said. "Nobody would be able to tell the difference."

While Kiki whined that Tanoshi was being mean, I was distracted by a large man standing against the wall. He looked at me and came forward, one hand hovering close to the opening in his suit jacket. He moved as one familiar with fighting. While his glare remained steady on me, he seemed fully aware of his surroundings. I knew, without a doubt, he was a trained fighter and carried a gun. Was there no end to these pesky goons? He was so close I didn't have time to ask questions, and we'd come to Kenji's house without weapons. I moved, using all my speed. Although he was strong, he didn't expect me to disappear and reappear at his side. In fact, I moved so fast I surprised myself—was this from my new magic ability? Anyway, a kick and a twist put him face down on the floor, pinned with one arm forced behind his back. I reached around and yanked the pistol from its holster and held it up so Kenji would know I wasn't just beating up on one of his guests.

"Stop," Kenji shouted. "He's my bodyguard."

Richard, fortunately wearing his policeman's dress blues, came over and took the gun from my hand. "Best let him up, Haruko, he thought you were threatening Kenji."

As everyone in the room stared at us, we disentangled ourselves and Richard explained to the bodyguard I'd never hurt Kenji. The man looked at me while rubbing the arm I'd twisted. "Kid must be some sort of ninja," he muttered and his hard eyes made me glad Richard still held the pistol.

Richard escorted the embarrassed bodyguard from the room to get cleaned up. I stood staring at Kenji and wondering what had happened to my friend. Why would he feel the need to hire a gun goon?

"They're animals," Kiki screeched at Kenji. "Animals! Send them away. They don't know how to act in polite society."

"What did you call us?" Tanoshi spun and spoke in a low voice, the threat behind it palatable in the hushed room. I believe ice crystals began forming in the wine Kiki held. We'd learned how dark-skinned people were once used as slaves in this country, and their owners had justified their greed by calling them animals. If there was one word Kiki should not have used, that was it. Tanoshi took two steps toward her rival and looked down at her face. The difference in their heights now obvious.

Seeing them so close, I realized there was a reason Kiki was a pop idol. Her exceptionally pretty face and small, shapely body seemed to be what Earth men looked for in a woman. Myself, I thought her waist too small. I'm sure I could encircle it with my hands and have my fingers touch. If anyone gave her a hoe and sent her out into a vegetable field, she would break. She now looked up at Tanoshi, a real woman with a lifetime of work which put a muscle beneath every curve. No one would call Tanoshi fragile.

Which woman did Kenji want? By every Earth standard Kiki was the most appealing, but Tanoshi and Kenji had a history, one I'd thought exceeded any shallow comparison of appearances. Kiki, dropped her wine, put her face in her hands and began crying and begging Kenji to protect her. My heart broke when Kenji went over and put an arm around her. Tanoshi, her mouth open, took a step back. It was a tribute to her inner strength she remained standing, and I knew never in her life had anyone hurt her so deeply. I rushed over and placed my arm on her shoulder, poor comfort but all I could offer.

Kiki, cradled in Kenji's arms, leaned over his shoulder, and confident only Tanoshi and I could see her face, stuck out her tongue.

"All right," whispered Tanoshi. "No more nice witch."

Tanoshi grabbed my hand. Her hand felt hot, almost burning hot, yet it seemed like she sucked the heat from my body. The room took on a red hue. I looked at Tanoshi, she was outlined with a red glow and I knew she was gathering magical power, even taking it from me. "Don't hurt her," I gasped, "that will turn Kenji and everyone against you."

She smiled. "Worse than hurt," she pointed a finger at Kiki. Despair washed over me. After a lifetime of battling against the evil trying to force her to embrace it, she'd finally yielded to temptation. I'd lost my beloved sister to hate.

The room became deathly quiet. All those little background noises that don't register but are always with us disappeared. The hum of the lights, the little sounds people make even when they're not talking. Even the pendulum in the wooden clock now swung silently. Such absolute silence made the hair on my head prickle. It was worse than the loudest scream. Then, alone, like a single candle glowing on a starless night, Kiki began to speak.

"You're a stupid pathetic half," she pushed Kenji away from her. "You were dumb in school and you're still just as stupid. It takes every bit of acting skill I have just to remain near you. Your only quality is money, and after I get my share, you're shit on the sidewalk." She looked at him, disgust visible on her pretty face. I watched Kenji staring at her as if he'd never seen Kiki before. We stood there, stunned.

The sounds returned, the silence shattered and the loud raucous cacophony made me jump. Everyone in the room was either shouting or screaming. To my left a woman slapped the man next to her. Another couple continued screeching obscenities at each other. In the back of the room two servers embraced, their little trays and their contents still clattering across the floor. Over by the food table, one woman was yanking her dress up while her companion pushed his pants to his ankles. Two men were shoving each other in a prelude to exchanging blows. One of the musicians smashed her instrument against the ground, stomped on it and cursed the day she'd taken up music. Andrea screamed at Airi, calling her a hussy and ordering her to stay away from John. All around the room insanity ruled.

I looked at Tanoshi. "The magic is out of control," I gasped. "We need to do something." I tried shouting for people to stop, but no one heard me.

"They can only hear the person they are with," Tanoshi said. "I thought I had only enough power to affect Kiki. The magic got amplified somehow."

I remembered her grasping my hand and how it'd felt as if she was pulling something out of me. I was an engineer. I built steam engines. I wasn't supposed to be magical. I felt Airi tugging on my arm. After Andrea's tirade, she'd run over to stand at my side. God, Airi looked beautiful. Beautiful far beyond what words could describe. From her personality to her intelligence, everything about her was beyond perfect. I'd known her my entire my life, and now I knew I'd loved her for every second of every minute of that time. How could I ever have considered marrying someone else? There was only one woman in all of creation for me, and she stood right there. I reached out to her. "Please," I shouted. "I love you."

Tanoshi yanked me back. "Yeah, yeah, you love Airi," she said. "We knew that years ago. Right now I need you to help me put a stop to this insanity. You two can make your marriage plans later."

Tanoshi grabbed both of my hands. "All right, think calming thoughts. Happy thoughts about peaceful sleep. I don't have much power left, but if I can draw some from you, we might stop this. Now, brother, let's do this."

As I held Tanoshi's hands, the room took on a red cast. I could feel something flowing from me and into Tanoshi. It made me feel weak and light-headed, and I feared I'd end up on the floor. Tanoshi kept her eyes closed, a look of intense concentration on her face. The red mist swirled around the room, settling on people and causing them to hesitate, even sag to the ground as though exhausted. All but Kenji, around him, a green mist, tinged with black swirls, kept the red at bay. The two colors fought each other, the red slowly penetrating the black. Finally, like the sound a falling tree makes, the black miasma was ripped away and Kenji stood staring at Kiki with his mouth open.

Tanoshi let go of my hands. I looked around and the red mist had disappeared. Everyone in the room either stood, or sat, looking dazed and confused among the scattered remnants of the elegant party. Kiki began shouting Tanoshi had made her say things that weren't true. Kenji only stared and didn't respond. After a few minutes he called for silence and said he thought there'd been an earthquake and it'd be best if everyone made their way home.

"Earthquake," Tanoshi echoed. "Go home now."

After the guests left, Kiki sat on a couch sobbing with her head in her hands. Kenji, we three, with Richard and Ono stood watching her. "Did you really force her to say those things?" Kenji asked Tanoshi.

"Not like that," she replied. "I only wanted her to tell you how she truly felt. I don't have much power, so I borrowed some from Haruko. When I reached out, he sent me too much and it made everything go extreme. I was so overwhelmed it affected everyone in the room. It released those feelings people keep so deep inside they don't know they have them. That's why it was different for everyone. Kiki was using you, but she doesn't hate you to that extent."

Kenji nodded. "Still, it made me remember how she'd treated me back when we were in school. I should have known she couldn't change that much. What was I thinking?" He turned and held out his hands to Tanoshi. "I was stupid, can you ever forgive me?"

"Something was affecting you," I said. "When Tanoshi's magic was working I saw a black and green cloud around you. Tanoshi ripped it away. It must be what was clouding your mind."

Kenji gasped. "An evil force was messing with me?"

"Kenji," Airi said. "Do you know how your father made his money? The money you now own."

"He made a lot of lucky investments in the stock market, but most of it came from his medical clinics. The lawyers told me they are amazingly profitable. Apparently, I own a big building downtown with dozens of employees who send out bills and deal with the claims they send to the government."

"He got rich by exploiting desperate sick people," Airi said. "It's tainted money. No good can come from money created by exploiting others. It might seem like you're enjoying it, but it blinds you to love and respect for your fellow humans. Tanoshi freed you for now, but as long as you own the evil money, it could return and make you forget who you really are."

Kenji stared at Kiki. "I think I understand. Kiki and I weren't even intimate, yet deep down inside, her subconscious was already planning our divorce. If Tanoshi hadn't lifted the curse, I'd have lived my life without ever knowing love, just an endless stream of cocktail parties and fancy toys." He turned to Tanoshi and took both of her hands in his. "Are you still mad at me? Before this money came to me, I had such a wonderful dream, an unbelievable dream of spending my life with most desirable woman in the world. Is there any chance I could get it back?"

Tanoshi drew him into her arms and they embraced with the same passion they'd shown after the fight at the beach.

CHAPTER 24

When you're a billionaire, disappearing isn't a good option. Besides, Richard couldn't come with us and we didn't want to abandon him to his poverty lifestyle. Airi, of course, found the answers. Kenji's money could redeem itself with charitable works. Richard and Ono agreed to become controllers of the Lawrence Bryce Charitable Foundation. Richard, now he'd lost Bruno, was happy to quit the force and take a job which paid well. After that, he and Ono began spending time in each other's company. It made sense, they were both about the same age and both had been betrayed by love. Perhaps together they could find something real. This was helped when Kenji learned that for a measly half million dollars, Richard's wife would happily hand over the children to their father.

I asked Tanoshi why I'd become capable of magic, she explained how, back on our world, I'd lived for sixteen of the long Moon World years and was now an adult. "You are our next monarch," she explained. "The monarchy has always held magic power. You've reached an age where it manifests."

"I'm an engineer. I don't think magic is going to do much for me."

"Probably not. But while we're here, I can tap into it to strengthen my own power. You said Sato's body took his Earth clothes with him when it disappeared, but they didn't weigh much. With your help, I might be able to determine how much Earth material we can carry and still have our own world pull us off this planet. Kenji intends to go with us, but it could mean leaving some seeds behind."

Of course there'd be a limit. We'd used Earth material before to hold us here. Obviously, if we held onto too much, we'd not leave. Over the next few days, the four of us spent time at the beach trying to get a feel for how much, besides ourselves, we could take into the nowhere place. At first, Kenji took Airi's sword into the sea with weights attached and found even the smallest additional material kept it anchored in this world.

Deciding the magic required human bodies, I became the next trial subject, using both a rope and a nearby Kenji to make sure I didn't disappear with my various loads of seeds. The results weren't encouraging. While standing on the shore, Tanoshi could feel the force trying to pull me away, and after many tests gave her depressing result.

"The amount of material we can take from this world is far less than we hoped. I doubt it's even a quarter of our combined weight."

"A quarter of our weight might be enough for us to take Kenji," Airi said, "but few seeds, maybe none." She didn't complete the thought. Without the life force in the seeds, we had no guarantee of dropping into our world's ocean close enough to land to survive. I looked at Tanoshi and by her depressed look, guessed she was being optimistic about even taking Kenji. We drove home in silence, each of us trying to come to terms with this unexpected turn of events.

Now Tanoshi and Kenji were in love, how could either of them live without the other? Tanoshi especially, back home, no one wanted to marry a terrifying witch. But here, she'd found Kenji, the first man who accepted and loved her. Once separated from him, would her depression and loneliness overcome her resolve to follow the Moon Goddess? Could this be the evil one's intention?

If we left Tanoshi on Earth, the nobles of Takamatsu would move to enslave Kyoto. I'm not sure what would happen to my mother, me and Airi, but it wouldn't be good. Besides, Tanoshi couldn't long survive in a world that worshipped money. By their silence I feared Tanoshi and Kenji hoped me, the idiot prince, would decide for them. There were some choices even a prince couldn't make if he wanted to live with himself afterward.

* * * *

"Do you really intend marrying me after we get home?" Airi whispered in my ear, waking me from a troubled sleep. It was late, sometime past midnight, and Tanoshi remained sleeping on my left, even in the dim light of the moon shining through the window, I could see moisture around her eyes. I guessed she'd cried herself to sleep. Yes, it'd probably been wishful thinking when she said we could take Kenji with us. Airi tugged on my arm, and I eased myself out of bed and followed her to the bathroom.

"I don't care what political problems it causes," I said once we were alone. "You're the only woman I could ever want. Besides, after dealing with Sato, there's no way I would marry his sister or any other damn noble. From this day forward, you are a princess." She looked at me and I realized I'd left out the most important part. "Airi, I love you, I've always loved you even if I didn't realize it before. Please consider marrying me, I promise to do everything I can to make you happy for the rest of your life."

"Promise to tell me you love me every day and I'll agree to marry you." She said and smiled. That was my Airi, practical as ever. I agreed repeatedly until she hugged me.

"All right," she said. "Now we can go back to bed and have wild, and very often repeated, sex. But first, I'll wake Tanoshi and tell her get her ass into Kenji's room and seduce him until he passes out."

"What?"

"Think about it, Haruko. Back in our world it's very difficult for a woman to become pregnant. Couples spend years trying before having success. Here it's just the opposite. On Earth, women take precautions because even a casual fling can result in a baby. So, if you and Kenji do your jobs properly, very soon both Tanoshi and I will be pregnant." She looked at me and shook her head. "Dummy. That means we'll have babies inside us—new life to come. We won't need to carry plant seeds. We're bound to land in a place where we, and our future children, will be safe."

"Oh," I said. "The chores a prince has to do to keep his people happy." I got punched, but not very hard. I suppose Princess Airi wanted me in top form when she returned to bed.

* * * *

Six weeks later, on the night of the full moon, the same fishing boat that had once brought us to Saint Petersburg, took us out into the gulf, far enough from land where we could no longer see the lights. Kenji and his mother remained down in the cabin, saying goodbye. I guess now the time had actually arrived it was hard for them both. We stayed on the fishing deck, trying to make small talk with Richard, his fishing buddies and Andrea. I tried not to show how nervous I felt. Even with all our planning much could go wrong. What if eating Earth food had made it impossible for our world to draw us back? I assured myself my father had lived on the Moon Goddess' world for many years, and he still needed to stay out of the ocean. But facing death, even hard logic felt weak.

Nevertheless, the last weeks had been fun in more ways than the obvious, since Earth's advanced detection methods now pronounced both Airi and Tanoshi pregnant. In the middle of this state they'd built some, what they called, amusement parks. We'd spent many days enjoying them all. Princess Airi met the pretend Disney princesses, and had managed to refrain from telling them she was the real deal. She also admitted if anyone made her smile that much her mouth would break.

Airi had spent much of the time studying physics and advanced mathematics. My dad, the high school teacher, could only take her so far in those fields. Now, she'd built on his foundation and probably knew as much as any Earth professor in what was, to me, a bunch of arcane symbols. I'd spent my time researching older steam and diesel engine technology, devices with a practical application in our developing world. Kenji followed my example and, when he wasn't reading web pages to me, learned all he could about geology, the subject he'd originally intended studying when he came to America.

All too soon the moon reached its zenith, and we could delay no longer. We stripped down, and before stepping off the transom and into the salty water, secured little seed packages around our waists. Rubber tree seeds were largish, but along with them we'd squeezed in a few cotton plant seeds and, at Kenji's request, some tiny Japanese daikon radish seeds.

We'd debated taking Airi's sword. Most of its magic was

exhausted, but Tanoshi feared leaving it on Earth might cause problems if it fell onto the wrong hands. As a thing, and not alive, it might not be drawn back to its origins, but Tanoshi said it wouldn't hold us back either. However, since we'd be naked except for those tiny seed pouches, one of us would have to hold it while swimming in the sea and keeping a tight grip on Kenji. Airi said, as it was her sword, she'd take the responsibility.

As agreed, the fishing boat pulled away, leaving the four of us alone in the deep water. They'd promised to give us a good half hour before coming back to make sure we weren't in trouble. The three of us encircled Kenji, pressing him as tightly against our bodies as was possible. Tanoshi, who'd spent time in the ocean regaining her little bit of power, began glowing blue almost immediately, Airi and I to a lesser extent. At least Airi's blue did spread over the sword she held relieving me of one of my fears. But, in those places where we touched Kenji or our seed packets, the blue refused to spread. After ten minutes, Airi asked me to drop my seeds. I did so, but if there was any change, I couldn't see it. Kenji's Earth mass was just too much.

Another ten or more minutes past, and in this awkward arrangement, even with our less-dense bodies, it became difficult to tread water. I wanted to believe blue covered more of Kenji's body, but it might have been wishful thinking. Airi sighed and asked Kenji to remove her seed packet since she was holding both him and her sword. As the seeds rose to the surface and floated away, I knew our only chance to grow rubber trees was around Tanoshi's waist.

"Release me and go home," Kenji said after a few more minutes. "You know you must, many people will die if you don't. I can see the boat coming back, our time is up. They'll fish me out after you're gone." He whispered to Tanoshi. "I'll always love you, never forget that." Then he tried pushing us away.

"No!" Screamed Tanoshi. "No, no, no!"

Surrounding the blue sparkles on our bodies, a red glow formed. I could feel it pulling on me, stronger and more insistent than ever before. It felt as if my essence was flowing from me. Tanoshi wanted everything I could offer. I didn't resist, but gave freely.

The water flashed warm, and then became a milky-white mist. Completely exhausted, I couldn't move, even breathing seemed to require more effort than I had. My arms hung limp and I'd have drifted away if the four of us hadn't been so tightly entwined.

"You did it," Tanoshi gasped. "You gave me the power I needed to break free. We're on our way home." I saw Kenji, he looked terrified, but he hung onto Tanoshi's waist as the four of us, one tightly held sword and a tiny package of seeds, tumbled through the nowhere place.

In a minute, if such labels could be given to a place where time didn't exist, we'd drop into the ocean on the Moon Goddess' world, swim to shore, and finally, our real lives would begin.

THE END

I hope you enjoyed the story. Any social media plugs or recommendations will be most appreciated. There might be another book in the works, as Haruko and his gang haven't made it home yet, and the evil one still hates their guts.

Don't forget, if you enjoy realistic Science Fiction, the first book in my **Rise and Fall of Synfood,** series; *Clericals, Courtesans and Superconductors* is now available.

Meanwhile, please consider checking out my website and learning about the new easy and cheap way solar energy could be converted into electric power.

WWW.FERROGENERATOR.COM

THANKS,

John

About the Author:

I hale from England, born during the post World War Two years. Just before my thirteenth birthday, an Aunt and Uncle offered me the chance to immigrate to America. A few years later, on America's first Law Day, I became an American citizen. Becoming an American, remains one of the proudest accomplishments of my life.

After marrying the most perfect women for me, a beautiful Florida cutie, we moved to Chicago to see snow and live in a big city. For a few fondly-remembered years our lives were happy and productive.

An accident left my wife in what doctors call a vegetative state and drove us back to Florida and family support. Being house-bound I began tinkering, curious to see if an idea I'd had about an alternative energy source had any merit. Plus, as I'd always enjoyed writing stores, the hours of sitting at a bedside gave me the time to indulge in this lifelong desire.

Made in the USA
Charleston, SC
21 April 2016